BLACK MAGIC WOMAN

A QUINCEY MORRIS SUPERNATURAL INVESTIGATION

Also by Justin Gustainis

The Hades Project

BLACK MAGIC WOMAN

A QUINCEY MORRIS SUPERNATURAL INVESTIGATION

JUSTIN GUSTAINIS

SOLARIS

Chapter One, in slightly different form, originally appeared as "A Fistful of Fangs" in the book The Ghostbusters: Vampire Hunters, *edited by G.W. Thomas. © 2004 by Justin Gustainis.*

First published 2007 by Solaris
an imprint of BL Publishing
Games Workshop Ltd
Willow Road
Nottingham
NG7 2WS
UK

www.solarisbooks.com

Trade Paperback
ISBN-13: 978-1-84416-541-4
ISBN-10: 1-84416-541-8

10 9 8 7 6 5 4 3 2 1

A CIP catalogue record for this book is available from the British Library.

Designed & typeset by BL Publishing

To
Libby Yokum,

who had magic
when I needed it.

“This agency stands flat-footed upon the ground, and there it must remain. The world is big enough for us. No ghosts need apply.”
Sherlock Holmes

“All that is necessary for the triumph of evil is that good men do nothing.”
Edmund Burke

“Thou shalt not suffer a witch to live.”
Exodus 22:18

PROLOGUE

Salem Village
Colony of Massachusetts
June 1692

ALTHOUGH SHE WAS sitting in a room full of people, Bridget Warren had never felt more alone in her life. She was surrounded by friends, relatives, neighbors, acquaintances, with her husband Nathaniel seated right beside her, and she might just as well be standing naked before the throne of God, so frightened was she.

In an effort to take her mind off what she would have to do in the next few minutes, she let her gaze wander around the interior of the village meeting hall, which doubled as a church on Sundays and had now been taken over for use as a courtroom.

The whitewashed walls, all Puritan starkness and simplicity, were broken up only by a few narrow windows and the oil lamps that were placed every ten feet. The ceiling was high, its unpainted beams clearly visible to any who might glance that way while seeking Heaven's guidance. The rows of hard wooden benches by design offered minimal comfort, lest anyone invite disgrace by dozing off in the middle of a sermon—in any case, dozing was unlikely to tempt many attending *these* proceedings.

Seated in the last row, Bridget could see that all of the benches were filled. No family in Salem was failing to pay heed to the trials by sending a representative. None would have dared.

Finally, Bridget made herself look to the front of the meeting hall, where the seven magistrates sat behind a series of tables placed end-to-end. Their expressions were both grim and righteous, as befitted the responsibility entrusted to them by the colonial governor—and, indirectly, by the Lord God Himself. Chief Magistrate William Stoughton, the colony's lieutenant governor, sat stoically at the center of this row of rectitude.

Twenty feet of open space separated the magistrates' tables from the first row of benches. The accused were always directed to stand there, midway between the people and their appointed guardians.

Chief Magistrate Stoughton stared at the woman who now stood before the court. His forbidding gaze seemed calculated to freeze the blood of any accused sinner subjected to it. Bridget had seen more than one poor wretch wilt under this merciless scrutiny, confessing to the charges without the ordeal of a trial—thereby saving the Colony no small amount of time, trouble, and expense.

Bridget Warren prayed that such would be the case this time—even while knowing in her heart that such an outcome was less likely than snow in July.

"Goodwife Carter," Stoughton declared solemnly, "ye stand accused of consorting with the Devil and of practicing witchcraft, despicable acts condemned by Sacred Scripture as well as the laws of this Colony. How answer ye these charges?"

The woman who stood before the court neither cowered nor looked away from Stoughton's piercing gaze. She sounded both confident and calm as she replied, "I am innocent of those crimes and of any other, Your Lordship."

"The truth of that will yet be determined," the Chief Magistrate said sternly. Raising his voice, he addressed the congregation. "Who gives evidence against this woman?"

The question was followed by uncharacteristic silence that seemed to grow heavier with each passing second.

Stoughton stared across the length of the meeting hall, and Bridget Warren fancied that she could feel the cold bite of his gaze. She tried to rise, but her trembling legs refused to obey.

Nathaniel placed a reassuring hand under her elbow, but did not try to lift her up. To stand or remain seated was her decision, and hers alone.

Grasping with both hands the back of the pew in front of her, Bridget pushed herself to her feet. In a voice louder and more resolute than she'd ever thought she could muster, she declared, "*I do.*"

NATHANIEL WARREN GINGERLY rolled off of his wife's naked body and arranged himself in the bed next to her, holding her close. He was waiting for his heart to slow to a normal rhythm and his hand, which gently cupped Bridget's left breast, told him that her pulse was racing, too.

After a few minutes had passed he said, "Your ardor tonight brings to mind our first months of marriage. You couple like one possessed, my love."

"Hush, you," she said softly. "Speak not such words—they're a danger, these days."

"What, 'couple?' Where's the danger in that?"

She slapped his leg, but not very hard. "No, idiot, I meant 'possessed,' as you knew full well."

"Aye, well, I suppose I did," he said with a smile.

"Still and all, I know whereof you speak. My passion did burn brighter this time. Mayhap I wanted to lose myself in pleasure, to forget that business of the trial today."

"Like enough you're right," he said, "but I'll not complain of the result." He gave a contented sigh.

A few peaceful minutes went by before he suddenly asked, "Will she hang, then?"

"Sarah? Aye, she will—as well she ought." Bridget's voice had lost all levity. "'Tis a sad thing, Nate, for all that she brought her doom upon herself. I had no joy over condemning her in the court. It were the hardest thing ever I have done."

"Still, the judges believed you. But then, they have done the same for every accuser who has come forward."

"I spoke the truth. You *know* I did."

"If only truth were enough to win the day," he said dryly.

"Yes," she said, her expression bleak. "So many good, blameless people condemned, by the words of crazy children, or jealous neighbors, or superstitious fools. But Sarah Carter..."

"'In league with the Devil.' I'd not credit it, had I not heard the words from your lips."

"I'd not credit it, myself, but that I saw her with mine own two eyes. She were sacrificing a goat, that day I came upon her in the wood, and she had the Devil's signs drawn in the dirt all 'round her—the pentacle, the inverted cross, and suchlike. I recognize the black magic when I see it, Nate, even if I practice only the white myself."

"Aye, I know." A frown appeared on Nate's face. "Does not Sarah have a daughter?"

"She does. Rebecca, her name is," Bridget said. "Aged... eight years, or thereabout."

"What's to become of her? The father died some time back, I think."

"Aye, a horse threw him and cracked his skull. Or so Goody Close told me."

"So, the girl's an orphan, once Sarah goes to the gallows." Nate shook his head sadly. "What's to become of her?" he asked again.

"They've relatives in Boston, or so the talk goes. Mayhap they will take the child in."

"I'll pray that they do. T'would be an injustice, were she turned out into the streets to starve. The daughter should not wear the blame for the mother's wickedness."

"Aye," she said. "There's been too many innocents ground up in the mill of justice already."

THIRTEEN DAYS LATER, Sarah Carter was hanged for witchcraft.

She died bravely, if her refusal to engage in the pleading, screaming, and crying that usually characterized such occasions may be said to constitute courage.

When asked for last words, Sarah Carter replied in a cold, clear voice that, some said, could be heard throughout Salem village: "*May you all be damned to Hell, and that right soon.*"

Then they kicked the ladder out from under her.

Bridget Warren stood at a distance and made herself watch. The expression on her face resembled that of someone about to vomit—which is exactly how she felt.

Nate stood with her, his arm around her shoulders. "We've no need of this," he said softly. "Why invite such sorrow into your heart?"

"I brought it about," she said firmly. "I'll not hide from the consequences, ugly though they be."

Nate squeezed her tighter. A few moments later, they were about to turn away and start for home when Nate suddenly growled, "Gah! I cannot believe they brought the child here!"

Bridget stared at her husband. "What child?"

He pointed with his chin. "Look yonder."

She followed his gesture to one of the little knots of people ringing Gallows Hill. It took her a moment to recognize the adults as Sarah Carter's Boston relatives, who had been pointed out to her a few days earlier. They clung together, the women weeping quietly.

But one who stood with them, a girl of about eight, was not crying.

She was looking at Bridget Warren.

It seemed to Bridget that she and the girl stared at each other for a long time, a contest that was halted only when the child raised her left hand, the first two fingers extended, and sketched a brief but complex pattern in the air.

Bridget gasped, then immediately brought up her right hand to make a gesture of her own—the sign that was the standard defense against the curses used in black magic.

Rebecca Carter continued to stare, expressionless, at Bridget until her aunt grasped the child's hand and pulled her away.

Nate Warren had observed the brief, silent exchange between the two females. Even if he had not, the expression on his wife's face would have told him that something was very wrong.

"Bridget, what means this?" he breathed.

It took his wife a moment more to tear her gaze away from the little girl—the youngest black witch she had ever seen, or even heard of.

"Mean?" she said finally. "Methinks it means but one thing, Nathaniel."

Bridget paused to look again at the lifeless form on the gallows, then sent one final glance after the retreating back of Rebecca Carter. After a few seconds she continued, in a voice that chilled Nate Warren's blood.

"*It means this wicked business is not yet done with.*"

PRIMUS
VISITATION

CHAPTER 1

Lindell, Texas
Population 3,409

"THEY SAID THEY was gonna be here *today*," Hank Dexter growled. "Fuckers done *promised* us."

He leaned his chair forward and spat a glob of tobacco juice onto the dust-covered asphalt of Main Street, where it immediately began to sizzle. Then he pushed his weight back against the chair, tilting it to rest once more against the front of Emma's Cafe. The chair, a cheap armless thing made of aluminum and plastic, normally graced one of the tables inside Lindell's best (and only) eatery. But Jerry Jack Taylor, who'd taken over the business after Emma passed away four years earlier, had raised no objection when Hank and his buddy Mitch McConnell brought a couple of the chairs outside. Emma's wasn't doing much business these days, anyway—and none at all, after dark.

Mitch made a show of looking at his watch. "Day ain't done yet," he said. "Shit, it's just past three o'clock."

"Yeah, and another hour it'll be just past four, then five, then six, and pretty soon after that the fuckin' sun'll be going down and it's gon' start all over again."

Mitch didn't say anything to that. But after a while, he asked, "Why'nt you just leave, man? Clear the fuck out like half the folks in town already have, seems like."

"Cause Jolene's in there, that's why. She's in there somewhere—with *them*." He was staring across the street at the Goliad Hotel, all two stories of it, and the hatred in his eyes was like a living thing. After a few moments he asked, "How 'bout you? Why you still hangin' around this shithole?"

"You seen what they did to my daddy. You was there when we found him."

"Yeah," Hank said softly. "Yeah, I was there."

"Folks say now he was one of the lucky ones, 'cause they killed him right out. Didn't... change him." Mitch gave a laugh that held no humor whatever. "Lucky, my ass. Ain't nobody deserve that kind of luck, no sir, and I ain't leavin' till I get back at them fuckers, somehow."

"Yeah, quite a few folks got scores to settle with the leeches. Good thing, in a way, 'cause without them, I couldn't have raised the money for them fuckin' experts, who was supposed to fuckin' *be* here—"

"Hey, what's that?" Mitch said suddenly. He was staring off to the left, where Main Street merged with Route 12.

Hank looked that way, his eyes narrowed against the glare. After a moment, he spat another wad of 'baccy juice. "Nah, that ain't nothin'. I hear tell them old boys travel around with a couple of semis, along with some four-wheel-drive jeeps and I don't know what all. Make a regular convoy out of it." He gestured up the street with his head. "That dust cloud ain't big enough for more than one vee-hicle, and it's just a car, most likely. Some damn tourist missed the highway turnoff, or somethin'."

Hank was right about it being a single car, as was proved a few minutes later when the dark blue Mustang pulled up in front of Emma's Cafe. But he was wrong about everything else.

The man who got out was tall and lean, with black hair and a heavy beard growth that looked like it needed to be shaved twice a day. He wore lightweight gray slacks and a white dress shirt with the sleeves rolled back a couple of turns to reveal strong-looking forearms. His sunglasses were the style made popular by those *Men in Black* movies, but he had the good manners to take them off before addressing Hank and Mitch. "Howdy," he said with a nod. He didn't smile, the way strangers usually do when they're about to ask for directions.

Hank and Mitch returned his greeting but said nothing more. The stranger did not seem bothered by their silence. He didn't come across as hostile or challenging, but there was a quality of stillness about him, as if he could have stood there all day and half the night, waiting for something to happen. It was the kind of patience you see in some hunters, the ones who always bag their limit no matter what's in season at any given time of year.

Finally, Mitch said, "Lost, are ya?"

The stranger seemed to consider the question seriously before shaking his head. "Not if this is Lindell, I'm not." He looked more closely at them. "And not if you boys are Hank Dexter and Mitch McConnell." His accent showed he wasn't local, but it didn't mark him as a Yankee or anything like that. Instead, he sounded like a Texas boy who had gone and got himself some education somewhere.

Hank sat forward suddenly, bringing the front legs of his chair down with a bang. "You ain't Jack—"

"No, I'm not," the stranger said. "Jack has a whole crew he works with, as you fellas probably know. And all of 'em are bogged down right now in one hell of a mess over in Waco. Way I hear it, what was supposed to be a simple job has turned out to be a major infestation, and Jack and his crew are about up to their ass in bloodsuckers."

The stranger twisted his head to the left and gave the Goliad Hotel a good, long look. Then he turned back around. "But Jack made a commitment to you folks, and he's a man keeps his word. So he gave me a call. Asked me to come on over and see if I could help out with your situation here."

"All by your lonesome?" Hank didn't bother to keep the scorn out of his voice. "And just who the fuck are you?"

"My name's Quincey Morris," the stranger said, not saying it as if he thought it would mean anything to them. And it didn't.

"You work for Jack, do you?" Mitch asked.

"No, I'm sort of an independent contractor," Morris said, smiling a little. "And it so happens that I owe Jack a couple of favors. Big ones." He glanced at his watch, then up at the sky. "But time's gettin' on while we're jawin' here, and there's a lot to do before sundown." He raised his thick black eyebrows. "I assume you fellas are still interested in doing something?"

"Bet your ass, we are," Hank said, and came to his feet at once. "Let's get to 'er."

"WHAT THE HELL is that?" Mitch asked, staring. "Flowers? We gonna fight the goddamn leeches with *flowers*? Mister, you are plumb loco."

Morris had popped the trunk of the Mustang, to reveal several bundles of thorny sticks, some with blossoms still attached. The odor released by opening the trunk was pleasantly reminiscent of a greenhouse, although it dissipated quickly in the hot, dry air.

"These are branches of wild rose," Morris said. "They've been demonstrated to have a binding effect on vampires—or leeches, if you like."

Mitch peered suspiciously at the bundles. "What's that mean—'binding effect?'"

"Well, for example, if you put one on a vampire's coffin, he can't leave it, even after dark. Has to stay inside."

"So, what, you 'spectin' us to go in there—" Hank made a head gesture toward the Goliad, "and put these things on a bunch of coffins? Are you fuckin' crazy?"

Before Morris could reply, Mitch said, "Mister, what he means is, we know a couple fellas went in the Goliad after this all started, lookin' to settle things with the leeches. Broad daylight an' all—they wasn't stupid. But they didn't come out again, neither."

Morris shook his head. "No, I wouldn't go in that place, day or night, and I wouldn't ask you fellas to do it, either. They've probably got booby traps, deadfalls, who knows what other devilment set up inside there. But, see, the binding effect of wild rose works in a number of ways."

He broke a bundle and picked up one of the branches. "Put this across a door and fasten it there, a vampire can't go out that way." He pointed across the street, at the front entrance of the Goliad. "Like that door over there, say."

Hank and Mitch were looking at Morris now with more interest than they had shown since his arrival.

"You take another branch," he went on, "put it across a window, and no vampire is gonna leave through that particular window, long as the branch stays in place."

Morris gestured at the contents of the Mustang's trunk. "Like you can see, I brought lots of wild rose branches with me—enough to seal up that hotel tighter than Huntsville Prison, at least as far as vampires are concerned. But I'll need you fellas to help me. I picked up some carpenter's staple guns, and I expect you know where to scare up a ladder or two."

After staring inside the trunk for a couple of seconds, Mitch scratched his head in puzzlement. "So what are you fixin' to do—keep the fuckin' leeches bottled up inside the Goliad forever? That dog just won't hunt, Mister. Sooner or later, these rose bushes of yours is gonna start to rot, and then—"

Morris held up a hand, palm out like a traffic cop. "That's not what I had in mind, not at all. I don't figure to keep the vampires penned up indefinitely. I just want them confined for three days—well, three nights, to be precise."

"Yeah, okay, say we can hold 'em for three days and nights," Hank said. "What happens after that?"

Morris told them.

Three days later
4:48am

MORRIS OPENED THE rear gate of the rust-spotted old cattle truck, and Hank Dexter helped him set the ramp in place. The four heifers were reluctant to move, but Mitch McConnell climbed into the truck bed with them and shooed them down the ramp, one at a time. Each cow already had a length of stout rope tied loosely around its neck, and Hank and Morris used these as leashes to lead the animals to predetermined positions and then tie them in place.

They tethered one of the cows to a lamp-post, another to a nearby parking meter. The other two were secured to the truck itself—one rope was tied to a door handle, and the other was made fast to the cattle truck's front bumper. The whole tableau was situated in front of Emma's Cafe, which placed it directly across the street from the Goliad Hotel.

Even though well used to people, the animals were skittish. This may have had something to do with the new sights and smells confronting them, but it probably owed a lot more to the enraged howls and screeches that were coming non-stop from inside the Goliad. The men were bothered less by it than the cows were—after all, they had been listening to that insane cacophony for the past two nights.

Mitch checked all the knots, then joined the other two men in the middle of the street. They were both looking toward the Goliad.

"Sounds kinda like a loony bin during a earthquake, don't it?" Mitch said.

"It's worse now'n last night," Hank observed.

"Sure it is," Morris said. "They're hungrier tonight. That was the whole point, remember?" He peered at his watch in the uncertain light of the street lamps. "I make it 5:06. How about you fellas?"

Hank checked the luminous face of his Timex. "Prid near, I'd say."

Mitch just nodded.

"Better get in position, then," Morris said. He looked at Hank, who was drawing a big hunting knife from a sheath at his belt. "You sure you're okay with this part of it, podner?"

"Reckon so," Hank told him. "I worked in a slaughterhouse for a while, when I was younger. Ain't fixin' to enjoy myself, but I'll get it done."

"All right then. You fall back to Emma's when you're finished, and Mitch, you'll let him in. Then the two of you are gonna uncork the bottle, right?"

"That's a big ten–four," Mitch said. He looked at Morris closely for a long moment. "You take care now, y'hear?"

"I was plannin' to," Morris said with a tight grin, and turned away. As he jogged off into the night, he called over his shoulder, "Remember the Alamo!"

Mitch McConnell stood inside Emma's Cafe and tried not to watch as Hank Dexter slashed each cow's throat. Hank moved so quickly that the last beast to receive his attention was only starting to low its distress when the sharp blade of the hunting knife flashed beneath its chin.

"I don't much like this part of it either," Morris had told them. "But we need blood out there, a lot of it, and it's got to be fresh. If it's any consolation, the poor damn cows won't have to suffer very long."

His butcher's work done, Hank ran for the front door of Emma's. Mitch let him in, then closed and locked the door again. Each of the double doors had a big glass panel in it, and those panels now bore a large cross, done in black paint. The same holy symbol had been painstakingly applied to all the windows in Emma's—and to every door and window along Main Street, as well as every structure in a two-block area. "That business about vampires having to ask permission to enter a dwelling the first time is bullshit," Morris had said. "But what you hear about the effect of crosses, now that's the truth. The gospel truth, you might say."

"You done good, podner," Mitch said, as Hank wiped his knife blade off on a napkin.

"Bet them cows don't think so," Hank said, his breath coming fast. "He said two minutes, right?"

"Yeah, more or less. Better check your watch—you got the one glows in the dark." They had left the lights off inside Emma's. Crosses or no, they had no desire to call attention to themselves during the next few minutes.

It seemed to Mitch they waited half an eternity, while the pandemonium coming from the Goliad seemed to double its crazed intensity, and then double again. Finally, he heard Hank say, "All right, I reckon it's time."

They felt around on the floor for the objects they had left there earlier: two metal tubes, which until recently had been legs of one of the cheap cafe chairs. Around each tube was now tied the end of a length of 150-pound test fishing line. Each thick black filament ran under the door, over the sidewalk, across the street, and right up to the front door of the Goliad Hotel. Both of the lines were knotted securely around the branch of wild rose that was stapled across the hotel's double front doors. One fishing line would probably do the job, but two was safer. "We can't afford any mistakes," Morris had told them.

"We take up the slack first," Hank said tensely. Each man began to roll a tube in his hands, which pulled the loose line in under the door and wound it around the tube. In a few seconds, both lines were tight, exerting tension on the branch of wild rose across the street, along with the big staples that held it in place.

"Okay, then," Hank said. "Slow and steady."

They braced their feet and began to pull, then harder, then harder still. Suddenly, the lines went slack again, which told Hank and Mitch that they had succeeded.

The branch of wild rose was now gone from the Goliad's front doors.

Nothing happened for a long time—two, maybe three seconds. Then the doors of the Goliad burst open like the floodgates of Hell.

THERE WERE SEVENTEEN of them, and they battened on those bleeding, frightened cows like sharks on a herd of fat seals. Some of the vampires went directly to the gushing fountains under the cows' throats, while others used their fangs to open fresh wounds of their own. A few went down on hands and knees in the street and began to lick from the spreading red puddles that had formed there. None spared a glance toward Emma's Cafe. They saw and smelled and thought of nothing but the blood. It was not the human variety that they preferred, but it was warm, and it was fresh—and it was *blood.*

Hank and Mitch were standing well back from the windows to avoid detection, but they could still see the spectacle outside. After a few moments, Mitch heard Hank mutter, "Ah Jesus goddamn piss-ass fuck. Goddamn it, shit!"

"What is it, podner? What's the matter?"

Hank shook his head a couple of times. "Jolene's out there with the leeches. She's one of 'em."

Mitch didn't know what to say, so he kept quiet.

"I kept tellin' myself, maybe they didn't do her yet, ya know? I was hopin' maybe they'd like, I dunno, *save* her, to fetch and carry for them in daylight, or somethin'." Hank shook his big head again, like a boxer trying to get past the effects of a haymaker before the next round starts. "Fuck, who'd I think I was kidding? Just myself, I guess. Like fuckin' usual."

He pulled out one of the chairs from a nearby table and sat down heavily. Still unsure what to say, and afraid of making it worse by coming up with the wrong thing, Mitch decided to leave Hank alone with his pain for a while. He turned his attention back to the carnage in the street.

Now that he started looking at the vampires as individuals, he could recognize Hank's wife Jolene easily enough. Along with Walt the barber, Tom Jesperson the sheriff, and three teenagers who used to hang around the pool room all day long when they should've been in school. In fact, every one of the creatures out there gorging on the cows' blood was someone Mitch had once known.

It took him a few seconds to realize what that meant.

"Where's the fuckin' Master?" he said out loud.

Hank took his head out of his hands and looked up. "Huh? What're you sayin'?"

"The *Master.* The dude that come into town and started all this vampire shit. That's what Jack told us they's called, remember? Masters. Well, I know every damn person out there, known 'em all for years, same as you. So, who's the fuckin' blooksucker that begun it? And *where is he?*"

Hank peered across the street, at the open doorway of the Goliad. Inside the hotel, back a little way from the door, he thought he could just make out something red... no, two somethings. He squinted hard, and suddenly knew what he was looking at—eyes. A pair of eyes, glowing red.

"Oh, fuck," Hank said quietly. "The bastard's still inside."

"*Fuck* is right," Mitch said, pointing to the left. "Lookee there."

Walking rapidly along the sidewalk across the way, staying in shadow whenever possible, was Quincey Morris. Carrying a fresh branch of wild rose in one hand and a big staple gun in the other, he was headed directly for the Goliad Hotel.

MORRIS WAS FEELING cautiously optimistic. Everything actually seemed to be going according to plan, and he knew how rare that was. Robert Burns has famously written, "The best laid plans of mice and men gang aft agley," and Morris's English Lit professor at Princeton had once interpreted that last part to mean "Things usually get fucked up beyond belief." Still—so far, so good.

If his luck held, this whole mess should be over in another fifteen minutes or so. Then he could help with the clean-up, maybe grab a few hours of sleep, and be back in Austin by evening.

The creatures across the street were still gorging themselves on cows' blood and paying no attention to what might be going on behind them. As he crept along, Morris mentally rehearsed his moves for the next few seconds: close the hotel doors, quickly staple on a fresh branch of wild rose, jump in his Mustang parked a few yards away, and take off before the vampires knew what was going on. Then let things take their course.

He had reached the Goliad and was just taking hold of one of the front doors when he realized that Bobby fucking Burns was proved right again, as the Master vampire leaped out from the hotel entrance and took him by the throat.

The impact of the Master's charge put them both on the sidewalk, the vampire on top. Morris had the breath knocked out of him, and the impact of the back of his head on the concrete hadn't helped, either. But he knew that unless he did something *right now* he was on his way to joining the ranks of the undead, and he was *not* going to let that happen.

He'd lost his stapler in the fall but still held the other object he'd been carrying, and as the Master vampire brought those predator's teeth down to tear out his throat, Morris jammed the branch of wild rose between the creature's jaws and pushed back, hard.

None of the experts who have written about the vampire's nature, not Van Helsing, or Blake, or Tregarde or any of the others, has been able to explain convincingly why the undead are repelled by certain natural substances, such as garlic, wolfsbane, or wild rose. Perhaps it is a sort of allergy, or there may be a deeper, spiritual meaning. But for pragmatists like Morris, wondering *why* these things work against the undead is far less important than knowing that they *do*.

The Master reared back, gagging. He yanked the branch of wild rose from his mouth and flung it aside, furiously spitting out small fragments onto the sidewalk. That only took a few seconds, and then the Master turned back to his victim—only to be struck hard by Morris's open palms, just above the eyebrows. The impact against the vampire's forehead was enough to break the small plastic bubbles, each about the size of a pregnant quarter, that were glued to Morris's hands.

Earlier, he had cut the bubbles from a sheet of packing material, and then used a small-bore hypodermic needle to carefully fill each one with about 50 cc of holy water—most of which was now running into the Master vampire's eyes.

The effect, similar to what you'd get from sulfuric acid splashed on a human, was immediate and devastating. The Master clutched his ruined eye sockets and fell sideways onto the sidewalk, howling in agony.

Morris did not waste time staring at the creature. He picked up the branch again, and, after a few moments' fumbling, found the stapler where he had dropped it. Scrambling to his feet, he hastily closed the Goliad's front doors and then affixed the branch of wild rose across them, putting on three staples, just for luck.

Then he turned around and saw that luck was something he was shit out of.

Seventeen vampires were standing in front of the hotel now, and they were all looking right at him, their faces full of rage—and hunger.

WATCHING FROM INSIDE Emma's, Hank and Mitch had been in turn worried and elated as Morris was attacked by the Master vampire and then bested him. But as the Master screamed out his anguish, they saw the feeding vampires finally began to take notice. One after another, they had abandoned the blood of the now-dead cows and turned toward the Goliad Hotel.

"Oh, shit," Mitch said. "He's fucked now. Some of them bloodsuckers is between him and his car."

"Yeah," Hank replied. His eyes were slits of intense concentration.

"Maybe he's got some more of that holy water he used on their Master. That might—"

"Shut up and listen," Hank said through clenched teeth. "Got me a idea." It took him only a few seconds to lay it out for Mitch, whose eyes went wide as he listened.

"You can't be serious about goin' out there, man," Mitch said. "Christ, there's a whole shitload o' them fuckin' leeches, and we're—"

"I'm goin'," Hank rasped. "Either alone, or with you to back me up, but I'm goin'. Which way's it gonna be?"

Mitch took in a big breath then let it out. "Okay, okay, all right." His voice sounded shaky. "Let's do it before I get me some sense and change my mind."

Hank nodded, and drew the knife from its sheath. "Just let me cut the line off of these here chair legs."

As the vampires advanced on him, Morris tried to formulate a plan of action. Trouble was, he seemed as fresh out of options as he was of holy water.

He decided to try a desperate dash through the crowd of undead, in the hope that surprise and momentum might allow him to smash through them before they could react. Then he could try for Emma's, or perhaps the cab of the cattle truck. Either way, he wouldn't have to hold out very long.

He knew that his chances weren't good. There were probably too many of the vampires for his half-ass plan to succeed. But he was *damned* if he was just going to cower there, like some heroine in a bad horror movie, and wait for them to take him. If they wanted his blood, they could damn well fight him for it. He was gathering himself for the rush when he suddenly heard Hank Dexter shouting: "Hey, you fuckin' leeches! Over here!"

Several of the vampires turned at the sound of Hank's voice. Morris could see Hank standing on the sidewalk in front of Emma's Cafe, and it looked like Mitch was positioned a few feet behind him.

"Still hungry, are ya?" Hank yelled. "Then how 'bout some of the *real* stuff?"

Hank held his hands out before him, revealing long, hairy arms in a shirt-sleeved shirt. The right hand held the hunting knife, and in a quick, economical motion Hank slashed the blade across his own left wrist. Arterial blood began to spurt immediately. Hank waved the wounded arm wildly back and forth, spattering his blood on the street in an arc that looked black in the streetlights. There was near hysteria in his voice now as he screamed, "*Come get your dinners, you low-rent motherfuckers!*"

All of the vampires were focused on Hank now, and as they began to surge toward him, Morris made his move. One vampire was still between him and the Mustang, and Morris hit him with a stiff-arm that Jim Brown might have approved of. He thought there might be a few drops of holy water left in the deflated bubble glued to his palm, and the scream from the vampire told him he'd been right. Unhindered now, he yanked open the Mustang's door, jumped behind the wheel, and quickly got the door closed and locked. He thought starting the engine might attract some of the undead's attention, but they were too interested in the sight and smell of Hank Dexter's fresh, pulsing blood to pay any notice.

Seeing that he'd accomplished what he wanted, Hank gripped his bleeding wrist tightly and began to back toward the open door of Emma's. The vampires started to follow, and that was when Mitch McConnell stepped forward.

He held one of the chair legs in each hand, and as the vampires approached he brought them together before him in the form of a cross. He had seen a guy do something similar in one of those old Dracula movies on TV, and it had done the job then, driving the evil count back like an irresistible force. Mitch silently prayed to God and Sonny Jesus that it would have a similar effect this time, too.

It worked just fine.

The vampires frantically reversed course, cowering back before the power of the holy symbol Mitch held in his trembling hands. Their dismay and confusion gave Hank Dexter the chance to get back inside Emma's, where he immediately began to apply to his arm the fishing line tourniquet he and Mitch had prepared a few minutes earlier.

Across the street, Morris gunned the Mustang and sent it hurtling up Main Street in a spray of dust. The front bumper caught one of the vampires, a woman, and knocked her sprawling. But Morris only went fifty or sixty yards before jamming on his brakes, turning the wheel hard left as he did so. These actions, combined with the film of dust on the street, allowed the Mustang's rear end to swing around 180 degrees in a perfect bootlegger's turn that had the car facing back the way it had just come. Morris hit the gas again, then flicked the headlights on high beam.

Earlier in the day, he had used the last of the black paint to paint a cross carefully on each of the car's headlamps. This meant that turning on the lights sent two cross-shaped shadows wherever the car was pointed.

Right now, it was pointed at the group of vampires in the middle of Main Street.

Smoke and screams arose whenever the cruciform shadows touched one of the undead. Morris aimed the Mustang right for the center of the mob, and the vampires scattered like tenpins. He drove through them, past them, and on for a couple of blocks before repeating the rum-runner's maneuver to turn the car around again. He let the car's powerful motor idle while he surveyed the scene he had just left.

The sidewalk in front of Emma's was empty, which meant that Hank and Mitch were both safely inside, protected by the crosses painted on the cafe's doors and windows. The vampires were milling around the street in apparent confusion. Since the Mustang's headlights were still on, Morris didn't think any of the vampires would be heading his way.

Then he raised his gaze a little and beheld a sight he had viewed many times in his life, but never with such profound relief.

Sunrise.

The vampires became aware of the coming of dawn at about the same time and they immediately began to scramble around in a desperate search for shelter. But there was none to be had. Every door and window they approached bore a painted cross that barred their entry as effectively as steel bars.

It was less than a minute before the vampires began to burn.

The first to go up was a man in a mail carrier's uniform, and even from two blocks away Morris could hear his screeches as the sun's purifying rays turned him incandescent. The others followed soon afterward—first one, then another, then two more, and finally all of them were ablaze, rending the air with screams of pain and rage. The Master, far older and stronger, went last, staring up at the sky with his ruined eye sockets, unable to see the great glowing orb that was turning him into a torch.

Then it was over.

Morris drove slowly back the way he had come and parked in front of Emma's. Up and down Main Street, people were starting to venture from their homes. They came out cautiously, a few at a time, the way folks will do after a tornado has passed through.

As Morris got out of the Mustang, the door of Emma's opened. Mitch came out first, followed by Hank, who now had strips of tablecloth tied tightly around his left wrist.

The three of them stood on the sidewalk staring out at the debris left in the street—the four dead cows, the pools of blood that were already starting to attract flies, and eighteen piles of ash that had once made up a colony of the undead.

After a while Mitch said, "Anything special we oughta do with them ashes?"

Morris thought for a moment. "You got a stream around here, or a creek—any kind of naturally running water?"

Mitch nodded. "There's a good-sized crick runs past the north edge of town."

"Put the ashes in there, then. Probably an unnecessary precaution, but it never hurts to be careful. You might say a prayer while you do it, too."

"I'd do that anyway, most likely," Hank told him.

"That was a brave thing you boys did, coming out there like that," Morris said. "Saved my sorry ass, for sure."

Hank twitched one side of his mouth. "I don't reckon a fella like you needs to talk much about *brave*. You got more guts than a pissed-off grizzly, Mister Morris."

Mitch was looking at Morris closely. "This ain't your first rodeo, is it? You done this kind of thing before."

"Yeah," Morris said, his voice sounding tired. "Yeah, I have. It's part of my profession, you might say."

"How's a fella end up doing this kind of thing for a living?" Mitch asked.

"It's kind of a family tradition," Quincey Morris told him. He reached inside his jacket pocket, found his Ray-Bans, and put them on. "Now, we've got some cleaning up to do here—but first, Hank, we better get the local doc to look at that arm of yours. I expect you're going to need some stitches, podner."

CHAPTER 2

May is a hot month in Texas, and Walter LaRue seemed grateful for the air conditioning in Quincey Morris's office. "I was wondering about something," he said, settling his bulk into the armchair across from Morris's antique oak desk. "When you file your income tax, what do you put in the box marked 'Occupation?'"

"Actually, I have a fella who takes care of all that for me," Morris said. The Southwest twang in his speech was slight but noticeable—at least it was to LaRue, who had lived all of his forty-two years well north of the Mason-Dixon line. "I tend to have a lot of deductions—travel, mostly—and trying to keep track of it makes my head hurt. Hell, it's all I can do sometimes just rememberin' to get receipts. But, to answer your question: on my tax guy's advice, I use 'Consultant.'"

"Not 'private investigator?'"

Morris shook his head. "That's a legal term, Mr. LaRue, and it's got a specific meaning under the law. The state of Texas, like most places, has pretty stiff requirements for a private investigator's license—you've got to show so many hours of law enforcement experience, and so on. I don't qualify for the license—but then, I can't say that I ever felt the need to."

"You don't advertise in the Yellow Pages, either." It was almost an accusation.

Morris smiled without showing any teeth. "No, I sure don't," he said evenly. "I doubt the phone book people have a category that would fit me very well. But there's quite a few folks out there in the world who know what I do. My clients mostly hear about me by word of mouth—as you did your own self. Or so I'm assuming."

Walter LaRue grunted softly in response. He was one of those big men who always seem untidy. His expensive gray suit had not known the touch of an iron for quite some time, the custom-made white button-down shirt had a button missing from one of the collar points, and LaRue's Hermes tie bore a small stain of what was almost certainly mustard. His hair, which was brown flecked with gray, was carelessly combed and unevenly parted.

In contrast, the slender, thirtyish man seated behind the big desk was carefully groomed and neatly dressed. Quincey Morris's black hair was combed back from his high forehead. His tropical-weight navy blue suit combined quality fabric with good tailoring. Although Morris didn't really care much about clothing, four years at Princeton had given him conservative good taste in attire. So, every January 2nd, he spent an hour online with the current catalogs from Brooks Brothers and Joseph A. Banks, ordering whatever he thought he might need for the coming year.

Quincey Morris may have been the only adult male Texan who had never owned a string tie.

After several moments of fidgety silence, LaRue said, "This is kind of... weird for me. I mean, six months ago, if you'd asked me to predict what I'd be doing today, most likely I'd say that I'd be at my desk in Madison, Wisconsin, running my software design firm. Sitting in Austin consulting a parapsychologist would have been pretty damn low on my list of possibilities."

"I'm not one of *them,* either, Mr. LaRue," Morris said patiently. "A parapsychologist—a real one, I mean, not one of the cranks or con artists—is a scientist, someone who studies the paranormal in an organized, controlled way. Now, I do try to keep up with the serious stuff as it's published. That's not hard to do, since there's so little of it. But I don't consider myself any kind of scientist."

"Then what *are* you?" LaRue asked with a frown.

"I suppose you could call me an interventionist, if you need to put a name on it. Let's say I've got a client who's experiencing some difficulty that he thinks is due to some supernatural entity." Morris shrugged. "That turns out to be the case, then sometimes I'm able to provide assistance."

"Only 'sometimes?'"

"Yep, afraid so. It all depends on the nature of the problem, and what the client expects in the way of a solution. For example, I've been asked more than once to raise the dead."

"Are you *serious?*"

Another shrug. "The people who asked me were sure enough serious. But necromancy is not something that I practice—and I mean *never.* That kind of thing comes strictly under the heading of black magic. I don't perform black magic, and I don't mess around with those who do."

"So, what does that leave?" LaRue asked. "White magic? Do you perform that, whatever it is?"

"I've got some very limited skills in that area, Mr. LaRue. But I have several associates whose expertise in that area is far greater than mine. I call upon them, from time to time."

"Maybe you should put 'warlock' on your tax forms," LaRue suggested with a tiny smile.

"That'd be wrong, too," Morris said. "But maybe we'd be better off identifying *your* problem, Mr. LaRue. I assume you're looking for some sort of... intervention?"

"Yeah," LaRue said, nodding slowly. "I guess that's what I need, all right. If 'intervention' is a fancy way of saying, 'help, and a lot of it, and right away,' then it could be that's just what I need."

Morris made a slight gesture. "Go on."

"There are these—these *occurrences,* these *events* that have been happening to my family the last three months. My wife and kids are terrified, and if I wasn't such a big, tough he-man, I suppose I would be, too." The second cousin of a smile appeared on LaRue's haggard face, but only for a second. "And the thing is, it's getting worse. It was puzzling at first, then annoying, but now I think it means us harm."

Morris kept silent but nodded his understanding.

"There were little things, in the beginning," LaRue said. "Objects falling over when nobody's near them, a door closing by itself, stuff like that. You tell yourself that it's just the vibrations from truck traffic, or a breeze getting in through cracks in the foundation. It's easy to explain it away at first."

"But you're not trying to explain it away any more," Morris said quietly.

"No, not for the last couple of weeks. Because now I'm pretty sure it, whatever *it* is, wants to kill us."

"Explain what you mean, please. Be as specific as you can."

"Well, one evening last week my wife and I were in the kitchen putting dinner together when our big carving knife jumped out of the rack and buried its point in the cutting board I'd just been using. If I hadn't jerked away, it might've pinned my wrist right there, just like a pin through a bug in some kid's science project."

"Dangerous, for sure," Morris said, nodding. "And frightening. But not really life-threatening."

"No? Not *life-threatening?*" There was anger in LaRue's voice now. "Then how about last Saturday night? My daughter Sarah, eight years old, was having her bath while my wife stood a few feet away in front of the mirror, using her hair dryer. She swears the dryer just *flew* out of her hand, sailed through the air, and splashed down into the bathtub, which, I might remind you, contained one little girl, surrounded by a whole bunch of water." The voice was almost a snarl. "Is that *life-threatening* enough for you? *Is* it?"

Morris held up a hand, palm forward. "Please, Mr. LaRue, I wasn't trivializing your concern for your family's safety." His voice was calm, soothing. "I tend to categorize paranormal events, and sometimes I think out loud. I meant no offense."

LaRue took a couple of audible deep breaths. "No, listen, it's not you, I'm sorry. I'm just on edge a lot these days. Not your fault."

"Your daughter, was she—"

"No, she wasn't electrocuted. The hair dryer's got a short cord—maybe they make 'em deliberately short, I don't know—so just before reaching the tub it yanked its own plug out of the wall. Hell, Sarah was hardly upset by it at all, just surprised. That is, until her mother became hysterical, and I really can't say that I blame her."

Morris scratched his chin. "Any other incidents since the one involving the hair dryer?"

"No. At least, not since the last time I called home, which was..." LaRue checked his watch, "about forty-five minutes ago." He spent several seconds examining the nail on his right index finger, as if he found it the most fascinating object in the world. Then he sighed, a sound that seemed to come from the cellar of his soul. "But I figure it's only a matter of time until it happens again, and that could be the one that kills my daughter. Or my son, who's five. Or my wife. Or me."

LaRue's face twisted, and Morris was sure he was going to cry—an understandable reaction, all things considered. But the big man reestablished control quickly. He spent some time staring at the pattern in the carpet before he said, without looking up, "Please help us." The voice was scarcely more than a whisper. "Please."

"Of course," Morris said. "Of course I will. Are you flying home today?"

"Yeah, I want to get back as soon as I can. My flight leaves at 6:40 this evening."

"All right, then." Morris stood and came around the desk. "I've got preparations to make here, but I'll fly out tomorrow morning. Depending on the connections, I expect to be in Madison sometime in the afternoon. I want to spend some time in your home, with your family. I'll probably pester you with a lot of questions, and I'll need to see the rooms where these incidents have occurred. Then we'll figure out what needs to be done."

He placed his hand on Walter LaRue's big shoulder and squeezed, just for a moment. "And then we'll go and do it."

As Morris walked him to the door, Walter LaRue said, "There's one more thing I've been meaning to ask you. No big deal, just something I've been kicking around in my head while I try not to think about what could be happening at home."

"What's that, podner?" Morris said absently, as if part of his mind were elsewhere.

"I was a Computer Sci major in college—I know, big surprise—but they make you do a certain number of credits in Humanities as part of that stupid General Education stuff. So I took this course in Gothic Literature. Seemed more interesting than most of the other choices they had."

"Uh-huh." Morris knew what was coming now; it had happened before.

"Well, one of the books we had to read was *Dracula,* which I ended up liking more than I thought I would. Thing is, there was a character in there, one of the guys who helped hunt Dracula down and kill him. I guess this fella was supposed to be from Texas." LaRue was looking at him intently now. "And, you know, I'm pretty sure his name was Quincey Morris."

Morris's mouth formed a small, wry smile. "Yep, that's true. That was his name."

"So, what gives? I'm no English professor, but I understand the difference between fiction and what's real. This guy in the book was a made-up character, just like Dracula, or Van Helsing, or any of the rest of them, right?"

"Many folks would call him that, no doubt about it," Morris said. Neither his face nor his voice held much expression.

"But what about you? What would *you* call him?"

"Me? I'd call him my great-grandpa," Morris said. "Now, y'all have a safe trip home, and I'll see you in Madison tomorrow." Then politely, but firmly, he ushered LaRue out of his office and closed the door.

BY 8:30 THE next morning, Quincey Morris had almost finished the preparations for his trip north. He had made airline reservations, arranged to have the mail and lawn taken care of, and brought the cage containing his only pet, a hamster named Carnacki, over to a neighborhood kid who would take good care of him. He had then packed a suitcase with clothing, several books, and a thick file marked "Poltergeists."

Now there was only one more thing left to do.

He took from the top drawer of his bureau a fireproof metal container a little bigger than a cigar box. Unlocking it, he carefully took out two envelopes, brown with age. From each one he gingerly drew out a multi-page letter, unfolded the brittle paper carefully, and placed the documents side by side on the bed in front of him.

He had thought more than once about photocopying these pages and placing the originals in a safe deposit box, but always rejected the idea. It was important that he handle *this* paper, that he re-read *these* words before going out on an investigation, especially if it promised to be difficult or dangerous. It helped remind him of what he was, and where he had come from.

He read each letter slowly. One was signed "John W. Seward, M.D." The other, written in a shaky, old man's hand, bore the signature "Abraham Van Helsing, M.D., D.Ph., D.Lit., etc."

It was these documents, along with the account given by Stoker, that had allowed the family to piece together the fate of the first Quincey Morris, who had fought and died in a place far from home.

The Carpathian Mountains
Transylvania
November 6, 1887

THE SUN WAS low on the horizon now, which lent greater urgency both to the pursuers and their quarry. The two parties were pushing their horses to the limit—they all knew that once that blood-red orb disappeared below the mountain peaks, continuing the chase would be futile.

The American was at the head of the pursuit. He rode hard and well, bent low over his mount's neck to decrease wind resistance and reduce the blurring of vision caused by the cold air whipping at unprotected eyeballs.

Unlike his companions, the American had some experience taking a horse into battle, although the brightly dressed gypsies up ahead bore little resemblance to the Apaches he had fought in south Texas as a young man, almost twenty years earlier.

The gypsies' cart was slowing to a halt now, under the rifles of Mina and the Professor, who had been hiding in ambush behind some rocks near the entrance to the castle. But the gypsies, although stymied, showed no inclination to surrender. Dismounting, they produced knives from within their clothing and formed a protective cordon around the cart and the large, rectangular crate that it carried.

The sun had crept lower still.

The American rode up on the scene and was out of the saddle before his mount had stopped completely. He sprinted toward the gypsies' cart, drawing the huge Bowie from its sheath on his belt. He could see Harker rushing forward from the opposite side, waving that great kukri knife of his like a scythe.

The two of them attacked without hesitation. There was no time to parley with the gypsies, even if a common language could somehow be found. There were at most a few minutes of daylight left, and then *his* time would be on the world again.

The American fought savagely and by instinct, which is the only way to go up against odds with any chance of survival. Slash, parry, thrust, parry, slash, feint, slash, thrust, parry, the big steel blade of the Bowie knife never still, thrust, parry, feint, slash, the left hand working as well, punching, clawing, blocking, pushing, gouging as he surged forward, forward, always forward. He knew nothing of fear, or pain, or mercy, and three gypsies lay twitching on the ground before the rest of them finally gave way before this madman, a moment after their kinsmen on the other side broke under Harker's equally desperate onslaught.

The two men clawed their way onto the cart's flat bed and immediately assaulted the nailed-down lid of the crate, the refuge and resting-place of the creature they had come so many miles to destroy.

Using their knives as levers, they tore the nails loose, wrenched off the lid and flung it aside—just as the last rays of the sun disappeared from the western sky.

He was inside, as they had known he would be, to all appearances a corpse but then, as the daylight fled over the horizon, the ancient eyes flew open, the sharp canine teeth suddenly visible as the face twisted in a triumphant smile—a smile that vanished an instant later as the blade of the Bowie slammed into the monster's heart while Harker's kukri bit deep of his throat.

The sudden blast of energy from the crate knocked the two men onto their backs, their knives clattering loose against the crude wood of the cart. A terrible sound filled the air around them, an immense bellow that somehow combined a screech of pain, a scream of fear and, strongest of all, an animal howl of rage. It lasted only a few seconds, but when the two men regained their feet and peered inside the makeshift coffin, there was nothing left but dust, a few scraps of cloth and a half-dozen gold buttons, each inscribed with a stylized letter "D."

The surviving gypsies had also observed their master's dissolution. Responding to a shouted order from their clan leader, they took to horse and fled, leaving their dead behind. As the sound of hoof beats faded into the distance, an unearthly quiet settled over this impromptu battlefield, a silence broken only by the wind and the far-off howling of wolves.

It was only then that someone noticed that the American was bleeding.

Both Seward and Van Helsing were physicians, but there was little they could do. One of the gypsy blades had found a major artery, and the hastily applied pressure bandages could not stem the flow of bright-red blood.

Mina Harker knelt beside the American, taking one of his hands in her own. She wept softly, and he turned his head toward her, probably with the intent of saying something manly and consoling. Suddenly his eyes widened. With an effort, he raised one unsteady hand, pointing at Mina's forehead. "Look!" he croaked. "It's gone! The scar..."

They looked, all of them: Harker, his hands still red from the Count's blood; Jack Seward, moustache quivering with emotion; Lord Godalming, the noble profile barely visible in the gloom; and Van Helsing, their leader, whose wise old face went from exhaustion to elation in the space of an indrawn breath.

Mina Harker's forehead, which had been scarred weeks earlier by the touch of a wafer of Holy Eucharist, was now utterly smooth. "God be praised!" Van Helsing said reverently. "Her brow is rendered clean as the virgin snow—the curse is lifted, by the death of the Devil that inflicted it!"

One by one, the men knelt on the ground, in respect for the miracle they had just witnessed.

It was sometime during that interval that Quincey Morris, of Laredo, Texas and many points east, lay back, closed his eyes, and quietly died.

Some time later, they loaded Morris's body onto the back of the cart that the gypsies had abandoned. "Should we put him in the coffin, Professor?" Godalming asked.

Van Helsing shook his head adamantly. "We should not the remains of our friend defile with the unholy resting-place of such foulness. He deserve better of us, I think."

In the end, they took coats and jackets from several dead gypsies and fashioned them into a semblance of a shroud. The gypsies themselves they buried in a common grave. While the Harkers and Lord Godalming labored at this, Seward and Van Helsing stood off a little way, talking quietly. "We shall have to make arrangements to have Quincey's body shipped back to Texas for burial," Seward said. "He would want that, you know."

The old man nodded. "He said so to me once, years ago."

"We should telegraph his family, as well. It wouldn't do to have the coffin simply arrive there unannounced."

Van Helsing sighed. "You are quite right. I will the telegram send from Bistritz. His family must learn the news, tragic though it be. We should also write at length, each of us, so they may know the true heroic end of him who they consign to the earth."

"Both his parents are still alive, I believe."

"Yes, and one child, also."

"*Child!* You mean Quince was *married?*" Seward's voice betrayed his shock. "But... but he sought Lucy's hand, just as Godalming and I did!"

The old Dutchman laid a gentle hand on Seward's arm. "Do not have distress, friend John. Quincey was married once, true. But his wife died, in childbirth. It has been, now..." Van Helsing calculated briefly, "about four years since. So, fear not. Our American friend was a gentleman. He was free to marry Miss Lucy, if she would have him. But, as matters developed..."

"Yes, quite." Seward closed his eyes tightly for a moment. The fate of Lucy Westenra was a wound on his soul that would need a long time to heal, perhaps a lifetime. "But the baby lived, you say?"

"Yes—lived, and is now in the care of Quincey's parents on their ranch, or so he did tell to me some months past."

Van Helsing saw that the others were done with Morris's body and preparing to leave. As the two men walked toward their horses, Seward asked, "Is Quincey's child a boy or girl? You didn't say."

"A boy. Strong and healthy, by all accounts." Van Helsing swung into the saddle. "We should pray that the son grow to be as brave and steadfast as was the father."

"Yes, we should," Seward said. "The world needs such men."

They turned their horses and joined the others on the road that would take them to Bistritz, and, in time, back to England. Behind them they left nothing but a ruined castle, a few gold buttons, and a handful of rags that were already scattering in the cold, Carpathian wind.

MORRIS FINISHED READING the letters, refolded them carefully, and placed them back in their original envelopes. He put the two envelopes in the fireproof box, and locked it. Then he returned the box to the bureau drawer.

The tall Texan who had died in the shadow of Castle Dracula was the first of the Morris family to stand against the forces of darkness that forever trouble the world.

He was not the last.

Quincey Morris closed his suitcase, picked it up from the bed, and went off to catch his plane.

CHAPTER 3

THE LARUE HOUSE certainly didn't look frightening. *But then, they never do,* Morris thought. The pleasant white Colonial with green and gray trim wouldn't even merit a second glance from some Hollywood production assistant out scouting locations for a new Wes Craven movie. Morris had been in a few certifiably haunted dwellings over the years, and none of them had borne the slightest resemblance to Castle Dracula—a place that Morris also knew a great deal about.

There was the house in West Pittston, Pennsylvania—the little one with the white siding. Nothing special to look at, but pure evil inside—as bad in its way as an equally nondescript place in Amityville, Long Island. And Morris had once spent an hour in a certain town house in Washington's Georgetown section. Walking through the elegant home, you'd never know that two Jesuit priests had once died there while performing an exorcism to save a little girl.

Morris had learned that evil doesn't advertise. It doesn't have to.

The fortyish blonde who answered his knock had probably been fairly attractive a few months ago, before fear and worry and sleepless nights had their way with her.

"Mrs. LaRue?"

"Yes, what is it?" she said impatiently. Clearly, she was ready to repel boarders, whether salesmen, Jehovah's Witnesses, or candidates for City Council.

"My name's Quincey Morris, ma'am. You're expecting me, I hope."

For an instant she gazed at him blankly, then comprehension dawned. "Oh, you're the—I mean, yes, of course, my husband told me. Please come in."

She led Morris down a short hallway and into the living room, where her husband sat on a couch next to a dark-haired boy of about five. They were watching a video that Morris recognized. It cleverly used stop-motion animation to portray the adventures of a wacky British inventor and his long-suffering dog.

LaRue stood up at Morris's entrance and walked over to shake hands. "Glad you made it. Good to see you, I see you've met my wife Marcia."

Morris nodded. Looking at the boy he said, "And who's this handsome young fella?"

"This is my son, Tim. Say hello to Mr. Morris, Timmy."

The boy turned his pallid face toward Morris long enough to say "Hi," before returning to the TV screen. "We're watching Wallace and Gromit. Wanna watch with us?"

"Maybe later, Timmy, thanks," Morris said. "I have to talk to your folks for a while first, okay?"

"Okay." The boy's gaze did not leave the screen.

Morris turned away and was about to ask LaRue something when the boy's voice from behind him said, "Are you gonna catch the ghost?"

Morris looked back at Timmy, who continued to stare at the TV. "Do you think there *is* a ghost, Timmy?"

A twitch of the small shoulders. "I guess. Mom and Dad say there's one." The boy's voice was utterly lacking in effect.

Morris stepped closer to the couch. "Have you *seen* a ghost?" he asked gently.

"Uh-uh. It's indivisible."

"Invisible, you mean?"

Another shrug. "Yeah, I guess."

"Then how do you know there is one?"

"It does things. Bad things. It makes Mom and Dad all scared. And Sarah. She's my sister. She's always cryin' and stuff." Timmy

LaRue's voice remained as empty as if he were discussing a dimly remembered comic book he'd read a year ago.

Morris took a casual-looking step to one side, so that he could see the boy's eyes straight on. "How about you, Timmy? Does it make *you* scared?"

"Uh-huh." Two syllables, delivered in a monotone. Morris was certain now.

Shellshock. The kid's shellshocked, or whatever they call it now—post-traumatic stress disorder. He's been so terrified that he's passed fear and come out on the other side. This goes on much longer, he'll be a basket case, probably for life.

Morris looked at the boy's too-placid face again. *If he isn't already.*

"If there's a ghost, I'll catch him, Timmy. I promise."

"Okay," the emotionless little voice said.

Morris walked back to the parents, who had watched this exchange with a mixture of sorrow and resignation. "I'd like you to give me a walking tour of the house, if you would," he said briskly. "Not just the rooms where the attacks have occurred, but the whole place. All right?"

"Fine, I'll do the honors," LaRue said. Looking at his wife, he said, "Do you want to...?" He made a small head movement in the direction of his son.

"Sure, I'll stay with Timmy," she said with a ghost of a smile. "We'll watch some more Wallace and Gromit together."

As the two men left the living room, Morris asked quietly, "Where's the little girl—at school?"

"That's right," LaRue told him. "She'll be home in a couple of hours."

"How is she dealing with this? Same as Timmy?"

"No, she's... jumpy. Nervous all the time. Has screaming nightmares three, four times a week." LaRue shook his head. "I don't know which is worse—watching her fall apart, a little at a time, or seeing Tim turn into a fucking zombie." LaRue's voice broke on those last two words, but he regained control quickly. Morris wondered what it was costing the big man to keep his emotions dammed up like that—and how much longer it would be before the dam burst.

They began their tour of the house.

* * *

"WHAT'S THIS HERE?" Morris asked. They had stopped on the second floor hallway, in front of a large oak bookcase. The top of the bookcase was at eye level for Morris, and it was there, among the usual family bric-a-brac, that something had caught his attention.

LaRue looked at the small object in Morris's hand. "Oh, my mother-in-law used to make those. Said they were good luck charms, or something. We're always finding them around the house."

Morris twirled the charm in his fingers. Its base was a three-inch length of wire twisted into a figure eight—which, laid on its side, is the mystical symbol for infinity. A bit of green thread was tied around it at the center, and through this had been inserted a couple of sprigs of some kind of flora, now long dead.

Morris rubbed a tiny piece of the vegetable matter onto his index finger, then brought the finger to his mouth and licked it. *Aconite, aka. wolfsbane. Well, now.*

"I'd very much like to talk to your mother-in law," he told LaRue. "Does she live in the area?"

LaRue shook his head. "She used to live with us," he said. "She died four months ago."

"I'm sorry for your loss." Morris thought for a moment. "And the attacks started occurring when?"

"About three months ago," LaRue said with a sigh. He ran a hand through his untidy hair. "I know where you're going with that," he said. "It's occurred to me, too, you know. I just haven't had the guts to say it out loud."

"Say what, exactly?"

LaRue made an impatient gesture. "That Greta's... ghost, spirit, whatever you want to call it, is responsible for all the shit that's been going on."

"Is that what you think?"

"Well, Christ, it's what *you're* thinking, isn't it?"

Morris shrugged, and said nothing.

"I mean," LaRue said, "if we're going on the assumption that all of this is being caused by some kind of spirit... and if you look at the timing, and all..."

Morris kept twirling the little charm in his fingers, watching it go round and round. Without looking up, he asked, "Was your mother-in-law on good terms with the family?"

"Yes. Yes, she was. I mean, I've heard all those jokes about mothers-in-law that people make on TV. But Greta was okay, you know? We all got along pretty well."

"Including the children?"

"Oh, yeah. She loved the kids. They loved her back, too. Her dying hit them both pretty hard—and then this other shit starts..."

"I assume she had her own room?"

"Sure, it's down the hall. Don't you want to do the rest of the tour first?"

Morris slipped the little charm into his pocket. "No, I've seen all I need to here."

"IT'S ALL PRETTY much the way she left it," LaRue said. "None of us has had the heart to start packing Greta's stuff up, and we don't really need the room for anything, anyway. Besides, after the... incidents started, we all got kind of preoccupied."

"That's good to know," Morris said, looking around the spacious bedroom. There were knick-knacks and mementos all over the bureau, nightstand, and bookshelves, but nothing that drew his interest for more than a second or two. "Listen, I'm going to have to search the room. I'll handle her belongings carefully, and with respect, and I'll put everything back exactly as I found it. But it's something I've got to do. Will that upset you?"

LaRue shrugged. "I suppose not. But what are you looking for?"

"I'll let you know, if I find it."

Eight minutes later, he did.

Morris stood looking into the bottom drawer of the dresser, contemplating what he had uncovered after moving some blankets and an old flannel bathrobe: the old book with its white leather cover, the small silver bell, and the hand-made candles in several colors and shapes. There were several other items that he also recognized.

Morris took from his jacket pocket the little charm that he had found earlier. As it twirled slowly in his fingers, he said to LaRue. "Well, it looks like I've got some good news and some bad news for you."

LaRue nodded cautiously, waiting.

"For one thing, I'm almost positive that your troubles here are not being caused by a poltergeist, or any other kind of resident spirit."

LaRue nodded again. "And what's the bad news?"

Morris looked at him for several seconds before saying quietly, "I'm sorry, Walter—that *was* the bad news."

CHAPTER 4

CECELIA MBWATO SAT sprawled in a chair in the cheap motel room, watching the sky through a dirty window and waiting impatiently for the coming of night.

She was not one of those creatures the stupid Americans called "vampires." She was human, more or less, and could function in the daylight as well as anyone. But she had long felt a certain affinity with the dark, especially since becoming *umthakhati* at age fourteen, an occasion she always thought of as embracing the Great Darkness.

Besides, certain deeds essential to her craft were best carried out under cover of night.

The sun had reached the horizon now, and begun to disappear below it. There were enough clouds in the vicinity to reflect the dying light, filling the sky with a roseate glow that some might have called beautiful. But Cecelia Mbwato knew nothing of beauty, and cared only for the falling of the black cloak of night.

Once it was fully dark outside, she picked up the telephone and tapped in two numbers.

A voice in her earpiece said, "Yeah."

"It's time," she said, keeping most of the eagerness out of her voice. "Get the car."

She hung up without waiting for a reply.

* * *

SNAKE PERKINS GUIDED the big, beat-up Lincoln Continental expertly through the quiet suburban streets, tapping the fingers of one hand on the steering wheel to the beat of music only he could hear.

His passenger didn't like the radio, but that was all right. Snake had a repertory of songs in his head that he could play whenever he wanted. It wasn't quite as good as listening to them from an outside source, like a stereo or something, but it wasn't half bad, either. Snake Perkins carried more tunes in his head than you'd find in the average teenager's iPod.

He was currently listening to Lynyrd Skynyrd's "Sweet Home Alabama," a song Snake had always liked even though he was a Mississippi boy, himself. He'd just gotten to the part where Skynyrd was pissing on Neil Young when Cecelia Mbwato said, "Up here, next to the park. Pull up beneath that big tree."

Snake did as she said. Part of him, the product of nine generations of dirt-poor, butt-ignorant, Klan-joining rednecks, bridled at taking orders from a woman who was just about the blackest nigger Snake had ever seen, and a damn foreigner besides. That part of him would have loved to punch the bossy nigger bitch in the face five or six times, get out, go around, and yank her out of the car. Then tie some rope around her ankles, the other end to his rear bumper, and take himself for a nice long ride, at eighty miles an hour.

But the Mistress he served had been very clear: he was to do whatever the nigger woman wanted, take her anyplace she wanted to go, and help her out however he could. And Snake Perkins dreaded his Mistress's wrath even more than he used to fear his mother.

He parked where he'd been told, killed the lights, and turned the engine off. When he saw that the woman wasn't getting out he asked, "Now what?"

"We wait. Someone suitable will come along soon, I think."

"How do you know that?" Snake was careful to sound only curious, not like he was giving her a hard time, or something.

She gestured with her chin toward the park. "Over there is a place for children."

"Yeah, a playground. So? It's dark, kids are all gone home."

"For now, yes. But the children, they feel safe here. A child who is not safe at home, the parents fighting, a big brother who is mean—may come here to feel safe again, for a little while. So we wait."

"Yeah, okay."

Snake went back to the jukebox inside his head. He had just finished grooving to the Oak Ridge Boys doing "Elvira" when Cecelia Mbwato said, "Why is it you are called 'Snake?' Because you are so tall and skinny? Or because you are deadly, like the mamba?"

Snake thought a mamba was some kind of dance that greasers did, but he said, "It ain't a nickname. It's my real name. They give it to me the day I was born."

"A curious thing to name a child."

"My folks seen this movie, *Escape from New York*. There's a character in it, guy called Snake Plisskin. They thought it was some kinda cool name, I guess."

"It must have brought you much mockery when you were small, from other children." There was no trace of sympathy in Cecelia Mbwato's voice.

"Yeah, I guess you could say that."

"If my parents had done such to me, I think I would be tempted to kill them, when I was grown."

There was something in Snake Perkins's voice that was almost enough to frighten even Cecelia Mbwato when he said softly, "How do you know I didn't?"

DEXTER GALVIN LOVED the playground, even at night, when there were no other kids to hang out with. In fact, night was better, because it was quiet. Dex liked sitting on one of the swings at night—not riding it, just swaying back and forth and thinking about stuff.

The stuff he thought about these days usually involved his Mom and Terry, her latest boyfriend. A couple of months ago, Terry had gotten Mom to try this stuff, crystal myth or something. The two of them would smoke it and pretty soon they'd get all weird, talking a mile a minute, laughing, crying, not sleeping for days. Then the myth would wear off, and they'd get all sad and mean until they had some more. Then it would start up all over again.

Tonight, Terry had tried to get Dex to have a puff from the pipe that he and Mom used. Mom heard him and started yelling, stuff like "Jesus, Terry, he's only nine fucking years old!" Then Terry had got mad and slapped Mom. A little while after that, Dex had sneaked out and headed for the playground.

There was a big, kind of beat-up car parked near the entrance to the park. Dex saw the silhouettes of two people in the front seat, one looking like it might be a woman. Dex wondered if they had been fooling around with each other, stopping when they saw him approach. Well, they could fool around all they wanted, as if Dex gave a shit. It was none of his business.

He had just passed the car when he heard one of the doors opening. He looked back and saw a tall, really thin guy get out. The man looked toward Dex and called, "Hey, kid, wait up a second. I wanna ask you somethin'."

Yeah, right. Dex had watched enough TV to know danger when he saw it. He turned and ran, flat out, toward the park.

He almost made it as far as the front gate.

SNAKE PERKINS SLAMMED the trunk lid and got back behind the wheel.

"He is no good to me if he is dead," Cecelia Mbwato said.

"I didn't kill him," Snake Perkins told her. "Just put him out with a sleeper hold until I could get the duct tape on him."

"What do you mean, 'sleeper hold?'"

Snake held out one hand, fingers shaped as if he were gripping a large glass. "Grabbed him around the neck and put pressure on the carotid arteries. Cuts the flow of blood to the brain, puts 'em right out. No permanent damage."

At that moment they heard the first of the muffled cries coming from the trunk.

"See?" Snake said. "Told ya."

Snake wasn't worried about the noise. You'd have to be either inside the car or standing right next to it to hear anything, and in a little while it wouldn't matter, anyway.

Cecelia Mbwato nodded. "Good. Now take us to the place I have selected. When we get there, and I have completed the preparations, you will assist me with the procedure." She paused. "I was told you are a man who is not bothered by the blood and pain of others."

"Long as it ain't my own, don't bother me a bit."

Another nod. "Very good. Now drive."

Snake started the car and headed off to the isolated spot near the lake that he and the woman had found the day before.

He wondered just how much blood and pain he was going to have to deal with when he got there.

CHAPTER 5

WHEN THE BUZZER sounded, the tall, brown-haired woman put down the ladle she was holding and went to answer the door.

Standing in the hall was a woman of medium height and rather chunky build. Her face, behind aviator glasses, was framed by thick black hair. The earnest expression that she wore went well with the tailored gray suit and slim briefcase.

"I'm a little early," the visitor said. "I hope that's okay."

"No problem at all," Libby Chastain told her, opening the door wider. "Come on in. Let me just turn off the stove."

They walked into the condominium's large kitchen, where Libby extinguished the blue gas flame that was burning under a large, black pot.

"Ah, a cauldron!" the visitor, whose name was Susan Mackey, exclaimed. "And what goes in there—tail of salamander, eye of newt, that sort of thing?"

Libby smiled slightly. "More like paste of tomato and leaf of basil," she said. "I'm making spaghetti sauce for later. But it can sit a while with no problem. Why don't we do the same?"

A deep furrow appeared between Susan Mackey's bushy eyebrows. "Sorry?"

"Sit a while, I mean. Come on in the living room."

The condo's living room was done in earth tones, the furniture mostly the comfortable variety of Scandinavian modern.

Once they were both seated, Susan leaned forward and said, "As I told you on the phone, I've got another job that would seem to need your, uh, talents. Are you interested?"

"That depends on the job, as always. The Devil—or, I should say, the Goddess—lives in the details. Is this gig like the last one?"

"In some ways, but on a bigger scale."

Libby thought for a moment. "What was the name of that old fraud in Cleveland? Sister Meredeth, or something?" There was amusement in her voice.

"Mother Josephine," Susan said. "You may not recall her too well, but I bet she still remembers you—not to mention that séance of hers we sat in on."

"You'd think someone who claims to call up the spirits of the dead would be prepared for a real ghost to show up."

"Apparently not, judging from the way she ran screaming from the room."

Libby studied the other woman for a moment. "You know, Susan, I sometimes wonder what the other folks at the Society for the Advancement of Rational Thought would say if they knew you sometimes debunk spiritualist scams by hiring a real witch."

"You're down on the books as a 'consultant,'" Susan said with a shrug. "As long as I get results, nobody's going to ask many questions about the exact nature of the consulting." She fiddled with the latches on her briefcase for a moment. "Besides, we're not opposed to spirituality, on principle, or even to belief in the supernatural. We're just against those who use beliefs in such things to exploit gullible people."

"And that's what you've got this time? Another con artist?"

"This guy is to con artists what Houdini was to magicians—the *crème de la crème*. Or maybe *crème de la creep* is more like it."

"So what's his particular angle?"

"That," Susan said, "is something I think you should see for yourself."

MANY SMALL, INDEPENDENT movie theaters have been driven out of business by shopping mall megaplexes, pay-per-view cable, and DVD players. Some of these former dream palaces have been torn down, while others have been converted to other uses—like the one in New York's East Fifties where the marquee now proclaimed "Tommy Timberlake Ministry," and, in smaller letters, "Healing, Testimony, Prophecy."

On the way in, Libby and Susan passed a table holding a tall box that read "Donations," guarded by a large man who looked more like a bouncer than a deacon. Since everyone filing in ahead of them seemed to be dropping in a "voluntary" offering, the two women each put in a few dollars. They did not want to draw attention to themselves.

The inside of the theater had probably not looked this good since the place opened in the 1940s. It had been extensively refurbished, with an eye towards opulence rather than good taste. However, the large placards bearing biblical quotations were not part of the original decor, nor was the giant cross that dominated the stage. The starkness of the plain, black cross was offset by the many large potted plants that were arranged around it.

The place was rapidly filling up, but the two women were able to find seats together about halfway down the middle section. The chairs were luxuriously padded and extremely comfortable. "Nearer my God, to Thee" was playing softly over the theater's sound system.

A woman with severely permed blonde hair, wearing a blue dress of elegant simplicity, was working the room. As she made her way around the seated crowd, she waved to many and smiled at all. Periodically she would pause to speak to someone in one of the seats for a minute or two before moving on.

"Who's that?" Libby asked.

"Winona Timberlake, the Reverend Tommy's wife," Susan said quietly. "Sort of a combination warm-up act and mistress of ceremonies. She does this meet-and-greet thing before every service."

"Looks like she's headed our way."

Winona Timberlake made her slow way up the aisle toward them, and paused two rows in front of where they sat.

"Hello, dear, and welcome to our church," she said to the middle-aged woman sitting in the aisle seat. "I'm Winona Timberlake."

"Oh, I know who you are!" the woman exclaimed joyfully. "I've seen you on the TV, I don't know how many times! I'm Madge Collier, and this is my sister, Rosie."

"Is this your first time attending our service here?"

"Yes, yes it is. I'm from Patterson, New Jersey. I watch your program every week, you know, but I thought coming in person might help me find the grace I need to, well, to get through some things."

"Is there something particular that is afflicting you, dear?" Winona Timberlake's voice radiated sympathy and concern.

"Well it's just that the doctor says I have a cancer of the—you know, the womanly parts. And he wants me to have an operation. But it's so expensive, and I don't have hardly any insurance, and I just..."

The woman identified as Rosie reached over and grasped her sister's hand where it lay on the armrest.

"Anyway," Madge Collier continued, "I was so hoping that being here with the Reverend, maybe the Holy Spirit might inspire me, you know, to help me figure out what I should do."

"I'm sure he will, dear," Winona Timberlake said with a brilliant smile. "There's absolutely no doubt in my mind that everything will work out for the best. The important thing is that you trust in the Lord Jesus."

"Oh, I do, I always have—" Madge said, but the other woman had already moved on to greet some new arrivals.

After another few minutes of mingling with the assembled worshipers, Winona Timberlake mounted the steps that led to the stage. She was handed a microphone by a minion, and by the time she reached center stage, a spotlight was waiting there to welcome her. The recorded music had stopped playing, and the crowd murmur quickly died down to nothing.

In the sudden silence, Winona Timberlake looked out at the audience. She held them with her eyes for a long moment before saying, "Friends, I'd like to welcome you to our service tonight. It feels so good, doesn't it, to come together with other Bible-believing Christians in the fellowship of the Holy Spirit? And fellowship is so important now, isn't it? Because we live in tough times, you and I do."

She paused for a beat. "Tough times where our spirits are assailed, our families are threatened, our schools are corrupted, and the streets of our cities are not safe for decent people." There were murmurs of assent from the crowd.

"But for those of us who believe in the Lord Jesus, there is always hope in our hearts. And here tonight with a message of hope, with a message and a vision and the blessed powers of healing and prophecy, is the man I am proud to call my husband and inspiration—the Reverend Tommy Timberlake!"

The applause that broke out would not have shamed a rock star.

Winona Timberlake's spotlight winked out and was instantly replaced by another that shone on a man standing stage left. He was medium-sized, although the subtly padded shoulders of his handmade suit made him seem bigger. His curly black hair seemed to shine in the light from overhead and he was a case study in barely controlled energy as he strode to the center of the stage, which his wife had quietly vacated. Even as he moved, the Reverend Tommy Timberlake was already talking. "I can feel the spirit of the Lord in this building tonight, friends." The applause faded at his first words. His voice seemed hushed, intimate, but the microphone he held carried each word clearly to every corner of the large theater.

"And why shouldn't He be among us, who have come here to praise Him?" There were a few shouts of "Amen" and "Praise his name" from the audience. "Didn't he tell us, 'Come unto me, ye who are afflicted and sore afraid?' Isn't that what the Lord, the God of Hosts, told us?"

"He did," "Yes, praise Him," and "It's the truth" came from various amen corners.

"Then we must believe," the Reverend Tommy Timberlake said. "We must trust in the Lord. We must have faith that the Lord sees our pain, knows our fear, understands our tribulation, and that He will deliver us from all of it if we will just ask Him to do so."

Reverend Tommy squeezed his eyes shut, like a man afflicted by a sudden migraine. He took in a sharp breath that was clearly audible over the microphone. "Is there a woman named Beatrice among us tonight? Beatrice, whose mother is so seriously ill"?

A woman off to the left suddenly screeched, "Yes, it's me! It's me!"

Reverend Tommy took a few steps in her direction. His eyes were open now, his gaze piercing. "Beatrice, your mother is ill with—is it colitis?"

"Yes, yes it is, Reverend! Oh, my Lord, yes!"

"I am in the way of knowing, Beatrice, that your mother will be healed, if only you have enough faith. Do you have faith, Beatrice? Do you love the Lord Jesus?"

"Oh, yes, Reverend Tommy! Praise His name!"

"Then if your faith is strong, if you truly believe, your dear mother will be delivered from her plight."

Reverend Tommy drew another noisy breath. "Is there a man here named Jimmy, no Jerry, from the Midwest, from, Iowa?"

It went on that way for another ten or so minutes, and then Reverend Tommy said, "Is there a woman named Madge, from New Jersey, I think it might be Patterson?"

The woman who had been speaking to Winona Timberlake jumped to her feet and began waving her hand frantically. "It's me, Reverend, over here!"

"Madge, the Lord is revealing to me that you have an illness, a cancer. That's right, isn't it?"

"Yes, Reverend, yes! Praise His name!"

"Do you believe the Lord has the power to cure your cancer, Madge?"

"Yes, I do, Reverend Tommy!"

"Can you feel his healing touch upon you even now?"

"Oh, my Lord, yes I do, I feel it now!"

"Can you sense those cancer cells shrinking, dying, disappearing from your body through the holy power of the Lord Jesus? I say, can you FEEL it?"

"Oh yes, yes, I do Reverend, YES!" Her voice was a scream now.

The Reverend Tommy looked up to heaven with puppy dog eyes of pious gratitude. "Thank you, Jesus, for healing this poor woman, thank you, Lord, thank you." Another loud intake of breath. "Is there someone with us whose son is in jail, a woman named... Nancy?"

"AND DID YOU notice," Susan said, "the collection plate, or whatever they call it, was passed at the end, even though we had already been hit up for a donation coming in?"

Libby Chastain nodded absently. They were sitting in a coffee shop a couple of blocks away from Reverend Tommy's tabernacle.

"And you can bet your bottom drachma that the take wouldn't be nearly so much if it weren't for that spiritual dog and pony show that Reverend Tommy puts on every time," Susan went on. "I don't know why he doesn't just call himself 'The Amazing Crisco' and start working Las Vegas, except there's probably a lot more money to be made by claiming that your feats of clairvoyance are courtesy of the Lord Almighty—and, by the way, have you heard a single word I said since we got here?"

Libby looked up from her coffee cup and with a tight little smile said, "I know how he's doing it."

A WEEK LATER, the two women were back inside the converted theater, watching Winona Timberlake make her rounds among the crowd before the start of the worship service.

"Winona's the key, of course," Libby said softly. "She's the source of the information that Reverend Tommy uses for his little 'divine inspiration' act."

"But the two of them have no contact in between her chatting up the audience and the start of the service," Susan whispered. "I mean, she doesn't even leave the stage until Tommy comes out to do his thing."

"Yes, and I'm sure that's deliberate. Otherwise, even these people, who want so desperately to believe, would start to smell a rat. But there are lots of ways to communicate these days, kiddo, and not all of them involve messages from the Almighty." She reached into her purse and pulled out a small bundle wrapped in cloth and bound with two slim ribbons—one green, the other blue.

"What on earth is that?" Susan asked.

"Something I prepared earlier this evening. It's been imbued with a spell for causing the hidden to be revealed. The spell is usually employed for treasure finding, that sort of thing, but I think it'll work very well for what I have in mind."

"I was kind of hoping you'd just wave your wand and change the Reverend Tommy into a toad, or something."

"If I did that, always assuming I could, all it would do is create sympathy for him. Winona would probably have these poor people bringing in flies every week to feed him." She gently patted the bundle in her lap. "This is better, trust me."

"If you say so. You're the expert."

"Were you able to get some media people to show up?"

Susan nodded. "The religion editor for the *New York Times* is here somewhere, and I also managed to interest a guy from the *Post.* He's sitting about six rows behind us. A woman I know at WPIX-TV wasn't sure she could make it, but promised to try."

"All right, good. Combined with the people who are actually in the audience, that should be—oh, look, Winona's getting ready to start."

The pattern of the service was the same. Winona Timberlake made a few pious-sounding remarks, introduced the Reverend Tommy, and then unobtrusively disappeared from the stage. The Reverend dispensed platitudes for a while, then once again begin noisily receiving divine inspiration concerning members of the audience and their various problems.

He had been going on for about five minutes when Libby leaned over toward Susan and said softly, "I guess this is as good a time as any." She carefully undid the two ribbons around the object in her lap, muttering in a language that Susan didn't recognize. The cloth wrapping parted to reveal a small collection of twigs. They were about six inches long and appeared to be coated with some kind of light blue powder.

Libby grasped the bunch of twigs in both hands, said something else in that foreign tongue, and repeated it twice more. Then, with a sharp motion of her wrists, she suddenly broke the twigs in two.

The microphone around Reverend Tommy's neck instantly lost power, but the theater speakers did not fall silent. Instead, they began to broadcast a different voice, one that sounded very much like Winona Timberlake's.

"Move stage right a little bit," the woman's voice said. "There's an old geezer from New Hampshire whose daughter's been diagnosed with AIDS, the little tramp. His first name's Martin, by the way..."

For a couple of seconds, the Reverend Tommy seemed unaware that the audience had stopped hearing his voice and begun to listen to another's. But then his eyes widened and his mouth dropped open. Instead of looking like a man in the middle of a migraine, he quickly came to resemble someone having a massive coronary. He frantically began to tap his microphone, then looked off-stage and snarled to someone, "Turn this goddamn thing back on!" But the mike remained silent, and the Reverend Tommy's unamplified voice was soon drowned out by the angry murmuring from the audience that soon grew into shouts, catcalls, and boos.

Meanwhile, Winona Timberlake went on and on: "Now you want a woman named Catherine, some fat cow from Wisconsin, who's been having a lot of trouble with high blood pressure, surprise, surprise. See if you can pray about fifty pounds off her..."

IN THE BACK seat of the taxi, Susan Mackey was still grinning. "You know, you were right," she said to Libby. "That actually *was* better than turning him into a toad. I don't think the Reverend Tommy is going to be ministering to many of the faithful next week, or in the weeks following."

"No, I expect he'll be lucky to draw enough of a crowd to fill a broom closet. Couldn't happen to a nicer guy, either."

"But how did you figure out how he and Winona were using a radio transmitter? Some sort of mystical divination?"

Libby snorted. "More like common sense, honey," she said. "He had to be getting the information from Winona—who must have a remarkable memory, to go along with that nasty mouth of hers. And since she clearly didn't talk to him before he came on stage, she had to be feeding him the stuff while he was actually up there. They make radio receivers the size of a shirt button these days, and he certainly had one in his ear. I couldn't see it, but then I didn't need to—uh, driver, this is my building coming up, on the corner."

Five minutes later, Libby Chastain, was unlocking the door to her condominium. As she went around turning on the lights, she was humming softly—a tune that the Reverend Tommy Timberlake would have recognized as "Rock of Ages".

Then the phone started ringing.

QUINCEY MORRIS SAT on the edge of his bed at the Holiday Inn and squinted at the plastic display card that bore the directions for making outside calls. After a moment, he reached inside his jacket and withdrew a slim address book. He looked up a number and began to punch buttons.

The phone at the other end was answered on the fourth ring. "I knew you were going to call." It was a woman's voice, alto and a little husky.

"I bet you say that to all the boys, Libby."

The woman chuckled. "Yes, I do, Quincey, and to the girls, too. Helps create that aura of mystery, you know."

"I've always found you eminently mysterious," Morris said. "So, how's business?"

"Well, I just got home from an interesting gig that a certain preacher and his wife aren't likely to forget soon. But, other than that, things have been pretty slow."

"Maybe you need to get your own 900 number."

"Sure, that's it. 1–900-ME-WITCH, maybe? I could have my own infomercial."

"It's got potential," he said. Then his voice became serious. "Listen, I'm on a case in Madison, Wisconsin, and I need you."

"All right. When?" Her voice had also lost its levity.

"Quick as you can get here."

She thought for a moment. "If there's a flight out tonight, I'll be on it. If not, I'll get the first one tomorrow."

"Okay, that'll be fine."

"So, what's the job? I need to know what kind of gear to pack."

"I want you to do a couple of things. First is to revive, and maybe strengthen, a network of warding charms in a house."

"How powerful do you need them to be?"

"The strongest you've got. The family's been under escalating magical attack over the last three months. With lethal intent, looks like."

"All right, that seems fairly straightforward. What's the rest of it?"

"Find whoever's responsible for this assault and stop it."

"Stop the assault—or stop the person?"

Morris thought about the LaRues, saw again the fear and exhaustion and despair etched into their faces, like copper engravings inscribed by acid.

"Whatever it takes, Libby," he said quietly. "Whatever it takes."

MORRIS DIALED ANOTHER number, this one a room-to-room call. When Walter LaRue answered, Morris asked, "Are you folks all settled in?"

"Pretty much. We decided to keep the connecting door open. Marcie's next door with Sarah, and Timmy, and I'll bunk in here. But I still don't get why you think we'll be any safer here than at home. I mean, if we're talking about something, uh, you know..."

"Supernatural?"

"Yes, right. I mean, what prevents it from following us here, whatever it is?"

"Because the attacks are all aimed at your living space," Morris explained. "Has your daughter reported any incidents occurring while she was at school?"

"No, she hasn't, you're right. Wait—what about the time in my car, when I damn near had a head-on with that truck?"

"Your car's part of your living space. You're in it every day, I'd guess, and at predictable times. Commuting, and so on."

"And you think that makes a difference?"

"I'm sure it does. We'll talk about that some more tomorrow. You and your family get yourselves a decent night's sleep, okay? Tomorrow we'll get to work making your home safe again."

"Who's 'we?'"

"Me, along with a consultant I've called in, who'll be here late tonight or early tomorrow."

"Consultant? What's this one's name—Van Helsing?"

"Her name's Elizabeth Chastain, and she's one of the best in the country at what she does."

"You mean she's some kind of... ghostbuster?"

"No, I mean she's some kind of witch."

CHAPTER 6

THE HUNTER ARRIVED in New York on a British Airways flight from London, although his journey had begun the day before, in the heat and dust of Johannesburg, South Africa. His lean body was aching after all those hours of cramming his six feet four inches into an airline seat in Coach that had clearly been designed with someone smaller in mind.

As he entered the main terminal building, he quickly scanned the ragged semicircle of people, each one waiting to meet a passenger, a few holding small signs with names on them. He didn't see his own name, but wasn't concerned. They knew he was here. They would find him.

The man's thin face had the weathered look of someone who spends a lot of time outdoors without the luxury of sunscreen. His eyes were the pale blue you sometimes see in fine Dresden china. They moved constantly, blinked rarely, and missed nothing. His tropical-weight gray suit, not cheap and not expensive, had already been rumpled when he'd boarded the plane in Jo'burg. By now, even its wrinkles had wrinkles.

He retrieved his big, battered suitcase from the baggage carousel and made his way over to Customs. He had been standing in line for less than a minute when he was approached by a well-dressed, thirtyish black man carrying a briefcase.

"Mister Van Dreenan?" The black man didn't sound the least bit tentative.

"Detective Sergeant Van Dreenan, *ja*."

The other man's eyes might have narrowed a little at Van Dreenan's use of the title, but if so, the expression was gone in an instant. He held up a small leather case containing a badge and a laminated ID card. "Special Agent Dale Fenton, FBI."

Fenton slipped the leather case into a pocket and extended his hand. "Welcome to America." His handshake was brisk, businesslike.

After shaking hands, Fenton stepped back and said, "Would you come with me, please?"

He led Van Dreenan to a nearby office marked "Authorized Personnel Only." Inside, a pretty Chinese woman who'd been working at a computer looked up.

"Oh, hi, Agent Fenton," she said pleasantly. "Is this the gentleman we spoke about?"

Fenton nodded. Van Dreenan put down his suitcase and stepped forward. "Garth Van Dreenan," he said. He shook the woman's hand carefully, as if well aware how easy it would be to break the bones.

"Veronica Chen," she said. "Welcome to the United States. May I have your passport and visa, please?"

She slowly slid his passport over a scanner that looked similar to the kind used in supermarket checkout lanes, and was rewarded by several electronic beeps and the illumination of a small green light. Then, consulting his visa, she typed something into the computer, waited, then typed some more. She clicked the mouse, and on a shelf behind her a printer came to life and began slowly disgorging a document.

Veronica Chen opened a drawer and produced a couple of pre-inked rubber stamps. She applied each one to both the passport and visa, then returned them to Van Dreenan. Pulling the sheet of paper from the printer, she placed it in front of Fenton. "Signature and badge number, please," she said to the FBI man. "And today's date."

Fenton filled in the information quickly and returned the document. "Thanks, Veronica, appreciate your help." Then he turned to Van Dreenan and said, "You've just cleared Customs. Let's go."

As they proceeded down a long hallway, Van Dreenan asked, "What was that form that you signed in there?"

"That was me sparing a visiting fellow officer the indignity of having his baggage searched, by attesting that he hasn't brought anything illegal into the country," Fenton said. He eyed Van Dreenan's suitcase. "I hope you're not going to make a liar out of me by having a machine gun in there." He did not sound like he was joking.

Van Dreenan smiled crookedly. "No," he said. "No... machine guns." The pause was similar to the one Bela Lugosi used to use in the movies when saying, "I never drink... wine."

THE FBI'S NEW York City field office occupies two floors of Federal Plaza on Ninth Avenue and West Thirty-fourth. Although space is at a premium, a couple of small offices are kept vacant for use by agents on temporary duty, and other federal law enforcement types passing through town on business.

In the room that had been assigned to him, Fenton sat down behind the scratched and battered metal desk, waved Van Dreenan to an equally cheap chair opposite, then took three thick files out of his briefcase and dropped them on the desk. "Three victims," he said. "All children."

"*Ja,* I know, three," Van Dreenan said. "So far."

Fenton shot him a look before continuing. "Two in Pennsylvania, the other one in West Virginia, all within a space of two weeks. Identical m.o. in each case. Uh, that's short for—"

"I am familiar with the term *modus operandi*, Agent Fenton," Van Dreenan said mildly. "Go on, please."

"The Bureau wasn't called in until after the third one. Murder isn't itself a federal crime in this country, but when it appeared that the killer or killers had crossed a state line, that made it our case."

"By 'our,' you mean the Behavioral Science Unit."

Fenton nodded. "The field offices handle most of the investigations the Bureau takes on. But serial murder often crosses jurisdictions. And so do we."

"Your department is quite well known within law enforcement circles, even in backwaters like South Africa." Van Dreenan's voice gave the last words a light coat of irony. "Justifiably famous."

"Just don't go thinking it's like in the movies or TV. That stuff is mostly crap."

"I don't go to movies," Van Dreenan said. "And I rarely watch television."

Fenton fussed around with the files for a few seconds. "I understand you were invited over here as a 'consultant' because your own outfit has got something of a reputation. I'd never heard of it, myself."

Van Dreenan's big shoulders twitched in something like a shrug. "Not surprising, really. We try to avoid undue publicity."

"The Occult Crimes Unit." Fenton shook his head. "I thought it sounded like *The X-Files,* or something."

"The what files? I don't know about them."

"Sorry, forgot you don't watch TV. Never mind. I read up on your unit, though, once I was assigned to be your liaison while you're here. You guys are into some pretty weird shit. Some folks over here might not take it real seriously."

Van Dreenan stared at him in silence for several seconds before he leaned forward. He blue eyes bore into Fenton's as he spoke, but he never raised his voice.

"There were a hundred and fifty-eight witchcraft-related crimes reported in South Africa last year, Mister Fenton. Many more surely went unreported. Of those, seventy-eight percent involved crimes against people believed guilty of witchcraft. In the outlying villages, the townships, sometimes even in the cities, a man or woman is accused of witchcraft, it is a serious thing. There are consequences."

Fenton drew breath to speak, but Van Dreenan went on in the same icy, quiet voice.

"Sometimes the village chief levies a fine, paid to the victim. But if the matter is more serious, the accused witch may be 'necklaced.' Do you know what that means, Mister Fenton, necklacing? It has nothing to do with jewelry, I assure you."

Again, Fenton was given no chance to answer.

"You tie someone up, good and tight, *ja?* Maybe to a tree, maybe not. Then you take an old tire, pour some petrol on it, soak it pretty good. You place that tire around the neck of the person you have tied up. Like putting a necklace on a woman, see? And then you set fire to it. It is one *fokken* ugly way to die, Mister Fenton."

"I've heard of it," Fenton said, when Van Dreenan finally paused.

"*Ach,* you do know something of my country. That is good. But do you know why such a method is used?"

Fenton shrugged. "As an example, to scare others? It's slow, agonizing, and the final result looks horrible."

"It does have such an effect, of course. But that is not the principal reason."

"What is, then?"

"Tribal beliefs hold that the only way to kill a witch for certain is through fire. Otherwise, it is said, they may come back, seeking revenge."

Fenton made a face. "Pretty goddamn barbaric."

"No doubt," Van Dreenan said. "But such barbarism, if it must be called that, has not always been confined to the continent of Africa, Mister Fenton. They did the same in Europe, beginning in the Fifteenth Century, you know. And always, they used fire. The *Malleus Maleficarum* was very clear—"

"The what?"

"*The Hammer of Witches,* is the English translation. It was a book that was, in effect, the Bible for witch hunters. It is flawed in many ways, but says very clearly that a witch must be put to death by fire. It caused much suffering for many innocent people, over the course of some two hundred years."

"Look, Van Dreenan, we're burning daylight, ourselves. Is there a point to this history lesson?"

"Indeed there is, Mister Fenton. You have said that you do not take my work seriously—"

"Hey, wait, I never said—"

"—and I simply wanted to give you some perspective on what I do. Of course, investigating such crimes as I have just described is only part of the work my unit does. The rest involves the activities of the witches themselves."

"I was wondering when we were going to get to that."

"The reason why I came here, *ja.* Understand, when I speak of witches, I do not refer to the *sangomas,* the traditional healers. They practice what you would call folk medicine. Much of what they do is quite sensible, and the rest of it does no real harm, most of the time. But witchcraft..." Van Dreenan shook his head a couple of times, "that is something very different. It refers to the practice of black magic—you use the same term in this country, I think? Black magic?"

Fenton shrugged. "Sure. In stories."

"Well, what we deal with in my unit are not stories, Mister Fenton. Witches are people who use black magic, and black magic has only one purpose—to hurt people."

"You mean they *think* it hurts people, right?"

Van Dreenan just looked at him.

"These witches you're talking about," Fenton said, "they commit crimes in the mistaken belief that doing so will give them this supernatural power, right?"

Van Dreenan remained silent.

"Or, are you talking about some kind of psychosomatic effect? Like in voodoo? I've read up on that, too. Guy finds out he's been cursed by a *houngan,* and because he and the *houngan* are part of the same belief system, the guy's mind causes him to develop symptoms consistent with the curse. That the kind of thing you're talking about?"

Van Dreenan produced a tiny smile. "Of course, Agent Fenton. What else could I be referring to? Some sort of genuine supernatural power? The ability to harness and direct the so-called 'forces of darkness?' If I said that, you would regard me as either a lunatic or a fool, I think, *ja?* Certainly not an experienced, professional police officer, which is what I am."

Fenton nodded slowly. "Yeah," he said, studying Van Dreenan's face. "Yeah, I guess I would, at that."

SECUNDUS INVESTIGATION

CHAPTER 7

WALTER LARUE HAD slept until almost 9:30, an indication of how exhausted he'd really been. At a few minutes after 10:00, freshly shaved and showered, he was just picking up the room phone to call Morris when he heard a knock at the door. After a quick look through the peephole, he opened up to admit Morris and the woman who was with him.

"This is Elizabeth Chastain, who I mentioned to you last night," Morris said. "Libby, meet Walter LaRue."

The hand the woman extended was free of jewelry and nail polish, and her grip was surprisingly strong. "Hello, Mister LaRue," she said, her voice a pleasant contralto. "I'm glad to meet you, although I deplore the circumstances that make it necessary." She was tall, slim, her dark brown hair worn shoulder-length. Intelligent gray eyes gazed out from a face that would never see thirty again. The woman was not what most men would call classically beautiful, but LaRue thought she had the kindest face he had ever seen.

"Thanks, I appreciate that, Ms. Chastain—or do you prefer 'Miss,' or 'Mrs.,' or...."

"Perhaps you should just call me Libby," she said.

"All right, I will, thank you. Please—come in and sit down."

After they were all seated, LaRue said, "I hope you'll pardon me for staring, Libby, it's just that you don't look much like my idea of a witch."

Libby Chastain laughed softly. "That's all right, Mr. LaRue," she said. "As Sigourney Weaver says in one of those *Alien* movies, 'I get that a lot.'"

"I mean no offense."

"None taken," she said. "I'm familiar with the image, believe me: conical hat, flying broom, warts, maniacal cackle, and all the rest." She looked at Morris and said, deadpan, "I've been working on my cackle, by the way, Quincey. It sounds quite fiendish now. Remind me to do it for you before I go back home."

LaRue gave that a small smile before saying to Morris, "You said last night that you would explain why we need the services of a, uh—"

"Witch," Libby said solemnly.

"Yes, right, a witch. I'm not arguing with you, understand, I'm not questioning your judgment." He looked from Morris to Libby Chastain, then back again. "I just want to know what the hell is going on."

"Don't blame you for that, podner," Morris said. He spent a few seconds gathering his thoughts, then said, "The first thing you need to understand is this: when I bring Libby over to your place later today, she will not be the first witch ever to cross the threshold."

"Are you talking about whoever's been doing this stuff to us? You mean, somebody snuck into the house—"

"No, Mister LaRue," Morris said. "I'm talking about your late mother-in-law."

LaRue's eyes narrowed. After looking at each of them for a second or two, he said, coldly, "I'm assuming that remark wasn't intended as humor, because I sure don't find it funny. I was pretty fond of Greta, and the kids loved her—not to mention my wife, who probably wouldn't care to hear you refer to *her mother* as a *witch*."

"No insult to her memory was intended," Morris said, shaking his head for emphasis.

"I think we have some explaining to do," Libby said patiently. "He wasn't using the term 'witch' in the popular sense, which, as you said yourself, has negative connotations. The word has a specific meaning, and it has nothing to do with the stereotype. When Quincey introduced me as a witch, he wasn't being either funny or cute. He was being accurate—just as he was in using the term to describe your late mother-in-law, rest her soul."

"See, there are two basic kinds of witchcraft," Morris said. "They each have several names, depending on who you talk to, but the basic distinction is one you've probably heard of: white and black."

"White magic and black magic," LaRue said. He didn't look pissed off any more, just interested. "So, what *is* the difference?"

"White magic derives its power from nature," Libby told him. "From the four essential elements of earth, air, fire, and water, as well as from the sun and moon."

"Is all that a fancy way of saying 'from God?'" LaRue asked.

Libby thought for a moment. "Well, it can be—although some of us might use other terms, including 'Goddess.'"

"And if you want to posit God as the source of white magic," Morris said, "it shouldn't be too hard to figure out where the other side comes from."

"No, I suppose not," LaRue said. He looked at Libby Chastain and asked, "Which is the stronger?"

"That's not an answerable question," she told him. "But there are some clear differences in practice. For instance, you can't use white magic to do harm to somebody."

"Why not?"

Libby shrugged. "It just isn't possible. There aren't any rituals in white magic that can be used to harm others. White witches, for example, don't do curses."

"That being the case, I'm kind of surprised that the bad guys haven't wiped you folks out a long time ago. I assume that black magic *does* allow curses."

"Oh, yes, hundreds of them," Libby said. "But don't assume that white magic is powerless. Self-defense is allowed, as is defense of others. And there are lots of ways that can be accomplished."

"You've already seen one of them," Morris told LaRue.

Although he was out of his depth, Walter LaRue wasn't stupid. "Those charms, you mean. The ones Greta made."

"That's right," Libby said. "They're warding charms, so called because they can ward off spells cast by others, including curses."

"That's what I meant when I referred to your late mother-in-law as a witch," Morris said. "I meant no aspersion, although I should have explained myself better. It's obvious from what Greta left behind that she was a white witch, and that term is *not* an insult."

"She was also your protector," Libby added. "Clearly, those warding charms were used to guard your family from attack by black magic. The problem is, many kinds of spells only retain their power while the witch who cast them is alive."

LaRue looked at her for several seconds, then nodded. "So when Greta was killed, the charms stopped doing their job. And then, somebody who practices black magic zapped us."

"Either that, or there was a spell already in place," Morris said. "You know, kind of like a plane in a holding pattern. And when your mother-in-law died—"

"The plane fell out of the sky," LaRue said. "Right on top of us."

"Yeah, something like that," Morris said. "Which leads us to the question of who's behind this. You've got an enemy, Mister LaRue. Or someone in your family has. Any idea of who it might be?

"An enemy who knows black magic? Can't help you there," LaRue said. "I didn't even realize there was such a thing, until now."

"Your enemy doesn't have to be a witch," Libby said. "Just somebody who knows how to find one. Quite a few witches, white and black both, are available for hire, if you know where to look."

"Any business rivals?" Morris asked. "Someone you beat out of a fat software contract, maybe? Or how about a former employee who didn't react too well to being let go?"

LaRue sat staring silently at the floor for the better part of a minute. "No, I'm sorry, but I can't come up with a single reasonable possibility. I have competitors in business, sure, but it's not a cut-throat kind of thing. And I haven't fired anybody in years. People leave, of course, for various reasons. But there's no bad blood that I can think of."

Later, as the two of them walked to the parking lot, Morris asked Libby, "Think he's telling the truth?"

"Yes, I do," Libby said. "He wasn't giving off any of the vibes that usually accompany deception."

"Damn. That's going to make it harder."

"Maybe so. But let's not neglect the obvious."

"Which would be...?"

"The protector was the wife's mother, right?"

"Right. So?"

"So, after we finish up at the house, I think we ought to talk to the wife."

QUINCEY MORRIS USED his borrowed key to unlock the house's front door. "Come on in," he said to Libby Chastain. "Welcome to Chez LaRue."

Closing the door behind them, Libby leaned her back against it. She and Morris stood silently in the hallway for almost a full minute. They appeared to be listening for something, but they could not have said what it was.

"Nobody home," Morris said finally, "but then we knew that. Come on."

"Wait," she said, grasping his forearm for a moment. "It occurs to me that we'd best keep our wits about us while we're in here—at least until the warding charms are back in place."

"Why? What's bothering you?"

She sighed once, softly. "Quincey, you've got the LaRues stashed over at the Holiday Inn. For their safety, you said, right?"

"Yeah, sure."

"And you did that for what reason?"

"Because it looks like the magical attacks are aimed at places the LaRues are known to—oh."

"Known to spend a lot of their time," she finished. "Exactly. So the spell that's causing all this trouble is directed toward places, not people. Which means the damned thing—and I mean that literally—may not be able to distinguish between the folks who live here and a couple of visitors."

"Like you and me, you mean."

"You got it, Sherlock. So we stay together, we watch each other's back, and we keep alert. All right?"

"No argument from me."

A smile lit her face briefly. "That *will* be a first. Oh—one more thing."

"Yes, mother."

"If, at any time we're in here, you hear me say '*out*'—and if I say it at all, I'll probably say it loudly—you get outside just as fast as you can. Door, window—whatever's closest, that's what you use. You don't ask questions, you don't hesitate, you don't worry about me. You're in a track meet, and that word's the starting gun. You hear it, you *go*. Understand?"

Morris looked into the gentle gray eyes, only a few inches lower than his own. "Libby, we've worked together, what, five, six times now?"

"Six, if you count this one," she said.

"I've never seen you like this before. We've always been careful, that's only good sense. But this little speech of yours—what the hell is *that* about?"

She held his gaze and shrugged. "Just a feeling. I get them, sometimes." A crooked smile. "Sort of witches' intuition."

Morris did not laugh. He had more respect for intuition than most. "And your feeling is—what?"

"There's a lot of power being used here, I can sense it." She extended her right hand, palm down. It trembled slightly. Morris realized that this was the first time he had ever seen Libby's hands anything but rock steady. "This is a bad one, Quincey."

"Scared?"

A nod. "Uh-huh."

"Want to go home?"

"You bet I do," she said.

"Yeah, me, too."

"So, what are we waiting for?"

They turned and slowly walked, side by side, into the LaRues' living room.

CHAPTER 8

EVERYTHING WENT WELL, at first—so well that it lulled them.

At nine different locations around the house—nine is three cubed, and hence a very powerful number in white magic—Libby Chastain was placing small objects made of straw, wood, and silver wire. They looked very similar to the one that Quincey Morris had found in the house the day before. Over each of the charms, Libby recited a brief incantation in a language that Morris didn't recognize. After the second time, he asked her about it.

"It's ancient Aramaic," she said.

"When did you start using that? Used to be, when you needed an ancient language for casting, you'd go with either Latin or Greek, right?" Morris had studied both, reluctantly, at Princeton.

She nodded. "I've been working on Aramaic for the last couple of years. Tough going sometimes, but worth the effort. It's got a lot of power associated with it, more than most of the other dead languages."

"Why's that?"

"Mainly because it was the language spoken by a famous Jewish preacher a long time ago. A guy called Joshua bar-Joseph."

Frown lines appeared on Morris's forehead. "Is this somebody I've heard of?"

Libby Chastain produced a small smile. "I expect you have. He's pretty well known, but mostly by his Greek name, for some reason."

"Which is—"

"Jesus. Jesus of Nazareth."

"Oh. Him."

LIBBY PLACED THE eighth warding charm on the top shelf of a linen closet, as far toward the back as she could reach. Closing the door, she said to Quincey Morris, "One more to go."

"Whereabouts, do you think?"

She considered briefly. "The kitchen. We haven't put any in there yet, and it will give us a nice balance of forces with the other charms."

As they walked down the hallway toward the stairs, things were already happening in the LaRues' kitchen. Drawers were slowly opening, seemingly of their own volition. Faced with an empty house, the spell cast by black witchcraft had lain dormant for a whole day, and it had gathered strength in that time.

It was strong enough to open drawers, certainly. But not all of the kitchen drawers, no indeed.

Just those containing the knives.

THEY WERE TWO or three paces away from the door of the LaRue's kitchen when Libby suddenly stopped.

Morris continued on for an additional step before his awareness of Libby's action brought him to a halt. He studied her for a moment before asking, softly, "What?"

Her eyes narrowed in concentration, she shook her head slowly from side to side. "I don't know," she said, and Morris could hear the tension in her voice. "Something—there's something stirring that wasn't here before, or maybe it just wasn't active earlier."

"Somebody else is in here?"

"No, it isn't human. It isn't even alive, not really."

"'Not really' isn't too helpful, Libby."

"I know, sorry. It's just that the impression I'm getting isn't well defined."

"Is it time for us to bail?"

She was silent for several seconds before giving vent to a long sigh. "No, we're almost finished. Getting the last warding charm in place may solve the problem all by itself. Even if it doesn't, we'll still be in a stronger position to deal with it." She looked Morris in the eye, and whatever she saw there seemed to give her some measure of comfort. "Come on," she said. "Let's go and do it."

She walked to the kitchen door, waited for Morris to join her, and opened it.

QUINCEY MORRIS, WHO had hands quick enough to pick flies right out of the air, never bragged about the phenomenal speed of his reflexes. To him, it would be like boasting about how tall he was. He'd had no control over either one—it was just part of the package that he'd been born with.

But even *he* might not have been fast enough, except that Libby Chastain's premonition had brought him to peak alertness.

The first thing he noticed as they entered the kitchen was four or five of the drawers on the far side of the room.

Open.

The second thing to get his attention was the faint sounds coming from those drawers.

Utensils rustling, moving, rubbing against each other.

What would the LaRues keep in there?

Spatulas. Forks. Whisks. Spoons.

Knives.

Because of these curious noises, Morris was looking right at the open drawers when something burst out of one to fly toward them with terrible, blinding speed.

Knives!

He sensed rather than saw the object's trajectory, identified its target by instinct rather than conscious thought, and was only just quick enough to snap his open right hand out to one side and block its path.

Which is why the razor-sharp paring knife did not bury itself in Libby Chastain's throat, as it seemed intent on doing.

Instead, the four-inch blade stabbed clear through Quincey Morris's right hand, stopping only when the plastic handle was jammed flush against his palm.

Throughout the kitchen, the sounds of metal rubbing against metal quickly grew louder.

LIBBY CHASTAIN MAY not have had Morris's lightning reflexes, but that didn't mean she was either slow or stupid. Rather than stand gaping at the knife that now transfixed Morris's bleeding hand, she grabbed his arm above the elbow and yanked him back out of the room with her.

Their legs got tangled up as they scrambled backward, causing the two of them to fall to the floor in the hallway outside the kitchen. This was what Libby had been trying for, and her reason was made clear an instant after they landed on the carpet—two more kitchen knives flew through the air where they had been standing and buried themselves in the wall beyond.

Libby hooked one foot behind the kitchen door and slammed it shut with a powerful movement of her leg. After a moment, she sat up and twisted around until her back rested against the door. Then she looked at Morris, whose hand was bleeding all over the carpet. "Can... can you sit up?"

"Yeah, I guess," he said through gritted teeth. A few seconds later, he was sitting next to her, his back supported by the kitchen door. They could both hear, and feel, the thuds as more knives struck the door from the kitchen side, like hungry animals eager for release.

"Let's see," she said, gently taking his impaled hand in both of hers. After a quick examination, she said, "We can't stop the bleeding unless we bandage it, and we can't bandage it with that knife in here." She looked at him and said quietly, "It's got to come out, Quincey."

Morris, whose face had gone the color of dirty milk, nodded slowly. "Do it, then."

"All right," she said. "But first, let me make it a little easier for you."

Still cradling his injured hand, she began softly reciting something in the language she had identified as ancient Aramaic. This went on for half a minute or so. After that, looking down at Morris's hand, she made a cryptic sign in the air just above it and said a two-word phrase. Then she gripped the handle of the paring knife and pulled the blade out in one quick, smooth movement.

Morris looked at her. "That should have stung like a bastard," he said. "But I didn't feel a thing." He looked at his injured hand in wonderment. "In fact, I still don't feel a thing. It doesn't hurt at all, now."

Libby nodded. "I've temporarily blocked your nerves from sending pain signals. It won't last long, though, so we'd better get you—"

They felt the bone-rattling impact behind them a fraction of a second before the crashing, grinding sound of it reached their ears. As they looked at each other, identical expressions of shock on their faces, they felt it—and heard it—again.

Something was battering against the kitchen door from inside—something that was a hell of a lot bigger than a butcher knife.

Libby Chastain was suddenly going through the voluminous pockets of her jacket, which she had not taken off since arriving in the house. As she searched, not quite frantically, through the objects she had in there, she said to Morris, "Brace yourself as well as you can! Dig your heels into the carpet, if that helps. *We have got to hold the door!*" Another smashing blow from within the kitchen followed hard upon her words.

Morris made his position against the door as secure as he could, trying not to think about the blood he was losing from his injured right hand. Libby's impromptu magic had stopped the pain of his wound, but had not done anything about the bleeding. "Not to argue with you," he said, "but why don't we just high-tail it out of here?"

"We wouldn't get far," she said, removing two small bottles from a pocket. "We move, the door's smashed open, and we're pincushions a few seconds later, believe it!"

"I do!" Morris said, as another splintering crash shook the door and its surrounding structure. There were cracks in the doorframe now. "But if the door comes down on top of us, we're pancakes *and* pincushions, right?"

"I'm working on it!" she snapped. "Be quiet and let me!"

Each of the bottles contained a fine powder, one gray, the other green. She poured a small quantity of the gray into her right palm, and an equal amount of the green into her left. Then she passed them back and forth between her hands to combine them. Another blow to the door at her back almost caused her to spill the stuff, but she held on. After nine such passes, she let the roughly mixed powder trickle out of the bottom of her fist onto the hall carpet.

She used the thin stream of powder to make a small circle on the floor, with an inverted triangle inside it. The remainder she let fall into the center of the triangle, where it formed a mound an inch or so high.

In the meantime, the assault against the kitchen door continued. Morris thought the blows were getting stronger, and there were cracks in the door itself now. Despite his desire not to distract a witch when she was working, Morris could not help what came out between his clenched teeth: "*Libbyyyyy…*"

"I know, I know!" she said tightly. From her left-hand coat pocket she pulled a disposable lighter, held it just above the small mound of powder, and flicked the ignition.

The powder caught fire immediately, but it burned slowly, with a flame of deep blue. Libby held her hands, palms down, an inch or so over the flame. "*Benedic Domine creaturam istam ignis,*" she chanted. "*Clarifica in me hodierno die, licet igno filio tuo…*"

Morris knew enough Latin so that he could have followed what she was saying, but his attention was distracted by the crashing impacts, behind him, each one a blow from a giant's fist. Every collision was bringing splinters and plaster dust down on them now, and he figured the door was good for another minute, tops.

Morris wondered whether he possessed enough grit to throw himself on top of Libby when the door went down. He would then most likely become what Libby had termed a "pincushion," pierced by every sharp object in the LaRues' kitchen. But Libby would survive, would be able to make the house safe again, and would then seek out whoever was responsible for inflicting this evil on the LaRue family.

And may God help you, whoever you are, he thought, *when this good, gentle woman catches up with you. For in her righteous anger she will be pitiless.*

Morris was working out the move in his mind, calculating the fastest way to knock Libby flat and cover her completely with his body when she suddenly cried, "*Finis!*"

Morris noticed that the oddly colored blue flame had gone out, seemingly of its own accord. The sudden silence was like balm to both his ears and nerves. There was no sound from the kitchen, no more blows against what was left of the door. There was nothing but blessed quiet, broken only by Libby Chastain's labored breathing.

Quincey Morris spent several seconds reveling in the sweet knowledge that he wasn't going to die, after all. Suddenly he said, "Latin!"

Libby looked at him.

"You cast that spell in Latin," Morris said. "What happened to ancient Aramaic, the language of Jesus, and all that?"

She shrugged. "Under stress, you go with what you know best. I've been working with Latin for a long time, and I'm not likely to make mistakes with it."

"Stress?" Morris grinned crookedly. "Were you feeling stressed about something?"

Libby started replacing her magical ingredients in her pockets. "I'd whack you one, if you weren't already bleeding," she said, with a smile of her own. "Come on, let's get that last warding charm in place, so the LaRues can come home. But first, I want to bandage that hand of yours."

CHAPTER 9

VAN DREENAN FINISHED looking at the last one of the three files and tossed it onto Fenton's borrowed desk. He was, in fact, familiar with their contents already, since the information, complete with crime scene photos, had been e-mailed to the South African Occult Crimes Unit a week earlier.

But it was always good to refresh your memory of the specifics of a case; sometimes, even the smallest detail could make a difference. Besides, Fenton seemed to expect him to examine the files before they talked, and Van Dreenan wanted to keep Fenton happy, within reason. He was going to need Fenton.

"All right, we've gone over the specifics," Van Dreenan said. "What are your thoughts on our case, Agent Fenton?"

"It's not 'our case,' Detective Sergeant. It's mine. You're here purely in an advisory capacity."

"Of course, yes. I was speaking out of old habit. But, in any event, what are your views?"

"For this kind of crime, it's... unusual," Fenton said, frowning. "I mean, BSU has run into ritual murders before. It's not nearly as common as a lot of people think, but it does happen. But this—" Fenton made a gesture toward the files strewn across the desk, "is outside any of the patterns we're used to."

"Not a surprise, really," Van Dreenan said. "Because what you have here isn't ritual murder."

"Oh, come on! Three kids butchered, all in the same exact way. Bodily organs removed and taken away, for God knows what purpose. And the free histamine level in the victims' blood shows that they were all alive when they were cut open, like fucking animals in a slaughterhouse! If that doesn't sound like ritual murder to you, pal, then maybe you better get back on—"

Van Dreenan had held up one hand, palm toward Fenton, in an effort to stem the tirade.

"Please, Agent Fenton, I did not wish to give insult to your intelligence. We are differing over a semantic distinction, although it is an important one."

Van Dreenan leaned forward in his chair. "Please, if you would—define a ritual for me."

A scowl remained on Fenton's face. "Look, I'm not going to play—"

The hand went up again. It was not a peremptory gesture, such as a traffic cop would make, but rather a plea for peace.

"I am not wasting your time with idle chatter, as you will soon see. For the moment, humor me, please. Now, then, what is a ritual?"

Fenton took a deliberate deep breath and let it out slowly. He looked at Van Dreenan for a few seconds before saying, "A ritual is a prescribed action having symbolic value, carried out as part of a ceremony, to achieve some predetermined purpose. That do you?"

"Full marks, Agent Fenton. That is good definition, and one that I agree with in all respects. Now, if you will indulge me just a little longer: what kind of ritual did these murders involve?"

"That's the point! We don't know. I thought that's what you were here for."

"Perhaps," Van Dreenan said. "Perhaps it is. But consider this question: if you do not know what kind of ritual was performed, how do you know there was any ritual involved at all?"

Fenton just stared at him. Finally he said, "Victim profile was the same in each case: kids. Modus operandi was the same: isolated area, kid stripped and staked out on the ground, cut open while still alive, bodily organs removed. That's pretty much the textbook definition of ritual."

Van Dreenan nodded. "In the psychological sense, yes. Any repetitive behavior can conceivably be considered ritualistic. But the religious meaning is somewhat different."

"I'm not sure I see the distinction." Fenton didn't sound angry any more, just interested.

Van Dreenan made a head gesture toward the desktop. "We have both read the files, *ja*? And seen the photos. So, tell me: were any occult or esoteric symbols found at or near any of the crime scenes?"

Fenton didn't have to consult the files. "No."

"Any evidence of candles, torches, or incense being burned?"

"No, none."

"Do we know how many people were present when these horrible acts took place?"

"Hard to say for sure. The people who discovered the crime scenes tended to walk all over them before the police got there. Our best estimate is, two."

"So, we have no symbolism, nothing burned, and the bare minimum of people necessary to do the deed. A strange kind of ritual, wouldn't you say?"

Fenton shook his head in frustration. "So if it wasn't a ritual, then what the hell was it?"

For the first time since he'd started talking, Van Dreenan seemed to hesitate.

"Agent Fenton, have you ever heard of *muti* murder?"

"Did you just say 'multi-murder?'" Fenton asked. "Multiple murders?"

"No, I didn't," Van Dreenan told him. "Although it is true that the one sometimes leads to the other."

"If you're trying to confuse the shit out of me, let the record show that you just succeeded," Fenton said.

"My apologies, it was not my intent."

Van Dreenan closed his eyes for a couple of seconds, as if trying to organize his thoughts. "*Muti* is derived from a Zulu word referring to a magic potion. That is why it is sometimes called medicine murder. You must remember that in many parts of Africa, magic and medicine are one and the same."

"Just a bunch of ignorant niggers, running around with bones through their noses, huh?"

Van Dreenan's eyes narrowed, although his voice remained mild. "I meant no slight, Agent Fenton, either to you or to your... ancestors. Cultures differ, beliefs differ. People are different. If I describe the beliefs of the tribal religions of South Africa, that does not mean that I sneer at them. It means I know them, and I know them because I deal with them every day."

"Yeah, all right. I'm sorry I snapped at you. It's just that... I used to read stuff in the papers about apartheid when I was younger. See things on TV, sometimes, that just..." Fenton let his voice trail off.

"I understand, I think." Van Dreenan let go a sigh that made him sound old and tired. "Apartheid was what it was. Neither of us can change history. And now it is gone. And neither of us need mourn its passing."

"Okay, look, let's just forget I brought it up, all right? You were talking about magic and religion."

"Yes, well, *muti* murder has been around a long time, quite possibly for centuries. It refers to the killing of a human being in order to obtain body parts, which are in turn used in magical rituals. That is what I meant when I said these murders we have here are not themselves ritualistic. The ritual comes at a later time, and the bodily organs that have been taken are a vital part of it."

"So, the victim isn't being used as a sacrifice at all." Fenton spoke so softly he might have been talking to himself.

"That is correct. In fact, you might say that death is almost incidental. The object is the removal of the organs."

"So there is a ritual involved, just not the kind we thought."

"Oh, there may be a few ritualistic elements to the murder. A special knife might sometimes be used, certain incantations might be uttered as the organs are taken, but that varies from region to region, and seems to be of little significance. Oh, except for two things that are considered important."

When Van Dreenan didn't continue, Fenton said, "You're going to make me ask, aren't you? Okay, mister expert, what are the two ritualistic elements?"

"You've seen them both, even if you did not recognize them as such, at the time. One of the bodies was found on a river-bank, *ja*? Another not far from a creek, the third close to a pond. That is not coincidence. *Muti* tradition holds that the body must be left outdoors, near water."

"That's not going to help us much," Fenton said. "Hell of a lot of rivers, creeks and ponds in this country. What's the other thing?"

"Most unfortunately for the victim, *muti* tradition requires that the organs be extracted while he or she is still alive."

Fenton shook his head. "Poor kids," he said softly.

"Indeed, yes, the poor children," Van Dreenan said. There was something odd in his voice that caused Fenton to look at him closely, but before he could say anything, Van Dreenan went on, "It was once the case that *muti* murder was confined to the outlying villages. But in the last decade or so, cases have been reported in urban areas, as well."

"All the victims children?"

"Not always, no. But some of the *umthakhati* believe that the organs of the young convey more power."

"Um-what?"

"*Umthakhati,*" Van Dreenan said. "Zulu for 'witch' or 'sorcerer.' In Sotho, the name is *baloyi.*"

"You speak Zulu?"

Van Dreenan shrugged. "Not fluently. Enough to get by."

"How about that other one you just mentioned?"

"Sotho? A few words and phrases, no more."

Fenton nodded, as if this made perfect sense. "This *muti* murder, is it unique to South Africa?"

"No, cases have also been reported in Lesotho and Swaziland. There have been unconfirmed reports of the practice in a few other places, such as Nigeria. But it seems to be most common in my country."

"So the killers are all black Africans. How about the victims? Same thing?"

"Not always. Sometimes they are white. Especially in recent years."

Fenton heard that change in intonation again. Then Van Dreenan had a coughing fit that lasted several seconds. Fenton offered to get him some water.

"No, I am all right, thank you," Van Dreenan said, and cleared his throat a few times. "I was about to say that a few incidents of *muti* killings have been reported abroad. They had a case of it in England, a few years ago."

"Same M.O. as ours?" Fenton asked.

"Only in the most general terms. The body of a child, a black male around seven years of age, was pulled out of the Thames, missing its arms, legs, and head."

"Local kid?"

"Probably not, although the body was never identified. The detectives referred to him as 'Adam,' just to give the poor lad the dignity of a name."

"Did they ever make an arrest?"

"Ultimately, no. Scotland Yard were very interested in a Yoruba woman from Nigeria, but the physical evidence was minimal and the woman refused to admit any involvement. Officially, the case remains open. But something good came of it all: Scotland Yard were prompted to initiate Project Violet, which is designed to investigate witchcraft crime in Britain. They have been very busy, I understand."

"Well, as you might imagine, Behavioral Science has searched every law enforcement database there is, and there's no record of this kind of crime being reported anywhere in North America before. These three cases are the first we've ever had."

Van Dreenan looked at Fenton very steadily as he said, "I wish I could assure you that they will be the last."

CHAPTER 10

QUINCEY MORRIS AND Libby Chastain walked with Walter LaRue through the ruins of his family's kitchen. Broken glass and bits of crockery crunched under their feet everywhere they went.

"Jesus Christ Almighty," the big man said softly.

"No, Mister LaRue," Libby said. "I think I can assure you that He wasn't responsible for any of this."

LaRue slowly took it all in: the knives and other sharp objects strewn everywhere—except for those protruding from the kitchen door or from the wall opposite; pots and pans all over the floor, having fallen, or been knocked off their wall hooks; the dinette table, which had clearly been used as a battering ram against the kitchen door and was much the worse for it; and the door itself—split, cracked, gouged, and close to coming apart altogether.

The massive damage to the kitchen door was a clear indication to Morris of just how close it had really been for him and Libby yesterday afternoon. *Just a few more hits with that table would have done it,* he thought. *Then the door would've gone and I'd have the chance to see how Davy Crockett felt there at the end, when the Mexican soldiers came at him with their bayonets.*

They had explained things to LaRue on the drive over from the Holiday Inn. It would have been cruel to just let him walk into his home to discover this carnage.

After carefully viewing the damage, Walter LaRue took a deep breath, let it out, and said mildly, "Well, it could've been worse."

Morris just nodded. He didn't look at Libby, although both of them had expected an explosion, considering the amount of tension that LaRue had been under lately.

"And if whatever caused this—" LaRue's gesture took in the whole kitchen, "allowed you to make my home safe again, then, goddamn it, it was worth it!"

"Of that I can assure you," Libby said. "The spell that caused those attacks on you and your family will not trouble you again."

"But the job's only half done," Morris said. "We've got to locate the source of the spell, before whoever cast the damn thing finds out what we've done and gets to working on another one."

Alarm clouded LaRue's face. "You mean what you set up here is only protection against one specific spell?"

"No, it's what you might call a broad-spectrum system," Libby told him. "Similar to what Greta had in place, but, if I may flatter myself, somewhat stronger. But no system is completely foolproof."

"As I understand this sort of thing, it's kind of like the arms race during the Cold War," Morris said. "The Soviets would come up with a new missile, and we'd develop a counter to it. Everything's fine—until they invent an even *better* missile."

LaRue ran a hand through his untidy hair. "Christ, just when you've got me thinking it's safe..."

"Besides," Morris continued, "there's no law that says your enemy has to stick with magic. What if he—or she—can't crack Libby's protection and then decides to come over here at 3:00am some night and firebomb the place?"

LaRue spoke calmly, but there were beads of sweat on his forehead. "Look, I want this fixed, for good. I want to be able to sleep at night. I want my kids to start feeling like kids again, instead of hunted animals." He looked from Morris to Libby and back again. "Now, how much more will it cost me to see that done?"

Morris pushed himself away from the kitchen counter he'd been leaning against. "Not a dime," he told LaRue. "You agreed to my fee in Austin, and paid it. Whatever we do now is all part of the service."

Morris paused and took a slow look around the ruin of a kitchen. "Although, you know what? All things considered, I'd probably do it for free," he said, and walked out of the kitchen.

Libby Chastain looked at LaRue for a second or two before saying, "Me, too." She followed Morris out of the room.

As Morris started the car, he said to Libby, "He's going to stay behind and clean up for a while, right?"

"That's what he told us. So, I assume, next stop is the Holiday Inn?"

"Yeah, Holiday Inn—and the wife."

"We can talk out here," Marcia LaRue said, opening the sliding door that led to the motel room's small balcony. "The kids are next door watching cartoons, but this way they won't disturb us, and vice versa."

Quincy Morris and Libby Chastain followed her, and Morris slid the door closed behind them. "Besides," Marcia LaRue continued, "out here I can smoke." As if to prove her point, she produced a pack of Winstons, shook one out, and lit up.

"Actually, I quit these disgusting things, about eight months ago," she said wryly. "But events've been putting a heavy demand on my nerves, lately."

"I can imagine," Libby Chastain said, nodding sympathetically. "But things should start getting better, now."

"Yes, so I hear. Walter called me from the house a little while ago." She tapped her cigarette on the balcony railing, sending a small flurry of ash down to the parking lot below. "He tells me the kitchen's going to need some major remodeling. But he says it's worth it, since you've given him the all-clear sign. Is that true?"

Morris and Chastain look at each other briefly before Morris shrugged and said, "More or less."

Marcia looked at him with narrowed eyes. "That's not quite what I was expecting to hear," she said. "I was under the impression that this insane business was over and done with. Are you saying now that it's not?"

"No, Ma'am, it's not over," Morris told her. "You should know that better than anybody."

Marcia LaRue took a long drag on her cigarette, her eyes never leaving Morris's face. "I have no idea what you're talking about."

"I'm afraid you do," Libby Chastain said quietly.

"Oh, Christ, now Madam Olga is putting her two cents in," Marcia snapped. "What the hell do *you* know?"

"I know the terrible burden you're psyche is carrying," Libby said. "I see how close it is to crushing you."

"You're a hoot, lady, you really are!" Marcia LaRue's voice dripped scorn. "What comes next—you offer to tell my fortune, for only $2.95 a minute? Haven't I seen you on late night TV, right after the Jamaican lady with the tarot cards?"

Libby's voice remained gentle. "I've been trained to read auras," she said. "It doesn't work all the time, but yours comes through loud and clear, Marcia. Ever since I met you, your aura's been dominated by the same two colors: green for fear, and violet for guilt. Strong as the fear is, the guilt is even stronger."

"How old were you?" Morris asked suddenly.

Marcia LaRue turned her glare on him. "How old was I *when?*"

"When you found out your mother was a witch," he said.

Marcia stared at him, then turned slowly and placed her hands on top of the wrought iron railing that bordered the little balcony. She stared out at the nearly empty parking lot for a long moment before the tears began to course down her cheeks. Without looking at Morris, she said softly, "You bastard. You fucking bastard. The woman's dead. She was my mother and I loved her and now she's dead. Can't you at least leave her in peace?"

"The dead are already at peace," Libby told her. "It's the living that Quincey and I are concerned about. Like you. Your husband. Your children."

"But Walt said you were going to *fix* it!" Her voice was breaking up, now. "He came back from Texas and said that you told him you could *make it stop!*" Her shoulders started to shake with the sobs that wracked her.

Libby went to her then, put her arms around her and held her close. "It's all right, let it out," her voice barely above a whisper. "Let it all out, it's okay, it's all right. Let it go."

As Marcia continued to cry, Libby looked up, made eye contact with Morris, then cut her eyes to the closed patio door. Morris looked, and saw the two LaRue children standing inside the room, silently watching their mother.

He looked back at Libby, who made the slightest of head movements in the direction of the room. Morris nodded and went to the door, slid it open just enough for him to slip into the room. He closed the door quietly behind him, then dropped to one knee to bring himself closer to the children's level.

"It's all right, podners," he told them. "Your mom's just upset with all this bad stuff that's been going on at your house, you know?"

They each nodded, solemn as judges.

"My friend Libby is a real nice lady, and she'll help your mom feel better soon. Why don't we all go back to the other room and watch some cartoons for a while? Your mom will come in when she's ready. She just needs to talk with my friend for a little longer, okay?"

"Okay," they answered together. As the three of them headed back into the adjoining room the girl asked, "Can we go home soon?"

"Yeah," Morris said, nodding. "Yeah, I think you can."

THE WOUND IN Morris's hand was throbbing, so Libby Chastain agreed to drive his rental car as they brought the rest of the LaRue family home. Although she had only been there twice, she found her way with minimal directions from Marcia LaRue.

As Libby pulled into the driveway, Morris unbuckled his safety belt and turned towards the back seat, where Marcia LaRue sat with her children. "I'm sure Libby has explained to you that the house is safe now," he said.

"Yes, she has," Marcia said. "And I'm very grateful to you both. We're all grateful to you." Her eyes, although red-rimmed from crying, were calm now.

"And as for that other matter we discussed," Libby said, "Quincey and I will start on it right away. We'll let you know when it's taken care of."

Morris shot Libby a look, but kept silent. Clearly, she was trying to be discreet so as to avoid frightening the LaRue children any further.

As Marcia and her children climbed out of the back seat, the front door of the house opened. Walter LaRue stood there, wearing a grin that threatened to split his face in half. The children ran to him, but Marcia stopped after a pace or two, turned to look back toward the car. She and Libby regarded each other through the windshield for several seconds. Morris was unable to interpret the expression on either woman's face, but he did see Marcia LaRue nod a couple of times before she turned away to walk toward her house, her family, and her life.

They sat in the car, watching while the LaRues went inside and closed the door after them. Then Libby said, "Are you hungry? We never did get lunch, what with one thing and another."

"We kept running into unfriendly kitchens," Morris replied. "Sure, I could eat."

"What do you say to an early dinner, then?" Libby started the engine and began to back down the driveway.

"That sounds good. And while we're eating, you're going to fill me in on what you learned from Marcia, right?"

"Absolutely. It's a fascinating story, in a grim sort of way."

"How about a hint, at least?"

Libby stopped for a red light. "All right," she said. "Remember the Hatfields and McCoys?"

"You mean those two families in—where was it, Tennessee?"

"Kentucky, I believe. Late Nineteenth Century."

"Sure, I've heard of them. Had this big feud, went on for God knows how many years."

"Well, Marcia LaRue is involved in a feud of her own. Only this one has lasted centuries."

LIBBY CHASTAIN SWALLOWED the last forkful of her vegetarian stir-fry and pushed the plate away. After a sip of water, she continued, "So, ever since Salem, each generation of Bridget Warren's descendants has come under magical assault by a descendant of Sarah Carter. Or so Marcia's mother told her."

"And Marcia didn't believe it." Quincey Morris was still working on his New York strip steak.

"Not a word—at the time. She thought it was 'superstitious bullshit,' to use her phrase."

"Well, it's a skeptical age," Morris said. "Lot of folks don't believe in anything they can't put under a microscope and look at."

"Sad, but true. And Marcia was apparently a skeptic's skeptic. In college, she took a minor in Philosophy—logical positivism, rationalism, and God knows what else. All those systems that claim the material world is the only one that exists."

"Yeah, there was a lot of that going around Princeton when I was there."

"But it didn't influence you?"

"With *my* family background? Are you kidding? No, my Dad clued me in on the way things really are long before I ever got to college." Morris pushed his own plate away and plucked the dessert menu from its holder next to the condiments. After glancing through it, he asked Libby, "Are you having dessert?"

"No, I'll just get some coffee. But you go ahead."

Without looking up from the menu, Morris said, deadpan, "They have peanut butter pie, it says here. With chocolate sauce."

He looked up to see Libby smiling crookedly at him. "You bastard," she said pleasantly.

"That's a matter between Mom and Dad, and they're not here."

A few minutes later, as they each dug into a serving of peanut butter pie, Morris said, "I take it that Marcia LaRue has abandoned her skepticism about matters supernatural."

"Oh, sure. Once the attacks started, she figured out what had to be the cause. But by then it was too late. She knew nothing of magic, and had no way to mount a defense."

"Sounds like Mom gave up pretty easy on enlisting Marcia in the ranks of white witches."

Libby shook her head. "No, she didn't, really. Marcia says that her mother would bring it up from time to time, in a gentle sort of way. But Marcia always refused to discuss it with her."

"Still, considering what was at stake, maybe the gentle approach wasn't the best way to go about it."

"I know. But Mom probably assumed there was a lot of time left to win Marcia over. The woman was only fifty-two when she died, Quincey."

Morris's brow furrowed in thought. "Which means she had Marcia when she was..."

"Twenty. I asked. Young, by today's standards, but not quite a child bride, either."

"No, I guess not. In good health?"

"Marcia says she was, yes. So it wasn't unreasonable of the woman to think she had quite a few years left to, what, *convert* her daughter." Libby forked the last piece of pie into her mouth, chewed, and swallowed. "Then along comes some drunk behind the wheel of a minivan."

"So Mom is suddenly gone home to Jesus, and along with her goes the protection of the warding charms."

"Which have now been reactivated, at no small hazard to you and me," Libby said. She pushed her empty plate away. "But, it's like you told Walter back at the house: it's only a matter of time before Sarah Carter's current descendant tries something different. A static spell is like a fixed defensive line in warfare. It's only good until somebody figures out how to get around it."

"And sooner or later, she will—whoever 'she' is."

Libby nodded. "Most likely. And, although the LaRues seem like nice enough people, I don't think I want to move in with them just so that I can be there for the next attempt, a month from now—or a year."

"So, we've got to find whoever's been doing this—and *then* what? You can't use white magic to destroy someone, even somebody who deserves it, big time. We both know that. All right, assume that, through luck or pluck or good karma or whatever, we manage to get a handle on this black witch who claims Sarah Carter as part of her family tree. What the hell *do* we do about her?"

Libby was using her napkin to wipe a small amount of chocolate sauce from her fingertips. "What you said to me on the phone last night."

She looked up then, and her gentle gray eyes were suddenly cold and hard as polar ice when she said, "Whatever it takes, Quincey. We do whatever it takes."

CHAPTER 11

THE CAR WAS a Hummer H2 Super Stretch limo, and it looked like the product of a carnal union between a Rolls-Royce and a Greyhound bus. Its polished black finish was so deep that reflections of the car's surroundings seemed to disappear into it, as if the limousine was some sort of omnivorous behemoth, absorbing and devouring everything that crossed its path.

The witch who was approaching the limo had no fear of being devoured. Christine Abernathy had little fear of anything or anyone—although, if pressed, she might have acknowledged that the man waiting inside the limousine could sometimes make her feel uneasy.

She opened the rear door, slipped inside, then pulled it shut behind her with a solid, satisfying thump. She knew that the heavily tinted windows would prevent anyone outside the car from seeing within, and the thick glass divider that had just been raised inside the car prevented the driver from hearing a word—as if he'd be able to pick up anything from thirty feet away. The man she was there to meet with preferred to do business in private—especially her kind of business. And what he preferred, he got. Always.

His name was Walter Grobius, and he had more money than God.

"What news?" His voice was raspy, as if someone had once drawn a file across his vocal chords.

"Preparations are well underway. I've completed much of the preliminary spellcasting, and I'm researching some other spells that I've never used before. It's taking some time—these kinds of materials aren't exactly available on the Internet."

"And the... other?"

"Also underway. I have contracted with a specialist in a branch of magic I'm not personally familiar with. She arrived in this country from Africa three weeks ago. I have reason to believe that she has started to harvest the materials she needs. When the fetishes are ready, she will bring them to me. When combined with what I've been working on, they should possess great power."

"How long?"

"It's impossible to say for certain. There is a procedure that she has to follow. Certain things must be done in specific ways, if the magic is to work properly. And she has to be wary of the authorities." Christine allowed herself the smallest of smiles. "They insist on calling what she is doing *murder.*"

Grobius nodded. "I have been in touch with the other specialists whose names you gave me. Most of them are part of the project now, busy with their own tasks."

"Only 'most?'" The idea that anyone could refuse him was difficult for her to grasp.

"Two of them were dead. Another appears to be incurably insane."

The witch thought that for this man to use the word "insane" was an exercise in irony that would have done Sophocles proud. But she kept her opinion to herself. Even one such as she understood the value of discretion.

"I am concerned," Grobius said, "whether everything will be ready by the target date."

"I think it will be, but you must understand that black magic is not an exact science. You have to take the dark forces as you find them, and they are not always cooperative, even for a skilled practitioner of the Art."

"Let there be no undue haste, then. I don't want any mistakes made. By anyone." His gaze fell on Christine Abernathy then, and she felt her heartbeat accelerate briefly. For her, this was equivalent to a normal person screaming in hysteria.

Maybe that's why I'm working for him, she thought. *He's the last person left alive, now that Mother's gone, who can make me feel fear.*

"If need be," he continued, "I'll sacrifice Halloween in favor of the alternate date in April."

"Walpurgis Night."

"Almost as good, for our purposes, or so you've said."

"Indeed, quite propitious. All Hallows Eve is better, but the switch shouldn't make a difference in the... ultimate result."

"Well, we had better get it right the first time, since another opportunity will, most likely, not be forthcoming."

"No," she said simply, thinking, *If it goes wrong, none of us are going to survive to try again later.*

Grobius appeared lost in thought, as if contemplating the wonder of what he was planning to achieve. Finally, he looked at Christine again, nodded, and said, "Very well. Proceed. You'll be notified when I wish to meet again."

Knowing she was being dismissed, she said, "I shall," and reached for the door handle.

Walking away from the limousine, she took in deep breaths of fresh air. She was glad to be out of there, and not just because of the effect the old man sometimes had on her. The car's generously padded and brass-fitted interior always reminded her of the inside of a coffin. It was, in some ways, as if the man inside were already dead. As if he were inviting her to join him.

ANOTHER CITY, ANOTHER cheap motel. Money was not a problem, but it was easier to pass unnoticed in lower-end accommodations, and Snake Perkins had been instructed to keep a low profile.

He lowered the comics page of the paper he'd been engrossed in and looked at what the woman was doing. On the room's rickety writing table, she had spread out a piece of cheesecloth about the size of a man's handkerchief. On this surface she was arranging a series of small objects, pausing to mumble over each one in a language Snake had never heard before. He assumed it was what they spoke back where she came from, wherever the hell that was. Someplace where they all ran around with bones through their noses, most likely.

Snake hoped she'd be returning there soon. He was sick and tired of being bossed around by someone who, to his way of thinking, ought to be cleaning up after white folks in an office building someplace.

He had been careful not to let his resentments come to the surface. Apart from the fact that he had strict orders from his Mistress, whom he feared greatly, the nigger woman was too damn handy with a knife. And not squeamish about using it, as Snake had reason to know.

He continued watching as Cecelia Mbwato added an oddly shaped twig and several bits of vegetable matter to the arrangement of objects on the cheesecloth. Then, from a red and white plastic cooler, the kind people often take to the beach, she brought out a gray, wrinkled lump of flesh, about the size and shape of a baby's fist. Snake recognized that one instantly.

It was the heart of the six year-old girl that Cecelia Mbwato had cut open the night before.

She sprinkled the gathered materials with two different kinds of powder, one fine and one coarse, muttering in that foreign tongue the whole time. Then, with infinite care, she rolled up the cheesecloth and tied it, at each end and in the middle, with a bright green twine that she had measured and cut into precise lengths.

Snake had known enough to keep silent while the ritual was taking place. But now that it was done, he asked, gesturing toward the tightly rolled bundle, "What do you call that thing, anyway?"

Cecelia Mbwato looked at him with her lizard eyes. After a moment she said, "In English, you would call it, I think, a fetish."

Snake's brow furrowed. "Ain't that some kinda kinky sex thing? Like gettin' turned on by woman's shoes, or somethin'?"

"I know nothing of the disgusting and perverse sexual practices of your people," she said primly. "And I do not want to. This fetish is a most powerful magical talisman, just like the other two that I have already completed."

Snake nodded respectfully. He knew about magic, and what it could do. He was smart enough to fear it. "Yeah, well," he said, "how many more of these things do you gotta make?"

"Two more. Just two, and then all will be ready for delivery to the one who sent you. Then I will receive my payment, and our time together will be done."

"Damn," said Snake impassively, "that'll be a shame."

CHAPTER 12

THE KINGSBURY BUILDING occupied one corner of a less-than-fashionable neighborhood two blocks off Boylston Street, the closest thing Boston has to a main drag. The ten-story structure had been built during the Truman Administration, and looked it: the red brick was crumbly, the wooden floors creaky, and the faded walls and ceilings gave off faint clouds of plaster dust whenever a bus or heavy truck drove by. A joke known by everyone who still did business there was that the Landmark Preservation Commission had considered declaring the Kingsbury an official historic site, until it was determined that nothing of historical importance had happened there—ever.

The building's only concession to modernity was the installation of automatic elevators. It was one of these, stopping at the ninth floor, that disgorged Quincey Morris, Libby Chastain, two women dressed like secretaries, and a small man with greasy hair who looked like a process server.

Morris and Chastain followed the numbered doors until they reached 936, which bore the legend "C. Prendergast and Sons. Genealogy." Inside, they were greeted by a pert woman in her mid twenties sitting behind an ancient oak desk. She had been using a jeweler's loupe to examine the faded page of an old ledger. "Hi, come on in," she said. "Have a seat, if you can find one under all the mess."

Morris looked at the young woman, who had short auburn hair and a face that was more interesting than beautiful. The huge lenses of her aviator-style glasses could not conceal either the intelligence in the blue eyes or the sprinkle of freckles that spread out from her nose to accent the high cheekbones. "We're here to see Sidney Prendergast," he said. "We have an appointment."

"That means you guys are Morris and Chastain, right?" Without waiting for an answer, she turned to Libby and said, "Just put that stuff anywhere on the floor, it's fine."

Morris saw that Libby was moving a pile of four or five books off a nearby armchair. "You're right," he said to the young woman. "I'm Quincey Morris, and this is Libby Chastain."

"Pleased to meet you. I'm Sidney Prendergast." She stood, and extended a hand to Morris. After a moment's hesitation, he took it. As they shook, he noticed that the woman was wearing a faded Harvard T-shirt and blue jeans. As Libby stepped over to shake hands, Morris moved a box full of files off another chair and sat down.

Once all three of them were seated, Sidney Prendergast closed the ledger before her and said, "Well, let's start by getting the FAQ stuff out of the way."

There was a moment's silence before Libby said, "You mean 'frequently asked questions?'"

"You got it," Sidney Prendergast said with a nod. "First-time clients usually have the same ones. Such as: 'Isn't Sidney a man's name?' Answer: yeah, usually, except among old-money WASPs, which my mother was before Granddad pissed away her inheritance."

"I see you *have* done this before," Morris said with a slight smile.

"Oh, sure. I don't mind, really. Let's see, what else? There's 'Why does the door read C. Prendergast and *Sons?*' That's 'cause Dad, Charles Prendergast, was both optimistic and stubborn. My two brothers never found genealogy interesting—one's a cop in Fall River, and the other one teaches high school—but Dad was too proud to have the sign changed." Her lips split in a grin. "Besides, he always used to say that I was his favorite son."

"*Used* to say?" Libby asked. "Past tense?"

"Afraid so. Dad passed away almost three years ago. I'd been working for him part-time for years, and he left me the business." She gave an exaggerated shrug. "It pays the bills while I finish my diss. After that, we'll see."

"Where are you getting your doctorate?" Morris asked.

She plucked at the front of her T-shirt, holding it out from her body for a moment. "The shirt tells the true tale," she declared with another grin. "*Veritas,* baby, *veritas.*" Letting the grin fade, she continued, "And considering the cost of tuition at Harvard, I hope you folks have some nice, complicated genealogical research you want done, thus allowing me to present you with a nice, fat bill. So, what's the deal?"

Morris said, "We're interested in tracing a woman who is a descendant of someone executed during the Salem witch trials."

Sidney Prendergast studied each of them in turn before saying, "You know, I charge by the hour, with any portion thereof rounded upward." The good humor was gone from her voice now. "So if this is your idea of a giggle, it's going to end up costing you some money."

"No, we're entirely serious," Libby said. "And we're prepared to pay for your time, no matter how much you have to put in."

The young woman looked at Libby for a long moment before nodding silently. Then she opened a desk drawer, pulled out a legal pad, and picked up a pencil from the desktop. "So, you want to locate someone who is living today, someone who had an ancestor die during that awful business in Salem, back in the 1690s."

Morris and Chastain both nodded.

Sidney Prendergast wrote rapidly on the pad. Without looking up, she said, "They've figured out what caused that, you know."

"Caused what?" Morris asked.

"The fits and other weird behaviors by some of the citizens that got interpreted as witchcraft." She looked up from her notepad. "Wheat ergot."

"Do tell," Libby murmured politely.

"Yeah, I read about it in my American Mythology class. Apparently ergot is some kind of fungus that infects grain in the field—wheat, rye, all kinds, I guess. It's not visible to the naked eye, and the heat you get from baking doesn't necessarily kill it."

"So, what does this sneaky fungus do?" Libby asked.

"Screws up your central nervous system. People who eat the bread, or cake, or whatever, can be afflicted with uncontrolled twitching of the limbs, paralysis, delirium, all kinds of weird behavior."

Morris nodded. "I've seen the results of ergot poisoning in the Middle East. It's not pretty."

"No, I guess not. So some of the wheat fields near Salem were apparently carrying ergot, and that wheat was picked, ground, baked, and eaten. Result: a lot of people start acting very strangely, and the authorities decide that they're either victims of witchcraft, or witches themselves. Then they start arresting and hanging people."

"I'm curious about one thing," Quincey Morris said. "How did the person who came up with this theory actually establish, after three hundred-some years, that ergot was in the wheat consumed by the people of Salem?"

"Well, they *couldn't* prove it, after all that time," she said. "But it stands to reason. I mean, *something* caused all that hysteria."

"It wasn't real witches, then," Libby said, her face as expressionless as her voice.

"No, not hardly," Sidney Prendergast said with a slight smile. "Sorry if that disappoints you."

"I think we'll both be less disappointed if you can identify the person we're interested in."

"You realize this usually goes the other way, don't you?" Sidney Prendergast said.

"How do you mean?" Morris asked.

"Mostly, my clients want me to start with the present—that is, with them—and work backwards. Sometimes they just want a nice copy of the family tree to being to a reunion. Other times, they're trying to claim a piece of some trust fund that's being distributed to 'all the living relatives of the late Mary Jones,' or somebody. And, pretty often, clients want me to establish that they're descended from some prominent, even royal, family. I can't tell you how much business Dad got when Princess Di was alive."

"No trust funds for us, I'm afraid," Libby said with a shrug.

"And I already *know* that I'm a bastard offspring of the British royal family, so we don't have to waste any time on *that,*" Morris added with a slight smile.

Sidney Prendergast shook her head in mock disapproval. "Well, let's see what we have to work with, here." She turned the legal pad to a fresh page. "What's the name of the person executed in Salem?"

"Carter," Libby said. "Sarah Carter."

"And the alleged crime?"

"Witchcraft."

IN A HOUSE miles away, in a room that no one except Christine Abernathy ever entered, a ritual was about to take place. Although some of the objects being employed were modern, the ritual itself was very, very old.

Amidst the swirling smoke of four sticks of incense, she picked up a two-foot length of insulated wire, the kind used in many electrical systems. She held the wire six inches above the low flame of a squat, black candle. "*Fiagra,*" she chanted. "*Fiagra, fiagra, fiagra.*" Although the wire had not come in direct contact with the candle, it began to smolder, then burst into flame. Dropping the still-burning wire onto the cold stone floor, Christine turned to another object—a smoke detector, the kind used in many homes and commercial buildings. She passed her hands four times over the device, each time repeating one word. "*Dormire,*" she chanted. "*Dormire, dormire, dormire.*"

On the floor, the length of electrical cord continued to burn, the smell of its insulation adding a harsh chemical overtone to the smell of the incense.

On the nearby table, the smoke detector, its battery intact, was silent as the dead.

"I CAN LOOK up Sarah Carter's exact date of death, if I need to. A lot of the records of the witch trials still survive." Sidney Prendergast wrote for several moments, then looked up. "Now then, Sarah's descendents?"

"One daughter," Morris replied. "Name of Rebecca. If there's a middle name, we don't know it."

"Okay, that probably doesn't matter. People didn't always have middle names in those days, anyway." She wrote some more. "Rebecca's date of birth?"

"Don't know that, either," he said. "We believe she was about seven years old when her mother died, so..."

Sidney Prendergast looked up again. "*About seven,* you say." Disdain for the imprecision was clear in her voice. "All right, what happened to the little girl after her mother's death?"

"She was taken in by relatives from Boston," Libby said.

"Their names?"

Libby shook her head. "No idea."

Sidney Prendergast blinked a couple of times. "Well, were they family on the mother's side, or the father's?"

"Same answer, I'm afraid," Libby said.

"Did they formally adopt Rebecca, or just let her live with them?"

Quincey Morris and Libby Chastain were silent.

Sidney Prendergast tapped her pencil on the desk a few times. "Well, then, what other information do you have about the family line?"

After another brief silence, Morris answered, "Nothing else, I'm afraid."

"*Nothing?*"

"Those are all the facts we have available to us," Morris said. "We were hoping that you'd be able to fill in the rest. That's why we want to hire you."

"To find somebody alive today, with nothing but *that*—" she slapped her palm lightly on the legal pad, "to go on?"

Morris nodded sheepishly.

"Hell, what makes you so sure the family line didn't die out, somewhere along the way? That happens all the time, especially with families this old. How do you know there even *is* a living descendant?"

"We know," Morris said. "I'm not at liberty to tell you how, but we know."

"Aw, Jesus..." Sidney Prendergast tossed the pencil onto the desk and leaned back in her chair. "Well, fortunately for you guys, my old man raised me to be ethical. So, instead of spending six months pretending to work on this piece of shit and then sending you a bill for ten to twelve grand, I'll tell you right now: it can't be done. Not with the limited—"

"Excuse me," Libby Chastain said suddenly. Turning to look at her, Morris saw Libby's eyes dart around the room, then rest on the door through which they had entered. "Sorry to interrupt," Libby continued, and there was something in her voice that made Morris suddenly, completely alert, "But I was just wondering—*do either of you smell smoke?*"

CHAPTER 13

"WAIT HERE," MORRIS said. He opened the door to the stairway and stepped out onto the landing. A few moments later he was back. "Stairway's already filled with smoke," he said tightly. "We'll never make it down—we'd either fry or suffocate."

People from the other offices were in the hallway now, calling to each other and dashing around. Tendrils of smoke eddied around them like angry ghosts.

Libby turned to Sidney Prendergast. "Is there another set of stairs on this floor?"

"No, but who *cares?*" she said frantically. "Let's just take the fucking elevator!"

"Bad idea," Libby told her. "The floor selector buttons work on a heat sensor. The elevator'll head right for the fire."

"Jesus, what'll we *do?*" Sidney Prendergast's voice was approaching hysteria.

Libby put a calming hand on the young woman's arm, then said to Morris, "Fire department ought to be here soon. Think we can hold out that long?"

Morris shook his head dubiously. "Fire's only one or two floors below us. Anyway, you hear any fire alarm, any smoke detectors going off, anything?"

Libby listened for a moment. "No, I don't," she said, and looked at Morris. "It's almost as if somebody wanted us trapped up here, isn't it?"

"Sarah Carter's descendant plays for keeps," Morris said grimly. "Look, can you do anything to put out the fire?"

Libby shook her head. "Not the way it's spread now. It would need gear I don't have with me, and a lot of preparation time."

"What are you two yammering about?" Sidney said angrily. "We've got to get *out!*"

Libby placed her hand on the back of the young woman's neck and muttered a few words that Morris couldn't hear. After a few seconds, some of the panic faded from Sidney Prendergast's face.

"She does have a point, Quincey," Libby said.

Morris nodded, his eyes narrowed. "Well, we can't stay here, and we can't go down. All that leaves is up."

He turned to Sidney Prendergast. "How many floors between us and the roof?"

Sidney thought briefly. "Three. Three floors after this one."

"There's a roof access door, right?"

"I—I don't really know, I never..."

Morris turned to Libby. "There's got to be a way to reach the roof, so they can repair leaks and so on. If the door's locked, think you could get it open?"

"Most likely," Libby said. "But say we do manage to get to the roof. What does that buy us?"

"Time."

EYES STREAMING, THE three of them stumbled out onto the Kingsbury Building's flat roof. They were all coughing and wheezing, even though they had used articles of clothing to cover their mouths and noses while climbing the stairs.

The fresh air eased their breathing within a couple of minutes. Sidney Prendergast collapsed face down on the roof's rough surface and lay there, breathing heavily.

Quincey Morris put his suit jacket back on and went over to the roof's edge, which was bordered by a four-foot-high retaining wall. He was peering over it when Libby Chastain joined him a moment later.

"Looking for a fire escape?" she asked.

"No, for fire trucks. Or cop cars. Or anything to show that the city even knows about this blaze."

"And...?"

"Not a fucking thing. And no sirens heading this way, either."

Libby looked for herself, then nodded bleakly. "She's thorough, whoever she is. Powerful, too."

"Powerful enough to keep the whole city from noticing this blaze indefinitely?"

"No, not indefinitely, but there's no way to predict just how long—"

"Hey!"

They both turned toward Sidney Prendergast, who had risen to her knees, palms flat against the roof. Panic was back in her voice as she said, "This thing's getting hot!"

Libby kicked off one sandal, placed a bare foot on the roof surface. "She's right. It's spreading faster than I would have thought."

"Old, dry wood," Morris said absently. "Stuff burns like kindling." He was looking at the adjoining building, which was the same height as the Kingsbury. It had an open, flat roof, just like theirs.

It was at least thirty feet away.

Libby followed his gaze and understood immediately. "Too far to jump," she said pensively. "Even with a running start, the retaining wall would kill your momentum."

"Yeah, I was kind of thinking the same thing." He was scanning the roof now, looking for rope, lumber, anything that would span the gap between the two buildings. There was nothing.

The first wisps of smoke were visible now, making their way through cracks in the roof surface. Morris gazed at the next building the way a drowning man looks at a distant shore. "Fire's a hard way to die," he said quietly. He looked again over the roof's edge at the concrete and macadam that lay twelve stories below. "Well, at least it's not the only way out." He flashed on photos he had seen of people jumping from the World Trade Center on 9/11, electing to fall to their deaths rather than burn. *Well, there are worse ways to go then defenestration. Plenty of them.*

He turned to Libby, who was staring intently at the next building, lower lip caught between her teeth. "What?" he asked tensely.

She began to go through the pockets of the light jacket she was wearing. "Gravity's a law," she said. "But laws were made to be broken."

Morris inhaled sharply. "You mean you can use magic to *fly?*"

Libby pulling small bottles and packets from her pockets. "I'm saying we *all* can. Maybe." She looked across at the other building again. "The three of us make for a lot to lift, and no time to do a proper casting. But—maybe."

Libby dropped her jacket on the roof surface, knelt on it, and began her preparations. A few feet away, Sidney Prendergast had rolled up into a ball, and was sobbing. Smoke was coming through the roof more insistently now, and Morris thought he could hear the crackle of flames from beneath them.

"Listen," Morris said to Libby, "if it was just you who was going to fly, would you be confident you could do it?"

"Reasonably confident, yes." Libby was using a mixture of powders to make a small circle.

"Then do it," he said harshly. "Better one of us makes it for sure, than all three of us end up splattered on the sidewalk. Take the sure thing, Libby."

Libby Chastain continued with the arcane pattern she was constructing within the circle. "Don't you go all Horatius-at-the-bridge on me now. Fuck that, and fuck you, Quincey Morris. Either we all make it together, or none of us makes it." She looked up at him, and her eyes were wild. "Now shut up and let me work!"

Four and a half minutes later, the three of them stood in a row atop the retaining wall. Libby had put the hysterical Sidney Prendergast into a light trance, and the young woman would do as she was told. She stood between Libby and Quincey Morris, the three of them holding hands like actors about to take curtain call. Behind them, the first flames were visible between the shingles.

"The spell went well, considering," Libby said. "And we don't really have far to go. I think we'll be all right."

"That's great," Morris said tightly. He was trying very hard not to look down.

"It's important that we keep our hands clasped," Libby said. "The spell is geared toward us as a unit, not three individuals. Understand, Sidney? Hold on to both of us, and don't let go."

"Yeah, okay," Sidney Prendergast said listlessly.

"I'm going to say a word of power three times. At the third time, we step off. We have to do it *together*, all right?"

"All right," Morris replied. His throat was so tight that he could barely squeeze the words out.

"*Levate!*" Libby said loudly.

Morris clenched his sphincter tight, afraid he was going to piss himself.

"*Levate!*"

Morris wondered whether his grip was breaking any of the small bones in Sidney Prendergast's left hand.

Libby Chastain, white witch extraordinaire, took a deep breath and called, for the last time, "*LEVATE!*"

Then the three of them stepped out into nothing.

ON BOYLSTON STREET, their taxi had to pull over to make way for fire trucks heading in the other direction.

"Day late and a goddamn dollar short," Quincey Morris muttered.

"Not quite a whole day," Libby Chastain said from beside him. "It just seemed that way."

Sidney Prendergast used a handkerchief to wipe soot from her face. "I don't know how to thank you guys for what you did back there. I guess I really lost my shit before I passed out."

"You were frightened," Libby said. "A perfectly understandable reaction, under the circumstances."

"I still can't remember exactly how we got away," Sidney said. "It's all... hazy, like a bad dream."

Libby rested her hand on the back of Sidney's head. "You're just in shock, it happens that way sometimes. I wouldn't be surprised if you forget everything that happened after the fire broke out. You'll feel better if you just forget it all."

"All I can remember is you saying some word, over and over. *Levate*? Was that it?"

"It's just something I say under stress. It's like a mantra, helps me stay calm."

"You know, to do genealogy, I had to learn Latin. Isn't that what your mantra is? Latin for '*Let us rise*?'"

"That's right," Libby said. She began to rub the back of Sidney's head, very gently. "But you'll probably forget that, too. Don't worry, it's all right."

"And *flying*," Sidney said suddenly. "It felt like we were flying, all three of us."

"People can't fly, Sidney," Libby told her. "You know that." Her hand continued rubbing. "It was just a dream you had. Best you just put it out of your mind."

"Well, can I at least buy you both dinner tonight, after we all get cleaned up?"

"We'd love to, Sidney, but Quincey and I have to catch a plane."

"Oh? Where to?"

"San Francisco," Quincey Morris said.

THEY HAD PUT Van Dreenan up in a Holiday Inn, which was all right with him. His room was clean and reasonably quiet, and he would have felt uncomfortable in one of those American palaces he'd seen advertised in slick magazines.

Van Dreenan tried to live an orderly life in private, perhaps in compensation for the disorder and chaos that his work plunged him into so frequently. He had been alone since the disintegration of his marriage, and, like many single men of middle age, sought what comfort he could find in structure and regularity.

His routine was the same, no matter where he was, or what he was doing.

After undressing down to his underwear, he went into the bathroom, urinated, washed his hands, brushed his teeth, and drank some water.

Then, sitting on the bed, he said his prayers, silently. He did not pray for himself, but rather for the souls of others.

Finally, Van Dreenan did what he had made himself do every night since the worst day of his life. From an oversized envelope, he removed several newspaper clippings that had been folded and refolded so often they threatened to come apart at the creases. Van Dreenan supposed he would have to mend them with tape when that happened. The thought of simply ceasing this nightly practice had never occurred to him.

He read the clippings again, even though he had their contents inscribed on his soul by now.

The first was headed "LOCAL GIRL GONE MISSING," and began, "Pretoria police are conducting inquiries into the apparent disappearance of a local girl from a playground near her home. Katerina Van Dreenan, age 9, was last seen by her friends..."

The second clipping bore the heading, "SEARCH INTENSIFIES FOR LOCAL GIRL." "Authorities have stepped up their efforts to determine the whereabouts of the daughter of a South African Police Force officer. Katerina Van Dreenan, age 9, has been missing since Tuesday, when she apparently disappeared from a playground near her home. According to police spokesman Pieter Jowett, the case is not yet being treated as a kidnapping, since no demand for ransom has been made. However, he stressed that every effort was being undertaken..."

"BODY OF MISSING GIRL FOUND," said the final news article. It went on, "The remains of Katerina Van Dreenan, age 9, were discovered today by a pair of hikers near the edge of Centurion Lake outside Pretoria. The girl, daughter of South African Police officer Garth Van Dreenan and his wife Judith, had been the focus of an intense search since she was reported missing on Tuesday. Authorities declined to comment today on unconfirmed reports that the girl had been the apparent victim of a 'muti killing,' since several organs were said to be missing from the body. A police spokesman would only say that a full investigation has been launched, and arrests are expected any..."

Having driven the dagger into his heart yet another time, Van Dreenan replaced the clippings in their envelope, got into bed, and turned out the light. After a while, exhaustion overcame grief and, mercifully, let him sleep.

He had been asleep perhaps forty minutes when the telephone rang. He answered it on the second ring, without fumbling or confusion—he had been awakened by the phone many times in his career, and none of the news had ever been good.

"*Ja*. Van Dreenan."

The voice in his ear belonged to Fenton, who did not waste time with polite preliminaries. "We've got another one," he said.

CHAPTER 14

ONLY A HANDFUL of people were working in the FBI field office at that hour, and a few looked up from their desks and stared at Van Dreenan as he quick-marched past them on his way to Fenton's glorified cubbyhole.

A few seconds later, Van Dreenan was leaning over Fenton's shoulder, asking, "What do we know thus far?"

"They're on the move," Fenton told him. "New Jersey, this time. Body was found this afternoon, in a wooded area outside Glassboro." Crime scene photos were still coming in online, and Fenton was downloading them into a USB flash drive he had attached to his laptop computer.

"Near water?" Van Dreenan asked.

"Yeah, looks like there's a little creek runs about fifty feet away."

"The victim—boy or girl?"

"Girl," Fenton said, and he felt rather than saw Van Dreenan stiffen for a moment. Then the big South African straightened up, went around to the room's only other chair, and sat down heavily.

Van Dreenan ran his hand through his thick hair a couple of times before asking, "What organs were taken, do we know?"

"Not yet. The local M.E.'s office is rushing the autopsy, but it's still not going to get done until tomorrow. For what it's worth, one of the first cops on the scene is saying, off the record, that it looks like they cut off the poor kid's labia. That's the—"

"External lips of the vagina, yes I know," Van Dreenan said. His voice contained no effect at all.

"And the male victims were missing their penises, among other organs," Fenton said thoughtfully. Then he shook his head. "How is that supposed to give power to some fucking witch? Jesus, it's not like these kids lived long enough to be sexually active."

"That is, in fact, the point, Agent Fenton. The organs, never having been employed for a sexual purpose, are thus pure, unsullied. They have lost none of their power as mechanisms of creation." Van Dreenan shrugged. "Or so some African sorcerers believe. It varies, by tribe and region. There is also the idea of luck."

"Say again? Luck?"

Van Dreenan nodded. "Some tribal belief systems hold that each of us is born with a certain amount of luck allocated by God. It is seen as a capital sum, reduced by expenditure. If a man has a lot of good luck when he is young, his well may have run dry, as it were, by the time he reaches middle age."

"Yeah, so? What's that got to do with killing kids?"

"Children, by definition, have not lived long enough to have expended a great deal of their luck. Most of it is still present. And some sorcerers will claim that they can capture that luck and transfer it to another person, by removing certain of a child's bodily organs and incorporating them into a religious totem, or fetish."

"Sick bastards." Fenton leaned back in his chair. "Yeah, I know, I know. I've got a Master's in Psychology from Stanford, and I've been with Behavioral Science for three years, and I'm not supposed to think that way about somebody's aberrant behavior, but, fuck it, these are just sick bastards."

"I could not agree more," Van Dreenan said. "I do not suppose one of the perpetrators was considerate enough to leave behind a wallet on this occasion, or perhaps a business card, or at least some usable fingerprints."

"Not fucking likely. We did get a few clear footprints this time, but that only helps us if we've got a suspect in custody to compare them to. Couple of interesting things about those footprints, though."

Van Dreenan raised polite eyebrows. "Indeed?"

"The feet were bare, for one thing."

"That is common in most such rituals, in Africa. It appears that someone has been doing his homework. Or—"

Fenton looked at him sharply. "Or what?"

Van Dreenen shook his head slightly. "Something for later, perhaps. Now, what was the other interesting thing about the footprints?"

"Well, the guy I talked to from the local FBI field office wasn't sure, because you can't be, really, but he said if he had to put money on it, it would be a pretty safe bet."

Van Dreenan made an impatient gesture. "Spare me the suspense, *mann*. What would be this safe bet?"

"That the footprints were made by a woman."

CHRISTINE ABERNATHY BLEW out the black candle and slammed her spell book closed in frustration. She cursed out loud, both obscenely and viciously, although even then she was careful of what she said. In this room, there were some names that must not be invoked, certain acts that should not be mentioned, lest they be considered invitations by someone—or something.

She had been trying for almost two hours to cast a spell that would bring death and destruction to the LaRue family in Wisconsin. Not only was carrying on the centuries-old feud a family obligation (a fact that Mother had beaten into her thoroughly), but Christine wanted to be the witch in her line to end it, once and for all. Her ancestors had managed to inflict considerable damage on the descendants of Sarah Carter over the years, but always some had escaped to continue the bloodline. She wanted to be the one to deliver the deathblow, as none before her had been able to do.

Christine Abernathy wondered if a cheer would go up in Hell on the day she finally destroyed the LaRues. There were enough of her family members there to create quite a din.

Clearly, that bitch Chastain had installed a strong system of wards and protections in the LaRue house. Well, Christine would be doing something about that meddling Wiccunt soon enough.

And, in any case, the collection of fetishes that was being prepared by the African woman, Mbwato, would be ready shortly. The child murders were starting to get national media attention, and you could follow on a map the progress of Mbwato and Christine's minion, Snake, as they harvested what they needed. Judging by the number of dead children they had left behind, the two of them were almost done.

Christine would, of course, deliver the fetishes to Walter Grobius, as agreed. He was paying her a great deal of money for them, and would not take well to being cheated. Although she was a black witch of considerable power, Christine Abernathy still understood the value of discretion. There were only a few people in this world who belonged on her list of Persons Not To Be Fucked With. Mother had been one. And Walter Grobius was clearly another.

But nothing said she couldn't use the power of the African fetishes to do a little spell casting of her own before turning them over to her client. The fetishes would not be diminished in any way by such usage. And their power should allow Christine Abernathy to go through Libby Chastain's defenses like a hot knife through a baby's arm.

She wondered if the LaRues would curse Libby Chastain in their final moments, when they realized that the white witch bitch had failed them. Christine rather hoped they would.

VIRTUALLY EVERY GAS station in America has a convenience store attached, and Drexler's Sunoco, on the east side of Glassboro, New Jersey, was no exception.

"Gonna go take a leak," Snake Perkins said, turning off the Lincoln's engine. "Then I'll fill 'er up and we can hit the highway."

Cecelia Mbwato looked at the brightly lit little shop just the other side of the gas pumps. "I am hungry, a bit," she said to Snake. "When you have emptied your bladder, go into that store there and get me some groundnuts."

Snake stared at her. "Some what?"

Cecelia clicked her tongue in annoyance. "Peanuts, you call them here. Buy me some peanuts."

"Yeah, sure, okay. You want regular or dry-roasted? Little bag, big bag, can, or maybe a jar?" Snake was jerking her chain, just a little.

She gave him a disgusted look and opened her door. "Go!" she said with an impatient gesture. "Do your business. I will get them for myself."

She walked briskly over to the white man's store, her flip-flops (one of the few things about this country that she liked) slapping against the asphalt. The handle of her large cloth bag, too big to be called a purse, was tightly clutched in one hand.

It took her a few minutes to find the section of the store she wanted, and a few more to make up her mind, given the variety of peanuts and packaging she was faced with. So many choices! Who needed so many ways to buy simple groundnuts?

She finally chose a bag of Planters cocktail peanuts and headed toward the front of the store to pay for it. The young man behind the counter was one of what back home were called "coloreds"—probably Indian or Pakistani. Another man reached the cash register ahead of her, and she stood a few feet behind him, waiting her turn.

Then the man in front of her reached under his filthy jacket and pulled out a gun.

He clutched the big revolver in both hands, pointed it at the clerk's face and screamed, "Gimme the money! All of it! Hurry up, motherfucker!"

He turned then, wagging the gun barrel as if to confront a horde of angry customers behind him, and saw that Cecelia was the only other person in the place. She noticed that his face bore five or six ugly scabs, some of which appeared to be infected. His eyes were those of a maniac.

He pointed his gun at Cecelia's chest. "You! Freeze! Get on your knees! Now!"

Cecelia decided not to point out the contradiction in his screamed commands, and knelt down obediently on the dirty linoleum. She let the packet of peanuts slip from her fingers and fall quietly to the floor. She wanted both her hands free, just in case.

The terrified clerk was pulling bills from the cash drawer with hands that shook.

"Get the big bills underneath the drawer, too, asshole! All of it! Move!"

The man turned back to Cecelia. "What's in the bag, lady?"

"Just my things," Cecelia answered calmly. She very much hoped that Snake Perkins, who had his own gun, did not come through the door in the next few seconds, or there was likely to be a bloodbath in here, and some of that blood might be hers.

"Gimme!" the man said. "Come on, gimme the fuckin' bag!"

"All right, just don't hurt me," she said. There were things in that bag that Cecelia Mbwato could simply not afford to lose. Not now. She faked a coughing fit, to distract the robber for a few precious seconds while one hand slipped into her bag. Fortunately, what she needed was in a small vial near the top.

The man turned to scream at the clerk some more, and when he returned his attention to Cecelia, she had palmed the vial she wanted and flicked the cap off with her thumbnail.

"I said gimme the fuckin' bag, or I'll blow your fuckin' nigger head off!"

"Here, take it, take it," she said in a voice that pleaded. She held the bag out to him, but just before his fingers could grasp it, she let the thing fall to the floor.

When he bent forward to pick it up, Cecelia Mbwato extended her other hand out to him, palm up, fingers together. There was a small quantity of fine gray powder on her palm.

Then, with a quick puff of breath, she blew the powder into his eyes.

The robber stepped back instantly, recoiling, and then Cecelia said a phrase, softly but very quickly, in Zulu.

A moment later, the man's eyes started bleeding.

He let out a screech and dropped his pistol—which fortunately, did not discharge when it hit the floor. He was reeling like a drunk now, clutching his eyes as the blood continued to flow through his fingers.

Cecelia Mbwato nodded to herself once and retrieved her bag, along with the package of peanuts. She got quickly to her feet, dodged around the staggering, screaming robber, and slipped out through the door.

Snake Perkins was just putting the gas cap back on the Lincoln as Cecelia hustled over to the car and yanked the front passenger door open. "Get in!" she snapped. "Quickly!"

Snake looked at her in bewilderment. "But I gotta pay for the—"

"Get in and drive!" she said, her voice cracking like a rhino-hide whip.

Snake sent one quick glance toward the convenience store she had just left, and saw that a little guy with brown skin and black, wavy hair was using a baseball bat to beat the shit out of some other dude who had his hands to his face and appeared to be seriously fucked up.

Then he got in the car and drove.

CHAPTER 15

THE GNOSTIC CHURCH of Satan occupied a converted storefront at the fringes of the Tenderloin, an area that most San Franciscans refer to simply as "the bad part of town." As he and Libby Chastain approached the old building, Morris thought he could detect faded lettering above the big front windows that appeared to read "S.S. Kresge & Co."

Just inside the door was a small foyer containing shelves full of pamphlets, a few chairs, and a battered old desk that looked like salvage from the front of some 1960s high school homeroom. Behind the desk sat a young woman done up in a good imitation of Morticia from *The Addams Family*. She looked at her visitors without much interest, took a drag on her Marlboro, and asked in a bored voice, "Help you?"

"We'd like to see Simon Duval," Morris said.

"He's awful busy. You got an appointment, or something?"

"No, but tell him Quincey Morris is here."

"Well, like I said, he's real—"

"Go ahead and tell him, dear," Libby Chastain said gently. "It'll be all right, I promise."

The girl stared at Libby, then stood without a word and went out through a nearby door.

"What was that?" Morris asked softly. "Magic mind control?"

"Just a little kindness," Libby told him. "She hasn't seen much of it in her life."

"How do you know that?"

"Really, Quincey—do you think anyone well acquainted with human kindness would feel the need to hang around a place like *this?*"

Morticia was back within a minute. "Okay, come on," she said, sounding surprised. They followed her along a dimly lit hallway that smelled faintly of incense, stopping at a red-painted door with black accents. Hanging from a nail was a small sign that read, "The Devil is IN—each of us."

The girl knocked, turned the knob, and stepped into the room. "This is them," she said to someone inside, then turned to Morris and Libby. "Come on in."

As he passed the door, Morris indulged his curiosity and turned the little sign around for a moment. On the back it read, "The Devil is OUT—to get YOU!"

The girl slipped out, closing the door behind her. Quincey Morris and Libby Chastain were left staring across a gleaming mahogany table at the Devil—or, at least, at the man who claimed to be his representative on Earth.

Simon Duval at least *looked* the part. He was thin to the point of emaciation, and his shiny black eyes were sunken deep in his skull. The jet-black goatee matched his hair, which was shaved in a monk's tonsure. He wore a black silk shirt buttoned to the collar, and he stared at his visitors over long, bony fingers that were steepled just under the thin, unforgiving mouth.

Then the fingers were withdrawn, and the mouth curved into a wide grin. "Quincey!" Duval said, with what sounded like real pleasure. He got to his feet and came around the desk, extending a hand. "*Que* fucking *pasa, hombre?*"

Morris, with a matching grin, approached and shook hands.

Duval stepped back and said, "You're looking good, man. Ghostbusting seems to agree with you." Then he turned to Libby. "And who's this lovely lady?"

After Morris performed introductions, Duval invited his guests to sit down, then returned to his own chair. "Would you folks care for something to drink?" he asked. "Coffee, tea, beer, soda, virgin's blood?"

They declined politely. With a perfectly straight face, Morris said to Libby, "It's not like you to pass up virgin's blood."

Libby's mouth crinkled at the corners as she said, "I've been trying to cut back. Gives me gas."

Duval gave a bark of laughter. "I see you're traveling with a better class of people than usual, Quincey."

"And I see you're still trying to make a buck off fake fire and brimstone," Morris said with a smile.

"Trying, and succeeding—big time," Duval replied. "You'd be amazed how many people are willing to pay serious money for the chance to put on a cowled robe and stand around in a circle chanting the Lord's Prayer backwards. Maybe piss on a crucifix as an encore."

"I can imagine," Morris said. "Or, rather, I can't."

"Oh, hell, it's just a harmless way for these jerks to feel wicked," Duval said. "Or maybe to rebel against their tight-ass upbringing. A lot of our members went to Catholic school as kids. They probably get a big thrill imagining what Sister Mary Paschal Candle would say if she could see them now. Although," he added, "some of them just join for the sex."

Morris and Libby both showed raised eyebrows.

"Well, naturally, you can't stage a black mass without having some kind of an orgy afterwards," Duval said. "People expect it. And as long as they're willing to pay for the privilege..."

Libby Chastain smiled. "I was just wondering," she said, "what Satanists might say at the point of orgasm. 'Oh, God!' hardly seems appropriate, does it?"

"Why don't you stick around for a while," Duval suggested, with a gleam in his eye. "You can find out for yourself."

"Perhaps another time," Libby said pleasantly.

Morris leaned forward in his chair. "We didn't come to join up, Simon. But we *could* use some help."

Duval sat back and spread his hands. "Whatever I can do, I will. You know that."

Morris described the problem they faced in trying to protect the LaRues. Libby chimed in whenever she thought a point needed explanation.

When they had finished, Morris summarized. "So we're trying to find a black witch, a powerful one, someone who's descended from a long line of left-hand path practitioners."

Duval nodded solemnly. "You realize, I assume, that what you've been talking about has got nothing to do with what goes on here. Nobody in this church, including me, knows the first fucking thing about real black magic."

Morris nodded. "I understand that."

"I mean, this whole operation is just a money-making scam, which means it's no different from a lot of Christian churches, if you know what I mean. And there's the added benefit that I get laid—a lot."

"You're being very frank," Libby said.

"Ah, Quincey and me, we go back a long ways. He knew me when I was still Seymour Lipschitz."

"I find that difficult to believe," Libby said.

Duval frowned. "What? That we've known each other for all those years?"

"No—that anyone was ever named Seymour Lipschitz."

Duval laughed again. "I like you, Libby, I really do. Hey, are you sure you don't want to stay for the orgy? I can promise you a good time, whether you like guys, or girls, or both."

An enigmatic smile in place, Libby just shook her head.

"How 'bout you, Quincey?" Duval asked. "You used to be quite the stud back at Princeton, at least to hear you tell it."

"I'll pass, Simon, thanks. What I really need is a line on this witch we're looking for. You're plugged into the occult underground all over the country. I was hoping you might have come across something."

Duval sat stroking his goatee for several moments, then shook his head. "Nope, haven't heard a thing that sounds like what you want, man. But I can make some calls, maybe talk to a few people who are closer to that side of things than I am."

"I'd appreciate it, especially if you can do it soon."

Duval checked his watch. "We finished tonight's service about half an hour ago, which means the post-mass orgy should be in full swing, as it were. I need to put in an appearance there for a little while, but I can probably start working the phone by midnight, or a little after."

"Isn't that rather late to be calling people?" Libby asked.

"No, not really," Duval told her. "Most people in the biz tend to be night owls. Comes with the territory, you know." He pushed his chair back and stood up. "Where can I reach you guys later?"

"We're at the Sir Francis Drake," Morris said. "Call any-time."

Duval led them out, but not the way they'd come in. "Might as well give you the quick tour," he explained. They passed various rooms that he identified as the chapel, robing room, library, and even a couple of classrooms. These last, he said, were used for lectures, orientation sessions, and even twelve-step program meetings.

"You have twelve-step meetings here?" Libby asked. "I would have thought that your church would favor most of the vices those programs are designed to control."

"You're right, we do," Duval said. "But we sponsor regular meetings of Fundamentalists Anonymous, and I've been thinking of starting a twelve-step for sex addicts, too."

"You're not the kind of guy who's opposed to sexual addiction, Simon—assuming there really is such a thing," Morris said.

Duval grinned at him. "'Course not. I just thought the meetings would be a good way to meet babes. Save a lot of time, you know?" He opened a door and motioned them inside. "Let's cut through here."

The big room consisted mostly of shelves containing all the impedimenta so vital to the conduct of modern Satanism: robes, incense, blasphemous books, videos, DVDs, sex toys—and a large cage containing a Burmese python. The snake, which appeared to be at least five feet in length, looked up at its visitors placidly.

In the lead, Duval was saying, "This is the shortest way through to the—*oh shit.*"

Quincey Morris had not followed the others into the room. Instead, he was standing in the doorway, looking with narrowed eyes at the reptile that was now ignoring him completely.

"My fault, I'm sorry," Duval said. "I forget we kept Percy in here. Otherwise I wouldn't have..."

Duval bustled about the shelves for a few moments before snatching up a large black cloth with red symbols woven into it. He quickly unfolded it and draped it over the glass cage.

Only when the snake was completely out of sight did Morris enter the room. "Sorry about that," he said. An embarrassed grin spread across his face.

"No, my fault entirely," Duval said. To Libby, he said, "See, my man Quincey has kind of a thing about—"

"Simon." Morris's voice was a little louder than it needed to be. "Just let it go."

"Sure, okay, no problem," Duval said. "Come on, let's get out of here. Maybe lighten the mood a little. Follow me."

It was another large room that he led them into, but this one was dimly lit by some small spotlights in the ceiling, along with dozens of fat black candles that were burning atop various tables and shelves. The walls were done in a red velvety material, and the floors appeared to be covered by a number of mattresses and futons, atop which at least two dozen naked people, in various combinations of twos and threes and more, writhed and strained and grunted in a fair approximation of ecstasy. The air was pungent with a combination of incense, marijuana, sweat, and sex. Especially sex.

Morris said through clenched teeth, "Simon..."

"Just giving you one last chance to change your mind," Duval said innocently. "As you can see, the party's still going strong, if you want to join in."

"No, but thanks anyway," Morris said firmly.

"Suit yourself," Duval said with a shrug. "How about you, Libby? Libby?"

Libby Chastain appeared not to hear. She was staring at a slim man with blond hair who was looking back at her intently even as he received vigorous oral sex from a slightly pudgy woman in a black garter belt with matching hose.

"Looks like your friend is thinking about sticking around, man," Duval murmured.

Morris stepped over next to Libby and took her arm gently. "Libby, are you all right?"

No response. Libby continued to lock eyes with the man on the floor.

Morris shook Libby's arm, then put his mouth next to her ear. "*Libby!*" he said sharply.

Libby turned her head toward Morris slowly, a faraway expression on her face. "Quincey?"

"Are you okay?" There was real concern in Morris's voice.

Libby closed her eyes tightly for a moment. When she opened them, they seemed more focused. "Yes, I'm all right, but, please, let's get out of this sleaze pit."

"You heard the lady, Simon," Morris said. "Which way's the exit?"

QUINCEY MORRIS TURNED the rental car onto Lombard Street and drove two blocks before being stopped by a traffic light. Without taking his eyes off the street he said to Libby Chastain, "So, what the hell was all that about?"

Libby stopped chewing her lower lip and said, "I don't know, Quincey. I really don't."

"I mean, you weren't really thinking about joining that Tijuana circus that Simon had going back there, were you?"

"Dear God, no. Not in a thousand years. I'm not a prude, you know that. And I've never begrudged other people their fun, as long as everybody's a consenting adult. But that kind of mindless rutting is definitely *not* my scene."

"Then what—"

"It was that man, the blond one. I mean, okay, I've never seen a real orgy before. So I was looking around, you know, at who was doing what to whom. Prurient interest, I suppose. But when I noticed the blond guy, there was *something...*"

"Did you know him, or did he maybe remind you of someone you know?"

"No, it wasn't that. And he's not even that good looking. But there was this instant, I don't know, *connection,* as if everyone else in the room had suddenly disappeared, or become irrelevant."

"Just like in the movies, huh?"

Libby snorted. "I don't usually have trouble separating the movies from real life. But for a few seconds there, I experienced such a surge of, well, *lust* is the only word for it, that I was seriously tempted to tear my clothes off, elbow the garter belt lady aside, and jump him right there, with all those people around."

"Goodness gracious," Morris said mildly. "Um, does this kind of thing occur often?"

"No, never. I mean, I've felt lusty before, everyone has, but nothing like that has *ever* happened to me."

“I’d almost wonder if Simon might’ve slipped something into your glass of virgin’s blood, except you didn’t have anything to drink.”

“No, you’re right, I didn’t,” she said pensively. “It’s an interesting idea, though.”

CHAPTER 16

THE KNOCK CAME as Libby Chastain was pulling on her nightshirt, a blue cotton garment decorated with little images of Shaun the Sheep. She went to the door, frowning. Quincey was in the next room, and he'd knock on the connecting door if he wanted something. Libby hadn't ordered anything from room service, and she certainly wasn't expecting company.

She peered through the fisheye lens into the hall then suddenly became very still. She stood looking through the glass for quite some time, then her right hand went slowly to the security chain and worked it loose, then dropped to the doorknob and turned it.

The door opened to reveal the blond man from the orgy at Simon Duval's church. He stood there in tight jeans and a white T-shirt with Jim Morrison's picture on it. The clear outline of his erect penis under the worn denim suggested he wore no underwear. Part of Libby's mind was acutely conscious that her nightshirt only came down to mid-thigh. The rest of her brain couldn't have cared less.

The man, who looked something like an older, taller Brad Pitt, gave Libby a lazy grin. "Aren't you going to invite me in?"

Libby found herself stepping back from the door, but the man continued to stand in the hall. Finally, she heard herself say, "Why don't you come on in?"

Only then did he cross the threshold, closing the door behind him. Libby kept backing up until she stood in the middle of the room. The man followed her, like a stalking leopard.

"What do you want?" Libby asked in a voice not quite her own.

"You, of course."

"But—why me?"

He smiled knowingly. "Unfinished business."

He reached behind his head and pulled off the T-shirt to reveal a hairless, muscular chest and flat stomach. He tossed the shirt on the floor, followed it with his sandals, then the tight jeans.

A long, aching moment later, they were joined by Libby Chastain's nightshirt.

LIBBY'S MIND SEEMED suspended in a red velvet fog, even as her naked body responded avidly to the blond man's kisses and caresses. Somewhere, deep in her consciousness, a voice was shouting out a warning, but Libby could not be bothered to pay attention.

The man had parted her thighs now, and she was gazing with fascination at the huge, engorged penis he was about to slide into her, when there was a knock at the connecting door.

The man kneeling above her turned his head toward the door in annoyance, and for an instant something showed in his face that was not quite human. The mists within Libby's mind parted enough for her to snatch a quick breath and yell, "Quincey!"

The blond man immediately clamped a hand over her mouth, and in tense silence they both listened to the doorknob rattle as the locked connecting door refused to open. The man looked back down at Libby then, and the smile was just returning to his handsome face when the door frame splintered under a mighty kick and Quincey Morris charged into the room like an avenging angel.

GETTING THROUGH THE connecting door had been relatively easy. A patient veteran of the Austin SWAT team had once taught Morris the basic techniques of what he called "explosive entry." But nothing in the training had prepared him for what he found in Libby Chastain's room.

There was enough light for him to recognize the man rearing up from the bed as the one from the group grope at the Church of Satan. Morris resisted the urge to stare at Libby's naked body and instead watched as the blond man slid off the bed to stand facing him.

For half a second Morris feared that he had just interrupted an intimate moment between two willing grown-ups, but then he remembered the urgency in Libby's voice when she'd called his name. Morris moved his feet a little, seeking perfect balance just as his *sensei* had taught him. Keeping his eyes on the blond man, he asked, "Are you okay, Libby?"

"Yes, I'm all right," she said shakily. "But there's something—"

"Quincey Morris, I presume," the blond man said smoothly. "A pleasure to make your acquaintance, although I would have done so later this evening, in any event. Still, there's nothing wrong with saving a little time..."

As Morris watched, the man began to *change*. The face became rounder and softer, the hair longer, and his entire body seemed to shrink a couple of sizes. Breasts began to bloom on the hairless chest, while the penis and testicles retracted and were soon transformed into female genitals, shaved bald as a baby's bottom.

It took only seconds for the handsome blond man to become a stunningly attractive blonde young woman.

Quincey Morris thought she was the most beautiful creature he had ever seen in his life.

"You like me, don't you Quincey?" The voice was a throaty alto, only a little higher than the man's had been. Morris found himself getting an urgent erection.

"Yes, I thought you might. Well, then, why don't we do something about it?" The woman stepped forward, holding Morris's eyes with her own. "All three of us, together."

She turned to look toward the bed. "You'd like that, wouldn't you, Libby? I know you like girls as well as boys; I could tell the minute I saw you. So what do you say, kids?" She returned her gaze to Morris. "Let's all have some *fun*."

Without consciously deciding to do it, Morris began to unbutton his shirt. He eyes saw nothing but the woman, his mind thought of nothing but having her, right now, this instant.

Sitting up on the bed, Libby Chastain slowly raised her left hand, the way some unlucky swimmers do when drowning. Then, using all the strength she could muster, she slammed it backhand against the edge of the night table.

The pain, as expected, was excruciating. It drove everything else out of Libby's mind, including the red fog that had enveloped it. She pointed her right index finger like a gun, and its target was the nude blonde woman. "Depart, unclean spirit!" she cried, sketching a sign in the air with her finger. "And return no more! I revoke my invitation! *Isa ya! Ri ega!*"

The door to the hallway opened, seemingly of its own volition. Morris never saw the woman-thing move, but one instant she was there in all her nude glory, and the next she was just—gone. Then the door slammed—loudly enough, it sounded, to wake the whole hotel.

Morris stood there for a couple of seconds, blinking like someone newly awakened. "Holy Christ," he said softly. He turned toward Libby Chastain, then quickly looked away. "Listen," he said to the wall, "I'm going to use your facilities, if you don't mind. Splash some cold water on my face, or something. Why don't you get dressed, and then we'll talk, okay?"

"Sure, Quincey, you go ahead." Libby's voice sounded a little unsteady.

He went into the bathroom and closed the door softly behind him.

"I THOUGHT I heard the phone ring while I had the water running in there," Morris said. He sat on the edge of Libby's bed, a few errant drops of water glistening in his hair like diamonds.

"You did," Libby told him. She had put on her nightshirt and covered it with a pink terrycloth robe. "The concierge wanted to know if everything was all right. He said he'd had reports of some noise."

"What'd you say?"

"That I'd heard the noise too, but it sounded like it was coming from further down the hall. I said that the racket had woken me from a sound sleep, and that I was just dropping off again when he called. He was quite apologetic after that."

Morris smiled briefly, then was serious again. He looked at Libby, who sat in the room's sole armchair. "What was that you said at the end of your dismissal of our visitor? I didn't recognize the language."

"Ancient Sumerian. It's part of a charm against demons."

"Is that what we were dealing with? A demon?"

She nodded. "An incubus—in its male form, anyway. The female side is called a succubus."

"I thought the legends describe those as two separate creatures."

"They do, but the legends are wrong. That's because the demon's victims are usually exposed to only one side of its nature. But, as you saw, it can take on either a male or a female aspect, depending on the person being targeted."

"That reminds me, didn't I hear it say something about you liking girls and boys both? It's none of my damn business, but do you play for both teams, Libby?"

Libby Chastain plucked at the hem of her bathrobe for a few seconds. "Yes," she said finally. "Yes, I'm bisexual." She looked at him then, one eyebrow raised in challenge. "But that doesn't make me some kind of a slut, Quincey."

"Jesus, Libby, of course not," Morris said hurriedly. "I didn't mean anything like—"

She held up a hand. "All right, okay. I'm sorry. I guess I'm feeling a little defensive at the moment."

"No, listen, like I said, it's none of my damn business, and anyway I wouldn't presume—"

She stopped him again. "Quincey, it's all right, just relax, okay?"

She leaned back in her chair. "We've never talked about our personal lives much, although I know we care for each other. At least, I know that I care for you, and I'm pretty sure it's mutual."

He gave her a lopsided smile. "Witch's intuition?"

"Something like that, maybe. Anyway, I'm a devout practitioner of serial monogamy. I've had romantic relationships with several people in my life. Some of them were men, some were women. But always one at a time. And I've never even considered something like that sexual free-for-all we saw at Duval's place."

"I understand," Morris said. "And I respect that, not that it matters."

"It matters to me, Quincey. Which is why I want you to understand that what you saw when you came bursting in here a little while ago was the result of an enchantment by that creature."

"You don't have to tell me. I felt it, too, remember? If you hadn't done something drastic, I swear she would have had me making the sign of the double-backed aardvark with her faster than you could say—"

Despite herself, Libby began to giggle. "The sign of the what? *Double-backed aardvark?* Who on earth calls it that?"

"A good ol' boy from down home, name of Joe Bob Briggs. Used to host his own movie show on cable, 'Joe Bob's Drive-In Theater.' Ever see it?"

"Guess I must have missed that one, I can't think how," Libby said with a barely suppressed smile.

Morris's voice turned serious again. "It raises an interesting question, though. What was the point of all this?"

"The point of sending an incubus/succubus, you mean?"

"Exactly. We're assuming it was sent by the black witch we're after, right?"

She nodded. "No other explanation makes sense."

"All right then. I can see why she'd want to set fire to the building in Boston. If we get burned to cinders, she's got no more problem. As you said, it makes sense, in an evil, twisted sort of way. But what does it matter to her whether we get laid, even by a minor demon? Succubi aren't killers, are they?"

"No, they're not. Not of the body, anyway."

"I'm not following you," Morris said.

Libby tightened the belt of her robe, as if against a sudden chill. "Intercourse with a succubus or incubus is said to rob the victim of vitality, ambition, and short-term memory."

Morris snorted. "Sounds like some pot heads I knew in college."

"It's much worse than a marijuana habit, Quincey. Some accounts even describe these creatures as devouring the soul. It's a form of psychic vampirism."

"Jesus."

"And it's like vampirism in another way, too."

"What's that?"

"After the first successful attack, there's nothing to prevent the creature from coming back, again, and again. And after each time, there'd be a little less of you left."

"So if you and I had succumbed to that thing, either together or separately..."

"Then tomorrow morning we'd have considerably less enthusiasm for continuing this expedition of ours. And the next morning, we'd have even less."

"Then I'd say we were pretty lucky you were able to come up with an incantation to drive that thing out of here. Talk about a demon lover!"

"That's exactly where the term comes from, I'm sure of it." Libby fussed with her robe some more. "Quincey?"

"Uh-huh?"

"Will you stay here, for what's left of the night?" Seeing his eyes widen, she added hastily, "Not for sex. I don't want to change our relationship that way, and I don't think you do, either. But, I don't know... I guess I'm scared to be alone."

"I'm kind of glad you asked me that, Libby," Morris said softly. "Since I've been sitting here trying to come up with a way to suggest the same thing without sounding like I was trying to put the moves on you."

They turned out all the lights but one, and Morris kicked off his shoes. The two of them lay together on the queen-size bed, close but not quite touching.

After a while, Morris drifted off to sleep. But Libby Chastain lay awake, wary and watchful, until dawn finally came to drive the night's evil away.

WHEN MORRIS RETURNED to his own room, the red message light on his telephone was blinking. He read the directions posted on the phone for retrieving voicemail messages, pressed the right buttons, and waited.

There was a click, then a familiar voice said in his ear, "Quincey, it's Simon. I don't know if this is what you need, but it's all I've got. There's a *mambo* in New Orleans, calls herself Queen Esther. I hear she might be involved in... all that shit you were asking about."

The line went silent, and Morris was about to hang up when Duval's voice continued, "Listen, man, don't bother to call back, and don't come over to the church any more, okay? In fact, if you're smart, you'll forget this whole witch hunt you're on and just go home. But either way, leave me out of it. I just dip my toe in these waters once in a while, but you—you're swimming with the fuckin' sharks, dude. Keep at it, and they are gonna eat you alive."

CHAPTER 17

THE WINDOW IN Fenton's borrowed office looked out over an airshaft, but at least it let in light and air. The bright morning sunshine that was coming through it did nothing to lift the spirits of either Fenton or Van Dreenan, who were combing through the reports on the Glassboro murder, looking for something, anything, that remotely resembled a lead.

Fenton's laptop, which was open on the desk, "pinged" to announce the arrival of an e-mail message. Fenton glanced at the screen, then looked away and went back to his work. Two seconds later he stopped, turned back to the laptop, and started reading more closely.

"It's from the Trenton field office," he told Van Dreenan. "Ever since you ID'd the killings as possible *muti* murders, I've asked our field offices, the ones that are closest to each of the four crime scenes, to go through the local law's incident reports for the periods before and after the murders, a week either way. I also asked them to keep an eye on current stuff as it came in."

"With a view toward accomplishing what?"

"Finding anything hinky that might connect up with our case." Fenton was rapidly opening the files that had been attached to the message.

"You did not, surely, use the word 'hinky' in your requests," Van Dreenan said with a tiny smile, his first in days.

"No, I believe I used words like 'unusual,' 'anomalous,' 'idiosyncratic,' and 'fucked-up.' Well, maybe not that last one." Fenton paused to read for a few seconds. "But this, my man, is some kind of seriously fucked-up." He turned the laptop around so that it faced Van Dreenan. "Check it out."

Van Dreenan read what was in front of him. A frown developed on his face and grew deeper as he continued. Finally, he looked up at Fenton.

"A woman apparently blunders into an armed robbery at a—" Van Dreenan glanced at the screen again, "convenience store. What is that, a 'convenience store?'"

"Small grocery store. Often attached to a gas station."

"Oh, of course. I know what you mean. So this woman, described as 'African-American'—how did the witness know that she was African? Or American, for that matter?"

"It's just a polite term for black people," Fenton said, with a small sigh. "Don't read any more into it."

"All right. The robber attempts to take the woman's purse away from her, and she blows some kind of powder into his face, blinding him."

"Blinding him, but good. Check out the ER doctor's report. The guy's eyeballs just about dissolved. He'll never see again."

"Yes, I read that part," Van Dreenan said. "But why is that of use to us? She blows some kind of caustic soda into the man's face, which has the expected effect. Good for her, I say. One less criminal on the streets."

"Yeah, I know," Fenton said. "I might even agree with you. But go a little further down."

Van Dreenan gave him a dubious look, but went back to the report, reading rapidly. Then he stopped. Scrolled back up. Read one part again, slowly. Then he looked at Fenton, and there was an odd expression on his face. "A chemical analysis of the blinding agent finds several kinds of herbs and some ground-up tree bark. That's all, nothing else." Van Dreenan shook his head a couple of times. "None of these ingredients should have done any harm to the man's eyes at all, beyond mild irritation—the kind you would have from any kind of dirt that gets in your eyes."

Fenton nodded slowly. "Yeah. Exactly."

"And this damage is rather too extreme to be considered a psychosomatic injury, even if the robber was a likely candidate for such, which he is not."

"Yeah," Fenton said again. "Told you this was fucked up."

Van Dreenan was looking at the screen again. "I recognize these herbs," he said slowly. "They are often used, in my country, in tribal magic rituals. One of them is even native to South Africa, I believe."

"Uh-huh."

Van Dreenan had long believed that "uh-huh" was one of the most useful terms in American English. It can express agreement, skepticism, indifference, or acknowledgment. It can also be used when you're so overwhelmed by circumstances that you can't think of anything else to say. Van Dreenan was betting that the last one of those applied to Fenton right now.

The two of them were silent for a while. "You know," Van Dreenan said finally, looking down at his hands, "of the many differences between your country and mine, one that I find most striking is the proliferation of surveillance cameras you have here, at least in the urban areas. I am not saying this is necessarily a bad thing, mind you. It can certainly make a policeman's job easier. But you have them everywhere, it seems. Office buildings, car parks, banks—" He paused then, and looked up at Fenton, "convenience stores..."

Fenton stared at him for a long moment. "You know," he said, "I would have figured that out for myself. Eventually."

"Of course you would have," Van Dreenan said graciously.

Fenton turned the laptop back so it was facing him and began to type quickly. After a minute or so, Van Dreenan asked, "What are you doing?"

"Getting us a road map." He clicked the mouse. "There. It's printing now." He gestured with his chin in the direction of the door. "Maybe you'd care to pick it up from the communal printer out there."

"Why do we need a road map?"

"So we don't get ourselves lost on the way to Glassboro, New Jersey."

THE MEDIA ROOM at Glassboro police headquarters contained a single TV/monitor that was hooked up to both a

VCR and a DVD player, and four chairs. Three of these were now occupied.

"I appreciate your letting us take a look at this without a lot of preliminary paperwork," Fenton said to Detective Hank Mulderig.

"It's okay, no problem," Mulderig said. He was a big, untidy man with white hair and bushy eyebrows, with a gut that showed he hadn't had to pass a physical fitness test in a while. "Thing is," he went on, "I don't see why the FBI should give a shit about some two-bit gas station hold-up, especially since we already got the perp in custody."

"We're less interested in the perp than we are in the woman who blinded him," Fenton said.

"Yeah, wasn't that somethin'?" Mulderig said. "Last I heard, the docs still haven't figured what was in that powder she used on him. Kid's a fucking meth-head, name of Tommy Carmody. I've busted him twice, myself. What happened served the bastard right, you ask me." He stopped, looked at Fenton, than Van Dreenan, and back to Fenton. "This some kind of terrorism thing?"

"In a manner of speaking, yes it is," Van Dreenan told him.

"Damn," Mulderig said softly, as if to himself. He picked up the remote and pointed it at the monitor, which came to life immediately. Then he aimed at the videotape player and pressed another button. "Okay, this is the footage from inside the store when it all went down."

The tape began to play, producing an image, black and white but very sharply focused, of the interior of the convenience store. There was, of course, no audio.

They watched the clerk taking packs of cigarettes from a carton and stocking the shelves behind the register. They saw the twitchy young man in the dark jacket, whom they now knew to be Tommy Carmody, approach the counter. And they saw the squat black woman who came to stand a few feet behind Carmody, holding a small bag of some kind of snack food.

Fenton thought he heard a sharp intake of breath from Van Dreenan, but didn't say anything.

They watched as Carmody drew down on the terrified clerk, then turned to train his gun on the woman. They saw him speak to her, yelling probably, threatening her with the gun. They saw her hold out the bag, saw it fall just short of Carmody's grasp, saw him bend forward to pick it up, then the woman's other hand coming up quick as a striking snake, the small cloud of powder suddenly in the air between them, Carmody staggering as he clutched his ruined eyes.

Each of the three men was privately glad he could not hear the screams.

They watched as the woman picked up her bag and scurried out the door, seemingly oblivious to the chaos she was leaving in her wake.

Mulderig pointed the remote again and stopped the tape.

Fenton was tapping a couple of fingers on his knee, a frown creasing his face. He said to Mulderig, "Mind if we see it again?"

"Sure, whatever." Mulderig pressed the rewind button.

Fenton noticed that Van Dreenan was rubbing the bridge of his nose between two fingers. "You all right?" he asked.

"Fine," Van Dreenan said, his voice sounding a little husky. "By all means, let us watch it again."

Fenton looked at him for a moment longer, then turned back to the monitor. When the tape reached the point where the woman blew the powder into Carmody's eyes, he said, "Stop. Run it back a little bit, then play it again, will you?"

Mulderig did as he was asked. This time, as the scene played out, Fenton said, "See that? The bag didn't slip out of her hand, she's letting it fall, deliberately. It's a sucker play. She wants what's-his-name, Carmody, to lean forward and get it."

"Why the fuck would she do that?" Mulderig asked.

"To decrease the range," Van Dreenan said quietly. "She wanted to make absolutely certain of her aim."

Mulderig's eyebrows went up, then he looked back at the video monitor. "Jesus. That is one cold, calculating bitch."

"*Ja,*" Van Dreenan said. "That is exactly what she is."

FENTON LOOKED AT Mulderig. "So, where did she go after she ran out the door? They've gotta have cameras covering the outside, too, right?"

"Yeah, they do," Mulderig said. "Gimme a second."

The detective changed tapes in the machine, and within a minute they were watching the black woman as she exited the convenience store. She made her way quickly over to one set of gas pumps, where a tall, very thin man had apparently just finished gassing up an old Lincoln Connie. The woman spoke to the man, who said something back and then looked in the direction of the convenience store. A moment later, he jumped in the Lincoln and sped off, the woman in the seat next to him.

As Mulderig ejected that tape, Fenton said thoughtfully, "The price of gas being what it is these days, they've gotta have a camera aimed right at the pumps, to get the license number of anybody who fills up and just drives away. Kind of like that guy did."

'Figured you'd wanna see that one," Mulderig said, as he slipped another tape into the VCR. "This is it right here."

This time, the camera gave them a good shot of the car from the rear. They watched as the tall, thin man approached and began to pump gas.

"Wonder where he just came from?" Fenton said.

"The john," Mulderig told him. "It's on another tape, if you wanna see it."

The camera angle gave them a clear shot of the Lincoln's license plate: PCL 976. Fenton squinted at the screen. "What state is that plate from? Can you tell?"

"Yeah, it's Mississippi," Mulderig said. "Guy's a long way from home."

"Assuming it's his car, and he didn't boost it someplace," Fenton said. "Have you got a registration?"

Mulderig shook his head. "Not yet. We put in a request to the Mississippi DMV, haven't heard back. Even with computers, they still tend to be a little slow down there."

"We'll see if they move a little faster when the request comes from the FBI," Fenton said. "I assume you've got a BOLO out on the car?"

"Bolo? What is that?" Van Dreenan asked.

"Acronym for 'be on the lookout,'" Fenton told him. "Kind of a general alert to area law enforcement."

"Yeah, we BOLO'd him this morning," Mulderig said. "We'd kinda like to talk to the woman, since what she did in that store was technically assault and battery. And the guy drove off with thirty-eight bucks' worth of hi-test unleaded he didn't pay for."

"If it's all right with you," Fenton said, "I'm going to have somebody from the FBI field office stop by for these tapes. He'll have them copied and brought right back to you. I want to see if I can get some blow-ups made of their faces."

"Yeah, sure, if you think it'll help." Mulderig chewed his lower lip for a moment. "Terrorism, huh? Those Al Qaeda bastards again?"

"Could be," Fenton said. "You understand, I can't talk about the investigation, not at this stage."

"Sure, I gotcha." Mulderig's face had taken on a grim cast. "I had a cousin, died when the twin towers went down. Knew him since we were both snotnose kids together. You get a chance, stick it to those motherfuckers good, will you?"

"Count on it," Fenton said.

AS THEY WALKED across the parking lot, Fenton glanced at Van Dreenan. "It's just the two of us here now," he said. "So, you want to tell me the nature of the bug that's crawled up your ass?"

Van Dreenan's mouth twitched, but what it produced was at best only an approximation of a smile. "Such elegance of metaphor, such poetry."

"Here's another one for you," Fenton said. "Cut the crap."

Van Dreenan produced a sigh that seemed to come from deep inside him. "Unless I am very much mistaken," he said, "I know who the woman is. When I see the enhancements from the video, I will know for sure. But, to use the American expression, I am ninety percent certain already."

"Okay," Fenton said cautiously. "This would be a good thing—right?"

"It is, and it isn't. Certainly, an identification may make it easier to apprehend her. But, given who and what she is, making an arrest may be both more difficult and more dangerous than you might think."

Fenton shook his head in bewilderment. "All right, let's start with the basics. Maybe this will all make sense, eventually. Who is she?"

"She is almost certainly Cecelia Mbwato, a citizen of South Africa—although, of course, she may not have entered the United States under that name."

"And you know her, how?"

"She is a fugitive from justice. She is wanted in South Africa on numerous charges, including five warrants for suspicion of murder."

"I think I already know the answer to this next one, but I'm gonna ask it, anyway," Fenton said. "What kind of murder is she wanted for?"

"There is evidence that she cut open the bodies of five persons, and, while they were still alive, removed certain of their bodily organs. The objects of her... attentions died, of course."

"*Muti* murder."

"Yes."

They had reached their government-issue sedan. The two men got in, Fenton behind the wheel. He did not start up immediately. Instead, he turned to look at Van Dreenan. "Just now, when you said the murder of five persons..."

"Children," Van Dreenan said bleakly. "She killed five children."

CHAPTER 18

LIKE THE REST of the French Quarter of New Orleans, Dumaine Street is inundated by hordes of tourists every day. They spill over from Bourbon Street in all directions, in search of fun, local color, and places to spend their money. They usually find all three—the Quarter largely escaped Hurricane Katrina, and the surrounding area was slowly regaining its *joie de vivre*.

But things change, once the sun goes down. The tourists move on to other parts of the Quarter, as if somehow sensing that their welcome has been withdrawn with the daylight. The few people who do venture down Dumaine Street after dark are almost always locals, and they walk rapidly, eyes straight ahead, as if they know exactly what they want and where they have to go to get it.

Quincey Morris and Libby Chastain knew what they wanted, but it had taken them most of the day to find out where it could be found. Quite a few people living in New Orleans are aware that real, authentic *voudoun* is practiced in their city, but they aren't always willing to talk about it. Those who know the most often have the least to say, and there are good reasons for their reticence. Nobody wants to come home late some night to find a white feather resting on his pillow.

Morris and Chastain each had contacts in New Orleans, and several hours of telephone calls had finally paid off. They knew now where to find the woman known as Queen Esther.

The cabbie who brought them to Dumaine Street was unable to find the address Morris and Chastain had given him, or so he claimed. He dropped them off at a corner, then stuffed his fare in a shirt pocket without counting it. "Place you want's most likely right around here somewheres," he said. "You find it pretty quick, I reckon—if you sure you wants to." And then he was gone, in a squeal of hasty tires.

They started walking, the warm, moist air enveloping them like a cocoon. "Can't blame the guy for being skittish," Morris said. "Of the dozen or so people I talked to today about Queen Esther, two of them called her a *bokkor,* which means a voodoo black sorcerer. Another one used the term *voudonista petro.* That's the name they give to a voodoo practitioner who serves the dark *loas.*"

"Demons, you mean."

"That's close enough."

"I'm not as familiar with voodoo as I probably should be," Libby said. "It's a very different tradition from the one I was trained in. That's not surprising, I suppose, since Wicca got its start in Europe, and voodoo's roots are African. How is it you know so much about it?"

"I worked a case in Baton Rouge a few years back that involved a voodoo curse. This professor at LSU took sick very suddenly, and all the doctors he went to were baffled. They had a whole bunch of tests run on him, I mean they did the whole nine yards, and every single result came back negative. Turned out the guy had been making fun of voodoo beliefs in one of his classes, and word had got back to a local *houngan,* who took umbrage."

"Local what? Hooligan?"

"No, *houngan.* A priest of voodoo. He'd put his mojo on the professor pretty good, too. Poor guy was in incredible pain—dying, really—but nobody could figure out why, or what to do about it. Well, turned out the professor had a friend in the Anthropology Department who knew me, and he gave my name to the family. They called me in."

"So, what happened?"

"The *houngan* died suddenly, which lifted the curse. The professor got better soon afterwards."

"Oh." Libby glanced at Quincey Morris, then looked away. "Do I want to know any more about that?"

"No, I don't reckon you do."

They walked on in silence for another couple of minutes, and then Libby stopped before a clapboard storefront. "This is it."

Morris consulted the slip of paper he'd pulled from his pocket. "So it is. Let's hope Queen Esther's in residence tonight."

"She's here," Libby said quietly.

"How do you know?"

"I can feel her."

They climbed two rickety wooden steps and opened a battered screen door, its spring screeching like a scalded cat.

The inside of Doctor John's Hoodoo Shop reminded Libby Chastain of the old Woolworth's she had regularly visited as a child. It had the same wooden floors, translucent globe ceiling lights, and split-level glass display cases. But the merchandise was very different here. The dime stores of Libby's youth had not offered their customers Four Thieves Vinegar, Hexing Powder, Graveyard Dirt, Cosmic Money Oil, or High John the Conqueror Root.

Libby's senses were attuned to magical power, and she knew instantly that the items in the display cases and on the shelves were mostly expensive junk designed to lure the superstitious.

But there was power somewhere nearby.

She thought for a moment that it might be coming from the big-boned young black woman who had just risen from a stool behind the counter, but rejected the idea quickly.

The young woman's face split in a smile that did not quite reach her eyes. "How might I serve you folks this evenin'?"

"We're looking for Queen Esther," Morris told her.

"Then your search has ended," the young woman said, drawing herself up into a dignified posture. "I am Queen Esther."

"No, you're not," Libby said matter-of-factly.

The young woman looked at Libby, her eyes narrowed. "Listen, now, I don't know what—"

"Martha!" The voice came through a doorway behind the young woman, an opening filled by a beaded curtain. It was a woman's voice, and to Libby it sounded old but strong, very strong.

Without another word, the young woman turned and slipped through the curtain into whatever room lay beyond it. A few moments later she was back, the smile gone now. "She say you come on back, de bot' of you." Her voice was sullen.

Libby Chastain followed Quincey Morris behind the counter and through the beaded curtain. It opened onto a short hallway. At its end was another beaded curtain, through which light could be seen flickering.

As she pushed through the curtain, Libby saw that the illumination came from dozens of candles that burned in every part of the room, the whitewashed walls making the light seem brighter than it was.

Against the far wall was a tall altar draped in red and black cloth. It held more burning candles, several paintings in small frames, a skull that was large enough to be human, and a machete, its blade covered with splashes and stains that had dried brown. Libby spared the structure only a glance before focusing her attention on the woman who sat in a rocking chair, her back to the altar. She sat rocking slowly, looking for all the world like somebody's grandmother on the family front porch, passing the time until *Murder, She Wrote* came on.

Libby felt the power coming off her in waves.

Morris didn't appear to notice, but to Libby's trained perception it was like standing in front of an open blast furnace, and just about as dangerous.

The woman didn't look like anything special. She was small, and old, her iron-gray hair worn short. Amid the many wrinkles in her brown face the dark eyes seemed to glitter, although that may have been an effect of the candlelight. Each finger of the knurled hands bore at least one ring; some had two or three.

She turned her head slowly toward the doorway and spoke to the tall young woman, who had followed Morris and Chastain into the back. The words were a fast stream of Creole dialect that was incomprehensible to Libby, although she saw Morris's head come up a few inches. If he had heard something meaningful in the words that sent the young woman scurrying back toward the front of the shop, he gave no hint of what it was.

The woman in the rocking chair turned back to look at her visitors. "Come closer, now, why don't you? These eyes of mine don't see so well like they used to."

They each stepped forward. The woman spared Morris only a glance before focusing on Libby. The two women looked at each other impassively for what seemed like a long time. It wasn't a staring contest as much as a moment of mutual assessment—and mutual warning.

Morris broke the growing tension by asking, "Queen Esther?"

The old woman turned her basilisk eyes back to him. "You know already the answer to dat, mistah. Now, why have you come to me?"

"My name's Quincey Morris, and this is—"

"Sidney Prendergast," Libby said smoothly. In black magic, names are power. No way was she going to let this old witch know hers.

Morris sent a surprised glance Libby's way, but recovered quickly. "We were hoping you could help us find someone," he told Queen Esther.

She nodded slowly. "I have helped many to find what they seek," she said. "But not all of them were made happy by their success."

"We're willing to take that chance," Morris said.

Another nod. "Very well. One hundred dollars, please."

Morris frowned at her. "And what does that buy us, exactly?"

"It buys you the chance to ask of me what you wish to know." Smiled, revealing expensive-looking dentures. "The white doctors call it a *consultation fee.*"

After a brief hesitation, Morris produced his wallet and pulled out some bills. He took another step forward, holding them out toward the old woman.

"No," she told him. "Place them there." She gestured toward the altar. They will be an offering to Baron Samedi. Perhaps *he* will answer your questions."

Morris placed the money next to the stained machete, then stepped back. "The woman we're looking for does magic," he said. "But she follows the left-hand path. The black arts have been in her family for many generations, handed down mother to daughter, even onto the present day."

"She sounds *très formidable,*" Queen Esther said, in a voice that did not sound at all impressed. "And what is her true name?"

"That's the problem, or one of them," Morris said. "We don't know her name. But she's descended from someone who was hanged for witchcraft in Salem, Massachusetts—a woman named Sarah Carter."

Queen Esther blinked once, slowly, the way a toad will. "I do not recognize that name. And I do not know the person you describe."

"Begging your pardon, ma'am, but I was told you did." The candles flickered again, although there was no breeze in the room.

"Then you were lied to." The bony fingers of the right hand began to worry one of the rings worn on the left. "So many lies there are in the world, such deception, so much evil all over." The ancient eyes locked on Morris's. "It can ensnare those who are unwise, you know, like the web of a great spider. Happens every day."

"But I wanted to—"

Libby Chastain laid a gentle hand on Morris's forearm. "We've troubled Queen Esther enough, Quincey. We really should go now." And after bending her head a few inches in the sketchiest of bows to the old woman, Libby led Morris out of the room.

As they traversed the short hallway leading back to the shop, Morris said quietly from the corner of his mouth, "I assume you know what you're doing."

Libby's murmured response was, "Trust me."

They passed through the beaded curtain into Doctor John's Hoodoo Shop.

The tall young woman was nowhere to be seen. The store was deserted.

"I think maybe we've got trouble," Libby said.

"Hell, I could've told you that." Morris went quickly to a set of shelves near the door. He spent a few moments scanning the items arrayed there. Then he took down a jar, checked the label, and unscrewed the lid.

"What are you doing?" Libby asked.

"Shoplifting." He dropped the lid on to the counter, but hung on to the jar, which had a garish green label that Libby couldn't read. "Come on, let's go."

Libby followed Morris through the noisy screen door and down the two steps. At the sidewalk, he turned right.

"Wait," Libby said. "We came this way." She pointed to the left.

"I know. That's why we're going the other way. Come on, hurry."

They had walked about fifty feet when two men stepped out of a doorway and into their path. They were black and big and they walked stiffly, as if unused to moving around much.

Each one held a large knife.

Libby's notion that these might be garden-variety muggers was quickly dispelled. The men didn't demand money, or anything else. And in the glow of a nearby street light she saw that their eyes looked completely white, as if the pupils had rolled back into their heads.

As if they were dead.

Heavy footsteps behind her caused Libby to look over her shoulder. Three more men, armed and disposed similarly to the two in front, were bearing down on them.

"Shit," Morris said. "Queen Esther likes to hedge her bets."

"I haven't got anything prepared to deal with this," Libby said tensely.

The men shambled toward them, knives ready.

"Fortunately, I have," Morris told her.

He held the jar from the voodoo shop in his right hand, three fingers spread over the mouth with space between them. He raised his hand, then suddenly swept it across his body in a wide arc, pivoting as he did so, and he sprayed liquid from the jar on all five of the men. "Get thee hence!" he cried, then brought his arm back the other way, causing more liquid to spew out between his fingers. "Leave us be, now and henceforth!" Then a third time, front and back, the last of the jar's contents splashing the men's faces. "Begone!"

The men cowered back, like the Frankenstein monster confronted with fire. Their knives clattered to the pavement and they brought their arms up over their faces. Then, making inarticulate sounds of fear and dismay, they turned and shuffled away—two down the alley, the other three back the way they had come on Dumaine Street.

Morris grabbed Libby's arm. "Come on." They crossed the street, walking rapidly.

"Where are we going?" Libby asked.

"Anywhere there's lights and people, the more the better."

"Then let's take the next left, if it looks safe. That's the quickest way to the center of the Quarter."

Less than three minutes later they were on Bourbon Street, surrounded by music and neon and drunken tourists. Libby noticed that Morris was still clutching the empty jar. "Let me see that, will you?"

"What? Oh, sure. Here."

She looked at the label, gothic black letters printed over a green background. "St. Louis Cemetery Black Banishing Oil?"

Morris nodded, looking pleased with himself. "Yep. Guaranteed to confuse, frustrate, and repel your enemies, whoever they may be, living, dead, or undead."

"I thought all that stuff was just a shuck. You know, like rabbits' feet and four-leaf clovers."

Morris took the jar back and tossed it in a nearby trashcan. "What, you don't think rabbits' feet are lucky?"

"Weren't too lucky for the rabbit, were they?"

"Good point. Well, a lot of those voodoo charms and potions *are* worthless, but not all of them. Obviously."

"*Obviously* is right. It's good you know what works and what doesn't."

"Most important thing is those zombies think it works."

"Is that what they were? I wondered."

They stepped into the street to avoid a group of fundamentalists who were handing out leaflets protesting against nude dancing in Bourbon Street bars. They would have done just as well to protest against the movement of the tides.

"Yeah, they were zombies, all right," Morris said. "The eyes are always a dead giveaway. So to speak."

"Wait a second," Libby said, frowning. "You picked that jar off the shelf *before* we ever saw what was waiting for us."

"Readiness is all, as somebody once said. Remember that stuff that Queen Esther rattled off to what's-her-name, Martha, when we first went into the back room?"

"Yes, vaguely."

"I don't really speak Creole, not well enough to carry on a conversation or anything, but I was able to pick the word for 'zombie' out of what she was saying. I didn't figure old Esther was dictating her Christmas list."

"She was lying to us, you know. About not knowing the current descendant of Sarah Carter."

"Yeah, I kind of tumbled to that, myself," Morris said. "But what the hell are we going to do about it?"

"As it happens," Libby told him, "I may have an idea."

WHEN VAN DREENAN walked in, Fenton said, without preamble, "We got a hit off that Mississippi license plate. Finally."

"From which?" Van Dreenan was frowning. "Oh, yes. The one from that surveillance camera at the petrol station."

"That's the one. I wasn't sure how much help it was going to be. Figured either the car or the plate had been stolen, but it looks like I was wrong, since the driver's license photo that they sent matches up pretty well with the guy's face that we can see on that surveillance tape. There's something else kind of interesting, too." Fenton worked his laptop's keyboard for a few seconds, then turned the computer around to face Van Dreenan. "See for yourself."

Van Dreenan sat down and peered at the screen. "Snake Perkins?" He looked at Fenton. "That sounds like an alias, but apparently it's his given name."

"Yeah, just a good ol' boy from Hattiesburg, Mississippi."

Van Dreenan thought he heard an off note in Fenton's voice. "Is there something about this town, Hattiesburg? Something I should know?"

Fenton made a dismissive gesture. "No, nothing important. I spent six weeks there, one night, a while back. Never mind. Read on."

"Um. Perkins was sent to reform school for auto theft at fifteen." He looked up again. "Reform school?"

"It's where we send juvenile criminals, instead of prison," Fenton told him. "Although with some of these places, there isn't much difference. The one Snake went to wasn't bad, though. I checked. More like a home for wayward boys."

"Wayward, indeed. And while he was at this reform school, I see, someone murdered his parents. Cut their throats while they slept, then set fire to the house. And in the charred ruins of the home, the authorities found—"

"Evidence that Mom and Dad had been in the kiddie porn business. Had a little studio in the basement, and everything. According to the arson investigators, that's where the fire started, with the help of about five gallons of gasoline.

Looks like somebody wanted to wipe out every trace of their product."

Van Dreenan read on. "Ummm. But someone, whoever it was, did not succeed. The parents had a large fireproof safe, whose contents survived the conflagration." A few seconds later, he shook his head in disgust. "They used their own son in some of the... performances."

"Yeah," Fenton said with a grimace. "Wish I could say I've never heard of that being done before, but apparently it's pretty common in the kiddie porn biz. Fucking scumbags. Give me serial killers any day."

"It hardly matters now, but do you happen to know the distance between this reform school the boy was in and the family home?"

"About forty miles, I looked it up," Fenton said. "Looks like you and I are thinking along the same lines."

"And this school was not a high-security facility?"

"Not that kind of place, no. Not impossible for the kid to sneak out, rip off a car, pay a visit to Mom and Dad with a sharp knife and a five-gallon can of gas, then sneak back into the school before he was missed."

"Well, if he did, one can hardly blame him," Van Dreenan said. He shook his head again. "Fifteen years old."

"The start of an active, if not illustrious, career," Fenton said. "How many arrests as an adult? Nine?"

Van Dreenan checked the screen. "Eight. Of those, two convictions—one for manslaughter and another for sexual assault. He served a total of, let me see... six years."

"Involved with the occult, too, it looks like. Hooked up with some voodoo coven, or whatever they call it, down in Louisiana. A New Orleans bunch headed by somebody called Queen Esther."

"Yes, so I see. That led to one of his arrests, on suspicion of murder. Apparently, the *voudoun* cult was believed to have engaged in human sacrifice during some of their rituals." Van Dreenan looked at Fenton. "That is very rare. Most practitioners of *voudoun* never sacrifice anything bigger than a chicken, or maybe a goat. They are law-abiding people, not killers. Although..."

"Although what?"

"Every religion seems to develop its own lunatic fringe. There have been reports, from here and there around the world, of *voudoun* cults devoted to gods who demand sacrifice of 'the goat without horns.'"

"The—oh, right, I get it."

Van Dreenan scratched his cheek pensively. "A very interesting chap, this Mister Perkins. At first glance, he would seem an unlikely traveling companion for Cecelia Mbwato. But the more I think about it, the better it sounds."

"A marriage made in Heaven," Fenton said with a sour smile.

"No, Fenton, not in Heaven," Van Dreenan said. "Not there."

THE SUN WAS shining brightly when Morris and Libby sat down to breakfast at an outdoor café. After they'd placed their order, Libby asked, "So, did you spend a quiet night, what was left of it?"

"Oh, sure. Thanks to those warding charms you put on the door and windows. The only zombies that bothered me were in my dreams."

She made a face. "I know what you mean. My subconscious seemed to spend most of the night in the middle of a George Romero film festival. *Not* a good time."

Morris took a sip of coffee and said, "You mentioned something last night about a plan for dealing with Queen Esther."

Libby nodded. "I think that, with proper preparation, I can cast a truth spell which should compel her to tell us what she knows about the witch we're after."

"Will it work on somebody like Esther? She's got pretty good mojo of her own, as we have reason to know."

"It shouldn't matter, as long as she's not ready for me," Libby said. "If she had time to put together a counterspell, that might well make a difference." She smiled tightly. "Which is why I'm not going to give her time."

"In other words, you're going to overwhelm her before she has time to set up a defense."

"Something like that."

"How long will you need to get ready?"

"I did some of the preliminary work last night. So, from this point, I figure I'll need—" she thought briefly, "another three hours, more or less."

"So, if you get started right after breakfast, everything should be set to go by early afternoon?"

"Most likely. And a good thing, too."

Morris looked a question at her.

"I mean, it's good we're going to do this during daylight," Libby said. "That's when white magic is strongest."

"And Queen Esther, being one of the bad guys, has the edge after dark."

"Exactly."

Their order arrived, and Morris dug into his eggs. "Good thing we got up early."

THEY HAD NO trouble this time finding a cabbie willing to take them to the proper address on Dumaine Street. Apparently the light of day made a difference to the taxi drivers, too. It was a little after two in the afternoon when they stood again in front of Doctor John's Hoodoo Shop and Apothecary.

Morris looked at the storefront for a moment, then turned to Libby. "Is she in there?"

Libby's brow wrinkled. "I don't know. I'm not sensing her the way I was able to last night, but there's something..." She shook her head uncertainly.

"Well, guess we may as well go on in and find out."

"But carefully."

"Don't have to tell me. I'm the fella who was driving off zombies last night, remember?"

There was no point in trying to sneak in. They knew that the steps would creak under their weight, and the spring in the screen door could be counted on to make a noise loud enough to wake the dead.

No one stood behind the counter. The shop appeared as deserted as when they had left it the night before.

But something was different, and it took Morris only a moment to realize what it was. "You smell that?"

Libby sniffed audibly. "Yes," she said quietly. "Yes, I do." The coppery odor was one they had each encountered before, and they recognized it instantly.

Fresh blood smells like nothing else in the world.

"Better let me go first," Libby said. "I've got a few things ready this time, just in case." She took a couple of small vials out of her purse and twisted off the lids. "Come on."

Morris followed, a tight feeling in his chest and stomach.

Moving slowly, carefully, Libby walked behind the counter and pushed through the beaded curtain. She turned to the right, then stopped suddenly. Morris could hear the sharp intake of her breath, and as he looked over her shoulder he saw the reason.

The young woman called Martha lay face down in the corridor, her head toward the room where Queen Esther had held court the night before. Martha's skull was split open, cut so deeply that gray brain tissue was clearly visible amidst the blood and bone and hair. Morris, who knew a thing or two about knife wounds, figured that you'd need something both heavy and very sharp to do that kind of damage.

Something like a machete.

Libby knelt and touched the back of her hand to one of the dead girl's legs. "Cold." she said quietly. "It's been several hours." Standing, she stepped gingerly over the body, careful to avoid the blood on the floor. There wasn't a lot of it; corpses don't bleed much.

Morris followed Libby down the short corridor to another beaded curtain—the one that marked the entrance to Queen Esther's chamber. He could see light coming from inside, but it was softer than he remembered from last night.

Libby used one hand to push some of the beads aside, but she did not enter the room. Instead, she stood in the doorway peering inside, and it seemed to Morris that she stood there for a long time before giving vent to a sigh that seemed to come from deep within her. "It's safe to go in," she said bleakly. "There nothing here to hurt us."

Morris followed Libby into the windowless room. More than half the candles had either burned out or been knocked over, and in the gloom he almost tripped over a body on the floor. Looking closer, he saw that it was one of the zombies who'd accosted them the night before. Unlike Martha, this corpse bore no obvious wound. Ten feet away lay another dead man, and Morris thought that one looked familiar from the night before, too.

In front of the altar, next to the overturned rocking chair, lay the bloody remains of Queen Esther. It was clear that, unlike Martha, the old woman had not died of a single, devastating wound. She must have tried to fight them. And so they had cut her to pieces. Literally.

The windowless room reeked of blood and shit and decaying flesh. The climate of New Orleans is not kind to the dead under the best of circumstances. Martha and Queen Esther were already becoming ripe, and the two zombies appeared to be in an advanced state of decomposition—their bodies probably making up for lost time since their natural deaths. Morris knew he was going to have to get out of there soon or puke.

Libby appeared to be having similar difficulties. She held a handkerchief over her mouth with one hand, then knelt over the body of Queen Esther. She seemed especially interested in the old woman's severed right hand, which lay some distance away from the rest of her. Morris wondered if she was going to take it for use as a Hand of Glory—a powerful talisman, when prepared properly. You need to start with the hand of a murderer, and Queen Esther almost certainly qualified. But Libby appeared to be focused on something clutched in the dead fingers, a piece of paper or cardboard that she pried loose, glanced at, then stuffed in her voluminous purse.

Standing, she put away the handkerchief and said, "Let's get the hell out of here, before I lose my breakfast."

Once they were back on the sidewalk, Morris said, "We'd better leave the area before some tourist looking for a love potion wanders in and starts screaming for the cops."

Libby nodded. "Let's walk back to Bourbon Street and find a bar, which shouldn't be difficult to do. I need a drink, maybe a couple of them. Then we need to talk."

They had gone less than a block when Morris asked, "What was that you took from Queen Esther's hand?"

"That's one of the things we need to talk about."

CHAPTER 19

LIBBY CHASTAIN PICKED up the glass of ice-cold Stolichnaya and held it against her forehead for almost a full minute. Then she brought the glass to her mouth and downed its contents in a single gulp.

Quincey Morris took a sip of his bourbon and branch water. "Feeling any better?"

"A little. At least I've got the smell of that place out of my nostrils." She signaled the waitress for another drink. "How about you?"

He let his gaze wander around the room before answering. Homer's Hideaway, like all the French Quarter bars, was doing a brisk business, even at three in the afternoon. Tourists from Kansas City and Pittsburgh sipped Hurricanes and listened to the cheesy faux-zydeco coming from the juke, telling themselves that they were doing the real Cajun thing now.

"I'm all right, I guess," Morris said. "Although I'm glad to be out of that slaughterhouse, too." He waited while the waitress served Libby's second vodka. "Damn, I bet old Esther was pissed, there at the end. Getting hacked up by zombies that you've created yourself has got to lend a whole new meaning to 'Hoist by your own petard.'"

Libby nodded pensively. "The two zombies didn't just decide to do that all by themselves, either."

"No, those poor bastards have no will of their own. The resurrection spell sees to that."

"And Esther certainly didn't induce them to do it."

"If she had, it would be the most bizarre suicide on record," Morris said. "Doesn't seem real likely."

"Then who did it?"

"I reckon you know the answer to that one as well as I do."

"The mysterious Ms. Carter." She said the name the way General Rommel used to say "Patton."

"Or whatever her real handle is these days. Somehow she got control of Esther's two shamblers and turned them on her—maybe as punishment for Esther's failure to kill us last night." Morris sipped his drink. "Or, could be she was afraid Esther might tell us something useful."

"And maybe that's just what she did, in her last few moments." Libby took something from her purse and tossed it on the table. It was a business card.

Morris peered at it. "This what you took from Esther's hand, back there?"

Libby nodded.

"*Randall and Carleton Special Services*," he read aloud. "*Investigations*. Got their office over on Bourbon Street." He ran his fingertip over the engraved letters. "Not a lot to go on, is it?"

"There's a little more than that," Libby said, and flipped the card over. Written in ink on the back was "Amos Gitner," followed by a question mark.

Morris frowned as he read the two words. "Amos Gitner?" He looked up at Libby. "Who the hell is Amos Gitner?"

"I have no idea," she said, counting money onto the table. "But I was thinking it would be a good idea for us to find out."

TULANE UNIVERSITY'S LIBRARY had the *New Orleans Times-Picayune* in one of its computerized databases. By entering "Amos Gitner" as a search term, they were able to find and read the only article containing the phrase that the paper had ever published. A few mouse clicks allowed them to print out a hard copy of the article, which was dated three years earlier:

> Sept. 6. The body of a missing Materie man was found in an abandoned building in the warehouse district

yesterday, under circumstances that cause local police to suspect foul play.

Amos Gitner, 26, had been reported missing by his mother three days earlier, authorities say. They discovered the body as the result of an anonymous telephone tip that a corpse had been seen in the building, which had been owned by Porterfield Imports until the firm went bankrupt last year.

Police officials have declined to comment on reports that the victim may have been involved with the local occult community, and that this somehow contributed to his death. Lieutenant Pierre Premeaux of the Homicide Division would say only that the death was considered "suspicious" and that the investigation was continuing.

Morris folded the single sheet of paper and put it in his jacket pocket. "Curiouser and curiouser," he said. "Think Queen Esther did this poor fella in?"

"Hard to know," Libby said with a shrug. "I wouldn't put it past her, but even she would need something that looked like a reason. We just don't have enough information."

"I wonder..."

"What?"

"I wonder," Morris said, "whether anybody is still at Randall and Carleton Special Services this late in the afternoon."

THE SECRETARY-RECEPTIONIST at Randall and Carleton was a petite blonde named Cindy Lee Mercell, who wanted to know whether they had an appointment.

"No we don't," Morris said. "Our problem came up kind of suddenly."

"We'd really like to see either Mister Randall or Mister Carleton for just a few minutes," Libby said with a pleasant smile. "Whichever one might be free."

"Well, I don't really know if I can—"

"It's about Amos Gitner," Morris said.

The receptionist looked at him for the space of three heartbeats. "Just a moment please," she said, and went through a nearby door

She was back within thirty seconds. "Mister Carleton will see you. If you folks would follow me?"

She led them into a spacious office whose furnishings were just old enough to look comfortable. The same might have been said for the man who rose from behind the antique desk.

Carl Carleton had a face like an old shoe, lined and seamed and showing a certain amount of wear and tear. There were smile lines around his mouth and eyes, but he did not smile as he shook hands with his visitors and invited them to sit down.

Carleton studied them in silence for a few moments, idly running a thumb and forefinger up and down the seam of his seersucker suit jacket. Finally he said, "You know, we normally set a lot of store by polite conversation 'round these parts, which means it generally takes us just one hell of a long time to get to the point. But since you two have practically barged in unannounced, maybe you'll forgive my manners if I ask just what the hell it is you want?"

"Are you normally so rude to potential clients, Mister Carleton?" Libby asked gently.

"No, ma'am, I'm not. But you two ain't clients, are you?" He spoke with that unique accent you find in some part of New Orleans that sounds more like Brooklyn than Biloxi, at least to Yankee ears.

Morris figured it was his turn to contribute something to the conversation. "What makes you say that?"

"On account of that name you used to get in here belongs to a dead man, as I expect you know full well. And I'm pretty sure you ain't relatives, since I met Gitner's family three years ago at his funeral, and you two weren't there at all. So I repeat my original question, which was, in case you've forgotten: what the hell do you want?"

"Amos Gitner's name came up in an investigation of our own," Morris said. "We're trying to locate a woman who's been making terroristic threats against a family in Wisconsin. We had reason to believe that she might have some ties to a woman in New Orleans known as Queen Esther."

Carleton nodded slowly. "Esther the voodoo queen. Yeah, I recollect we talked to her, back when we were tryin' to get a line on young Mister Gitner. She send you over here?"

"In a way, yes," Libby told him. "We got this from her." She handed over the business card with Amos Gitner's name written on the back.

Carleton held the card delicately, turning it over with his big, square-tipped fingers. "Yeah, I like to leave cards with the folks I interview, especially if they haven't had a lot to say. Sometimes I hear from them later on, more often not." He shifted in his chair, causing it to creak under his weight. "You know, Queen Esther didn't strike me as the real friendly type, that time I talked with her. Fact is, I had the distinct impression she'd as soon kill me as look at me. But you're sayin' she just up and give you this business card? Just like that?"

Morris and Libby exchanged looks. After a moment, Libby said, "Not exactly. Quincey and I discovered her body earlier today, and this card was in her hand. She'd been murdered, chopped to pieces."

Carleton stared at her, then slowly reached for the telephone, picked up the receiver, and punched in a single number. After a moment he said into the mouthpiece, "Lex, can you come on over a minute? Yeah, if you would. Thanks."

Replacing the receiver, Carleton said, "I've asked my partner, Mister Randall, to come join us. It looks like we're about to go swimming in some serious shit here, and I make it my practice never to go swimming alone."

There was a perfunctory knock at the door, which opened to admit a tall man, slim, almost skinny, with dark hair combed down flat. He looked about ten years younger than Carleton's mid-forties. *Ivy League,* Morris thought. *Or maybe University of Virginia, which in the South they regard as the same thing.* Morris figured the man's tropical-weight gray suit must have cost three times the price of Carleton's seersucker, even if it did require only half as much fabric.

Carleton performed introductions and Lex Randall shook hands with the visitors. Carleton then handed him the business card.

"Miss Chastain here tells me that she took that from the dead hand of Queen Esther. You recollect her, don't you?"

"That voodoo priestess, over on Dumaine Street," Randall said, nodding. "I haven't seen anything in the papers about it—when did she die?"

"Overnight, or perhaps early this morning," Libby said.

Randall stared at Libby, then at Morris, then looked over at his partner. "Are we talking about a natural death, here?"

"She'd been hacked to pieces with a machete," Morris said. "Along with a young woman named Martha who apparently worked for her."

"There were two other corpses on the premises," Libby said. "Although, in a sense, they died some time earlier."

"I'm afraid I'm not following you," Randall said.

"I mean they were zombies, who returned to their natural state after the death of their reanimator. That would be Queen Esther, of course."

There was silence in the room that went on for some time. It was finally broken by Carleton, who said to Morris, "You know, I thought your name rang some kind of bell, and I've been trying to recollect where I came across it. Tell me, you ever been up to Baton Rouge?"

Morris nodded cautiously. "A few years back."

"Thought you might've." Carleton looked at his partner. "That professor at LSU, three, four years ago. Fella took sick, looked fit to die, and nobody could figure out the cause of it. Some folks even thought there was voodoo involved."

"I remember now," Randall said. "They practically had the man measured for a casket, and then he got better. Just as suddenly as he'd taken ill." He turned to Morris. "Was that you? The one they sent for?"

Morris nodded again. "Uh-huh."

"And what about you Ms., uh, Chastain, is it?" Randall asked. "Are you Mr. Morris's partner in these investigations he takes on?"

"No, not exactly," Libby told him. "I'm kind of an independent contractor, but I've worked with Quincey before. He calls me in when he needs me."

"And what is it you do," Carleton asked, "when you're not helping out Mr. Morris, here?"

Libby shrugged, but her voice was polite when she said, "I do a certain amount of consulting work. Different clients have different problems. Not unlike your own profession, I would imagine."

"Um." Carleton used his big forefinger to nudge the old business card with Amos Gitner's name written on the back. After staring at it for a few seconds, he looked up at Randall and said, "I'm gonna tell 'em."

Randall looked closely at his partner, and Morris decided that some kind of unspoken communication was going on between them. He was sure of it a few moments later when Randall nodded slowly and said, "All right, then. Tell them."

Carleton swiveled his chair so that he was facing Morris and Libby squarely. "Never talked to nobody about this mess before," he said. "Lex here knows, 'cause he was there when it all transpired. Anybody else, they'd probably think I was just funnin' 'em. That, or they'd nominate me as a prime candidate for the booby hatch. But knowing what I do about you, Morris, I'm guessing that you just might understand. And you, Ma'am, if you hang around much with this fella, I expect you've had *beaucoup* experience of some pretty strange goings-on yourself."

Libby Chastain smiled a little but said nothing.

"Yeah, well," Carleton went on, "you should know off top that when Amos Gitner's mama hired us to find him, that wasn't the first occasion he'd gone and made himself scarce for a few days. Way she told it, he'd go off somewheres every month for three, four days. Then he'd show up home again—he still stayed by his mama, even though he was in his middle twenties—and she'd say, where the hell you been, so forth, and he'd tell her he just plain didn't remember. Some kind of amnesia, apparently, although it never seemed to show up at any other time. She wanted him to see a doctor about it, but he just wouldn't go. Said it was his problem, and he'd work it out himself."

"I take it this wasn't simply a case of Gitner sneaking off on a three-day drunk every once in a while," Morris said.

"I did raise that question," Carleton told him. "But his mama said 'No how, no way.' Seems her own father had been an alcoholic, and she was more than a little familiar with the signs—and the smell, for that matter. And she claimed the boy was showin' no hint of a drug habit, neither."

"Gitner's mysterious absences had been going on for almost a year when his mother hired us," Randall said. "A long-suffering woman, you might say. Plus, she's fairly well off financially, and she was in the habit of indulging her son something awful."

"Spoiled rotten," Carleton said, nodding. "Still, even Mrs. Gitner had a limit to her forbearance. One day, when she noticed sonny-boy was gone again, she came huffin' on down here and said she wanted us to find him, drag his ass home, and report to her on what the hell it was he'd been up to."

"I'm no detective," Libby said, "but it seems to me that it would have been easier for you guys to follow Gitner when he left on one of these jaunts, rather then try to track him down once he was already gone."

"I mentioned that to Mrs. Gitner, you know," Carleton said with a sour smile. "Even suggested that we might best wait until the following month and get in on the beginning of her son's next little excursion into the unknown. But she wouldn't hear of it. Her blood was up, and she wanted us to find the little bastard now, not wait until the next time and do it the easy way." He shrugged his meaty shoulders. "What the hell, she was willing to pay us to look for him. And so that's what we did."

"How did your search bring you into contact with Queen Esther?" Libby asked.

"Oh, his mama told us that Amos had been spending time with some of our local occultists," Carleton said. "She recollected that he'd once said something to the effect that voodoo had a lot more to it than the tourists ever see. So we had a word with some of the more prominent practitioners, including that old sweetheart Queen Esther. But either none of the *voudinistas* we talked to knew young Mr. Gitner, or none of them were sayin'."

"But then we had some luck," Randall said. "Mrs. Gitner had provided the license number of her son's BMW, and a nice lady I know down at the parish DMV ran the license plate for us. Nothing unusual on his record, but there were a number of parking tickets over the last year or so. They had all been paid—Mrs. G. had seen to that—but we were more interested in when and where the tickets were issued. Almost immediately, we began to see clusters."

"You mean the tickets had all been written in the same area," Morris said.

"Yeah, you right," Carleton said, nodding. "They were all in the Ninth Ward, down near the river. Lots of warehouses and garages 'round there, along with some abandoned buildings and burnouts. And the dates matched up, too. The tickets had all been written up during times that sonny boy was off doin' whatever it was he did."

"There were a couple of other factors we might have considered, but didn't," Randall said. "Well, it probably wouldn't have made any difference. Even if we had somehow reached the proper conclusion, we wouldn't have let ourselves believe it." His voice contained equal proportions of bitterness and regret.

"Lex learned to talk like that at that fancy college of his," Carleton said. "But what he means is, there'd been occasional news reports that homeless folks in that ward had been disappearing, in ones and twos, for some time. Understand, we ain't talking banner headlines in the *Times-Picayune* here. Nobody makes much of a fuss about the homeless, and besides, they come and go all the time. Some poor bastard hasn't been seen for awhile, who's to say whether he's gone missing or just moved on to try his luck in Shreveport or someplace?"

"You mentioned two factors," Libby said. "What was the other one?"

"The dates of young Mr. Gitner's little excursions," Carleton told her. "There was a pattern to 'em, but we missed it—until it was too late, anyway."

"The full moon," Randall said quietly. "They were all during the period of the full moon."

Libby Chastain and Morris looked at each other but said nothing.

Carleton explained how he and Randall started driving around the area where Amos Gitner had received his parking tickets, and on the second day spotted a blue BMW with license plates that matched what Mrs. Gitner had told them. They staked out the car, and just before dusk were rewarded with the sight of a man who looked an awful lot like the one in the photos they'd been provided with. The man drove off in the Beamer, and the two detectives followed him to what looked like an abandoned warehouse. He parked and then went inside.

"We waited a while," Carleton explained, "'case he was just making a quick stop for some reason. But after about a half hour, when he didn't come out, we decided to go have ourselves a look."

"It was full dark by then," Randall said, as if it meant something important.

Carleton nodded agreement. "So we come up on this place, trying to keep to the shadows. Wasn't hard to do, since most of what you *had* around there was shadows. Blacker than the boots of the High Sheriff of Hell, is all it was. Course, the moon hadn't come out yet."

"No," Randall said softly. "That was a little later."

Carleton then told them that he and Randall had gone through the same side door that Amos Gitner had used. With Randall's penlight, they were able to see the trail of footprints in the thick dust on the floor. It led them to a set of metal stairs that the two men climbed slowly, carefully, and quietly.

The second floor of the warehouse was strewn with junk—scraps of lumber, abandoned tools, and a couple of old shipping containers. "It looked," Carleton said, "like whoever used to own the place had cleared out fast, and just left behind anything they couldn't see a use for."

"And it was from behind one of those shipping containers that Amos Gitner appeared," Randall said. "Nothing melodramatic about it. He didn't jump out suddenly or act aggressively or anything. Just strolled right on out. Of course, he *was* buck naked."

"Like the day he was born," Carleton said. "He had set up three of those big nine-volt flashlights in different parts of the room, along with a couple of those electric lanterns that campers use, so we could see him pretty good. Boy was hung like a stud mule, too." He looked at Libby and inclined his head slightly. "Your pardon, Ma'am."

Libby gave him a pleasant smile. "References to the penis don't usually offend me, Mr. Carleton," she said. "Please go on."

"Well, I introduce myself and Lex to this naked fella, then tell him we're private investigators his mama hired to find out what the hell he's been up to. 'You may as well get dressed, Mr. Gitner,' I tell him. 'We need to talk some.'"

Carleton shook his head at the memory. "He just stares at us. Then he says, 'You two have no idea what you've stumbled into.' And, you know, he doesn't say it like a threat—and take my word, I've heard plenty of threats in my time. Fella actually sounds like he *means* it. Then he glances toward the window, and I'm wondering if he's thinking about trying to make a dash in that direction. But then he looks back at us and he says, 'The absolute best thing y'all could do for yourselves right now is to clear out of here just as fast as you can. And then forget you ever found this place, or that you ever saw me.'

"So, I try to explain to him that it doesn't work that way, that we don't intend him any harm but that we took his mama's money which means that we have to do the job she hired us for."

"He didn't seem to find any of that very interesting," Randall said. "He hardly seemed to be paying attention."

"Yeah, you right," Carleton said. "He's acting pretty bored by my little discussion of the ethics of our profession. Then, all of a sudden, he looks back toward the closest window. The moon must've come out from behind the clouds about then, because it's suddenly a whole lot brighter in there, and Gitner just looks at us and says, 'Too late, now.' He sounds almost sorry about it.

"And that's when the *real* shit starts."

Carleton fell silent then, staring down at his desk blotter. After a bit, Morris said, "If you're waiting for someone to feed you the next line, I'll be happy to oblige. *What* started?"

Carleton shook his head. "No, it ain't that. I'm not tryin' to drag this out, to make a better story of it. It's just that I never talk about that night, and I feel like an ass tryin' to describe something that I didn't used to think even *existed,* not in real life, anyways."

He took a deep breath and look up at Morris. "You ever hear the term *loup-garou?*"

Morris nodded. "French name for 'werewolf,' isn't it? The Cajuns use it, too." He didn't say this as if he were surprised, because he wasn't.

Carleton looked at him with narrowed eyes. "You ever seen one?"

"That doesn't matter," Morris told him. "But it seems pretty clear that *you* have."

Carleton shifted in his chair. "Yeah, I reckon I did," he said finally. "Damnedest thing—maybe literally, I don't know. But we watched the moonlight shine on young Mr. Gitner, and within a couple of seconds he started sprouting fur, claws, the whole nine yards. Nothing that you can't find in a dozen different videos available at your local Blockbuster, but this was by God *real.*"

"The whole process took about two minutes, I'd guess," Randall said. "I suppose we could have used the time to run. Hell, we might even have gotten away." He shook his head ruefully. "But we were just... *transfixed* by what we were seeing."

"Like we were paralyzed," Carleton said, nodding. "Leastways, until the fucking thing came at us. Looked more animal than human by that time, and seemed like it was about ninety percent teeth and claws."

"It must have been terrifying," Libby said. "Were either of you armed?"

"Yeah, I had this ten-millimeter Glock that I keep on my belt around back. Lots of folks carry the nine, but I like the extra stopping power. Lex doesn't carry a piece most the time, and he didn't have one that night. Can't blame him for that, really. Hell, we was just running down some rich boy with a bad habit or two, or so we thought. No need for heavy artillery."

"Did you reach your gun in time?" Morris asked quietly.

"Yeah, I did, for all the difference it made. I got a shot off, and I hit the sumbitch, too, I'm sure of it. Square in the chest." Carleton shook his head. "Didn't even slow him down. And a second later he was on me. Knocked me to the floor, the Glock went flying off somewhere, and then he's doing his best to tear my throat out with his teeth. I was able to get my forearm under his chin, and that gave me some leverage. But I knew I wouldn't be able to hold him off for long. *God* he was strong. Then, all of a sudden, he kind of rears up and lets out this howl—not a scream, understand, but a *howl,* just like you'd expect from an animal."

"That was because I'd noticed an axe on the floor when we came in," Randall said, "along with all the other junk that had been left there. So, I grabbed it up and then did my best to bury the blade in that thing's spine."

"Did that kill it?" Morris leaned forward in his chair.

"Not even close," Carleton said. "The damn thing rolls off me, jumps to its feet, reaches back, and just *yanks* that hatchet right out of there. Throws it aside like it was a toothpick. And then it starts toward Lex."

"I'd about run out of options," Randall told them, "so I figured that I was looking at the last thing I'd ever see. But then the shooting started."

Libby looked at Carleton. "You'd found your pistol again?"

The big detective snorted in disgust. "Hell, no," he said. "At that point, I'd have been lucky to find my head with both hands. No, I wasn't the one doin' the shooting. That was the fella who'd just burst through the door."

"He must have come up the same stairs we had used earlier," Randall said. "We hadn't heard him—not surprising, really, with all the commotion going on. He had a revolver, and he put three rounds into that werewolf, or Amos Gitner, or whatever you want to call him, in as many seconds."

"And he must've been doing something right," Carleton said, "because that thing did nothing but rear up, fall over and die. Right then and there. Next thing that happened was right out of the movies, I swear. The transformation reversed itself, and pretty soon we were lookin' at the naked body of Amos Gitner. Same as before, apart from the bullet holes. And the blood, o' course." Carleton shook his head at the memory. "After a little while, I manage to sit up, and I ask this fella, you know, 'How the hell'd you stop him, when we couldn't do diddly-squat?' He just shrugs and gives me this crooked kind of smile. Then he says, '*Silver bullets.*'"

Randall, still leaning against the doorjamb, said, "He told us that he was a private investigator from New York. Apparently one of the homeless men who had disappeared had a brother up North who was worried about him, and who had heard wild stories about some creature that was preying on the street people down here. This investigator told us that he sometimes took on cases involving what he called, 'the unusual.' So he'd agreed to come to New Orleans and try to find out what was going on."

"Sounds like he found out just in time," Morris said.

"Yeah, for sure," Carleton said with a slow nod. "He gave us his business card before we all left the warehouse together. We've called him on the phone a couple of times since then, sort of on a consultant basis. But we haven't set eyes on the fella since that night."

"This investigator," Libby Chastain said thoughtfully. "What did he call himself?"

"Unlikely as it may sound," Randall told her, "the card said his name was Barry Love."

CHAPTER 20

THIS TIME, THE cheap motel was in Connecticut. Snake Perkins figured that being a state away from where all the shit went down might buy them a little breathing room.

"Got us a problem," he said to Cecelia Mbwato.

Cecelia was ensconced in the room's only armchair, eating salted peanuts, one at a time. She looked at Snake, who sat on the bed, with a mixture of scorn and indifference. "What problem is this?"

"Gas stations these days, they all got cameras trained on the pumps, case somebody decides to just take off, instead of paying. They must've had 'em at that place in Jersey."

"So the authorities will have a movie of us driving away. As you would say, 'Big deal.'"

"The big fuckin' deal is that they most likely got my license number. Which means by tomorrow, and maybe sooner, every cop in six states is gonna have it in the little computer in his squad car. I ain't saying there's gonna be some big manhunt for us. But there just ain't a lot of cars on the road look like mine. All we gotta do is drive past some Dudley Do-Right who ain't too busy eatin' doughnuts to notice the car and decide to run the plates, and then it's WBF, for sure."

"What means this 'WBF?'"

Snake gave her a crooked grin. "Lady, it means 'We Be Fucked.'"

Cecelia thought for a few moments. "Then you should get rid of your car, and steal another for us."

Snake shook his head. "Nope, bad idea."

"And why is that? Do you love so much that piece of junk we have been riding in?"

Snake felt his gorge start to rise. The Lincoln meant more to him than this ugly nigger bitch ever would, but he had just enough control not to say so. Instead, after a deep breath or two, he told her, "There's a couple of reasons. One is, I'm no car thief. Sure, I can hot-wire a car, any kid can do that. But cars these days, shit, they got alarms, and steering wheel locks, and remote ignition switches, and GPS systems, and all kinds of other shit that I don't know how to deal with. I try to steal us a ride, I'd end up busted, for sure."

"How terrible that would be," she said, her face expressionless.

"Yeah, and the other reason is, even if I do rip off a car, there's no way of knowin' when it's gonna be reported. Any car that's good enough to be worth stealin' is good enough for somebody to miss it. We'd never know for sure if the car was hot, until we saw them red flashing lights in the rearview mirror, and then it's too fuckin' late. Trying to outrun the cops is for suckers. You see that on TV all the time."

"Then what are you suggesting that we do?" She waved a hand around the dump of a room. "Spend the rest of our lives hiding in here?"

"No, not hardly. I got me an idea, and it ain't half bad. I don't steal a car—just a set of plates. And I don't only steal 'em, I replace 'em with the plates off the Lincoln. I mean, who goes out to his car in the morning and checks his damn license plates? The guy might not notice the switch for weeks. Meantime, we'd be drivin' around with a nice, clean set of plates that ain't on any cop's hot sheet."

"It makes sense," Cecelia said grudgingly. She glanced at the cheap watch she wore on her wrist. "There are several hours of darkness still left," she said to Snake. "What are you waiting for?"

* * *

FENTON AND VAN Dreenan were braving the traffic on the New Jersey Turnpike, thus proving that neither was lacking in courage.

Van Dreenan broke several minutes of silence by saying, "Once we get back to New York, I have some phone calls to make."

Without taking his eyes off the road, Fenton produced his cell phone. "Here, use this if you want."

"Thank you, no. I already have my own. But one of the calls requires that I look up a number in my address book, which is currently in my suitcase, at the Holiday Inn."

"You want me to drop you there, then?"

"If you would, please. For the other call, I know the number, but it is in South Africa. For that, I should use a landline. As you are aware, cell phones are often unreliable at that sort of distance."

"Yeah, for sure." A pause. "You mind if I ask, has this got to do with our case?"

If Van Dreenan noticed that Fenton was now referring to it as 'our case,' he did not say so. Instead, he said, "Oh yes, very much so. I want to ask a colleague of mine to send, by the quickest possible means, a hair sample we have on file. It came from one Cecelia Mbwato."

"They found some bits of hair at two of the crime scenes," Fenton said thoughtfully.

"*Ja,* I know. A DNA comparison might be very informative, don't you think?" He let Fenton think that was the real reason.

"Damn right, it would. When it gets here, I'll ask my boss to press the FBI lab, make them give it priority."

"That would be very helpful, I think," Van Dreenan said.

"Um, what about the other call? The one where you have to look up the number?"

"That one, my friend, should be local. The lady in question used to live in New York. I can only hope that she still does."

"Our phone system here has Directory Assistance, you know. Just hit four-one-one and talk to the nice computer."

"Her number is almost certain to be in the X directory."

"The what?"

"Sorry. What you call here an unlisted number."

"Oh. This somebody who knows Cecelia what's-her-name?"
"Mbwato. No, probably not. But she *is* someone who knows a great deal about magic."

CHAPTER 21

BARRY LOVE'S OFFICE was near Ninth Avenue and Forty-Eighth Street, in a dilapidated brick building whose lobby smelled strongly of cat piss. Morris found that the structure reminded him of the Kingsbury Building in Boston, and he hoped there wouldn't be any fires to contend with this time.

As the self-service elevator clanked and groaned its way to the fifth floor, he quietly said to Libby Chastain, "Think she knows we're here?"

Libby didn't have to ask who *she* was. She bit her lip for a moment before answering. "Hard to say, since I don't know what precise magical mechanism she's been using to keep track of us. It's some sort of scrying, obviously, but there are lots of different ways to do that. I've been putting out some cloaking spells since New Orleans, but the only way to know for sure if they're working is if nobody tries to burn us up or hack us to pieces."

"Or seduce us," he said, thinking of San Francisco.

"That, too."

"So, you like girls, huh?"

"Leave it alone, Quincey."

Barry Love was expecting them, and within a couple of minutes they were in his office and settling themselves into worn and faded client chairs that looked like they'd been bought cheap from a bankrupt funeral parlor. The chairs fit in well with the battered old desk where the detective sat down, and with the unpainted wooden shelves that jutted from the wall behind him.

Love had been on the phone when they'd arrived, and politely asked their indulgence for a minute while he finished with his caller. As the detective muttered into the receiver, Morris found his gaze drawn to the shelves and their unusual contents.

Books were crammed together on the top shelf, and Morris found that he recognized several of them. There were two Bibles (the Latin Vulgate and King James Version), Stone's *Practical Demon-Hunting,* an expensively bound copy of the *Bhagavad-Gita,* Newman's *The Vampire in Victorian England,* Wellman's biography of John the Balladeer, a couple of volumes by Hegel and one by Sartre, Black's *Approaching the Millennium*, and the third edition of *Investigating the Occult: Principles and Techniques* by Scully and Reyes.

The other shelves contained an odd assortment of bric-a-brac, including a statuette of what Morris believed to be the goddess Shiva, an economy-size bottle of Vivarin, an ornate silver crucifix that looked like it properly belonged in a cathedral, an African witch doctor's mask, a small stuffed toy bear with a dirty face, a bronze Star of David, a shrunken head that looked genuine, two autopsy knives, a large can of Maxwell House coffee, and several objects that Morris couldn't identify at all.

Barry Love was listening intently to the voice on the phone, and had begun to write notes on a yellow legal pad that rested on the worn desk blotter. The private investigator appeared to be in his late thirties, so the touches of gray in his hair were probably premature. Morris thought they might have been brought on by the same experiences that had put all those lines in the man's face. It was a thin face, with prominent cheekbones beneath a two-or-three-day growth of beard. A broad forehead stood sentinel above red-rimmed blue eyes that looked like they hadn't known a good night's sleep since the Reagan administration.

Love was wearing a wrinkled blue dress shirt with a button-down collar and short sleeves. His pale, wiry arms bore several tattoos, which Morris recognized as sigils against demons. Barry Love, it seemed, was a man who took his work seriously.

Love completed his call and hung up. "Sorry about that," he said to Morris and Libby, "but I thought that guy might have a line on something—somebody—I'm interested in finding, and he doesn't get in touch very often. I can't call him, since he moves around a lot and doesn't trust cell phones. Now then," he said, leaning back in his chair, "you said when you called yesterday that you were interested in some information."

"Information that you could have provided over the phone, if you have it at all," Morris said. Jet lag and the strain of the last few days had made him irritable.

Love shook his head solemnly. "I never discuss important things over the telephone with strangers. A voice on the phone—hell, you could have been anyone, even one of Them."

"Them?" Libby Chastain said politely.

"From the other side." Love's voice was matter-of-fact.

"You've had some experience of the 'other side?'" Libby asked.

Love nodded slowly. "More than I ever wanted. Like a guy I once knew used to say, I seem to have a knack for the weird shit. I've been finding it, or maybe it's been finding me, for a long time now."

"What might Quincey and I do, or say, to convince you that we're not from the 'other side'?" Libby asked.

"You don't need to do anything," Love told her. "I already know you're not."

Libby tilted her head a little. "And how do you know that?"

"I can tell, that's all." Love shifted his gaze to Morris for a moment, then looked back at Libby. "Just like I can tell the two of you have had some dealings with the weird shit yourselves. But what I *can't* tell is what you want from *me*."

"We're here because a couple of fellas in New Orleans thought you might be able to help us." Morris said.

"New Orleans." Love smiled a little. "That would be Carleton and what's-his-name, Randall."

"It would, indeed."

"Help you with what?"

"The weird shit," Morris said, and grinned at him. "What else?"

Morris and Libby took turns telling Barry Love about the black witch they were looking for, and why. It took quite a while. Their narrative was twice interrupted by the ringing phone, but each time Love brusquely told the caller, "I'll get back to you later," and hung up.

When their tale was done, Barry Love sat back in his chair. "This lady you're looking for sounds extremely dangerous," he said.

"She is," Libby told him. "That's why we need to find her quickly, before she manages to destroy the LaRues."

"Or us," Morris said.

"Or us," Libby agreed. "We've done all right so far, but the aggressor always has the advantage—that's true in war, football, and magic, too. If this game of cat-and-mouse keeps up, sooner or later we're going to get careless or she's going to get lucky. So we need to move fast."

Love's thin fingers pinched the bridge of his nose for a long moment. Then he said, "I don't know her, not personally. There have been rumors for a long time about a powerful black witch who's descended from a long line of them, a line that extends all the way back to Salem. I've never heard her called by name, but I might be able to get a line on her for you."

Barry Love was rubbing one of the mystical tattoos on his left arm absently. He may have derived comfort from it, or perhaps it just itched.

"I'm familiar with most of the people in the city who deal in black magic," he went on. "The real stuff, I mean, not tourist crap. Some of them owe me favors, and the others would probably be only too happy to have *me* owing *them* one. Let me make some calls and see what I can find out."

"How soon do you think you might have something for us?" Morris asked.

Love glanced at his watch then thought for a moment. "Come back around ten tonight. With any luck, I should have some news by then."

"We haven't discussed your fee yet," Libby said.

Barry Love looked at her with his bloodshot eyes and grinned crookedly. "If I do manage to turn up this lady for you, I guess that would mean you'd owe me a pretty big favor, both of you. That true?"

"It certainly is," Libby said, and Morris nodded agreement.

"Okay then," Love said. "That'll be enough."

* * *

SINCE LIBBY LIVED in New York, she invited Morris to have dinner at her condo while they waited for Barry Love to work his contacts in the occult community.

"You've been here before, so you know where everything is, Quincey," she said, while walking around turning lights on. "Make yourself at home, while I see who's been demanding my attention the last couple of weeks."

Morris made himself a weak Scotch and water before flopping onto the couch in Libby's spacious living room. She had several magazines strewn across her coffee table. Among these, Morris was glad to see, was the latest issue of *Cemetery Dance,* which he tended to view as a news magazine. Libby picked up the pile of mail that had accumulated in her absence and sat down next to her telephone answering machine. She pressed "Play" and gave half her attention to the recorded messages while sorting through her mail, much of which ended up in a nearby wastebasket.

The fourth message, however, quickly engaged her interest.

"Elizabeth, this is Garth van Dreenan. You may remember me from that nasty business in Mozambique we dealt with several years ago. I am in New York temporarily, and I wish to ask your help on a matter of considerable importance. I would be most grateful if you would call me as soon as you can, at one of the following numbers." There followed a series of phone numbers. The first one Van Dreenan's voice identified as his cell phone, the second as his room at the Holiday Inn, and the third as the FBI's New York City field office. The answering machine then produced a mechanical voice announcing that the call had been received at 2:18pm the previous day.

Libby Chastain finished scribbling the numbers on the back of an envelope, then turned the answering machine off. She noticed that Morris was looking at her.

"I didn't mean to eavesdrop," he said. "But it was hard not to."

"No, that's all right," she said. "Garth is with the South African Police, their Occult Crimes Unit."

"Thought I recognized the accent. I've heard of the Occult Crimes Unit, too."

"Garth's a good guy," she said. "He brought me in to help out with a case he was working a while back, and we eventually ended up in Mozambique." She made a face, as if tasting something bitter. "It turned pretty messy."

"Do I want to know any more about that?"

"No," she said after a brief pause. "You probably don't."

"Fair enough."

She tapped her pencil on the envelope she was holding. "Garth picked a bad time to need help from me. But maybe it's something that I can take care of quickly. Failing that, let's hope it can wait."

She picked up her phone and started with the first number.

"SO YOU SEE," Van Dreenan said, "in order to locate Cecelia Mbwato, I will need some magic of my own."

Libby nodded slowly. "You realize that the kind of locater you're talking about won't work over great distances. Probably not more than a few miles."

"I understand that," Van Dreenan said. "I plan to put myself in her general vicinity. Of course, for me to do that, she must kill again. That is the only way to know where she is, or, at least, has recently been. Rather a macabre dilemma, I recognize."

"I think I know how you feel," Quincey Morris said. "Friend of mine has a son with cystic fibrosis. The boy's only hope was a lung transplant, from a donor the right age and general size. My friend hoped and prayed for that transplant, even knowing that if it was going to happen, somebody else's child had to die. It bothered him some."

"Life can be cruel," Van Dreenan said.

"It can, for sure," Morris said. "But I'll say to you what I said to him. You're not taking anybody's life. That's outside your control. All you're doing is trying to use the means available, to save somebody else's life."

"You said she's killed four?" Libby asked.

"Four, yes," Van Dreenan said.

"Then there'll be one more," Libby said. "You know why as well as I do, Garth."

"Indeed," Van Dreenan said glumly.

"Powerful number, five," Morris said. "Especially in black magic."

"As much in the African variety as in the European," Van Dreenan said. "Cecelia Mbwato must have something very nasty in mind. And if she does commit one more murder, that will probably be my last chance to... apprehend her, and I want to be ready." He looked at Libby. "That is why I am here, Elizabeth."

Libby picked up the small plastic bag that was resting on her coffee table and held it up to the light. "You're sure this hair is Ms. Mbwato's?"

"As sure as I can be," Van Dreenan told her. "It was taken during a police raid on her home last year. She lived alone and had, of course, long since departed, but she left some items behind—including a hairbrush that had her fingerprints, and only hers, all over it."

Libby shook the bag slightly, watching the curled black hairs bounce around. "I'm surprised the FBI doesn't want this," she said. "For DNA analysis, or whatever."

"They do want it," Van Dreenan said. "But the police back home were able to get a rather substantial sample from that brush, and I persuaded one of my colleagues to rush some to me, in two separate bags. The FBI lab has what it needs to work its magic."

Libby stood up, still holding the plastic evidence bag. "Well, let me see if I can work some of my own. This may take a little while." She looked at Morris, "Quincey, do you mind keeping Garth company while I try to assemble this thing?"

"My pleasure," Morris said. "I figure the two of us ol' boys have quite a few interests in common. Failing that, I guess we can always watch soft porn on your Pay-Per-View cable."

Libby left the room, smiling and shaking her head. When she was gone, Van Dreenan looked at Morris. "I understand soft porn," he said, "but what is this Pay-Per-View cable?"

NINETY MINUTES LATER, Van Dreenan was gone and Libby and Morris sat down to dinner. Libby was a vegetarian, so dinner consisted of a casserole made of rigatoni, three kinds of cheese, and portabella mushrooms. Although Morris was descended from a long line of Texas beef-eaters, his wide travels had given him an appreciation for a variety of cuisines. He thought the casserole delicious, and said so.

"I have a bottle of Chablis that would go with this very nicely," Libby said, "but maybe that's not such a good idea, under the circumstances."

"I know what you mean," Morris said. "Getting mellow on that wine could make us slow, and it seems I recollect an old saying that makes a clear distinction between the *quick* and the *dead*."

"Maybe I should make coffee."

"Good idea."

They ate in silence for a while until Libby said, "What are we going to do if Barry Love can't come up with some kind of lead for us?"

Morris chewed another mouthful of casserole and swallowed before shaking his head. "Damned if I know, Libby," he said softly. "Damned if I know."

CHAPTER 22

It was a few minutes before ten o'clock when they returned to the lobby of the old office building.

Libby was reaching for the button to summon the elevator when Morris gently grabbed her arm and said, "Let's take the stairs."

As they started up the chipped and creaking steps, Libby asked tensely, "Something?"

"Maybe."

"What?"

Morris shook his head. "Wait."

When they reached the second landing, Morris said, very quietly, "Do you smell that?"

Libby took a long sniff and made a face. "That's not cat pee. Unless the cats around here have started drinking sulfur water." Her voice was as hushed as Morris's had been. "I don't recognize it. Do you?"

"Could be I do. Come on."

As they climbed, the smell grew stronger. Pausing at the fourth floor landing, Morris asked, "Got your gear with you?" He was looking upward, toward the fifth floor, where Barry Love had his office.

"Of course," Libby said. She was already slipping the catch on her large handbag.

"Anything in there that'll stop a demon?"

Libby's eyes widened. "A *demon?* Why do you think—?"

That was when the door to the fifth floor landing burst open to reveal something out of a nightmare.

It had the body of an orangutan and the head of a hyena—except for the jaws, which would have looked at home on one of the larger species of crocodile. It crouched on the landing looking down at them, and from its mouth came the sound that a Doberman makes just before it goes for your throat.

Libby Chastain's disciplined mind quelled the panic that was trying to rise within her. She kept her eyes on the demon while quickly sorting by touch through the objects in her bag. After a few seconds that seemed much longer, her fingers closed around the vial she had been seeking. She nudged the stopper off with her thumb.

"Whatever you do, *don't run,*" Morris said tightly. "It expects that—that's why it's waiting. Damned thing will jump on your back, then reach around and tear your throat out from behind."

Morris took from his pocket a small bottle that bore the label of a health food store. The contents rattled as he twisted off the cap.

Libby risked a quick glance in his direction. "What's that?"

"Sea salt. They don't like it. Something to do with Solomon's bottle, when it was cast into the sea with a demon imprisoned inside. Have you got something ready?"

"Yes. It's—"

"Never mind, save it—we'll probably need it. This one's mine."

"*This* one?"

"They travel in packs. This ol' boy's probably not alone."

The prospect of more of these creatures made Libby swallow hard. "So, how do we play this?"

"Like Sam Houston at San Jacinto—we charge. *Come on!*"

And with that he was pounding up the stairs. Libby pulled the vial from her purse and followed, offering a quick prayer to the Goddess as she ran.

When Morris was two steps below the snarling demon, he flung a handful of the sea salt up toward the hideous face. "Be thou bound, Hellspawn, as with Solomon's seal!" he shouted.

The demon threw its paws up to its face and staggered back, making a sound very much like a whimper. Morris immediately took the last two steps and closed in, wrapping one strong hand around the creature's massive snout, which rendered the killer teeth briefly useless. With his other hand he grabbed a handful of loose skin and fur along the demon's back.

Then, in one smooth motion, he pivoted and threw the squirming monstrosity over the railing. Its enraged screams echoed through the stairwell until they were abruptly cut off by a wet sound of impact, five floors below.

"Is it dead?" Libby asked.

Morris shrugged. "Maybe. Out of action, anyway." He shook the bottle of sea salt, as if checking how much was left.

"I thought demons were immortal and couldn't be killed."

"*Killed* might be the wrong word, but they can at least be sent back where they came from. Especially if you destroy the physical body they're manifesting in. Listen, we have to—"

From the other side of the door came the *boom* of a gunshot, then another.

"Shit!" Morris said. "They're after Love, too. We'll have to play this by ear. Keep one thing in mind," he told Libby. "Demons aren't smart, most of them, and they don't adapt quickly. Keep them off balance, and you've got a chance."

He took Libby's hand and squeezed it tightly. "Once we go through that door, we're like an egg on a hot griddle. If we stay put for more than a second or two, we fry. Maybe literally. Okay?"

Libby Chastain's mouth was set in a thin line of concentration. She nodded once.

"All right," Morris said. "Let's go." He took a deep breath, then yanked open the door to the fifth floor.

What greeted them could have been a scene right out of Dante, if only the great poet had written *The Inferno* while tripping on LSD.

The door to Barry Love's office was open, and something that looked like a puke-colored Teletubby with fangs lay in the hallway, dead in a pool of its own slime. Its guts were being eaten by another demon that resembled a naked human dwarf, except it had the head of a goat, and a living snake in place of a penis. Two other monstrosities were peering cautiously into Love's office from either side of the doorway. One looked something like the Creature from the Black Lagoon except that it had the breasts of a voluptuous woman. The other was dressed like a Nazi storm trooper, except that under the peaked cap was the head of a boar, complete with sharp-looking tusks.

The two demons at Love's door ducked back suddenly, and an instant later came a shot that blew a piece of the doorframe into splinters. Morris wondered how many rounds Barry Love had left, and whether his bullets were silver.

Then the dwarf-thing noticed them standing near the hallway door. It pulled its head from its cohort's intestines and bellowed something in a language that neither Morris nor Chastain recognized. Then it bared its fangs and charged.

Libby Chastain stepped forward as the demon ran at them. "Mine!" she said to Morris. "Go on!"

As the dwarf-thing closed in on Libby it growled, in English, "Gonna eat your cunt first, bitch!"

Libby smiled tightly and said, "Eat this!" She raised her right hand, palm up, to reveal some violet-colored fine powder. Extending her hand, she blew hard on her palm, spraying the powder all over the approaching demon. She then said a quick phrase in Latin and the dwarf-thing instantly froze in place, an expression of astonishment on its goatish countenance. Libby then made a complex sign in the air with two fingers of her right hand and cried out, "*Ignis!*"

The demon immediately burst into flame, screaming horribly.

White magic can't be used to harm people, but it works just fine on Hellspawn.

Burning demon flesh gives off an odor so putrid and vile that it can induce vomiting in humans who aren't used to it. Libby, who had little experience with demons, was caught unprepared by a wave of nausea that hit her like a punch to the solar plexus. She was, for a few seconds, defenseless.

While Libby was dealing with the dwarf-demon, Morris went for the two creatures that had positioned themselves outside Barry Love's office door. He had already poured the remaining sea salt crystals into his left hand and dropped the bottle. With his right he pulled out a switchblade knife that was illegal in twenty-eight states. Thumbing the button on the handle produced a six-inch blade that glittered brightly even in the corridor's uncertain light. The sharp steel was silver-plated, and the weapon had been blessed years ago by the Archbishop of Albuquerque, after Morris had rendered the archdiocese a singular and very discreet service.

Keep moving, don't stop, Morris was thinking. *We stop we fry. We fry, we die.*

The two demons were waiting for him, so Morris decided on misdirection. He made a sudden head fake toward Barry Love's office door. When the creatures started moving that way, Morris suddenly threw the sea salt into the face of the pig-faced storm trooper and was rewarded with an outraged bellow. He slashed at the lagoon creature with his blade, but the green monstrosity was quicker than it looked. Webbed fingers locked around Morris's knife hand, and the demon's fangs went for his throat. Morris blocked the horrid face with a forearm, and the two of them staggered into Barry Love's office and fell hard onto the cheap carpet.

Despite his effort to twist as they went down, Morris ended up on the bottom. He kept trying to use the knife on the creature while protecting himself, but demons are strong. The scaly, amphibian face was pushing inexorably against Morris's forearm, the sharp teeth drawing closer to his throat, when Barry Love placed the barrel of a Colt .38 revolver against the thing's head and blew the contents of its skull all over the nearest wall.

Love helped Morris to his feet. "Sorry that took me so long," he said. "I was watching the door to see if any more of them were going to try a rush while we were distracted. Where's your girlfriend?"

"She's not my—" Morris began, but then there was a cry from the corridor outside. It was quickly stifled, but he knew that voice. "Libby!"

Morris rushed into the hallway, Barry Love close behind him. The sight that greeted them caused each man to come to a sudden stop and then to become very still.

The storm trooper demon with the boar's head clutched Libby Chastain from behind and was using her for a shield. One hairy hand was clasped tightly over Libby's mouth. The other held a Nazi ceremonial dagger, its needle point just touching Libby's throat. If a boar's face can be said to grin, then this one was doing so.

"So the game has changed," the demon said. Its voice was raspy and nasal, reminding Morris of the late Peter Lorre. "But now I hold the best cards, including, it would seem, the Queen." It dug the dagger's point in a little, causing a drop of blood to make its way down the column of Libby's throat. "You will drop your weapons! At once!"

"You've been watching too much TV," Barry Love said conversationally, as he took a slow step to his left. "Or do they have TV in Hell?"

"Yes, but only *The Jerry Springer Show,*" the demon told him. "Now cast away your weapons, or watch me gut her!"

Morris thought he knew what Love was doing. He moved a little to the right as he asked, "What happens if we do as you ask? Will you let her go?"

"All you need know is what happens if you do NOT do as I say!" the demon bellowed. "And stand still, both of you!"

"Libby," Morris said, locking eyes with her, "Don't worry, we'll get you out of this." He paused a beat before continuing, "And whatever you do, *don't faint.*"

He thought he saw understanding in Libby's eyes, and knew he was right a moment later when she suddenly sagged at the knees, making herself dead weight.

Demons are strong, but not smart. The boar storm trooper was not prepared for the sudden shift in Libby's weight, and she was slipping toward the floor before the creature could adjust its grip to prop her up.

Suddenly, the demon's great ugly head was unprotected.

Barry Love fired at once. The .38 bullet chipped the top off one of the boar tusks and continued on into the porcine face.

The demon staggered back, releasing Libby in the process. A moment later, its throat was pierced by the silver-coated switchblade, which Morris had thrown with all the skill and strength that long practice could give him.

The demon went down stiffly, like a felled tree, and was still.

"*Hades über alles?*" Morris said softly as he looked at the prostrate form in its brown uniform and swastika armband. Then he shook his head. "Not this time, podner."

BOURBON WAS NOT Libby Chastain's favorite drink, but she didn't complain when Barry Love handed her an almost-clean glass containing three fingers worth of Jack Daniel's.

Love gave another glass to Quincey Morris and picked up a third one for himself. Sitting wearily on the edge of the desk, he raised his glass in a silent toast to the other two.

After taking a long swallow, Libby said, "You're probably going to need some help disposing of those—things before morning."

Love shook his head. "They usually discorporate very quickly, once destroyed. Look there." He gestured with his chin to the spot on the carpet where he had shot the lagoon creature. All that remained was a large, amorphous stain on the fabric. "You'll find something similar when you get out into the hall, I expect," he said. "It's about the only decent thing that demons ever do, and that one's kind of involuntary."

"We're sorry to have brought this shit down on you, Barry," Morris said.

Love looked at him with a puzzled frown. "Say what?"

"We told you earlier today how this black witch we're lookin' for has tried to kill us several times already. Fire, zombies, and now demons. People who do black magic tend not to be fussy about collateral damage, as you almost got to find out. Good thing you're fast with that pistol of yours."

"I've been putting out cloaking spells in an effort to hide us from her," Libby said. "And, in any case, we'd hoped to be in and out of your life before she could zero in on us. But it didn't work out that way. So, as Quincey says, we're sorry."

Love shook his head slowly. "I appreciate the apology, but I'm afraid it's kind of misplaced."

It was Morris's turn to be confused. "What do you mean?"

"I mean, I'm not the innocent bystander here. You guys are. Those demons were after me, not you."

"What makes you so sure?" Libby asked.

"I've been involved in an ongoing conflict with the Nether World for quite some time now. Started out with a case I had in Brooklyn about six years ago. Looked straightforward enough at first, just another adultery thing, but it all went to Hell. Literally. That was my introduction to the weird shit, and I still dream about it."

"And demons have been coming after you ever since?" Libby seemed appalled at the prospect.

"Not constantly, but sometimes, yeah." Love produced a grim smile. "Other times, I've been the one coming after *them*."

Morris frowned. "I don't know, Barry. It just seems like such a huge coincidence, after what Libby and I have had aimed at us recently. When was your last demonic encounter, before today?"

"Um, let me think—yeah, it was just before Christmas, which tends to be a busy time for the Infernal forces, though you might not think so."

"No, I believe you," Morris said. "It makes a certain amount of perverse sense."

"Well, I don't suppose we'll ever really know for sure who those monstrosities were after," Libby said. "But I do know that Quincey and I, not to mention the LaRue family, are going to be a lot safer once we find this black witch and do something about her. Were you able to...?"

Barry Love smacked the desk lightly with his palm. "Shit! In all this craziness I completely forgot." He started searching through the collection of papers, files, and clippings that was strewn over his desk. "I talked to several people familiar with the black magic scene. Most of them didn't know anything about the witch you asked me about, or so they claimed. But two others each gave me a name—*and it was the same name.*"

A moment later, he said, "Yeah, here it is," and pulled a smudged four-by-six index card out of the desktop mess. He handed it to Libby, who was closest.

Libby looked at the card for much longer than it could possibly have taken her to read what was written there.

Finally, she passed it to Morris, who saw that the card contained only four words:

Christine Abernathy
Salem, Massachusetts

CHAPTER 23

"SHE WILL KILL once more," Van Dreenan said. "And when she does, we must be ready."

"How do you know she's only gonna do it one more time?" Fenton asked. "I mean, I agree she'll do it again. She's getting something out of it, something that matters to her. But why would she stop after just one more?"

"The next death will be her fifth. The fifth in this cycle, at any rate." Van Dreenan's eyes took on a faraway look, not unlike the "thousand yard stare" you find in soldiers who have seen a lot of combat and are approaching their breaking point.

Fenton was staring at him. "You all right, man?"

Van Dreenan blinked several times. "Yes, I'm sorry. I was thinking of something else."

"You know, I've noticed it before. You get kinda weird every once in a while, and it seems to happen whenever we're talking about *muti* murder, and no other time."

Van Dreenan shrugged, but said nothing.

When he spoke again, Fenton's voice was gentle. "Is there something you're not telling me?"

Van Dreenan looked at him hard for several seconds before dropping his gaze. "It may be that there is," he said slowly. "And, under other circumstances, I would tell you. I have come to respect you, Fenton, in the time we have worked together. Indeed, I find that I rather like you."

"I guess you could say that it's mutual. In both aspects."

There followed the embarrassed silence that usually occurs whenever two men in this culture talk about such matters. Van Dreenan broke it by saying, "I thank you for that. And I do not wish to—what is the expression?—hold out on you. But you are a professional and a man of integrity. If you were working on a case with someone who had an emotional involvement, a personal stake in the outcome, you would feel obliged to report it to your superiors, *ja?*"

"I guess I would, yeah."

"And the reaction of your superiors would be what?"

"Most likely, they'd remove the emotionally involved person from the investigation. On the grounds that emotional involvement clouds judgment, and clouded judgment impairs the investigation."

"Precisely. Now, tell me something. Would you say that I have been an impediment to the investigation thus far?"

"Hell, no. We wouldn't be nearly as close as we are now if it weren't for you."

"That is kind of you to say. So any hypothetical emotional involvement I might have has not adversely affected the investigation, is that a fair assessment?"

"Sure."

"Then I would prefer not to speak with you about certain matters. Not now, in any case. It would be better if you are able to say later, under oath if necessary, that you had no direct knowledge of any personal feelings of mine that might relate to the subject of this investigation."

"I see."

"I must not be removed from this case, Fenton. *I must not.* And not only for my own sake, but for yours, as well."

Fenton ran a hand over his face. "All right, now you've *really* lost me."

"I know, and I regret that. I hope all will become clear to you in time. But for now—" Van Dreenan leaned forward in his chair, "I ask you to trust me. No, I *need* you to trust me. For a short while, only."

In the space of the next few seconds, Fenton's agile mind considered a variety of factors. But it returned, over and over, to his memories of the crime scene photos. The blood soaked earth.

The ravages of insects and wildlife. The pathetic, pale, savaged bodies.

He kept thinking about dead children.

Fenton had children of his own, three of them. Girls, eight and three, and a boy, six.

All were within the age range of Cecelia Mbwato's victims.

He met the South African's eyes with his own. "All right, Van Dreenan. All right. I'll go along. Don't you make me regret it."

"It is my sincere wish," Van Dreenan said, "that neither of us will come to regret it."

THE PHONE RINGING next to his ear brought Snake Perkins out of a restless sleep. He glanced at his watch, and saw he had been in bed just over four hours.

Jesus, why couldn't the bitch leave him *alone?*

"Yeah?"

"Did you take care of the car?"

"Yeah, sure. Found just what I needed and made the switch. Look why don't we—"

"We must leave here and find another place. Closer to where we have to go later."

"You mean Sa—"

"Hush! Not over the telephone!"

"Oh, for God's sake, lady. You're fuckin' paranoid."

"We have to leave here," she said again. "Keep in your mind that we are nearly done with this. It will soon be finished. Then you can sleep as much as you want."

Snake sat up in the lumpy bed. "Yeah, all right, okay. Give me half an hour."

"Take less than that. We have much to do."

"SO, WHY ARE you saying she just wants one more?" Fenton asked. "Because she killed five the other time, in South Africa?"

"No, that's not it," Van Dreenan told him. "Rather, I believe she will kill five here for the same *reason* she chose five victims the last time."

"Which is..."

"The number five is very significant in black magic rituals, Fenton. No one is sure why, although the pentagram is, of course, a five-pointed star, and it has a long association with the dark path. Perhaps that has some bearing."

"Yeah, I've seen plenty of pentagrams, although most of the 'occult crime' reported in this country is nothing but bullshit."

"Role-playing young people, combined with panic and rumors? *Ja,* we have the same problem back home. It is one of the reasons behind those witch murders I told you about earlier."

"Murders of witches, you mean. Or rather, people accused of being witches."

"That is correct. A great tragedy, since the vast majority of them are guilty of nothing more than saying the wrong thing in anger, or having a sinister-looking face, or making enemies of the wrong kind of person."

"People deliberately use accusations of witchcraft, knowing they're false, just to pay off scores?"

"*Ja,* exactly," Van Dreenan sad. "The same thing that happened in Europe during the Middle Ages, and in your Salem, Massachusetts some years later. Most of those poor souls were certainly innocent."

"You keep saying stuff like 'the majority' and 'most people.' What does that make the rest of them?"

Van Dreenan seemed to hesitate before he finally spoke. "Real witches, of course."

Fenton sat scratching his cheek for a few seconds. "You know, we had this conversation before, when you first got here."

"*Ja,* I recall as much."

"This is the part where I say something like 'Oh, you mean people who think they're practicing real witchcraft, even though you and I know it's superstitious nonsense,' and you give me this 'Oh yes, of course, what else could it possibly be' crap."

"I was not planning to say that, this time."

"Yeah? How come?"

"Because," Van Dreenan said softly, "this time, I think, you are ready for the truth."

"WELCOME TO RHODE Island," the sign read. "Please Obey Speed Limits."

Snake Perkins was grooving to some early Eric Clapton in his head, but he made a face as they crossed the invisible line separating Rhode Island from Connecticut. "You sure it's a good idea, doin' the last one this close to her?"

"It is a very good idea," Cecelia Mbwato said. "The closer we are, the sooner I can make delivery once the package is ready."

"Want your money, huh?"

She gave him another of her contemptuous looks. "Just like you want yours, I think," she said. "But it is more than that. There is the matter of safety to consider."

Snake blew air out his nose. "What we been doin' ain't exactly what I consider real safe," he said. "That's why we gettin' paid so much to do it."

"You say the truth. But there is no reason to make the risk last longer than we must. If all goes well tonight, we will have with us the evidence of five murders. These American scientists, they can prove what person a piece of flesh comes from. They catch us with these things... they hang us for sure."

"Most places don't hang ya any more," Snake said. "They use lethal injection or the electric chair. But I get what you're sayin'."

"I have heard of this electric chair," she said musingly. "It is said that people being killed that way sometimes catch fire and burn."

"Yeah, I guess I heard that, too. Don't matter, though. They ain't gonna be doin' it to us. We got this down to a science, now."

"A science. Yes, I suppose so." Cecelia Mbwato consulted the road atlas she had open in her lap. "Drive another thirty, forty miles, then find us a motel." She closed the atlas with a sound like a slap, and tossed it in the back seat. "Then we go to look for playgrounds."

"THE TRUTH," FENTON said scornfully. "You actually think this black magic shit is real, don't you?"

"I trust what I have seen with my own eyes," Van Dreenan told him. "And so should you."

"What's that mean?"

"You viewed the videotape, as did I. You saw what happened in the convenience store. And you have read the toxicology report, just as I did."

"Yeah, okay, I admit that's puzzling, but it doesn't—"

"Puzzling?" Van Dreenan's voice held some scorn of its own. "The woman blows powder in the robber's eyes, *ja?* Almost immediately, the robber's eyeballs start to... dissolve. Later, the powder is analyzed—by professionals, people who do this sort of thing every day. Hardheaded American science, the best in the world, is brought to bear on the problem. And what do they find?"

"Look, I know it might not—"

"What do they find in the man's eyes, Fenton? Sulfuric acid, maybe?"

Fenton raised his eyes to the ceiling. "No, no acid."

"Some derivative of lye? Anything like that?"

"Stop badgering me, Van Dreenan. We both know what the tox report said."

"Herbs, wasn't it? Several different ones, ground to powder. And tiny bits of tree bark. And nothing else."

Fenton rubbed his eyes with a thumb and forefinger. "Yeah, I know."

"The scientists did not believe it, either. The report said they were going to perform the analysis again. They should have completed it by now. Do you wish to check the results?"

Fenton looked at him. "I guess I'll do just that."

He turned the laptop toward him and began to type. Van Dreenan didn't bother to look over his shoulder.

It was less than three minutes before Fenton logged off and turned away from the computer. "Same results," he said with a scowl. "Exactly the same. Now the lab people are making noises about how the sample must have been mislabeled, or maybe contaminated at the crime scene. It's all CYA stuff now."

"CYA?"

"Cover your ass. A practice beloved of government employees everywhere." Fenton shook his head, as if trying to deny what he had just read. "Look, man, this just isn't possible."

"Except that it has happened," Van Dreenan said gently. "Believe me when I say that I know exactly how you are feeling. I went through the same process myself. As a Christian, and yes, I admit it, a white South African, I was raised to regard the tribal religious beliefs and practices of the native blacks as no more than superstitions—proof, supposedly, that their culture had not advanced as far as ours. No man's mind was more closed than mine."

"So, what opened it?" Fenton asked sourly.

"My investigation into the deaths of Miles Nshonge's wife and children."

"Miles? Cecelia? How is it that these native blacks, as you call them, all have English-sounding first names?"

"During apartheid, the government required it. No person's birth could be registered without a Christian first name. And without a birth certificate, it was impossible to later obtain a work permit, driver's license, and so on." Van Dreenan had the good grace to look embarrassed. "Once the African National Congress, Mister Mandela's party, took over, the practice was abolished, of course. But that had no effect on the millions who had been born before, unless they took the trouble to change their first names legally. Some have, but most have not."

"All right, so how did this Miles what's-his-name make you a believer in black magic?"

Van Dreenan ran his big hand slowly over his face, like a man bracing himself for something unpleasant. Then he leaned forward in his chair. "It was like this..."

Thokoza Township
Republic of South Africa
February 2003

THE AIR CONDITIONING in the unmarked police car wasn't working, as usual, so Van Dreenan and Sergeant Shemba kept all the windows down, except when the dust was particularly bad. Van Dreenan had never been to Thokoza before, but as they drew near he found that it looked like all the other black townships he had seen. The usual mixture of one-story mud-brick buildings and corrugated tin shacks, broken-down cars, small businesses operating out of converted cargo crates, and children running around playing—children who should be in school, except there was no school for them to go to.

Every urban area of any size in South Africa has a township outside it; bigger cities like Pretoria and Cape Town have more than one. The townships came into existence during apartheid, when blacks and "coloreds" were not allowed to live in the cities with whites. Those who had jobs in the cities wanted to live close by, so the townships evolved.

Apartheid disappeared in 1994, but the townships did not. The charitable referred to them as suburbs. The realists, who had seen them, called them slums.

The first two people Sergeant Shemba asked for directions just shrugged and walked away. But then he found a boy, aged about ten, who told them how to find the house of Miles Nshonge. The boy had not yet learned to hate and fear the police. In time, he probably would.

The boy's information proved accurate, and a few minutes later they pulled up in front of the mudbrick house that had been the home of the Nshonge family. Only Miles Nshonge lived there now, which was why the two policemen had come to see him.

Once they were out of the car, Sergeant Shemba popped the hood and raised it. Using a rag to avoid burning his fingers, he removed the distributor cap from the engine, wrapped it in the rag, and stowed it in a pocket of his khaki uniform. The poverty and desperation in most of the townships was such that no unattended car was safe, even one belonging to the police. As it was, the two men would still keep an eye in it, lest they come back to find it stripped down to the bare metal.

Detective First Class Van Dreenan and Sergeant Shemba had been partners for just over three years. Van Dreenan valued Shemba's insight, courage, integrity, and the fact that the big man spoke four of the tribal languages, including Xhosa, which was the dominant tongue in Thokoza.

The two men positioned themselves on either side of the house's front door before knocking. People in the townships sometimes shot right through the door if they did not know it was the police outside—and sometimes even when they did.

Following Sergeant Shemba's vigorous knocking, a male voice inside called out something in Xhosa. Sergeant Shemba answered, in a tone that brooked no nonsense.

A few moments later, the door was opened by a narrow-shouldered, very thin man of about forty with a sad, careworn face. Sergeant Shemba asked a question that contained the name "Miles Nshonge" in it. The sad-faced man answered, then stepped back to allow his visitors entry.

The house's large main room was sparsely furnished but spotlessly clean. The principal decoration was a large framed photograph on one wall showing Nelson Mandela being sworn in as President of the Republic of South Africa. Nshonge waved the two policemen into mismatched wooden armchairs with thin, frayed cushions on the seats; he sat facing them on an ornately carved wooden bench about the size of a European loveseat.

Van Dreenan said to Sergeant Shemba, who would act as translator, "Please give him our condolences on the deaths of his wife and children."

After Shemba spoke, Nshonge nodded his acknowledgment, but said nothing.

"Tell him we appreciate his being willing to talk to us today."

Nshonge replied briefly, shaking his head as he did so.

"He says it does not matter, because he is a dead man already."

"Ask him to explain that."

"He says that the same curse that killed his family will soon take him, also."

"Ask about the curse."

Nshonge spent some time looking at the floor without saying anything. Then, without raising his head, he began to talk. He spoke at length, as if he were letting something out that he had kept inside him for a very long time. Sergeant Shemba translated after every few sentences.

"He says he liked to gamble: cards and betting on horses. He has a good job as a carpenter, but the last five years, he had been gambling more and more. He lost much money playing cards with his friends. And he would go to the racetrack sometimes, but it is far away and hard to get to. So most of the time he placed his bets with a local broker."

Shemba looked at Van Dreenan. "I believe by this he means what we would call a 'bookie.'"

"Right," Van Dreenan said. "Ask him to go on."

"He says the broker would extend to him credit, to let him keep betting even when he owed money. But the day came when the broker said there would be no more credit, and wanted the debt paid. He says at that time he owed the broker almost eight hundred rand."

"I bet I know what happened next," Van Dreenan muttered.

Shemba turned to him again. "Sorry?"

"Nothing, never mind," Van Dreenan told him. "Please continue."

"He says the broker has some big, tough men who work for him. Threats were made—against him, and against his family. He says he became quite desperate. He says he tried to borrow the money he owed, but none would loan it to him, even the moneylenders who charge very high interest. So, out of fear for his family, he went to a *tagati*."

"Sweet Christ," Van Dreenan said softly. A *tagati* is a witch, of either gender. Unlike the *sangomas*, who practice benign folk medicine, the *tagati* deal in one thing only: black magic. They were notorious for being utterly ruthless, and people who did business with them usually ended up getting hurt, in one way or another.

"He says the *tagati* listened to his tale very closely, very carefully. When he finished, the *tagati* asked him how much money he wanted—not how much he owed, but how much he wanted. He said he would like twelve hundred rand. That would pay his gambling debt and allow him some left over for his family.

"He says the *tagati* then asked him if he would swear a High Oath, in return for the money."

"High Oath? What's that mean?"

For the first time since they had arrived, Sergeant Shemba showed signs of distress. Being a disciplined police officer, he was not obvious about it, but Van Dreenan knew something was wrong.

"The High Oath," Shemba said, "is something that can be invoked by only the most powerful of *tagati*. If you swear the High Oath, you are bound to the sorcerer until he releases you, and to make the bond, you give him your soul. You belong to him. Or to her."

Superstitious claptrap was Van Dreenan's reaction, but he kept it to himself. He liked the Sergeant too much to show disrespect for tribal beliefs, some of which Shemba still bought into, despite being nominally a Methodist. He said to Shemba, "Ask him if he took this High Oath."

The Sergeant did so. After listening to Nshonge's response, he said, "Yes, he did. He says that he was desperate, that he had no other choice. In return for the money, he pledged to perform any service that the *tagati* might demand of him in the future."

"So, the *tagati* just gave him twelve hundred rand?"

"He says no. Instead, the *tagati* instructed him to wait two days, and on the third day to bet on the daily number, with five-three-five as his choice."

Van Dreenan nodded. The local numbers syndicates had their counterparts worldwide, and were always more popular among the poor than the legal state lotteries.

"He says he did as the *tagati* told him, and five-three-five was the winning number that day. He was the only winner in the township. The pay-out was exactly twelve hundred rand."

Van Dreenan raised his eyebrows at that, but said nothing, as Nshonge continued speaking.

"He says all was well, then, for almost two years. He paid his debts for gambling, and gambled no more after that. He became a different man, he says. Then the *tagati* came to him in a dream, demanding payment. The *tagati* wanted Mr. Nshonge's eldest child, a boy of seven years. He says the *tagati* told him to deliver the boy to a certain crossroads, at midnight, on the first night of the next full moon."

"In a dream, eh?"

"Yes, but you must remember, that dreams are very important among these people. They are considered a means of communicating with the spirit world, with their ancestors, and so on."

Van Dreenan nodded. "Ask him what he did about this dream he had."

"He says in the dream he refused. He acknowledged his debt to the *tagati,* but said that repayment take some other form. He would not give up one of his children. He says the *tagati* was insistent, reminding him of the High Oath he had taken, and told him that he would have the boy, one way or another."

"I think we may be about to get to the heart of the matter, and about time," Van Dreenan said. "Ask him what happened then."

"He says the moon became full three nights later. He was very vigilant the first night and stayed awake until dawn to keep watch, lest the *tagati* send minions to take the boy by stealth or by force. He borrowed a shotgun from a neighbor, and kept it close to his chair. But the night passed without incident. However, when he went to wake his family, he found the eldest boy having convulsions. He says blood was coming from the boy's mouth, his nose, his bumhole, and his ears, and they could not stop it. He sent for the local *sangoma,* who came at once, but the boy was dead by the time he arrived."

"Ask him if he notified the police."

"He says 'no.'"

"What about the Health Service?"

"Also 'no.'"

"Then ask him *why the bloody hell not!*"

Once the question was translated, Van Dreenan saw Nshonge gesture helplessly before answering.

"He says the boy was already dead," Shemba said. "There was nothing for the police or the white doctors to do. He says they buried the boy in the local graveyard, with due ceremony."

Van Dreenan shook his head in disgust at the man's abysmal ignorance. The boy could have been carrying an infectious disease that might have wiped out the whole township, and beyond, if left untreated.

Except that nobody else had died. Apart from the rest of Nshonge's family.

"Ask him what happened to his other two children, and his wife."

Shemba spoke to Nshonge, then listened in return. He turned to Van Dreenan. "He says before he speaks of that, there are two other things we must know.

"He says that the day after the boy's funeral, Mr. Nshonge's wife went to the grave, to pray that her ancestors would receive the boy's spirit in welcome.

"He says that when she got there, she found that the grave had been dug up, and the boy's body removed."

Van Dreenan frowned. "Animals?"

Sergeant Shemba translated the question.

"He says it could not be. The grave had been dug deeply, to keep animals away. And there were marks in the earth of hands, human hands."

"His poor mother, it must have broken her heart," Van Dreenan said softly. Then to Shemba: "He said there were two things. What's the other one?"

"He says the *tagati* came to him again in a dream. The *tagati* was very angry, saying that the High Oath had been broken. He said that Nshonge would watch his remaining two children die, then his wife, before he, too, would succumb to the *tagati*'s power."

"Ask him to give us the rest of it. Briefly, if possible."

"He says the next full moon, the same happened, This time it was his middle child, who was found dead in her bed, in a pool of her own blood. After the funeral, he hired guards for her grave. But the next morning, the guards were found in a deep sleep, from which it was hard to rouse them. The grave of his daughter was empty."

"Someone drugged the guards?"

"He says the guards swore not. They ate and drank only that which they had brought with them, and saw no one, the whole night long."

"They would have said that, anyway," Van Dreenan muttered. "All right, get to the end of it."

According to Sergeant Shemba's translation, Nshonge said that he had sought the help of the most powerful *sangomas* he could find. They had sold him all manner of charms, amulets, ointments, and potions to protect his last child from the *tagati's* vengeance, but to no avail. The first night of the next full moon, the girl had died, in the same manner as her siblings.

Nshonge had again hired guards for the child's grave, but this time he had accompanied them himself, bringing a large thermos of strong tea that he had brewed himself, to help everyone stay awake. But, after sunrise, he had awakened, groggy, from a dreamless slumber, to find the guards also asleep and the grave once again plundered.

When the time of the next full moon approached, Nshonge said, he had urged his wife to leave for a few days, perhaps to visit relatives in a distant village. However, she had insisted that her proper place was with him, and had refused to go. The two of them vowed they would both stay awake all night, to keep the *tagati* from coming in their sleep. They had made tea, so strong that was almost undrinkable, kept the radio on all night, and played cards (not for money) to pass the time.

Although he had been determined not to assume any posture that would permit sleep, Nshonge awoke in the morning sitting at the table where he and his wife had been playing a variation of gin rummy. His head had been pillowed on his folded arms, which were resting on the table.

Across from him, his wife was in a similar position. Except that she was covered in blood, as dead as Nshonge's last hopes.

That had been three weeks ago. As he had feared, his wife's body had been stolen from her grave, despite all precautions, and Nshonge was alone now, waiting for the next full moon so that his torment, along with his life, could finally end.

Once Nshonge stopped talking, there was quiet in the room for the better part of a minute. Looking at Sergeant Shemba, Van Dreenan could tell that his partner was seriously perturbed by what he had heard. Van Dreenan thought he knew exactly how the big man felt. He said to Shemba, "Ask him for the name of this *tagati,* and where he may be found."

When the question was put into Xhosa, Miles Nshonge appeared agitated for the first time in the interview.

"He refuses," Shemba said. "He says the *tagati*'s vengeance is already terrible enough—he does not wish to make it even worse."

"What the hell could be worse than what he says he is facing now?"

"He says he does not know, and does not wish to know. He will not speak the *tagati*'s name to us."

After a few more attempts to coax the name of the sorcerer out of Miles Nshonge, Van Dreenan gave it up. As they left, Sergeant Shemba gave the man his card, inviting him to call if he changed his mind. Nshonge accepted the card, but neither policeman seriously thought he was going to be getting in touch with the law.

The car was, fortunately, still in one piece. As they drove off, Van Dreenan asked, "When does the next full moon start, do you know?"

Sergeant Shemba thought for a moment. "Not tonight, but tomorrow night. Yes, I am sure of it."

Van Dreenan nodded slowly. "I was thinking," he said, "that the day after tomorrow might be a good time to come back, pay Mister Nshonge another visit."

Shemba looked at him, before turning back to watch the road. "Assuming he is still alive, you mean."

"*Ja,*" Van Dreenan said glumly. "Always assuming that."

Two days later

VAN DREENAN AND Sergeant Shemba got an early start, which meant they arrived in Thokoza a little after 9:00 in the morning.

The unspoken question that had occupied their thoughts during the drive over was answered as soon as they saw the small crowd gathered in front of Miles Nshonge's house.

The locals gave way to the two policemen as they walked to Nshonge's front door, which stood open. The buzzing of flies inside the house was loud, as if something within had attracted their interest. Van Dreenan was pretty sure he knew what it was.

Miles Nshonge lay on his back, upon the bench where he had sat during his interview a few days earlier. He might have seemed asleep, were it not for the pool of blood that spread out from underneath the bench to cover a good portion of the floor.

Taking care not to step in the small lake of gore, Van Dreenan prowled the room, although he could not have said exactly what he was looking for. There were no signs of struggle. Nshonge's body bore no visible wound. The blood smelled fresh, and a careful touch of Van Dreenan's finger revealed that it was just starting to become tacky. Nshonge had been dead no more than a few hours.

Van Dreenan made a gesture toward the open door with his chin. "Have a chat with that lot outside, will you?" he said to Shemba. "See if anybody saw or heard anything, the usual drill—for all the *fokken* good it will do."

Van Dreenan took the small police radio that he wore clipped to his belt, flicked it on, and prepared to follow procedure for reporting a suspicious death on his patch. *And they don't get much more bloody suspicious than this,* he thought.

While he spoke into his radio, he let his eyes wander idly around the room, taking in the blood pool, the flies that were gorging themselves on it, the sparse decorations, the cheap but serviceable furniture...

It was then that he noticed the piece of paper.

The Nshonge family's dining table looked old but of good quality, as if it were an heirloom handed down through several generations. On it rested salt and pepper shakers, a few small bottles probably containing other spices, a cheap-looking necklace with some carnivore's tooth attached, and, underneath it, a half-sheet of paper.

Van Dreenan finished his radio conversation while making his slow way over there, careful to avoid the blood. Out of habit he touched nothing on the table, but he doubted forensics was going to be much help to him this time.

He wondered if the amulet on the table was one of those that Miles Nshonge had purchased from a *sangoma*, in a desperate and futile effort to keep what was left of his family alive.

The piece of paper beneath the amulet had writing on it. Van Dreenan bent closer and saw that someone, probably the late Miles Nshonge, had written two words there in a clean, precise hand: Jerome Lekota.

PATROLMAN GEORGE DEBRINE had a mate, a Yank to be exact, who worked at one of the big game preserves outside the city. The two of them would get together sometimes on a weekend, have a booze someplace and trade lies about the supposed excitement of their respective jobs. And this mate of his, Bennie Prescott, had an expression he'd use about somebody who'd gone and pissed him off. "That bastard," he'd say, "is on my shit list now." It never failed to give George a good laugh, especially once he'd got some beer inside him.

Patrolman DeBrine's current situation had given him a whole new perspective on that phrase, and its implications. Because George was on his sergeant's shit list now, good and sure. Late for roll call three times in a month, George had been. Showed up for his shift once or twice a bit under the weather (all right, hung over and fit to die, truth be told). And when Sergeant Wilson had upbraided him about all of this (got right in his face, the bastard had, and told George he was a disgrace to the uniform), George had experienced a sudden attack of near-suicidal bad judgment and told the sergeant to fuck off.

Which is how George had found himself stationed outside the double doors of this hospital morgue, with orders to make sure that nobody made off with some *kaffir's* dead body. Eight bloody hours, apart from his lunch and two piss breaks, standing there. And if that wasn't bad enough, he was also expected to visually check every corpse that was removed from the room, to be sure that the remains of said *kaffir,* one Miles Nshonge, was not among them.

That detective, Van Dreenan, had been very explicit in his instructions. Maybe too much so. He'd taken George inside the large, cool room and pulled open one of the sliding metal drawers, looking for all the world like a bloody great filing cabinet. Made him study the face of the dead *kaffir,* as if they didn't all look alike.

"You don't go just by the morgue tag," Van Dreenan had told him. "Somebody wheels a corpse out of here, you make them zip open the body bag far enough for you to check who's inside it. Got that? The autopsy on this gentleman is not scheduled until the day after tomorrow, maybe later, so there is no reason for his body to leave this room until then. *And it had better bloody not.*"

George DeBrine liked his job—most days, anyway. He certainly didn't want to lose it and have to start fresh with something else that would probably offer less money and far less authority. So he had decided, reluctantly, to reform. No more boozing. At least, not when he had work the next day. He'd not had a drop of anything stronger than his tea the night before this boring, useless assignment.

Which is why George was so astounded when he groggily awoke to find himself in a corner, back against the wall and his legs straight out before him, hands folded peacefully in his lap, his neck with a painful crick in it. He got unsteadily to his feet and began brushing dirt from the filthy floor off his khaki uniform. He had no memory of getting down there to have a snooze in the corner. Christ, he couldn't remember even *thinking* about doing something so incredibly stupid. It was only by a stroke of luck that none of the hospital staff had come along and found him—

George stopped brushing himself off and just stood there like a statue, as a horrible thought flashed through his mind. He looked toward the double doors of the morgue and then, after a long moment's hesitation, began to walk slowly toward them.

Ordinarily, being in this room all by himself would have given George the creeping willies, but this time he was glad to be alone. He remembered clearly the number of the drawer containing the remains of Miles Nshonge: 1408. A few seconds later he stood in front of it, one hand wrapped around the cool metal handle. George knew that, one way or another, the course of his life from this point forward was going to be determined by whether the dead *kaffir* was in there or not.

In his mind, he offered a brief, beseeching prayer to his Creator, whom he had not addressed in quite some time. Then he took a deep breath and pulled the drawer open.

Apart from the bloodstained sheet upon which the body of Miles Nshonge had once lain, the drawer was as empty as George DeBrine's future with the South African Police Force.

"IF THIS ISN'T a *fokken* cock-up, then I don't know what one would look like," Van Dreenan said. "The Chief is so pissed off he's about ready to spit blood. Trouble is, he isn't quite sure who to be mad *at*. Apart from that poor bastard DeBrine, that is. He's for the chopper, that much is for sure."

"And well he should be," Sergeant Shemba said, as he slid into the chair behind his desk; his and Van Dreenan's were pushed together front-to-front, so the two of them sat facing each other from a distance of about four feet. Shemba twisted the cap off a cold bottle of mineral water he had brought in with him.

"Think so?" Van Dreenan asked. "I'm beginning to wonder."

"Are you? Why?"

"Tell you in a bit. First things first. Jerome Lekota is as clean as they come—officially, anyway. I found the record of his birth from forty-six years ago, and that's all. Never been convicted, arrested, questioned, or even farted in public, far as I can tell. Model citizen, is our Mister Lekota."

"Officially," Shemba said.

"Right. And, as everybody knows, that's all that bloody matters. How about you? Turn up anything?"

"I know that Lekota is a *tagati,*" Shemba said. "He lives in the next township over from Thokoza. Those who know what he is, and they are few, fear him."

"Works powerful witchcraft, eh?" There was a time when Van Dreenan would have said that with a condescending smile. He was not smiling now.

"Most powerful. Those who have incurred his anger, they are said to have died, all most unpleasantly."

"Any particular way?"

"My informants mentioned several, although it is impossible to separate rumor from fact when one speaks of such things." Sergeant Shemba took a long swig of water, then placed the bottle on the desk in front of him and stared into it glumly, as if it were a crystal ball revealing a future he didn't much care for. He did not look up when he said to Van Dreenan, "But two different people did say to me they had heard of enemies of Lekota who developed uncontrollable bleeding in the night, from all their bodily orifices, and soon bled to death."

The two men were silent for a time, until Van Dreenan cleared his throat and said, "*Ja,* well, in addition to checking Mr. Lekota's nonexistent criminal record, I spent some time with the tapes from one of the hospital surveillance cameras."

"They had one pointed at the morgue?" Shemba looked surprised.

"No, but they've got one covering the corridor just around the corner from it. There's a storeroom there where they keep drugs, so they want to know who's coming and going. I went over there this morning and walked around a bit, just to be sure that my memory of the place was correct, and it was. There is no other way out of the morgue except through that corridor. No doors, no windows, not even a bloody mouse hole. Nothing. It's in the cellar, remember."

Shemba nodded slowly. "That would appear to simplify matters for us."

"Think so, wouldn't you? Well brace yourself for the bad news, my friend, because nobody took a body out of that morgue between when I was there the first time and when DeBrine sounded the alarm."

"No autopsies were done? None at all?"

"They've only got one pathologist on staff, and she's sick. Flu, or something. Been out a couple of days. Several bodies went in, all right. They're all on the tape and supported by the hospital records. But nobody wheeled a corpse out of there, or brought out anything that might have hidden a corpse inside it, like a crate, a trash container, or even a bloody steamer trunk."

"Could Nshonge's body have been moved to another drawer in the morgue, perhaps?" Shemba asked. "Whether by accident or design?"

Van Dreenan shook his head. "The hospital people thought of that, too. Checked every *fokken* one. No Miles Nshonge."

"Is there an incinerator near the morgue, where the body could have been burned up?"

"No, sorry. Oh, they've got an incinerator, all right. But it's on the other side of the building, with no access from the morgue that doesn't take you right through that corridor with the video camera. And before you ask, I checked with the video boffins upstairs: there's no sign that the tape has been tampered with. None."

Shemba took another drink, then sat back in his chair. He was looking right at Van Dreenan now.

"Almost like it was magic," Shemba said quietly.

Van Dreenan would have, not so long ago, greeted such a pronouncement with derisive laughter. Now he only grunted.

"This man, this *tagati,* has wiped out a whole family. Five human beings. And who knows how many others before that?"

Van Dreenan just stared at him.

"Left alone, this Lekota, he will surely kill again in pursuit of his dark purposes."

"We can't arrest him," Van Dreenan said. His voice was now as soft as Sergeant Shemba's. "There's no *fokken* evidence a crime has even been committed. And I don't fancy asking the Prosecutor to charge some bloke with murder by witchcraft."

"I agree. We cannot arrest him, even though we know he is guilty of murder."

Van Dreenan leaned forward suddenly, his mouth a thin hard line. "Then what the bloody hell *can* we do?"

Shemba hesitated before saying, "If you wish to know, I will tell you. But be certain, my friend, that you really wish to know."

In the space of the next few seconds, Van Dreenan thought fleetingly about many things—his pension, his wife and children, his deep regard for Shemba, his own conservative Christian upbringing. But mostly he thought about Miles Nshonge and his family.

Van Dreenan walked slowly to the office door, and closed it. Then he sat back down and said to Sergeant Shemba, "Tell me."

From "The Pretoria Times"
March 8, 2003

MOB KILLS ALLEGED "WITCH"

Umlazi Township (SANS). A mob of local residents attacked and murdered a man here last night, using a method often associated with so-called "witchcraft murder."

Jerome Lekota, 46, died from being "necklaced," meaning that a gasoline-soaked tire was placed around his neck, then set alight. He received massive burns about the face and upper torso, which proved fatal. He was pronounced dead at the scene.

Several residents of the township, who did not wish to be identified by name, said that Mr. Lekota was believed to be a "tagati," or practitioner of black magic. Residents say he was alleged to have been responsible for several murders in recent years, all using magic as a means.

The question of why local sentiment seemed to turn against Mr. Lekota only recently has not yet been answered to the satisfaction of investigating officers.

Rumours that a white male was part of the mob that killed Mister Lekota are being discounted by police as unsubstantiated and highly unlikely.

The murder by mobs of alleged "witches," usually using the method known as "necklacing," has been an unfortunate aspect of life in the country's black townships for many years. A police spokesman said today that...

CHAPTER 24

"AND THAT IS why," Van Dreenan said, "I began to reassess my views on what I once considered 'superstitious nonsense.'"

"Wait a second," Fenton said. "You're telling me that you and this African cop—"

"Sergeant Shemba is his name. And we both consider ourselves to be 'African cops,'" Van Dreenan said mildly.

Foley made an impatient gesture. "Whatever. The two of you went out there and killed this guy? Burned him alive?"

"I said no such thing, Fenton. A mob killed Jerome Lekota. Just as the newspapers said."

"But you and this Sergeant Shemba, you got them stirred up."

"Did we? Even if such were the case, I would not burden your sense of professional responsibility with such an admission."

"Yeah, but you're a—"

"Fenton, as you sometimes say, give it a rest. Whatever happened out there, it is outside your jurisdiction, beyond your responsibility, and, in any case, long over with."

"Then what the fuck did you bring it up for?"

"Now you are being deliberately obtuse. Stop it, please. You know why I brought it up."

Fenton angrily swiveled his chair so that it faced the window. He looked out for several seconds, and did not appear pleased by what he saw. Without turning back, he said to Van Dreenan, "Yeah, I guess I know why. You think this voodoo shit is real."

"It is not voodoo, *per se*. In any case, I am not presuming to say what is and is not real. I tell you only what I have seen with my own eyes."

"Yeah, right." Fenton was still not enjoying the view.

"The experience which I have related to you was my first with... such matters. It was by no means the last."

Van Dreenan sat and waited. Eventually, Fenton turned his chair back around. Most of the anger was gone from his face now. "The business with this Lekota guy, it that what got you into the Occult Crimes Unit?"

"I applied to join shortly afterwards, yes. Look, Fenton, the members of the Occult Crime Unit are not a bunch of superstitious 'ghostbusters,' although the tabloid newspapers like to use that term. As I told you the day I arrived here, we are experienced, hardheaded police officers. The principal difference between us and the average member of the South African Police Forces is that we try to keep open minds—to let the evidence determine our beliefs, not the other way around."

Fenton came up with the ghost of a wry smile. "Must've required quite an adjustment."

"You can have no idea. I was raised in the Dutch Reformed Church, Fenton, and compared to them, your Christian Right over here are a lot of timid, liberal agnostics. But I reached the point where I had to make a choice—between what I had been taught, and what I had seen." Van Dreenan's big shoulders twitched in a shrug. "I chose the latter."

Fenton nodded slowly. "An open mind, you say."

"That is all that is necessary, I think."

"Let's say I'm willing to try for this open-mindedness we're talking about. That doesn't mean I'm going to just stand by and let you administer vigilante justice to a couple of criminal suspects in this country—if we can even catch the motherfuckers."

Van Dreenan spread his hands. "I never thought you would. Or indeed, should."

"All right, then."

"But that is why we must be ready to move quickly when—if—we receive word of a fifth child murder."

"Hard to move fast when the whole damn country is the target zone."

Van Dreenan rubbed his chin. "Not the whole country, I think. They could have gone anywhere, thanks to your marvelous highway system, but they have chosen to stay in the East."

"Maybe they're just lazy."

"Do you really believe that?"

"No," Fenton said after a moment. "I guess I don't."

"There is a reason why they are staying in this part of the United States. It is probably tied in with the purpose behind these *muti* murders."

"I thought you said she's doing it to gain magical power."

"Yes, but why here? If all she wanted was the power, she could have—" Van Dreenan's voice caught for a moment, "she could have committed these atrocities in South Africa. But she made a long, expensive journey to an unfamiliar country. There must be a reason. And I'll wager that it is the same reason she and her associate are remaining in the East."

"All right, assume that's the case. I can put out an alert online to all police departments in, say, a twelve-state area. I can request to be notified immediately if a child's body is found, matching the details we have for the other victims."

"*Ja,* that will help. And once we hear something, we must be able to get to the scene quickly. Can you have a helicopter standing by? On the roof of this building, perhaps?"

"Jesus, do you know how much money that's gonna cost? To have a chopper just sitting there, idle, maybe for days?"

"Do you not think it will be money well spent?"

"Of course I do, but, shit, it's not my money to control. My boss will have to authorize it, and probably clear it with *his* boss, and budgets are tight these days, especially for anything that doesn't have to do with terrorism."

"This is terrorism of the very worst kind, my friend."

"You know that, and I know that, but my boss doesn't."

"Then you should explain it to him. Ask him to visualize the positive publicity, if the Bureau should succeed in bringing two serial killers, murderers of children, to justice."

Fenton chewed his lower lip. "Yeah, that might get his attention."

"You might further suggest he imagine the intensely *negative* publicity that would result if it should become known that the FBI had the opportunity to apprehend such vicious criminals, and did not take it."

"If I leaked something like that, my career would be over. I know it, and they *know* I know it."

"*Ja,* probably so," Van Dreenan said. "But if *I* leaked it, *my* career would *not* be over."

A slow grin made its way across Fenton's face. He turned his chair and picked up the nearby telephone. "Let me see what I can do."

CECELIA MBWATO AND Snake Perkins had abducted and murdered four children without any witnesses or interference—either before, during, or after their evil deeds. They had taken great pains to remain unobserved, of course, but they had also had, perhaps literally, the Devil's own luck.

On a moonlit night near Cranston, Rhode Island, their luck ran out.

"JESUS CHRIST, TOMMY, this is starting to remind me of high school," Marcie said. The dirt road was reasonably wide, but still overhung by trees. The only illumination came from the car's headlights and the full moon that peeked between the branches as they drove.

"Not my fault your fuckin' roomie decided not to go home this weekend," Tommy Hambledon said. He proceeded slowly, looking for a good spot—something private but not too spooky. "We could've gone to my room, you know, like we did last time."

She made a snorting sound. "I am not going to walk past those assholes in your suite when I'm leaving. Uh-uh." She made her voice deeper and husky. "Hey baby, how about sloppy seconds? Show you what a *real* man can do."

"I took care of that, just like I told you. I made it real clear to Mitch that I was gonna kick his ass from here to Providence, he ever talked to you like that again. He knows I'll do it, too."

The sign they had just passed read "County Reservoir, 1/4 Mile."

"Fine. So now him and the other two jerks can just give me those shit-ass grins as I walk past. I don't think so."

"Okay, okay. Hey, this looks like a nice spot, huh? Real quiet, moon shining on the water and stuff. Kinda romantic, dontcha think?" He brought the car to a slow stop and turned off the engine.

Marcie gave serious consideration to just calling the whole thing off and making Tommy drive them back to campus. There was a movie showing at the Student Union that she'd wanted to see when it first came out, or maybe she and Tommy could go to the Rathskeller, have a few beers, and dance instead. But then she thought about the way Tommy's big cock felt inside her, and the things he could do with his tongue...

"Turn on the radio, not too loud," she said. "I always liked that, in high school."

SNAKE PERKINS DIDN'T see the pothole in this crappy dirt road until it was too late, and the Lincoln jolted a little as its big, soft springs compensated for the sudden dip. Cecelia Mbwato shifted position, which caused the knives and other metal implements in her bag to rub against each other audibly.

She bit back the acid comment she was going to make about Snake's driving. Their association was almost done, and there was no sense in provoking the white fool unnecessarily. Instead, she asked, "You are sure there is water up here?"

"Sure is," Snake said. "A whole damn reservoir full of it—least, there was this afternoon, and I don't figure they drained it since then. Nice and quiet, too. Nobody hardly comes up here at all, far as I can tell."

"All is very well, then," she said. It was the closest thing to a compliment she had ever paid him.

Snake went back to listening to Jerry Jeff Walker in concert, a show that he alone could hear. He was quietly relieved that his job was almost over. After four deaths, soon to be five, even he was starting to get sick of the constant smell of blood in his nostrils.

MARCIE TUCKER HAD removed her skirt and the thong she wore underneath it. She lay sideways on the front seat, her head and shoulders against the passenger door, one arm braced on the dash and the other clutching the seat back, her legs spread wide and Tommy's head between them.

He was taking his time, teasing her the way she liked, licking fast then slowly, up and down, then side to side, the tip of his tongue making circles and zigzags and figure eights, and Marcie was building toward one hell of an orgasm when from between her half-closed eyelids she saw the headlights.

"Tommy!" she whispered urgently.

"What is it? What's wrong?"

"Car!"

"Oh, fuck goddammit shit!"

He squirmed up past the steering wheel and looked out through the windshield. The other car had come to a stop on the opposite side of the reservoir, maybe 300 feet away. It was parked at an angle, so its headlights did not shine directly toward them.

"Cops, do you think?" Marcie asked.

"I dunno. If it is, he hasn't got his red lights going."

"How the hell did he get up here? He didn't pass us!"

"There's another road up, from the Cranston side. Must've come up that way."

"And how do you know about that?" she asked archly. "Brought a lot of girls up here, did you?"

"A bunch of us guys used to swim in the reservoir during the summers, all right? Jeez!"

Marcie looked over at the headlights again. "Why's he just stopped there?"

"Maybe it's a couple, came up here for the same reason we did, before we got so rudely interrupted." He started to slide his hand up her bare thigh.

"Stop it!" The sudden appearance of the other car, along with the fear of imminent arrest, had been like a bucket of cold water thrown on Marcie's libido. "If they came up here to fool around, then why keep the lights on?"

"Beats the shit out of me," Tommy said, irritation creeping into his voice. "Look, why don't we just—"

"Somebody just walked in front of the lights. See? And now another one. There's two people over there, Tommy. What the hell are they doing, this time of night?"

"Maybe they want to get busy outside, instead of in their car. Who cares? Speaking of getting busy—"

"In the wet grass? It rained most of the day."

With an effort, Tommy managed to sound patient as he said, "Could be they brought a blanket, or something. Marcie, come on. Forget about those—"

Then the awful screaming started from across the reservoir. Tommy Hambledon didn't know it yet, but it was a sound that was going to haunt his nightmares for a long time to come.

"NINE-ONE-ONE operator. How may I assist you?"

"Uh, I—I need the police, I guess."

"And what is the nature of your emergency, sir?"

"I guess, uh, I don't know exactly."

"I will need more information if I am going to dispatch someone to your location, sir."

"Cranston Reservoir. Send 'em to the Cranston Reservoir. The uh, west side, yeah, the west side of Cranston Reservoir."

"I need to know why you require police assistance at this time, sir."

"Somebody was, I mean there was like screaming, it just went on and on. Sounded like a kid, maybe, but we couldn't be sure. Oh, God, please, just send the cops, will you?"

"You are reporting screams from the west side of Cranston Reservoir? Is that correct, sir?"

"Yeah, yeah, how many times do I have to fuckin' say it? Some kid was screaming, not like he was fooling around, like kids do, I mean, it was like he was *dying*, or something. Or she, I dunno, I couldn't tell. And then it just, like stopped, as if he had, oh Jesus, God. And there was a car over there, we saw two people get out of this big car, and then the screaming started and for Christ's sake, will you just fuckin' *send* somebody? Please?"

"I am dispatching a unit to your location now, sir."

VAN DREENAN LOOKED at Fenton's haggard face and said, "You should go and get some sleep, my friend. It's late."

Fenton waved away the suggestion. "I grabbed a couple of hours this afternoon. Besides, if this is gonna go down, it'll be at night, just like all the others."

Van Dreenan nodded slowly. "Yes, I expect you are right."

"How about you? You could go back to your hotel, catch a few z's. I'll call you if anything breaks."

"Thank you, but no. I find that I do not sleep much anymore."

Ten minutes later, Fenton was amusing himself, and possibly even Van Dreenan, by telling a very involved and highly obscene joke.

"So now they're all standing there, right? Dad, Mom, the two kids, Grandma, and the family dog. Naked, panting, dripping with sweat and two or three other fluids, besides. And the talent agent says, 'That's quite an act you've got there. What do you folks call yourselves?' And the father says—"

Then the phone rang.

Fenton grabbed it on the first ring. "Yeah?"

He spent the next minute or so listening intently, occasionally making notes on a legal pad.

"How far a drive is it from the field office to the scene, for somebody using lights and a siren? Yeah? Okay, have a car meet us at the Providence airport, the chopper pad. I want it gassed up, and somebody behind the wheel who knows the way to the crime scene and can get us there fast, okay? Appreciate it."

As soon as the line was clear, Fenton tapped in a three-digit number.

"This is Fenton. Get the chopper warmed up. Destination is the main landing pad at the Providence, Rhode Island airport, whatever its name is. They can't have more than one, a dinky state like that. I wanna be there ten minutes ago. Right, thanks."

Van Dreenan was already on his feet. "I take it something has happened."

"You take it right." Fenton was quickly stowing items in his briefcase, including case files, his laptop, and two clips of 9 mm ammunition for his Glock. "Cranston, Rhode Island," he said tersely. "Some kids from URI were up at the reservoir, gettin' it on in a parked car. Then our perps came along, oblivious, and did their last victim, like a hundred yards away. Kids heard the screams and called nine-one-one."

Fenton looked at his watch. "We're less than an hour behind them. Let's roll."

Van Dreenan had a briefcase of his own that he had taken to carrying around with him lately, although he had never opened it in Fenton's presence. He quickly grabbed the handle and his voice was tight with excitement as he said, "Ready when you are, *baas*."

CHAPTER 25

"CAN'T GO TOO fast up here," Special Agent Spencer said. He had a broad Down East accent that made him sound like he should be selling "clam chowdah" on TV. "Too damn many potholes. The county doesn't exactly spend a mint keeping these access roads in shape."

"Just do the best you can, man," Fenton said. "Nobody's interested in having us getting a punctured oil pan." He peered through the windshield, trying to see ahead, past the reach of the headlights. "Looks like we're almost there, anyway."

"Ayuh. Couple of minutes, max."

The road soon began to level off; shortly afterward, they could see moonlight on water.

"This is it," Spencer said.

Van Dreenan had sat silently in the back seat during the urgent drive from Providence. Now he leaned forward and placed a hand on Spencer's shoulder. "I want to thank you for getting us here so quickly, Agent Spencer. If you ever decide to leave law enforcement, I believe you might easily find employment in Hollywood, as a car handler."

Seeing the quizzical expression on Spencer's face, Fenton said, "I think he means 'stunt driver.'"

"Oh, right. Hey, it was kind of fun. I don't get to use the flashing light and siren much. It was cool, watching everybody get out of the way."

"You know we're taking the car, right?"

"Sure, no sweat. I'll get a ride back with one of the other guys."

Spencer brought the car to a stop amidst half a dozen other official vehicles—state, local, and unmarked federal. They all had their lights flashing, which turned the crime scene into something that looked like a fundamentalist's notion of Hell.

Fenton and Van Dreenan got out of the car and followed Spencer to the ranking FBI man on the scene, who turned out to be a woman.

Special Agent Rita Garber was a taller-than-average blonde with short hair, a dark suit, and a hard-looking face. Van Dreenan thought the hardness might be temporary, caused by what she had been dealing with for the last hour. He wondered what she looked like when she relaxed, assuming she ever did.

Spencer performed introductions. Agent Garber looked at Van Dreenan longer than she needed to, clearly curious about what a South African cop was doing at the crime scene.

"You didn't say anything on the phone about leaving the body of the vic in place," she said to Fenton, "so I let the local law send her to the morgue. Coroner'll do the autopsy tonight or tomorrow—I can find out when and where, if you guys want to be there."

"That won't be necessary, but thanks," Fenton said. He looked over at the patch of ground that was cordoned off by the yellow tape. "Is forensics done with the scene?"

"Done and gone," Agent Garber said. "Theirs and ours, both."

Fenton looked at Van Dreenan, then without a word the two of them went over to the bare patch of earth, lifted the crime scene tape, and ducked under it.

It didn't take them long to observe the essentials: the four tent stakes driven deep into the ground, the torn-up earth around it, the footprints in the muddy soil. The blood had long since soaked into the earth, but each man would have sworn on a Bible that he could still smell the thick, coppery odor.

They had seen it all before. Four other times, to be exact—either in photos, or up close and personal.

Van Dreenan had produced a small but powerful flashlight and was shining it around the immediate area. Suddenly, the moving beam of light stopped. "Fenton."

Van Dreenan's light was focusing on the array of footprints in the soft earth. There were many around the crime scene, made by the police, the coroner's people, the forensics techs, and God knows who else. But one set of footprints stood out clearly from all the others.

The feet that had made them were bare.

They walked quickly back to Agent Garber. "Pictures?" Fenton asked.

"Over here," she said. They followed her to one of the unmarked cars. A laptop computer was open on the hood, a thin, balding man wearing FBI creds hunched over it, typing.

"Connor, show these officers the photos of the scene that our people took earlier," Garber told him.

"Sure, boss, no prob," the man said. He worked with the mouse and the keys for a few moments, then a photo of the area, a wide-angle establishing shot, appeared on the computer screen. The resolution was good, the details clear.

"We've got, I think, forty-eight, all told," he said. "You guys want to see 'em all?"

"No," Van Dreenan told him. "Just the photos of the body, please. Close-ups of the wounds, if you have them."

Agent Connor stared at the South African for a moment, then said, "Yeah, sure, we got 'em. Give me a second."

Four minutes later, Van Dreenan and Fenton were in the car that had brought them, heading back down the hill as fast as Fenton could safely drive.

"All right," Fenton said. "We've been to the scene, and we're sure it was Snake and Cecelia again. The witnesses said the car went back down this way, so we're following the same route the perps took. But we're almost two hours behind them now, man. It's a pretty cold trail."

"Not as cold as you might imagine. They will not have left the area immediately following the murder."

"Why the fuck not?"

"Because she still needs to perform the ritual of incorporating the stolen organs into the fetish she is making. That is the object of the murders, remember."

"Yeah, but they could drive a hundred miles before they stop to take care of business." Fenton swerved to avoid a pothole the size of a garbage can lid.

"But they won't. For maximum effectiveness, the ritual must be performed while the organs are still... fresh." Van Dreenan swallowed hard, hoping that Fenton didn't notice. "And, bear in mind that our friends are in no great hurry. They have no idea that they were observed this time by those university students."

"How can you be sure?"

"Because those two young people are still alive."

"Yeah, I guess you've got a point," Fenton said. "So, okay, the trail is fairly fresh, then. What the hell do we do about it?"

"We track them, of course." Van Dreenan had his briefcase in his lap and was fiddling with the latches in the uncertain light.

"And just how do we do that, O great detective?"

There was a loud "click" as the lid of the case popped open. "With this."

CHRISTINE ABERNATHY WAS watching a documentary on the History Channel about medieval torture devices when a thin yellow banner appeared at the bottom of the picture. It was a function of the news alert service that she subscribed to as part of her cable package. A moment later, the story began snaking its way from right to left across the foot of the screen:

> R.I. POLICE REPORT FINDING THE BODY OF A MURDERED CHILD NEAR CRANSTON RESERVOIR IN THAT STATE. PRELIMINARY REPORTS SUGGEST THAT THE VICTIM WAS THE LATEST IN A SERIES OF CHILD MURDERS/MUTILATIONS THAT HAVE PLAGUED THE NORTHEAST IN RECENT WEEKS. THE VICTIM, SUSAN ANN MAISANO, 11, WAS REPORTED MISSING FROM THE YARD OF HER PARENTS' HOME EARLIER TODAY. ACCORDING TO THE PROVIDENCE FIELD OFFICE OF THE FBI, AGENTS ARE PURSUING A NUMBER OF LEADS AND ARE EXPECTED TO MAKE...

Christine Abernathy now had a contented smile on her face. Unless she was very much mistaken, that made five victims, which meant that all of the components of the magical fetish would soon be ready for her. And Rhode Island—so close! She might even be able to take delivery tonight.

Walter Grobius would be eager to meet with her—and would be sure to bring his checkbook. And before passing her prize along to him, Christine would use its power to smash the wards protecting the LaRues, and then to crush the LaRues themselves, putting an end to her family's centuries-long vendetta. Afterwards, she would see about those interfering dilettantes Chastain and Morris.

Christine Abernathy looked at her watch and frowned, wondering if she had time to wash her hair before company arrived.

IN YET ANOTHER bargain-basement motel room, Cecelia Mbwato tied the last string to bind her fifth and final sorcerer's fetish. Then she blew out the squat, black candle and extinguished the stick of incense she had been burning.

She had started putting her implements away when Snake Perkins came out of her bathroom, where he had been washing away the blood that had got on his hands while he assisted in the ritual.

"You may as well go to your room and pack," she said, sounding almost polite. "I will be ready shortly, and then we can be off to Salem to deliver the material and collect our payment."

"Sounds good," Snake said. He left, and walked the twenty feet to his own room. Packing his grip wouldn't take long, but he turned on the TV, anyway. The late local news should be doing their sports segment right about now, and Snake wanted to see if his Braves had beaten the despised Yankees.

He had just opened his small suitcase on the bed when he realized that the news broadcast wasn't doing sports, after all.

CECELIA MBWATO ANSWERED the knock at her door, wondering why Snake's rapping sounded so urgent. Her insides went tight when she saw his grim expression. "Got us a little problem," he told her. "Put the TV on, Channel 5."

She wasted no time in questions, and a few moments later they were watching a young woman with a microphone, doing a live report from a location that looked all too familiar.

"—are releasing few details at this time. They have refused thus far to confirm or deny that this horrible murder fits the pattern of the so-called 'Water Killer,' who has abducted, murdered, and mutilated several other children in Eastern states over the last few weeks, leaving their bodies near water each time. The college students who observed the crime from a safe distance have declined to be interviewed on camera, but one of them has told Channel Five Action News that she has never heard anything as horrible as the—"

Cecelia Mbwato swore a series of terrible oaths in Zulu. Then she took a couple of deep breaths to calm herself before saying to Snake, "The car. Have they said anything about the car?"

"Nothin' that I've heard so far."

"They may still have knowledge of it—the car and the license number both." She began to pace, although the size of the room only allowed her three steps in each direction. "With these computers they have, that Internet, every policeman in this cursed country may know by now."

"Well, maybe, but I don't reckon it's real—"

"We were seen." She stopped and stood facing him. For the first time since he had known her, her face showed something besides contempt, or malice, or simple concentration. Now it was showing something that looked a lot like fear. "Do you not understand? We were *seen!*"

Snake Perkins actually experienced a momentary urge to comfort her in her distress. But he crushed it, as he had always done with such feelings, and instead put his mind to the problem at hand. Cecelia Mbwato had resumed pacing, and she had made four more trips back and forth across the worn carpet before Snake said, "Be right back," turned to the door, and went out.

He was gone just long enough for her to start wondering whether he had decided to cut his losses and run, leaving her for the police. Then he came back in, carrying the battered Rand-McNally road atlas that she remembered seeing in the car.

He went over to the rickety table they had earlier used to perform the ritual, quickly flipped through the atlas's pages, then put it down, open, on the table. "Lookee here," he said to Cecelia Mbwato.

She saw that he had opened the atlas to a double-page spread showing Rhode Island and Massachusetts. Snake's index finger stabbed down to a point near West Warwick, Rhode Island. "We're here, okay?" Then the finger moved six or seven inches. "Over here's Salem."

His finger traced along the line indicating Route 95. "Most direct route, and the fastest, is along the major highways. If they's watchin' for us, that's mostly where they gonna do it. Hell, there's state cops along there all the time anyways, lookin' for speeders. We pass one of them ol' boys, and he's got us on his hot sheet, then we're fucked, plain and simple."

Cecelia Mbwato had regained some of her composure now. "You should steal another license plate and switch them, as you did the last time."

"I was plannin' to do just that," Snake told her. "But that don't buy us as much as you might think. Can't be that many '97 Connies painted British racing green on the road. And those with a white guy and a black woman inside, gonna be even less. Cops might just pull over anything matches that description, so's they can check IDs and registration. They do that, and we're right back to being fucked again."

"So what do you suggest we do?"

"First thing, we travel only at night. Make it harder for anybody to see who's inside the Connie. That means we ain't gonna hit Salem until tomorrow night, seein' as it's about two hours 'til sunup right now."

"All right," she said. "That makes sense, even if it does delay us."

"Second thing," Snake said, "is we forget about the interstates and turnpikes. We use secondary roads only, the more secondary the better. Smaller towns, the cops is less likely to be keepin' their eyes out for us. Can't spare the manpower. And if one of 'em does pull us over—" he glanced toward what he had taken to calling Cecelia Mbwato's "bag of tricks," "well, we got a better chance of dealin' with him 'fore he puts out a call for help to the other little pigs."

She pulled in a big breath and let it out. "Very well. That is a sensible plan. I agree."

Snake grinned at her. "Figured you would. Well, you'd best finish packin'." He went to the door, then turned back before opening it. "Me, I got some license plates to liberate."

CHAPTER 26

IN ORDER TO avoid wrapping the car around a tree, Fenton was only able to spare quick glances toward the object that Van Dreenan had produced from his briefcase, but the first glimpse was enough to tell him that it was like nothing he had ever seen before.

"I was just about to say," he said, watching the road again, "that you have got to be kidding me. But by now, I guess I know better. You're serious as hell, aren't you?"

"I am," Van Dreenan replied. "And Hell is very serious, indeed, as we both have reason to know."

"And we're going to use that thing to find two serial murderers."

"Such is my devout hope. And didn't we agree that you were going to keep an open mind?"

Fenton shook his head a couple of times, a gesture that said as clearly as words, "What have I gotten myself into?" "Yeah," he said. "I guess I did." The headshake again. "Just remind me not to put any of this in my report."

He glanced again at the apparatus that Van Dreenan was now holding in his lap, atop the closed lid of his briefcase. "You wanna tell me how that contraption is supposed to work?"

The main part of the device was a carved wooden semicircle, like a capital "C," that was about six inches from tip to tip.

Arcane symbols had been carved into the wood, and one arm was flattened on the bottom so that the whole thing could stand upright by itself. The two ends of the "C" were connected by a thin length of rigid filament that might have been piano wire. Before being attached to the frame, the wire had been used to skewer another piece of wood that was the general shape of a pencil or stake, an impression strengthened by the sharp-looking point carved at one end. This component was able to pivot freely in the frame, using the wire as an axis. The pencil-shaped piece of wood was wrapped with something that looked like black thread.

"I cannot explain the magical aspect," Van Dreenan said. "For that, you would need to talk with Elizabeth Chastain, the woman who made it for me, or to some other practitioner of so-called 'white' witchcraft. But for practical purposes, this device is a locator. It has been attuned to one person only, and that person is Cecelia Mbwato."

Fenton risked another quick look before turning back to the road. "How the hell did she do that?" he asked. "Or is that part of the magic stuff you can't explain?"

"This pointer here—" Van Dreenan touched the pencil-shaped piece of wood, "—is wrapped in hair belonging to Cecelia Mbwato. Elizabeth used what she called an affinity spell on it. Simply put, like attracts like."

"I remember you gave me some of that bitch's hair to pass on to Forensics for DNA analysis. What'd you do, hold out on me?"

"I did no such thing, my friend. The FBI lab got all the hair it needed for its various procedures. I simply asked Sergeant Shemba to send along some extra from the evidence file."

"Sergeant Shemba. I think I remember hearing about him."

"Indeed you did," Van Dreenan said. "A good man."

"So this thing is supposed to act like a compass, except instead of pointing due north, it points toward Cecelia fucking Mbwato?"

"An excellent analogy, and very astute. That is precisely what it does."

"How can you be sure the thing's gonna work?"

"It is already working."

There was a moment's silence in the car. "And you know that how?"

"You did not notice, because you were wisely concentrating on this miserable road," Van Dreenan said. "But when I removed this device from my case, the indicator happened to be pointing toward you. Observe, please, which way it is aiming now."

Fenton glanced over. "It's pointing out the windshield, toward the front of the car."

"And we already know that our quarry left the reservoir using this route. The witnesses have said so."

"Uh-huh. I don't mean to be the pimple on the ass of this little expedition, but that could be just coincidence, man."

"Indeed, it could. But the end of this road is coming up, I am glad to see. Let us see what happens when we reach the point where it intersects with the perpendicular road below, and a choice of directions must be made."

As the car approached the paved thoroughfare that ran left to right across the end of the access road, Fenton slowed to a crawl. He wanted to watch the locater without risking an accident with the car. The moon was bright enough that he could see without having to put on the dome light and ruin his night vision.

Just as the car's front wheels left the dirt road for the asphalt of the newer one, the pointer, of its own volition, turned to the left. Van Dreenan's hand, Fenton was sure, had not touched it, or tilted the frame.

Fenton blinked rapidly a couple of times. Then he took in a big breath, let it out, and said, "Guess we'd better turn left, huh?"

"A wise choice."

And so they went, off into the darkness.

THE SUN HAD been up for about half an hour when Snake Perkins came out of the Shamrock Motel's office dangling a room key between two fingers. He walked the fifty or so feet to where he had left the Connie, opened the door, and slid behind the wheel. He said to Cecelia Mbwato, "Usual check-in time's noon or later, so I had to pay the bastard extra, but it's worth it for us to get out of sight for a while."

"Just one room this time, yes?"

"Yeah, like we talked about. It'll draw less attention. So I registered us as Mr. and Mrs."

Cecelia Mbwato made a grunting sound that could have meant anything.

"And since I parked out of sight from the office window, Mister Motel Manager didn't get a look at who the 'Mrs.' is. Not that he probably gives a damn."

Snake started the engine and drove around to the back of the one-story building, where he pulled up in front of room 119. "I told the guy we wouldn't be needin' any maid service. Kinda gave him a wink when I said it, so he most likely figures we're gonna be spending the day in there, well, you know."

"Fucking," Cecelia said. Her voice and face were both lacking in expression.

"Well, uh, yeah, something like that."

Snake pulled the room key out of his pocket. "I'm gonna get the door open and bring our stuff inside. Then I'll take a quick look around, to be sure nobody's paying us any attention. When I give you the wave, come on in the room. Don't run or nothin', but don't dawdle neither. Okay?"

"Yes, fine, go ahead."

A few minutes later, Snake was closing the door of room 119, Cecelia Mbwato safely inside with him. "There's some fast food restaurants down the street," he said. "Later on, I'll take a walk over there, get us something to eat, and bring it back. But right now, I could use a shower and some sleep. How 'bout you?"

She nodded. "Yes, I am very tired, also."

Snake hesitated briefly before saying, "Well, there's just the one bed. But we're both grown up and all. I reckon we can manage without getting all dainty about it."

"Yes, no doubt."

Twenty minutes later, freshly showered and wearing only his undershorts, Snake slipped into the double bed, where Cecelia Mbwato appeared to be already asleep. He had, in fact, been feeling a little uneasy about the sleeping arrangements, but not for the obvious reason.

Snake had grown up believing that all black people smelled bad, even when, like Cecelia, they had recently showered. That was just how they were. In the car, he had kept his window down to avoid having to smell her, but now it was unavoidable. However, he was pleasantly surprised to find that Cecelia Mbwato did not stink. She smelled faintly of cinnamon, and nothing else. *Just goes to show you,* he thought.

He turned on his side away from her and was, in fact, on the point of dropping off when he felt her weight shift on the mattress next to him. A moment later he became aware of her arm sliding around his waist. Then, after a few second's fumbling under the sheet, he felt her fingers encircle his penis, which immediately began to come erect.

Her voice in his ear was hardly louder than a whisper when she said, "There is more than one way to pass the time."

QUINCEY MORRIS FOLLOWED Libby Chastain out the front door of her apartment building and onto the sidewalk. Both of them had to squint against the morning sunlight.

"Where's our best bet for getting a cab?" he asked.

"Down the street and around the corner," Libby said. "It'll be quicker than phoning for one, this time of day."

As they walked, Morris adjusted the strap of his carry-on bag. "Your sofa is more comfortable than it looks," he said. "Thanks for the use of it."

"My pleasure. No point in running up expenses on the LaRues unnecessarily. Besides, I think it's wise for us to stay together until this business is settled."

"Yeah, I hear you. Well, maybe we can *get* it settled, now that we finally know where to go."

They moved to one side to make room for a pretty young woman who was walking six dogs at once, three leashes per hand.

"Salem, of all places," Libby said, once the dog walker had passed. "Talk about hiding in plain sight." She frowned briefly. "Who said that, anyway? 'Hide in plain sight?'"

Morris thought for a moment. "Don't know. It was Poe came up with the idea, in 'The Purloined Letter.' But I don't think he used that expression. I have a feeling it originated later."

"Well, Christine Abernathy's days of hiding would seem to be just about over," Libby said. "Did you know she's even listed? I called Directory Assistance and checked while you were in the shower."

"Bet she doesn't advertise in the Yellow Pages, though."

"No, I don't think even Ms. Abernathy has that much in the way of balls."

"Sure you don't mean 'ovaries?' That's the politically correct term when referring to a woman, isn't it?"

"I suppose it is," Libby said. "But what I meant was *balls*."

TERMINUS
CONFRONTATION

CHAPTER 27

In the basement of a house in Salem, Massachusetts, Christine Abernathy sat peering into a large ceramic bowl on the table before her. The vessel was decorated with a variety of cryptic symbols that had been applied with fresh baby's blood shortly after the bowl had been made, some two hundred and eighty years earlier.

Five squat black candles burned on the table, their light reflecting on the surface of the dark liquid that filled the bowl almost to the brim. The odor given off by the liquid was a pungent combination of kerosene and sulfur.

She added ingredients from several jars and bottles nearby, making complex signs with each addition and murmuring all the while in ancient Chaldean, a tongue that was archaic when Christianity was still young.

Some say that it was the language used by a certain serpent when it came to tempt a naive young woman, in a garden long ago.

After the fifth ingredient had been added, the liquid suddenly cleared. On its surface appeared a moving image, almost as if a small television had been somehow turned on within the bowl itself.

The image showed a slim man with black hair and a tall, brown-haired woman. They each carried a suitcase and appeared to be walking along an urban sidewalk.

The powerful fetish she had been expecting from Cecelia Mbwato had not been delivered the night before. Christine Abernathy very much hoped, for everyone's sake, that nothing had gone wrong, and that her two associates had only been delayed. She would wait until she had the fetish in her possession before taking definitive steps against the LaRues, but overnight she had developed an idea for dealing with Morris and Chastain. It was now time to make it work.

Christine Abernathy spoke three more words and made a gesture with both hands over the bowl. The focus of the image began to broaden, as if a lens were being adjusted and pulled back for a wider view.

She could see the street now, and the busy traffic that traversed it, stopped now for a red light. She scanned the line of cars quickly, then seemed to settle on one, a blue SUV. Eyes narrowed, Christine began to speak loudly and very fast, all her considerable power focused on that one vehicle—and its driver.

ARCH TRACY WAS worried. Traffic was backed up, and if he was late again, which would be the third time this month, he was going to get a load of shit from Puckett, the foreman. They wouldn't fire him, not for that—he was one of the best welders they had, even that fucking Puckett had said so once. Besides it was a union shop, which meant to get fired Tracy would have to stick his torch up Puckett's fat ass and then give the gas valve a good, hard squeeze. A smile twitched across Arch Tracy's face as his mind entertained the image. *Might almost be worth it. Hell, I can always get another job.*

Some impulse caused him to look off to the right, where the pedestrians were making their way along the sidewalk. This being New York and rush hour, most of them were moving along pretty briskly.

Cooper's gaze suddenly focused on two people walking together, a man and a woman. He'd never set eyes on either one before, but somehow looking at them now set his teeth on edge. He couldn't have said what it was—they were probably just a couple of wage slaves on their way to work, a tall guy and a woman who was almost the same height.

But there was something about them that just pissed Arch Tracy off.

As they drew closer to where the SUV sat stuck in traffic, Tracy's irritation quickly progressed to anger, and then rage. He found himself consumed with irrational hatred for that tall asshole and the bitch with him, and they were suddenly all the people who had ever hurt him, scared him, embarrassed him, made him feel like nothing more than a dog turd fit only to be scraped off your shoes.

Tracy was staring at the couple now, seeing them as if through a red haze. His breath was coming in short gasps, his pulse pounding like a crazed drummer in his ears.

Suddenly, without any conscious decision on his part, Arch Tracy wrenched the wheel of the SUV hard to the right, making the power steering scream with the strain. A moment later his foot, seemingly of its own volition, moved from the brake pedal to the gas.

And then he floored it.

IT WAS THE screech of overburdened power steering that caused Quincey Morris to glance toward the street, and that was the only thing that saved him. He saw the blue SUV suddenly pull out of the line of idling cars and make a screaming beeline for the sidewalk, picking up speed alarmingly fast.

It was headed right at him and Libby.

Even Morris's hair-trigger reactions gave him precious little time to do anything. As the SUV bore down on them, he yelled "Libby!" and shoved her hard to his left, an instant before making his own desperate dive to the right. In the midst of this flurry of movement he got a fraction of a second's glimpse of the SUV's driver, whose face was distorted into a mask full of the kind of rage and pain that you rarely see outside of an asylum.

Morris tried to turn his dive into a tuck and roll, but the small suitcase hanging on his shoulder made that impossible. He hit the pavement with the suitcase underneath him, bounced off it, and slid several feet—until he was abruptly stopped by the impact of his head against the base of a lamppost.

After that, things got kind of hazy for a while.

He was vaguely aware of the sounds of impact as the SUV smashed headlong through the front of Del Floria's Tailor Shop, which lay just beyond where Morris and Libby had been walking. He could hear the SUV's horn then, a blaring monotone that went on and on until somebody must have pulled the driver's body off the steering wheel. A while after that, Morris couldn't have said how long it was, came the peal of sirens which gradually grew louder before suddenly ceasing altogether, to be replaced by a hurly-burly of flashing lights, slamming doors, and shouted orders.

And, semiconscious though he was, Morris lay there on the pavement and grieved. Because from the section of sidewalk where he had desperately shoved Libby Chastain, there was silence. And silence. And silence, still.

IT HAD JUST gone one in the afternoon when Fenton and Van Dreenan followed Route 1 through Peterborough, Massachusetts. The pointer on Van Dreenan's magical device was aimed straight ahead, so they assumed they were still on the right track.

"I don't know where our friends are headed," Fenton said, "but they sure as hell don't seem to be in any big hurry to get there. We haven't hit anything bigger than a two-lane road since we left Cranston."

"It is curious," Van Dreenan said. "Regardless of where their rendezvous is, there are surely faster ways to get there than the route they are following. One assumes they would be in a hurry."

"I don't suppose this would be a good time for me to wonder aloud whether that magical doohickey is doing what it's supposed to?"

Van Dreenan shrugged his big shoulders. "You either believe, or you don't," he said. "Me, I believe—perhaps because I have nothing else left. In any case, my friend, we are surely committed now."

"I just hope somebody in the upper echelons of the Bureau doesn't end up deciding that we ought to *be* committed." Fenton have a shrug of his own. "You're right, though. Fuck it. The cards've been dealt, and we put down our bets. All we can do now is play them."

A few minutes later, Van Dreenan's stomach made a noise like a small building collapsing. "Excuse me," he said with a grimace.

"Hungry?" Fenton asked. "Me, too. I haven't eaten since dinner yesterday, which was—" he checked the dashboard clock, "about seventeen hours ago."

"I don't think that stopping for food is a good idea, considering the circumstances. I imagine you have been hungry before, as have I. We survived it. We will this time, too."

"Yeah, but hunger equals low blood sugar, which equals loss of concentration and slower reaction time. And if we do catch up to these motherfuckers, we had damn well better bring our 'A' game, 'cause from what I've seen we are sure gonna need it."

"I did not understand that in all its particulars," Van Dreenan said, "but I believe I grasp your meaning. And I do not disagree. But I still do not think we can spare—"

"Tell you what," Fenton said. "Let's keep our eyes open for a fast food place that doesn't look busy. We stop, run in—well, maybe I run in, while you stay here and babysit that thing—I buy a bunch of food to go and bring it back here. Since eating while driving isn't real safe, you eat while I drive, then I pull over someplace, we switch places, and I eat while you drive. Total time lost, five minutes, tops. What do you think?"

"I think I want you at the table the next time my police union is negotiating its contract with the government," Van Dreenan said. "You're right, it's a good idea. Let us, as you say, keep our eyes open for a likely place."

A few minutes later, Fenton was stopped for a red light at an intersection and peering ahead through the windshield. "That looks like a Wendy's, up there on the right. See it? I'll cruise the parking lot, and you take a look inside, see how crowded it is."

"Fine with me," Van Dreenan said. He began to stow the magical tracker back inside his briefcase.

The light changed, and Fenton eased into the intersection. Perhaps his blood sugar really was low, or it may have been that thoughts of a double cheeseburger and large fries had him distracted.

For whatever reason, he reacted slowly, far too slowly, when the teenage boy in the pimped-out Camaro ran the red light and came streaking right toward them.

THE SMALL, BRIGHT light shined into Morris's right eye, went away, then came back. A moment later, the same procedure was repeated with his left eye.

"You're a lucky man, Mr. Morris," the doctor said, replacing the penlight in the pocket of his starched lab coat. "There's no sign of concussion, your reflexive responses are normal, and the EEG results are negative. How's the head feeling?"

Morris rubbed the back of his skull, where he could feel a lump the size of a ping-pong ball. "I've had a few hangovers that were worse," he said. "Although not recently."

The doctor nodded without smiling. He was a short, freckled redhead who reminded Morris of a leprechaun. His name-tag read "Rosenbloom."

"Lucky, as I said." Rosenbloom glanced at the file he was holding. "I understand you've been asking about the woman who was with you, Elizabeth Chastain."

"Yes."

"I'm afraid Miss Chastain was not so fortunate."

Morris felt a tight, hard knot form in the pit of his stomach. Trying to hold his voice steady he asked, "Dead?"

"No, she's alive, although I'm told it was touch and go there for a while."

The knot loosened, a little. "Is she going to make it?"

"She's not my patient, you understand. Doctor Stanhope headed the team that treated her, and he's currently in the middle of treating a gunshot victim. But I was able to get a look at Miss Chastain's chart before I came in here. She sustained severe injuries, but they've got her stabilized now. I'd say the prognosis is... fair."

"You said 'severe injuries.' How severe?"

Rosenbloom frowned with concentration. "The chart mentioned a ruptured spleen, perforated large bowel, and some kidney damage. Internal bleeding, but that's under control. Plus two, no, three cracked ribs and a fractured right fibula."

"Come again on that last one?"

Rosenbloom made a face. "Sorry. Broken arm."

"Can I see her?"

"She's in the ICU. Normally, they don't admit visitors who aren't members of the immediate family. They're pretty anal about it."

Morris closed his eyes for a moment. Through clenched teeth, he began, "Doctor—"

"Of course, since Miss Chastain was unconscious when admitted, they were unable to ask the usual questions about marital status, and so on. Lots of women keep their last names when they get married. If you were her husband, I could get you into the ICU to see her."

Rosenbloom looked at Morris for a long moment. "Tell me, Mr. Morris, are you Elizabeth Chastain's husband?"

Morris nodded, his face expressionless. "Yes, Doctor. Yes, I am."

"All right, then." He made a note in the file. "I'll see that you're informed as soon as she comes out of the anesthesia. In the meantime, I believe there are some people waiting to talk to you."

"Who's that?"

"A couple of detectives from the NYPD."

"You sure you don't want to go to the hospital? Either of you?" Sheriff's Deputy Tom Bernardi's eyes went from Fenton to Van Dreenan and back again. "You guys don't look so great."

"You should've seen the other guy," Fenton said, then remembered what the teenager had looked like when the emergency rescue crew had peeled him out of the wreck of his Camaro. The kid had not, apparently, been wearing his seatbelt, nor did he have the protection of airbags. "Sorry," he said. "Bad joke. No, Deputy, we're all right. Really."

Fenton had developed a bloody nose from the car's air bag exploding in his face, but the bleeding had just about stopped now. Van Dreenan, who was sitting next to him in the back of the deputy's cruiser, had a welt on the side of his face from slamming into the side window, but the ice pack provided by one of the EMTs was helping to reduce the swelling, and the South African was not exhibiting any signs of concussion. Their car, however, was likely headed for the junkyard.

"Well, if you gentlemen are going to decline transportation to the nearest medical facility, I'll need to get some information from you for the accident report."

Bernardi produced a clipboard with a number of forms clipped to it. Long, complicated-looking forms.

"Deputy, I would be really grateful if you would let us get back in touch with you later to complete the paperwork," Fenton said. "I understand that you have rules and procedures to follow, and I'm not disrespecting those. But as I told you, we're on official business, and Detective Sergeant Van Dreenan and I really need to get going."

"Are you claiming the existence of an emergency, Agent Fenton? Keeping in mind that I will be obligated to ask you for the nature of that emergency, which I will later have to verify with your superiors?"

Fenton thought about trying to explain that he and Van Dreenan were pursuing a couple of serial killers using a magical device made by a white witch, and then he thought about asking his boss at Behavioral Sciences to back him up on it.

Fenton dabbed at his nose, which no longer needed his attentions. "Can we at least expedite this as much as possible?"

"Yes, sir," Deputy Bernardi said impassively. "I'll sure do my best."

CHAPTER 28

THE YOUNG DETECTIVE with dirty-blond hair said that his name was Clark. He was tall, with the wiry build of someone whose idea of weekend fun is running in 10k races. Morris didn't quite catch the other detective's name, except that it ended in "witz." He had receding brown hair, mean-looking eyes, and a potato nose above a broad, untidy mustache. He looked twenty years older than his partner, and fifty pounds heavier.

"So, you've never met Archie Tracy, the driver of the Bronco?" Clark was consulting his notes.

"No, never," Morris told him.

"What about your friend, Miss Chastain? Did she know him?"

"Can't say for certain, but I have no reason to believe she did."

"But she lives here in the city, right? So she could have known him and just never mentioned it?"

"I reckon that's possible, yeah," Morris said.

Something-witz had been prowling the room impatiently, but now he stopped and faced Morris. "Was there any kind of interaction between you and this Tracy just before he pulled out of traffic and decided to take that shortcut on the sidewalk?"

"No, I didn't even notice him until he was heading right for us."

"Uh-huh. He didn't maybe say something through the car window when you two walked by? Something insulting to your lady friend, maybe? Something that you might've responded to by flipping him off, or saying, 'Hey, fuck you, asshole.' Something like that?"

"No, he didn't say anything," Morris said. "There was no communication at all. He just headed right for us."

Something-witz nodded, as if he found all this about as credible as the Easter Bunny. "So this hump just decides to run down a couple of people chosen at random, for no reason at all?"

"I suppose he had a reason that made sense to him, Detective, even if to nobody else. Why don't you ask him?"

"Yeah, well, we would," Something-witz said with a scowl, "except the son of a bitch is in a coma."

"From the crash?" Morris asked.

"They don't think so," Clark said. "The air bag deployed the way it was supposed to, and he had his seat belt and shoulder harness on, too. The guy's brain seems to be just—fried."

"Could be the result of a drug overdose," Morris said. "The same one that might have caused his homicidal impulse."

"Gosh, we never woulda thought of that." Something-witz's sarcasm was as ponderous as his belly.

Clark sent a long-suffering look in his partner's direction. "The toxicology reports haven't come back yet," he said to Morris. "In the meantime, we're checking to see if Tracy had any kind of mental health history. Could be that today was the day the voices in his head told him to come home to Jesus, and you and your friend were just in the wrong place at the wrong time."

"Voices in his head," Morris said thoughtfully. "Could've been something like that, couldn't it? Well, good luck with finding out."

As the two detectives left, Something-witz looked back toward Morris, saying, "Yeah, and thanks for all your *help*, pal."

FENTON WAS IN a fury as he drove the rented Ford Focus out of the Hertz lot, the tires screeching. It was 4:12pm.

"Deputy Dawg can't even loan us an official car," Fenton snarled. "All in use, he says. On official business, he says, every fucking one."

He made an abrupt left turn without signaling, cutting off two other cars and prompting much blaring of horns.

"Providence field office can't give us a car because we're outside of their area of operations. We're Boston's problem now, they say. Boston field office says they'll be *happy* to have someone bring us over a car—tomorrow, or maybe the day after."

"It will not help our situation if you marry this vehicle to a light pole by driving like a maniac," Van Dreenan said mildly. "Besides, I believe I have good news."

"Well thank God and Sonny Jesus for *that,* because I could sure as shit use me some good news right about now!"

Van Dreenan said nothing, and it was quiet in the car for a few moments. Then Fenton carefully reduced the speed to something more reasonable, and took a couple of deliberate deep breaths.

"Sorry," he said. "You're the last person in the world who deserves to get a bunch of shit from me. I'm sorry, man."

"Entirely understandable," Van Dreenan said. "Forget it. Now as to the good news, there are actually two items."

"I'm listening."

"The first is that Elizabeth's locator was protected by my briefcase and undamaged in the accident. I have checked it, very carefully."

"That's good, although I don't know what fucking difference it makes now."

"The other item is in the context of what you Yanks call 'good news and bad news.' The bad news is that you and I are idiots."

"I've been suspecting that about us, especially lately."

"The good news is that I think we might still be able to catch up with Cecelia Mbwato and her companion."

MORRIS STOOD WATCHING Libby Chastain for what seemed like a long time. Her bed in the Intensive Care Unit was surrounded on three sides by expensive-looking machines that peeped and beeped and traced wavy lines on a series of small screens. An IV drip slowly fed some kind of clear liquid into her left arm.

Libby's blackened eyes were so prominent they made her look like a raccoon, or a burglar out of some old animated cartoon. A large gauze bandage covered much of the left side of her face. Her right arm was in a cast, and Morris could only speculate on the other damage that was hidden underneath the thin hospital blanket.

The nurses had vowed to chuck him out instantly if he tried to wake Libby up. And so he waited.

Then he noticed the pattern on one of the electronic monitors changing. The shallow curves it had been tracing gradually became deeper. Morris was wondering what it meant, and whether he should call for somebody, when Libby said softly, "How you doing, kiddo?"

Morris stepped closer to the bed. "You don't know how glad I am to hear your voice—even if you do sound like you've been gargling with Drano."

"Kind of feels like it, too."

Morris shook his head slowly. "Libby, I am so sorry about this."

"Could be... worse, I guess. Would be, too, 'cept for those... lightning reflexes of yours. That's twice, now. I owe you."

Morris felt his throat tighten, and he had to wait a long moment before trusting himself to speak again. "You don't owe me a thing, Libby. I haven't been keepin' score about who's saved whose ass how many times on this job, but I reckon it's pretty much even."

Libby's eyes closed again, and he was wondering if she had drifted back into unconsciousness when she suddenly asked, "How bad am I?"

Morris related what he'd been told by Doctor Rosenbloom. Then he added, "Most likely it'll be a while, but once you're feeling better, we can sit down and figure out what we're going to do about old Christine, up there in Salem. In the meantime—"

"*No!*" The vehemence in her voice took him by surprise. "We can't wait. *Can't.*"

"Libby, you're in no shape to travel, let alone deal with a full-fledged black witch when you get there."

"I know. That's why you have to go. By yourself."

Morris stared at her, wondering if the injuries she'd suffered had somehow affected her brain.

After a moment, Libby shook her head—about a half-inch either direction. "No, I haven't lost my wits, along with everything else. You have to go, it's the only way to end it."

"Libby, you need to rest."

"Yes, but not eternally. Not just yet, anyway. And if she makes another run at me now, I'm helpless to stop her. Which means I'm dead."

"That's why I should stay with you. To protect you."

"The way you did this morning?" Her voice was gentle.

"Libby, I—"

"No, hear me out, I'm starting to feel woozy again. I know you saved my life today, Quincey. But she *almost* killed me. And the hospital won't let you stay here twenty-four seven. Even if they did, you still have to sleep sometime."

Morris's mouth tightened in frustration.

"And remember," Libby said, "if I die, so do the LaRues."

"Christ, I forgot." Libby's death would render all her warding charms in the LaRue house useless. The family would be utterly defenseless against another magical assault by Christine Abernathy.

"Only chance is an end run." Libby's voice was starting to sound slurry. "Remember... aggressor has advantage. This time, you be... aggressor."

Morris nodded reluctantly. All right. He would go to Salem by himself, although what he was going to do against a black witch of Christine Abernathy's power....

Libby seemed to read his thoughts. "My bag," she mumbled. "In the locker thing... there. Get it."

Morris found the black leather purse and brought it over.

"Inside pocket," Libby said. "Zipper. Feel it?"

Morris fumbled, then said, "Yeah, okay."

"Open. Find the mirror."

Morris unzipped the little compartment and located the small oval mirror, about four inches from top to bottom. He held it up where Libby could see.

"Take it," she said. Her gaze was losing it focus now. "Prepared... last night. Keep with you when you meet... Abernathy. Mirror spell. Should help, if she...."

And then she was out again.

A few minutes later, the head ICU nurse made Morris leave, and told him not to come back to tire her patient for at least twenty-four hours.

Twenty-four hours? he thought. *It'll be over long before then, lady.*

USING HIS TURN signal, Fenton slowly and carefully pulled over to the side of the road, well clear of traffic. Then he shut off the engine. "Tell me," he said. "The short version."

"We've been assuming that for the locator to work, we had to follow the same route that they did. Since they had a head start, we were always behind them. I take responsibility for that stupid assumption, by the way."

"Whatever." Fenton waved an impatient hand. "What's the rest?"

"The locator, Elizabeth said, should work over a distance of several miles. Which means it should still be able to detect them if they are on one those secondary roads they like so much, while we are speeding along an adjacent highway. The locator will tell us when to leave the highway by indicating that we have passed them."

Fenton rubbed his chin dubiously, but there was something like hope dawning in his face. "They've got one mother of a lead on us, man."

"Did you have anything else planned for tonight?" Van Dreenan asked him.

Five seconds passed. Ten. Then Fenton broke into a grin and said, "Fuck, no."

Van Dreenan grinned right back at him. "Me neither," he said. "Me, neither."

"The Hertz lady said there was a map in the glove compartment," Fenton said. "Dig it out, and let's figure out how to get to the nearest Interstate."

SNAKE PERKINS WAITED until it was full dark before loading up the Connie with their sparse luggage. Then he went back inside their room.

"All set," he said to Cecelia Mbwato.

She nodded, then went around the room, turning off the lights. They had agreed that there was no reason to have light from the room illuminate her when she came outside to get in the car.

A few minutes later, they were on their way.

"Got that road atlas handy?" Snake asked.

"Yes, right here."

"Good. We don't wanna get lost now. I'll need you to navigate for me."

"To what?"

"Tell me when to turn, so's we don't end up on the wrong road. I been to Salem before, but I never went this way. I can't check the map and drive at the same time."

"Very well."

"There's a pen light in the glove box, I think. Can't risk driving with the dome light on—it'd light us up like we was on stage, or somethin'."

After a few moments' fumbling, she said, "Yes, I have it."

They were talking about everything but what they had spent the whole day doing on the motel bed, with brief breaks for food and naps. Neither would admit to themselves, let alone to the other, that they had just had the best sex of their lives.

Sex between two people who love each other can be hot, passionate, even transcendent.

Sex between two people who don't like each other, oddly enough, can sometimes be almost as good.

But it leads to some awkward moments afterward.

They had been in the car over a quarter-hour before Snake said, "Uh, listen, about what we—"

"Let us not speak of it. We did what we did, and now it is in the past, to be forgotten, or remembered, as we wish."

Coming from Cecelia Mbwato, Snake thought, that was almost poetic. But what he said was, "Yeah, you're right. I was just gonna say that, myself. Good."

After a little while, though, she said musingly, "There was one thing that was a surprise to me, today."

"What's that?"

"Your cock. It is not nearly as small as I thought a white man's must be."

CHAPTER 29

MORRIS HAD THOUGHT about just getting on an airplane. New York to Boston, there must be a dozen flights leaving JFK every day. Then rent a car and drive the last thirty-five miles or so to Salem and whatever awaited him there.

But then he thought some more.

It doesn't really take a lot to bring an airliner down, as the 9/11 hijackers demonstrated all too vividly. Morris didn't know what Christine Abernathy might be able to manage in the way of sabotage—electrical failure, some kind of attack on the cockpit crew, a flight of geese sucked into the engines—but he supposed there were any number of possibilities. And the black witch didn't seem much concerned about what the military calls "collateral damage."

Morris wasn't eager to die, although he thought there was a good chance that he would not survive the confrontation to come. But he wasn't interested in putting a planeload of innocent passengers at risk, just so he could take the most convenient route to his own funeral.

The folks at Avis, he found, were still trying harder. They were not only willing to rent him a fairly new Oldsmobile, but also provided a computer-generated set of maps and directions. The pretty blonde behind the counter, seeing his destination was Salem, even made a cute little joke about witches.

She seemed disappointed when Morris didn't laugh.

He located the blue Olds in the lot without much difficulty, and stashed his suitcase in the trunk. Then he started the engine, took a deep breath, and headed out into the Darwinian chariot race that is New York City traffic.

Morris wondered whether he would ever return to New York, and whether Libby Chastain would still be alive when he did.

Following the directions that Avis had given him, he beeped, butted, and bluffed his way out of the city. Within half an hour he was on Route 95, the great north-south interstate that spans the east coast from New England to Florida.

He had been on the highway for only a short time when it started raining toads.

The first of the small creatures landed on the Oldsmobile's hood and just squatted there, looking in at Morris impassively. A couple of seconds later, another one hit the windshield and bounced off, leaving a wet, yellow smear. Just for a moment, he thought the amphibians might have dropped from an overhanging tree—then he realized that state highway departments don't allow trees to grow that close to the interstates. A quick glance in the mirror confirmed that there wasn't a tree within fifty yards of the stretch of road he had just passed over.

Then the toads began to fall in earnest. He could see them strike the hood and windshield, and hear them on the roof and trunk, sounding for all the world like the record-setting hailstorm that Morris had driven through back in Texas years before, when some of the chunks of falling ice had been the size of billiard balls.

The toads were all over the road in front of him, too. Morris wasn't trying to run them over—he was fond of animals, and tried to avoid hurting them when he could—but their sheer numbers made it impossible to avoid squashing some, and he could both hear and feel their bodies striking the undercarriage as they were flung there by the rotation of his wheels. Thinking about the carnage he was causing made his skin crawl.

Visibility quickly became so bad that he turned on his windshield wipers, but GM hadn't designed them to cope with this kind of precipitation, so the improvement was minimal. Morris was giving serious thought to pulling off to the side of the road when the green deluge suddenly ceased. Unlike a rainstorm, there was no gradual slowdown of the shower. It just—stopped. He checked the mirror again to see if amphibians were still coming down in the area he'd just left, but he could perceive nothing out of the ordinary, and the road behind him ran straight for more than a mile.

A minute later, he saw the sign for an upcoming service plaza, and decided to stop there and assess the damage to the car.

Except that there wasn't any damage.

He'd parked the Olds a little apart from the other vehicles in the huge lot, then walked around it twice, slowly.

There was nothing at all on the car to reflect the bizarre downpour he'd just driven through: no scratches, no dents, nothing green adhering to any of the tires. Even the slime on the windshield was gone—if it had ever been there to begin with.

Morris looked up at the cloudless sky for a long moment. Then he shook himself, the way a dog will when it comes in out of the rain, and walked into the plaza's main building in search of something to eat.

Half an hour later, after putting away a mediocre cheeseburger and some over-brewed coffee, Morris was washing his hands in the restroom when he suddenly realized there was something oddly familiar about the man standing to his left. Morris turned his head and looked more closely, his eyes widening. The middle-aged man with slicked-back brown hair was wearing the kind of jumpsuit you often find in institutional settings. He turned from the sink and stared back at Morris with eyes of a soft, luminous blue. He smiled gently.

The man was an absolute dead ringer for that British actor who has played a homicidal psychiatrist in a series of scary, gory movies.

"I knew a fellow once who tried to interfere with Christine Abernathy's plans," the man said in a soft, cultured voice. "She ate his kidneys with a plate of lima beans and a nice glass of Merlot. Or was it Chardonnay? Yes, I rather think it was." He pulled his lips back from his teeth and made a staccato sucking sound like someone inhaling a long strand of spaghetti.

From somewhere, the man had produced what looked like a police nightstick. He slapped the business end against his palm as he said, "Ready when you are, Mr. Morris."

Morris took a quick step back, then flicked his gaze toward the mirror, to see if there was anyone else nearby who might be either a potential ally or enemy. Two men were standing at the row of urinals, apparently unaware of the confrontation taking place behind them while they emptied their bladders. Morris's glance took no more than half a second, and he was already assuming the fourth defensive posture of Shotokan karate as he looked back toward his adversary.

The demented doctor was gone.

Morris blinked a couple of times, then put his arms down. One of the men who had been relieving himself turned away from the urinal and looked at Morris curiously for a second before leaving the restroom.

Morris turned back to the sink and finished drying his hands—which, he noticed, were not quite steady.

When he returned to his car, there was a gray Toyota parked a couple of spaces away. A woman with long black hair was fussing with the window of the driver's side door. As Morris approached she looked up, an anxious expression on her face, and he could see that she was holding a bent coat hanger. She was tall, slim, probably around thirty.

She was the most compellingly attractive woman he had ever seen in his life.

"Listen, I'm sorry to bother you, but could you help me?" Her voice sounded a little shaky.

"What's the trouble?" Morris was wary, unsure if this was genuine or another of Christine Abernathy's attempts to play with his head.

"I feel so utterly stupid," she said. "I locked the keys inside." She gestured with the wire hanger. "I found this in one of the trash cans, and I've been trying to reach the inside door handle, but the window's only open an inch at the top, and I just can't *do* it!" The eyes glistened with incipient tears.

Morris glanced inside the Toyota and confirmed that the keys were, in fact, still in the ignition. He made a decision.

"That's because you're going about it wrong, that's all," he said. "Here, let me see."

He took the hanger from her and bent the curved top into a tighter, smaller loop. "Now I'll show you a trick that every good car thief knows. Uh, you don't have a car alarm, do you?"

She shook her head.

"Good."

He began to work the wire loop between the driver's window and the rubber molding that ran along its base. After a moment's initial resistance, he was able to force it down into the door itself, just forward of the handle. He moved the hanger back and forth a couple of times then suddenly stopped and said, "Gotcha!"

He pulled upward, and the lock button in the door popped open with a loud "click."

"Oh my God, that's incredible!" she said. "And when I think of how long I've just spent fussing over the damn thing..."

"You just have to know the trick," Morris said, working the hanger back out of the lock mechanism. "If I'd had a shim with me, the kind of tool that professionals use, I would've had it open even faster."

"You've been very kind," she said, placing her hand on one of his. "I don't know what I can do to repay you."

As she looked at him with those big green eyes, Morris suddenly realized who she was.

She was Mary Beth Sturnevan, who he had loved utterly and completely for most of his junior year at Sam Houston High School. He'd never tried to do anything about his infatuation, except in his fantasies. After all, she was the prettiest, most popular girl not just in the junior class but in the whole damn school. The young Quincey Morris, who was referred to by many of the other kids as "that weird guy," had known that his chances with her were somewhere between ridiculous and none.

And this woman was Mary Beth Sturnevan writ large. She was older, of course, but also taller, more beautiful, infinitely more desirable than the original had ever been.

Alarm bells started going off in the back of Quincey Morris's mind.

He stepped back, forcing her to let go of his hand. "No repayment's necessary, ma'am," he said. "Glad I could help out."

She smiled then, and to him it was like the angels singing. "Let me at least buy you lunch." She gestured toward the building he'd just left. "This place doesn't look like Wolfgang Puck works here, but the food probably won't kill us." She tilted her head a little to one side. "Unless you maybe have a better idea?"

Better idea? Yeah, I just might. How about we break the land speed record between here and the nearest motel and then fuck each other until our ears bleed? How about we get married, raise a family, and never go near Salem, Massachusetts for as long as we both shall live? How about we just ride off into the sunset together and see if we can find ourselves a whole bunch of that "happily ever after" stuff I'm always hearing about?

Morris took a deep breath and let it out slowly. Then he backed up another step, and his face never showed how much that effort cost him. The one after that was easier, a little. "That's mighty kind of you," he said with the best smile he could manage, "but I just finished eating, and I'm kind of behind schedule as it is. Thanks for the offer, though."

He went around to his car and got in. After starting up, he looked back and saw that she was still standing there, staring at him. She wasn't smiling now.

He rolled down the window and with forced cheerfulness said, "You have a good trip now, hear?"

Her voice didn't seem very loud, but it carried well enough for him to hear clearly. "She's going to kill you, you dickless bastard. She'll tear your guts out and tie them around your neck in a bow tie. She's going to make you—"

Morris put the car in gear and accelerated away. After a while, he couldn't hear her voice any more.

Except inside his head.

He drove on for another forty minutes or so and reached his exit without further incident.

He was on I-91 heading toward Hartford when he noticed a hitchhiker up ahead who looked vaguely familiar. As Morris drew closer, he realized it was the Nazi demon from Barry Love's building, the one with the boar's face. The creature was holding a hand-printed sign that read, "Going to Hell?" Its porcine head swiveled to stare at Morris's car as he drove by.

It was half an hour later that he encountered the motorcycle gang.

He wasn't sure where they'd come from, but suddenly the choppers were in his mirror, coming up fast. There were at least twenty of them, and, as Morris watched, the customized Harleys began to drift left into the passing lane.

Morris thought briefly about trying to outrun them, but realized how futile that would be—this was an Oldsmobile he was driving here, not a Porsche Carrera. And, besides, the bikers hadn't made any hostile moves so far. Could be they were just another bunch of macho louts on their way to a beer blast somewhere.

And if it came to trouble, Morris had one big advantage. The Harleys had speed, but the Olds had weight. In the event of any kind of collision between a bike and a car, the bike was going to be the loser—and that held true for whoever was riding it, too.

The lead motorcycle in the pack began to pull even with the Oldsmobile. At highway speeds, you can't safely take your eyes off the road for very long, but Morris figured he couldn't afford to be ambushed, either. He risked a glance to his left, to get a better idea what he was dealing with. After a couple of seconds, he returned his gaze to the road in front of him. His normally mobile face bore no expression, none at all.

What he'd seen atop the Harley was in many ways a standard-issue outlaw biker type: stocky body clad in boots, filthy blue jeans, and a sleeveless denim jacket with some kind of club insignia sewn on the back, the whole ensemble topped by an imitation Nazi coal-scuttle helmet, complete with swastika insignia on the side. The only thing that didn't conform to the stereotype was the face.

Because there wasn't one.

Even with his hurried look, Morris had seen that the biker's helmet topped a naked skull, without a scrap of flesh or hair left on it. After a moment, Morris risked another glance, and this time the biker was staring back, his black, empty eye sockets seeming to contain endless night. The skull-face still had all its teeth, though, and they seemed to grin at Morris as the biker waved in a friendly way, then accelerated and pulled ahead, followed by the rest of his too-dead crew.

As they passed, Morris could see that each denim jacket bore the same emblem: a stylized skull with blood dripping from the eye sockets. Atop the image, gothic-style lettering spelled out "Hell's Angels," and underneath the skull was added: "For Fuckin' Real."

As the last skeletal biker rode by, he turned a fleshless face toward Morris and yelled, "See ya in Salem, motherfucker!"

Then, almost casually, he tossed an open can of beer at Morris's windshield.

The almost-full can hit the glass with a sharp "crack" and bounced off, spewing foaming Budweiser all over Morris's field of vision. He swerved the car instinctively to the right, which caused it to skid. Morris took his foot off the gas, but had the sense not to touch the brake pedal. The Olds veered off the road, onto the shoulder, and hit the guardrail a glancing blow. Morris overcorrected, which brought the car back across the road and into the left lane. He still did not brake, but inertia and engine compression were slowing the car now, and he was able to regain control, thanking his stars that no other traffic had been coming up right behind him.

He eased the Olds into the right lane and then finally applied the brake, bringing the car to a gentle stop on the right shoulder.

He sat there for several minutes, waiting for his heart to return to something like its normal rate. He did not bother to look down the road to see if there was actually a pack of outlaw bikers receding in the distance. It didn't matter, really. If he needed evidence that he hadn't imagined it all, the thin crack in the windshield would do nicely, along with the splattered film of beer that was already drying across its surface.

After a while, he got out and went around to the passenger's side. Sure enough, the impact with the guardrail had left a good-sized dent in the door and messed up the paint badly. Morris found himself wondering how he was going to explain this to the folks at Avis, but then gave a mental shrug. In his situation, worrying about cosmetic damage to the Olds was like Custer at Little Big Horn fretting about grass stains on his buckskins.

CHAPTER 30

IT WAS DARK by the time Morris reached I-90 and noticed that the gas gauge had fallen below a quarter of a tank. He was getting close to Boston, and signs at every exit offered gas, food, and lodging in some form. Morris took the next off-ramp and followed the sign to a nearby Mobil station.

A few minutes later, he was waiting in the station's convenience store to pay for his gas when a nearby rack of newspapers caught his eye. It held not only the Boston papers but the *Providence Journal,* the *Hartford Courant*, and even the *New York Times*.

Since the customer ahead of him seemed to having some trouble getting his credit card approved, Morris reached over and plucked the *Times* from the rack, wondering if it had a story about the attack that morning that had nearly cost him and Libby Chastain their lives.

He didn't find any mention of what he was looking for. Instead, on the front page of the Metro section, he saw: "Patient Raped, Murdered in Hospital ICU."

Morris felt his heart start to thud against his chest wall even before he read, "Elizabeth Chastain, 34, of Washington Square, was sexually assaulted and murdered in the Intensive Care Unit of Cedar Sinai Medical Center earlier today. A hospital spokesman confirmed that Ms. Chastain had been brought in to the hospital as an emergency room patient several hours—"

FENTON AND VAN Dreenan, tearing north on Route 95, an hour after sunset.

"Damn, I wish this was an official car," Fenton said. "I could take it up to ninety or so, and if a state cop gave chase, I could get on the radio, find his frequency, and explain I'm on official business and in pursuit of suspects. Hell, he might even give us an escort."

"But if we're stopped, you still have your FBI credentials to show," Van Dreenan said. "That should get us out of trouble." He held the locator steady on the lid of his briefcase, and it was pointing straight ahead.

"Yeah, but getting cleared would take time. He'd want to know why I'm in a civilian car for starters. Then, after I explained that, he'd have to radio my name and badge number in to his barracks, who would call the local FBI field office, Boston I suppose, who might well decide to contact Behavioral Science at Quantico to make sure I was legit. Christ only knows how long all that palaver would delay us."

"Well, we could always just shoot him."

Fenton looked at Van Dreenan without turning his head. "I'm going to have to watch out for that sense of humor of yours."

"Always assuming I was joking," Van Dreenan said with a tiny smile.

"Yeah, assuming that. No, we're better off keeping it at seventy, which is more or less within the legal limit. Just let me know as soon as that pointer starts moving again."

They were approaching the exit for someplace called Peabody when it did.

"Pointer's moved!" Van Dreenan said. It's at two o'clock now. Best take this exit coming up."

"Right, got it." Fenton put on his turn signal and began to move into the right lane.

As they made the turn off Route 95, Fenton said, "What do we do when we hit the end of the ramp?"

"Let us hope the device will answer that for us." Van Dreenan said. His voice had grown tight with tension, and he kept fiddling with the clasps of his briefcase.

"Well, it fuckin' well better."

It did. The sharpened stick moved smoothly to the left, sending them north along Route 128. Fenton brought the speed down to forty-five, out of concern for both safety and the local cops.

They had just passed the Northshore Mall on their left when the indicator turned to the right again.

"Take the next exit," Van Dreenan said.

"Gotcha."

A few minutes later, van Dreenan muttered, "Gott!"

"What? What's up?"

"Did you see the sign?"

"Which one?"

"Salem, 3 miles."

"Well, fuck me," Fenton said softly. Then, more loudly: "You don't suppose—"

"Yes, I do suppose. I suppose very much that this is not mere chance."

They were on something called Peabody Avenue now, but soon the indicator moved again, sending them on a turn into Marlborough Road. The indicator continued to point ahead, but now it was vibrating softly.

Fenton glanced over and noticed the sudden oscillation. "What's it doing that for?"

"It means they're close," Van Dreenan said, and flicked open the clasps of his briefcase. Putting the locator aside for a moment, he raised the lid and rummaged inside. He removed several objects, closed the case up again, and put the locator back in place.

Van Dreenan suddenly leaned toward Fenton. "Hold still!" he said, and raised his hands over Fenton's head. A moment later, he withdrew and Fenton realized that Van Dreenan had placed around his neck a leather thong with something hanging from it. He grasped the small object now resting against his chest and raised it to eye level.

It was the tooth of a large animal, the tip still sharp. Some odd-looking symbols were painted on it in red. Fenton looked over at Van Dreenan, and saw that the South African had just put on what appeared to be an identical necklace.

"What the fuck is this?" Fenton asked.

"An amulet, made of a lion's tooth. Blessed by a very powerful *sangoma.*"

"What's the point?"

"It will protect us from her magic. Maybe."

"Oh, man, for Christ's sake—"

"Just leave it in place, will you? It is no more insane than chasing all over creation because a magical stick tells you to, is it?"

"Well, when you put it like that..."

"We're coming to an intersection," Van Dreenan said. "Be ready to turn."

"Which way?"

"I'll tell you. Wait for it."

As soon as they reached the end of Marlborough Road, the pointer moved again. "Left!" Van Dreenan said. "Turn left here!"

Fenton made the turn, then picked up speed. The area appeared to be semi-rural, the houses they passed few and far apart. Soon, he could see another vehicle ahead of them. They were gaining on it, and Fenton hoped the road would remain straight enough let him pass them when the time came.

"Fenton! Does that car ahead look familiar to you? From a certain videotape?"

Fenton flicked on the high beams. "Sweet Christ, it's a fucking Continental! Can you make out the color?"

Van Dreenan spoke again a few seconds later, but this time his voice was quiet and calm. "Unless I am very much mistaken," he said, "it is British racing green."

"MISTER, YOU GET gas?"

Morris tore his eyes away from the newspaper. "What?"

The teenager behind the counter had finally finished with his other customer. "Gas," he said again. "Ain't that blue Olds yours? The one at number four?"

Morris stepped forward, trying to focus on what he was supposed to be doing. "Uh, yeah, sure. That's me. What do I owe you?"

"Thirty-two eighty-five. Plus another dollar for that paper, if you're plannin' on buyin' it."

Morris ignored the sarcasm and reached for his wallet with an unsteady hand. *Libby, oh dear Jesus, I'm sorry. It's all my fault for dragging you into this fucking mess in the first place.*

Then the small part of his mind that was not reeling with shock and grief came up with an interesting fact and presented it to his forebrain for inspection:

The New York Times is a morning paper.

Which meant that something newsworthy happening in mid-afternoon, which was when Morris left Libby Chastain's bedside, is not going to show up in the *Times* until the next day's edition. It just wasn't possible.

Morris pocketed his change and looked at the teenage attendant. "Listen, could you do me a favor real quick?" He folded the Metro section in half and held it out. "Could you just read me the headline on this story right here? Just this one."

The attendant glanced at the paper, then looked up suspiciously. "You can't read, then what the hell you buyin' the paper for?"

"I can read. It's just that I'm dyslexic."

"What's that mean?"

"It means I have trouble understanding what I read sometimes, that's all."

"Look, man, I'm tryin' to run a business here, ya know?"

Morris glanced around the store. They were the only two people in the place.

He pulled out his wallet again and tossed a twenty on the counter. "That ought to make it worth your time."

The bill disappeared so fast it might never have been there at all. "This story right here, you mean?"

Morris nodded.

"It says, 'Mayor Opposes New Bond Initiative, Threatens Veto.'" He had trouble pronouncing "initiative."

Morris let out the breath he hadn't been aware he was holding. "Thanks," he said, and turned away.

"Hey," the attendant called, "don't you want your paper?"

"Keep it," Morris said from the door. "Maybe there's comics in there somewhere."

CHAPTER 31

SNAKE PERKINS WAS silently listening to the Rolling Stones doing "Brown Sugar" when he saw the headlights in his mirror, coming up fast. He looked for the flashing light of a police car, but saw none. Then the guy back there turned on his brights.

"Jesus, what the fuck is that?" he said.

Cecelia Mbwato turned and looked back, but only for a moment. "Trouble," she said, and reached down for her bag.

"NOW I KNOW how the guy felt who had a tiger by the tail," Fenton said. "I mean, now that we've found 'em, how do we stop 'em? I can't call for backup, because we've got no fucking radio! And if we chase these bastards into Salem at high speed, civilians are gonna get killed, maybe a whole bunch of 'em."

"Can you run them off the road?"

"That Connie's way heavier than we are, man. I try that, he'll most likely run *us* off the road."

"Just bring us as close as you can, then" Van Dreenan said, his voice icily calm. "Let us see what develops."

CECELIA MBWATO WAS chanting something in the same language Snake Perkins had heard her use during the rituals for preparing the fetishes. She had removed a small leather pouch from her voluminous carpetbag. From the corner of his eye,

Snake watched as she poured some of its contents, which looked like a coarse powder, into her cupped hand, chanting all the while.

Then she dropped the pouch back in her bag and used her free hand to lower the window next to her.

"Jesus, what are you doing?"

"Just drive!" she snapped, and flung the handful of powder out straight up into the night air.

FENTON SAW A hand and arm, blacker than his own, extend from the Connie's passenger-side window, and wondered if he and Van Dreenan were about to come under fire. But the hand did not hold a gun, and in any case it quickly disappeared back inside the car.

"Was that her?" Fenton asked. "Mbwato?"

"Very likely," Van Dreenan said, "but I do not know—"

Something flickered in the air between the two cars. There, and gone. Then it reappeared again for an instant and winked out again. Fenton thought, crazily, that it looked like the face of George McDougall, a serial murderer who had almost killed Fenton during an arrest attempt eighteen months earlier. Fenton still had nightmares about George McDougall, and about what they had found in his basement once the man had been shot dead.

Beside him, Van Dreenan started in surprise. Fenton didn't know that the South African was seeing brief images of a black mamba, the deadliest snake in Africa. The bite of one of these reptiles had almost ended Van Dreenan's life when he was a young policeman.

"You're seeing something, aren't you?" Van Dreenan said. "Something you're afraid of?"

"Yeah, how'd you know?"

"It's a common trick among African sorcerers. The spell brings up visions of whatever you fear the most, causing panic. It would be far worse, for both of us, were it not for the amulets we are wearing. Ignore what you think you see—there is nothing there. Remember that!"

"Yeah, okay." Fenton found the brief apparitions unsettling, but he was a long way from panic.

Van Dreenan had produced a small bottle and was pouring liquid from it all over the pointer of the locator device.

The pointer that was covered with the hair of Cecelia Mbwato.

Fenton glanced over before returning his gaze to the road. "What's that?"

"Something else I brought from Africa, courtesy of the same *sangoma.* I'm going to try a little sympathetic magic. Elizabeth would be angry with me for using this, but desperate times..."

Now that the hair wrapped around the pointer was saturated, Van Dreenan put the bottle aside and reached inside his jacket pocket to remove a small cardboard box.

"What's that?" Fenton asked, after another quick look. "More magic?"

"No, just matches," Van Dreenan said. "A box of matches I have been saving for a long time."

He removed a wooden match and lit it. Then he passed the flame under the pointer, saying a word in a language Fenton didn't recognize. He said the word three times, and at the third utterance the hair wrapping the pointer began to burn.

"Hope you know what the fuck you're doing, man," Fenton said tensely.

"Oh, I do, my friend. I do, indeed."

Sixty feet ahead, inside the Continental, Cecelia Mbwato's hair suddenly caught fire.

WHEN HER HAIR ignited, Cecelia Mbwato let out a screech. Snake Perkins yelled "Holy fuck!" and began to slap at her head in an effort to extinguish the flames.

"No, let me!" she yelled, and quickly grabbed from her bag a bandana with arcane symbols written all over it. She immediately used the cloth to cover her hair while saying a word in Zulu, the same one, five times.

The fire instantly went out; it had not done her any serious damage.

But in yanking the bandana out of her bag so hurriedly, Cecelia Mbwato had also pulled out the pouch containing the remainder of the powder that she had just used against her enemies in the car behind. Some of the powder spilled out, and the air vents immediately began to blow it around inside the car. Cecelia Mbwato was too busy tending to her burning hair to notice, and, in any case, was immune to her own spellcasting.

Relieved that the fire was under control, Snake Perkins faced forward again.

There, staring at him through the windshield, twice as large as life, was a vision of what he had once feared more than anything else in the world.

"Mama?" he screamed. "No, Mama, don't hurt me, I'll do what you want, whatever you want, please Mama!"

Snake began frantically waving his hands in front of him, as to ward off a blow, or worse. The car, whose speed was pushing seventy, immediately began to veer off the road.

Cecelia Mbwato grabbed for the wheel while yelling a word that would counteract her terror spell and return Snake to something like sanity.

The magic worked on Snake, who stopped yelling. But it was unable to overcome the laws of physics.

The Connie careened into a road sign that said "Salem 1/2 mile." The sign bent with the impact, just as it was supposed to, but then the rear wheels ran over it. At the speed they were traveling, that was enough to send the car hurtling sideways—off the road, and off balance.

The Connie turned over twice before coming to rest on its roof, fifty-some feet in front of a billboard that bore the image of a crone in a conical hat and read, "In Salem, be sure to visit the Witch Museum. Fun for the whole family."

FENTON BROUGHT THE rented car to a slow stop, staring at the wreck. "No fire, anyway," he said. He reached into a pocket and brought out his cell phone. "Don't need a police radio to call nine-one-one, fortunately."

He had just flipped the phone open when Van Dreenan said, "Look—help is coming," and pointed out the driver's side window.

Fenton looked to his left, saw nothing, then turned back just in time to catch Van Dreenan's big fist along the side of his jaw.

VAN DREENAN GOT out of the car stiffly, rubbing the knuckles of his left hand. He had been an amateur boxer when younger, and had twice reached the finals of the Police League championships. He still knew how to hit. The punch had done exactly what he'd intended it to do—knock Fenton unconscious without inflicting any lasting damage. Or so Van Dreenan devoutly hoped.

He hoped the FBI man would forgive him; he had come to like Fenton a great deal. But what he had to do now was bigger than friendship.

He checked to make sure that the big Sig Sauer automatic was securely anchored behind his right hip, patted his right jacket pocket to check for something else, then closed the car door.

As he walked toward the wreck of the Continental, Van Dreenan made a quick survey of the surroundings. No houses close by. A golf course, closed at this hour, across the street. No traffic for the moment, or pedestrians. He looked for flashing lights in the distance. None, so far. Good.

As he approached the wreck, he brought out the small flashlight he always carried, although the full moon provided considerable illumination.

Glass crunched under his feet now, and the smell of gasoline was strong. The tank must be ruptured somewhere—not surprising, considering the damage that the vehicle had sustained.

He checked the driver's side first. The Continental had been too old a model to have air bags, and it soon became clear that Snake Perkins had not been wearing his seatbelt. Van Dreenan was no physician, but he had been around a lot of dead bodies; he recognized a crushed skull and a broken neck when he saw them.

He went around to the passenger side then, and observed that the door had burst open in the crash. Cecelia Mbwato, unlike her companion, had been wearing her seatbelt, and it had undoubtedly saved her life. Of course, since the car was upside down, she was now dangling from the lap belt and shoulder harness, trying to free herself with the one arm that seemed to be working properly. The other, Van Dreenan could tell, had received a compound fracture and was virtually useless to her.

He crouched down, careful not to step in the puddle of gasoline that was under the car and growing larger.

He'd wondered if she would beg for help, but she just stared at him, like a great venomous toad, and kept trying to unlatch the seatbelt with her one good arm.

Van Dreenan wondered why he felt no pleasure at this moment, the one he had prayed for and dreamed about so many times over the last four years. Looking at Cecelia Mbwato, all he felt was empty, as if the thing that had been driving him for so long had finally died.

But still, he had a debt that must be paid. And a promise that must be kept.

Van Dreenan started to speak, but his throat was constricted. He tried again, and this time he found his voice.

"Cecelia Mbwato, you do not know me, but you and my family are nonetheless closely connected. You have met, I know, at least one member of it."

There were sirens off in the distance now. Van Dreenan had only a little time left.

"My daughter, Katerina, was only nine years old when you took her. Katerina Van Dreenan. Do you recognize the name? Or do you even learn their names before you... use them?

"Did she scream when you cut her open that night? Did she struggle and bite and fight you as much as she could? I'll wager that she fought. She had spirit, Katerina did." Van Dreenan's voice broke, and he stopped and swallowed hard, then again, before going on.

"I had to identify her body, at the morgue, you know. Her mother could not face it, and for this I did not blame her. I identified Katerina's body, what else could I do? But that night I also made her a promise. Now, I know that I am a weak man, a sinner. I have, in my life, broken many promises."

Van Dreenan stood, his knees cracking like gunshots. He reached into his coat pocket and brought out the box of wooden matches. He had used them to light the candles on his daughter's birthday cake. Her final birthday.

The sirens were closer now.

"But not this one."

He opened the little box, removed a match.

"They say that fire purifies."

He dragged the match alone the box's side, igniting it.

"Perhaps it can make pure even one such as you. But I have my doubts."

Van Dreenan dropped the match into the gasoline.

"Now go to your Father, in Hell."

Then he turned and walked away, toward sirens that sounded like the screaming of the damned.

CHAPTER 32

Morris left Route 128 at the Salem exit. He missed the turn that would have taken him directly into the city, and ended up on Marlborough Road, instead. But when it brought him to Highland Avenue, he checked the map and realized that a left turn would take him where he needed to go.

To the right, he saw a good-sized fire blazing, a little way off the road. Two fire trucks were trying to deal with it, accompanied by a number of police cars, their lights flashing. From the illumination provided by the flames and the fire trucks' floodlights, it looked as if a good-sized car had done a crash-and-burn and ended up on its roof.

Morris shook his head. He hoped that no one had been trapped in the car when it blew. Burning was a very nasty way to die.

Another few minutes brought him to Washington Street and a sign that read, "Welcome to Salem." Fifty feet beyond, a billboard urged, "Visit the Witch Museum."

"No museums for me, pal," Morris murmured. "Only the real thing will do."

As it turned out, the only decent place with a vacancy was the Hawthorne Hotel, which put him right across the street from the Witch Museum, anyway. Shit, might as well get into the spirit of things, Morris thought as he signed the registration card. He wondered whether there were other places around the world raking in big bucks from the memory of old atrocities. Is there an Auschwitz Hilton over there in Poland, with tour buses leaving for the crematoriums every couple of hours? Maybe they have a little gift shop that sells refrigerator magnets reading "Arbeit macht frei."

Morris had originally planned to seek out Christine Abernathy as soon as he arrived. But he'd gotten there later than he had anticipated, he was dead tired, and his nerves were stretched to the breaking point. And, upon reflection, he concluded it might be unwise to confront a black witch at night, when her powers were at their strongest. *Or maybe I'm just scared shitless of her.*

Morris called the hospital to check on Libby's condition—which he learned, was still "critical." Then he unpacked, took a quick shower, and went to bed. Mercifully, he did not dream.

DOCTOR MELLING LOOKED at the unconscious woman in the hospital bed. She had an IV needle going into each arm now, and was hooked up to a number of monitors that hummed, beeped, and blinked quietly. All around the ICU, similar machines did their work with other severely injured patients.

Melling scanned the medical chart that had been hanging from the front of the woman's bed. He turned to the man next to him. "She went comatose about three hours ago?"

Doctor Gujral checked his watch and nodded. "Almost exactly. Not surprising, really, considering her injuries." Short and intense, he was Libby Chastain's attending physician. Melling, a tall Dane with wire-rim glasses, was Gujral's relief.

"She's the one who was hit by some maniac who drove his car onto the sidewalk, right? I heard it on the news."

"Yes, that's her," Gujral said. "The vehicle must have been moving quite fast, judging by the severity and extent of the trauma."

"Well, given her comatose state, I'm going to update her condition—from 'Critical' to 'Grave.'" Melling looked up from the chart he was writing on. "Okay with you?"

"Sure, makes sense." Gujral stared at his patient for a long moment. "I wonder if she'll survive the night."

Melling replaced the chart on the front rail of the bed. "If I were the kind of doctor who was insensitive enough to give odds on something like that, I'd probably put them at five to three against."

Gujral looked at Libby Chastain's unconscious form one last time. "Yes," he said glumly. "So would I."

AFTER BREAKFAST, MORRIS went back to his room and looked over the material that AAA had given him about Salem. It included a map of the city, and he located the street he wanted without difficulty. It was only six blocks away.

Morris put down the map and held his hands out in front of him, palms down. He was gratified to see that they were steady. There was said to be at least one professional gunfighter in Morris's family tree, and some traits persist through the generations. Morris wondered what that old gunslinger would make of the opponent his descendant was going to face here in Salem.

This town ain't big enough for both of us, witch lady. Draw!

If it were only that simple.

HE KNEW BETTER than to expect a house out of *The Addams Family*, so he wasn't surprised to find that 338 Chestnut was a pleasant-looking brick colonial with azaleas and rose bushes growing in the front yard.

But he still wasn't prepared for what opened the front door in response to his knock.

She looked to be about seventeen, as she stood there in tight shorts and a black "Nine Inch Nails" T-shirt. Both eyebrows and one nostril were pierced with small gold rings. The spiky black hair was bisected by a set of lightweight headphones connected to an iPod player at her waistband. Her head bobbed a little to the beat of whatever she was listening to.

She looked at Morris with the utter indifference achievable only by civil servants and teenagers and asked, "Whatcha want?"

After a moment's hesitation, Morris said, "I'm looking for Christine Abernathy."

"Who?"

Morris began to wonder if he had the right address. But the young woman had now removed her headphones, so he repeated, "Christine Abernathy."

"Oh. Um, yeah. Come on in."

Once Morris was inside, she said "This way," and led him down the length of a carpeted hallway toward the back of the house. The hall ended at the entrance to a big, open room that was flooded with sunlight from several large windows. Morris followed the girl inside, and saw that it was clearly some kind of family room, containing mismatched couches and chairs, a fireplace, a big screen TV and a half-size billiard table. Posters from the *Shrek* and *Spiderman* movies decorated the walls, and potted plants were placed under each of the windows.

Apart from Morris and the teenage girl who'd brought him here, there was no one else in the room.

He turned to ask the girl something—but she was gone. He had not heard her leave.

Keyed up as he was, he should have heard her.

He went back to the door he'd just come through and opened it. The long hallway was empty.

From behind him, a female voice said, "Welcome to Salem, Mr. Morris. I trust your journey wasn't lacking in moments of… interest."

Morris whirled toward the sound of the voice, and saw that the pleasant family room was gone.

He now stood in a windowless chamber of rough stone walls, with a slate floor that was dotted by a few rugs with cabalistic symbols woven into them. The chamber was dimly lit by candles placed here and there, and by the flames that flickered in the fireplace beneath what looked for all the world like a bubbling cauldron. Shelves and cabinets held dusty jars and bottles, and devices whose purposes might only be guessed at. Some old-looking tapestries hung from the walls, depicting scenes that Morris decided he didn't want to look at too closely. In any case, his gaze was drawn almost instantly to the woman sitting in the large, throne-like chair who was looking at him with an expression of amused contempt.

She was the same teenage girl who had answered the door. Except that she wasn't.

This young woman's black hair was long and flowing, not cropped short as in her other incarnation. The piercings were gone, and now she appeared to be wearing pale makeup, along with a shade of lipstick that seemed to be the exact color of fresh human blood. The contemporary teen clothing had been replaced by a simple black dress with bell sleeves and a long, flared skirt. Feet clad in shiny black boots were visible under the hem of the dress.

Morris made an effort to push aside this latest mental shock. He took a couple of paces forward, his steps audible on the hard floor. In a voice that was as calm as he could make it, he said, "Christine Abernathy, I presume?"

The young woman inclined her head in acknowledgment. "Do you like the effect?" she asked, making a small gesture that took in the whole room. "We're nothing if not traditional, here in Salem."

"Very impressive," Morris said. "Almost as impressive as all those other little tricks you played on me while I was on my way up here. I assume they were all just illusions. Conjuring tricks, right? Like they have in those Las Vegas shows?"

Her eyes narrowed a little. "Well, there are all kinds of 'conjuring tricks,' as you put it. And not all of them involve illusions. I believe your car has a cracked windshield and some body damage that the people at Avis are going to be very unhappy about. That's not quite an illusion, is it?"

She looked toward the fireplace, and the large vessel that bubbled there. "And if you believe that cauldron to be just an illusion, I invite you to go over and stick your hand in it, as deeply as you like. The third-degree burns you receive will be, I assure you, no illusion."

The fire under the cauldron roared high for a moment, then subsided. It sounded to Morris like the growl of a large, hungry animal.

"And don't expect any help from me afterward, for the pain and scarring," she continued. "I don't usually heal pain and scars, anyway." The smile returned. "I much prefer to cause them."

"You've caused plenty for the LaRue family already," Morris said.

"You think? Oh, but I've barely begun."

"But *why?*"

"I'm tempted to say, *because I can,* and there's a certain amount of truth to that." She shifted position in the big chair. "But you know the real reason, you must. You wouldn't be here, otherwise."

"What, all because of something that happened during the witch trials, three hundred-some years ago? Everybody involved in that business, on both sides, has been dead a long, long time."

"Yes, but the memory lingers, like a festering sore. As it will continue to do, until every last descendant of that Warren bitch is wiped out. The coven that my family owes its allegiance to has a motto, Mister Morris: 'No slight forgotten, no injury unavenged.'"

"And you're expecting to accomplish your vengeance through black magic?"

"Of course. I would have thought that obvious, by now."

"The practice of black magic—that comes with a pretty high price tag, doesn't it?"

"What are you talking about?"

"I'm talking about eternal damnation, the inevitable result of selling your soul to the Devil. Which is what anyone has to do who wants to use black magic."

For a moment there was something in her face that made her look older than her years. Morris thought it might have been despair, but it was gone so quickly he could not be certain.

"I was raised to be what I am from the cradle, if not from the womb, Mister Morris. I never had the choice to be anything else." She sat up a little straighter. "Not that I would, given the chance." After a moment she said, reflectively, "And who knows, there may yet be an escape clause in the agreement you referred to. If there is, I'll find it, in time."

"Somehow, I don't think you're the first black witch to console herself with that particular fantasy," he said. "Sounds to me kind of like somebody whistling her way past the graveyard."

"You're starting to bore me, Mr. Morris. Is that why you made your determined way to Salem? To bore me to death?"

"I came here to ask you what it is you want in order to leave the LaRues alone."

"What I *want?*" She seemed amused by the notion. "You came here to *bribe* me?"

"No, I came here to bargain with you."

"To bargain? How charming! And what do you believe you have to bargain with?"

"That goes back to the question of what you want."

She thought about it, or pretended to. "All right, how about this? Your little friend Elizabeth Chastain has proven a more formidable adversary than I had first reckoned. I doubt she's going to survive her injuries, but it's possible she might. And if she does, she could eventually pose a problem for me. Only a minor one, but still..."

Morris thought he could see where this was heading, but he kept silent.

"Very well, then," she continued. "Go back to New York, and kill that Chastain bitch for me. That should present no real problem. Apart from her grievously weakened condition, which should make her easy prey, she seems to trust you, the Devil knows why."

"And if I do that, if I kill Libby, then you'll give up your vendetta against the LaRue family." Morris's voice was utterly without inflection.

"Yes, I will," she said gravely. "I give you my word."

"No, I don't think I can accommodate you on that one." Morris let the anger into his voice now. "And even if I thought for half a second that you'd actually keep your word, the answer would still be 'no,' you twisted little monster."

"Oh, well." She seemed neither surprised nor disappointed. "Can't blame a girl for trying. But now let me ask you something, Quincey Harker Morris: what is the one thing you fear the most in this world?"

Snakes.

Morris said nothing.

Snakes.

He tried hard to keep his mind a blank, too—but that's like telling yourself you're not going to think about pink elephants.

Snakes.

Morris had been eight years old when he'd stumbled upon the Diamondback rattlesnake in the grassy field that abutted his family's back yard. It was a toss-up as to which one of them had been more surprised by the encounter—young Quincey or the rattler. But the snake had quicker reactions, and it bit the boy on the ankle before slithering back into the undergrowth. He'd run home screaming, and his mother, after tying a hasty tourniquet just below his knee, had proceeded to break every traffic law in Texas getting him to the emergency room. Although the doctors and nurses knew just what to do, and did it well, the pain had been excruciating, and he had been forced to stay off the foot for weeks afterward. Ever since then, he had been terrified of—

"Snakes, is it?" Christine Abernathy said, as if Morris had answered her out loud. "How wonderfully Freudian. Well you don't have to worry, Mr. Morris. There are no poisonous snakes in this part of Massachusetts." Her smile caused an icy finger to trace its way down his spine. "And, of course, no witches, either."

Morris started to speak, but she shook her head. "No, this has become tiresome. I really think it's time for you to go." She made a slight gesture with one hand, and Morris was suddenly standing outside, looking at the front door he had knocked on minutes earlier. He felt no inclination to knock again.

On the way back to his hotel, Morris replayed the encounter in his mind over and over, wondering what he should have said or done differently. After a while, he concluded there was nothing in his power that would have made any dent in Christine Abernathy's implacable malignity.

He had not come to Salem with any clear objective in mind. He had intended to confront Christine Abernathy, and he had accomplished that, for all the good it had done him. And he had wanted to take her measure. He had done that, too, and found her formidable—and terrifying. But he had no idea what his next move should be. Libby had said that it was imperative he travel to Salem immediately, and so here he was.

He wished Libby were there to tell him what he was supposed to do now.

CHAPTER 33

MORRIS SPENT MOST of the day in his room trying to figure out his next move. He had come up with several ideas, but had ending up rejecting each one for being either impractical, impossible, or suicidal. He called Cedar Sinai to check on Libby's condition, and his stomach did a slow somersault when he learned that it had been changed from "critical" to "grave."

Finally, by six o'clock he had had enough, and went out to dinner at a Ponderosa Steakhouse that he had passed on his way into town. Normally, he liked to sample local cuisine in the places he visited, but he was afraid that the independent restaurants here might be boosters of the city's witchcraft tourism industry. He was in no mood to look at a menu containing fare like "broomstick beef stew" or "cauldron custard."

Back in his hotel room, he restlessly channel-surfed the TV for a while, then decided to take a shower. He often had his best ideas while under hot running water, and an idea was something he definitely could use right about now.

Morris clicked the TV screen to black, and started taking off his clothes.

CHRISTINE ABERNATHY CAREFULLY laid out on her worktable the implements and ingredients she would need. She was vexed that the African magic fetish she was expecting had not yet been delivered, but she knew that she could cast this particular spell without it. She had meditated first, for a full hour, to clear her mind—the spell she was about to cast was a difficult one, and required utmost concentration. Considering what she was about to conjure up for Quincey Morris, she had no interest in making any mistakes.

Finally, everything was ready. She did a brief scrying first, to confirm that Morris was in his hotel room. The image that appeared in the ensorcelled bowl showed Morris, nude, turning on the taps in a shower stall. All the better—let him be wet and naked when he confronted the little gift she was sending him.

Christine Abernathy's gaze did not linger over Morris's naked body, but this was not due to any vestigial sense of decency on her part. Once you've had sex with demons, the charms offered by humans of either gender will hold very little appeal ever again.

Using a long wooden match she had made with her own hands, she lit the five squat black candles, which were also her creation. Then she touched the small flame to a chunky, yellow substance that she had placed in a small brazier, which immediately began to emit a thin stream of aromatic smoke.

She then combined several ingredients from a number of different bottles, jars, and small boxes. These she crushed with a mortar and pestle until they were reduced to a fine powder, which she transferred to a small, blood-red bowl.

She brought the bowl over to the part of her work table that contained the pentangle. This was not drawn on the table, but rather carved directly into the wood itself. Christine Abernathy had done this years ago, with painstaking slowness and care, so as to avoid having to redraw the symbol each time she wished to work magic. She thus saved considerable time and also protected herself against the ever-present dangers of a miscalculation in the pentagram's construction.

Reaching into the bowl with her left hand, she took a handful of powder and began to trace with it, letting the material trickle out to form a specific pattern within the pentagram. Then she repeated the process, took more powder, and did it again. And again.

After a few moments, the pentagram was full of the lines she had drawn there, long and sinuous and winding, each one the same shape: the shape of a snake.

Then she brought over to the table a very old book. Cabalistic signs were inscribed on its cover, which was made of material that only a handful of forensic experts would have recognized as human skin. Christine Abernathy opened the book to the page she had marked previously with a black ribbon.

She began to read aloud the first words of the spell.

QUINCEY MORRIS TURNED off the water, slid the shower door open, and reached for a towel. Drying himself off, he decided that although he was cleaner than he had been, he was no closer to solving his problem. He still didn't know what the hell to do about Christine Abernathy, to whom the terms "witch" and "bitch" might both apply with equal accuracy.

Once he was done, he tossed the towel in a corner and went into the other room to get dressed. He was just opening a bureau drawer to get clean underwear when he heard a sound that puzzled him.

For an instant, he flashed on his parents' old house in Austin, with its archaic steam heating system. Even Texas gets cold sometimes, especially when a blue norther makes its day down from Canada. There were plenty of January mornings when young Quincey would wake up to hear the radiator in his bedroom hissing away with the build-up of steam that had come from the boiler in the basement.

Morris frowned. This place was far too modern to use steam, and besides he had the damn air conditioning on, not the heat.

Suddenly he heard it again—that prolonged, inexplicable hissing sound.

Then he saw the snake crawl out from under his bed.

Morris was no expert on reptiles, but anybody who watches TV or goes to the movies learns what certain kinds of snakes look like, especially the varieties that present an instantly recognizable threat to the hero, or some other character on the screen.

Morris had seen the first Indiana Jones movie, *Raiders of the Lost Ark,* three or four times. As a result, he was pretty sure he knew just what he was looking at.

Shaking off a momentary sense of disbelief, Morris made himself focus on the two most salient facts of his situation.

One: there was a King Cobra in the hotel room with him.

Two: the large reptile was between him and the door.

There were more hissing noises from under the bed. A moment later, another snake crawled out to join the King Cobra. Morris did not recognize this one, but a few seconds later it was joined by something that he did find familiar.

Even after all these years, he had not forgotten what a rattlesnake looked like.

Morris was about to run back into the bathroom and slam the door when a stir of movement from in there caught his eye. He looked just in time to see a deadly Water Moccasin crawling out from the shower stall he had so recently vacated. He'd seen those in Texas, too.

Two seconds later, a naked Quincey Morris was crouched atop the hotel bureau, watching in horror as more and more snakes appeared from underneath the bed. He recognized at least one more variety of cobra, this one smaller than the first and differently colored, and he was pretty sure he saw a couple of Copperheads among the growing collection. The others weren't familiar to him, but he had no doubt they were deadly poisonous, just as he had no illusions about who had sent them. Christine Abernathy, he realized, was done creating illusions. She had decided to play for keeps this time.

He looked around desperately. The phone was across the room, which meant it might as well be on the moon. Besides, what would he tell the hotel operator—"I'd like to report a couple of dozen snakes in my room." She'd probably just tell him to sleep it off.

The snakes were slithering around the room now, examining the furniture, and each other, curiously. They were showing little interest in Morris at the moment, since he was too big to eat, and was posing no immediate threat to them. Morris thought he probably had a few minutes' grace to figure some way out of this predicament.

Then he heard the thin "crack" as the cheap wood of the bureau began to give under his weight.

Several of the snakes were looking Morris's way now, reacting to the sound. Their two-pronged tongues flickered in and out, testing the air for more vibrations.

Panic screamed for attention within Morris's brain, and he crushed it down savagely. He then tried to figure out what he could do to survive if the bureau collapsed and sent him tumbling into that mass of crawling, squirming death.

He knew that snakebite, even from the deadliest reptile, is not instantly fatal. It often takes an hour or more for an untreated adult victim to die.

But that was from one bite. What about twenty bites? Thirty? And even if he made it into the hall, how long would it take to persuade someone to call an ambulance for the naked lunatic who was raving about a room full of poisonous snakes? And what hospital anywhere near Salem was likely to have a supply of antivenin on hand? Eastern Massachusetts was hardly snake country.

Until now, that is.

There was a grinding sound as more of the cheap wood that made up the bureau began to give way beneath his feet.

Morris realized the bare toes of his right foot were touching something hard on the bureau's top. He glanced down, saw that it was the hand mirror that Libby Chastain had given him back at the hospital.

What had she said? "Keep it with you, when you meet Abernathy," something like that. He had thought at the time that Libby was trying to say that the mirror had a spell of some kind on it.

Moving cautiously, he reached down and grasped the little mirror. Bring it up to his face, he looked in it, and was unsurprised to see the face of a man who looked scared shitless.

He didn't know what he was expecting the mirror to do, but nothing happened.

A few feet below, the snakes kept writhing and swarming.

AT THAT MOMENT, in the Intensive Care Unit of a New York City hospital, the monitors connected to patient Chastain, Elizabeth J. (Condition: Grave) began to exhibit sudden changes that would have puzzled any medical professional, if one had been standing nearby to see them.

The EEG showed a marked change in brainwave activity, while the blood pressure cuff around one arm recorded a spike in both systolic and diastolic pressure. Respiration began to increase significantly, as did pulse rate. Although her eyes remained closed, a low moan escaped the patient's lips.

But no alarm was tripped by the monitors, and no doctor or nurse came by to observe these highly unusual events.

In her basement workroom, Christine Abernathy blew out the five candles and began to put her equipment and materials away. There was a smug expression on her coldly beautiful face.

She wondered how long it would take Quincey Morris to die.

The cheap hotel bureau gave one more loud crack, and that must have been one of the legs snapping, because the whole thing suddenly tilted forward as it began to collapse. In desperation born out of sheer terror, Morris leaped from the top of the falling bureau, across the five feet of space and onto the bed.

He had thought the distance too far to jump, but fright is a powerful motivator. Landing on the mattress, Morris used the momentum to go into a tuck and roll and came to his feet at once. Somehow, despite his exertions, he had managed to hang onto Libby's little mirror—for all the good it was doing.

The bureau had fallen on top of some of the snakes. Morris wasn't sure if any had been killed or hurt, but it was clear that the rest had been thrown into a frenzy by the crash. Several of the reptiles had reared up, hissing like mad, while the rest glided restlessly around the room, looking either for something to attack, or for a way out—Morris wasn't sure which.

Then something appeared at the foot of the bed—the head of the King Cobra. Morris had noticed earlier that the deadly snake was at least six feet long, and it was using some of that body length to rear up and examine this large, warm-blooded creature that was causing all the fuss in its new territory.

Morris and the snake stared at each other for a long moment. Then the King Cobra began to crawl up onto the bed.

Libby Chastain was breathing hard now, and a sheen of sweat covered her body, soaking into the hospital gown and bedclothes. Her lips moved rapidly as if she were speaking, but no sound came from her mouth. Although her eyes remained shut, the lashes fluttered rapidly, like the wings of a trapped bird.

Libby began to writhe upon the bed, twisting and straining as if in the throes of some mighty effort. Her exertions increased, and it did not take long before newly sewn surgical stitches began to part under the kind of pressure they were never meant to withstand. Libby Chastain started bleeding in several places, then other stitches started to give way and she began hemorrhaging internally. This did not stop her struggles, or even slow them down.

Some of this frenetic activity finally tripped one of the alarms wired to Libby's monitors, and an ICU nurse came hustling over to see what had happened. Nurse Greta Beck's eyes widened as she took in the patient's convulsions, as well as the monitor readings, which appeared to have gone completely haywire.

Greta Beck wasted no time gawking. She sprinted to the nearest telephone and called a Code Blue for the ICU.

MORRIS BACKED UP as far as he could, moving slowly so as not to antagonize the King Cobra that had just slithered onto the bed with him. But there was only so much room on a double bed, and in a second or two Morris's back was against the wall.

There was nowhere else to go.

Morris had just decided that his best chance, such as it was, lay with a sudden dash to the door of the room. He would almost certainly pick up several poisonous bites on the way, but at least he would then be out of the room, and able to close the door against these crawling horrors.

Then maybe he could get someone to call an ambulance. And maybe Morris would still be alive when it arrived. And maybe they would have something at the local ER that might be useful against snakebite—even multiple bites from the kinds of snakes that had never been seen around here.

Yeah, and maybe pigs might fucking fly.

But the alternative was to give up—just roll up and die in the middle of this snake pit.

You just didn't do that—not in Morris's family.

The first Quincey Morris had fought the good fight right up to the very end, and the hell with the odds. He had been the start of a long line of Morrises, men and women both, who had devoted themselves to the struggle against the darkness. Not because the Morrises were a bunch of sanctimonious Holy Joes with martyr complexes—but because once you have looked upon the true face of evil, you have no choice but to fight against it, assuming you want to retain any self-respect at all.

Many in Quincey Morris's family had suffered for their commitment. Some had lost their lives over it.

But not one of them had given up. Ever.

Morris began to flex his calf muscles in preparation for the leap off the bed. It was likely that his sudden movement would prompt an attack by the King Cobra. Morris would just have to take the huge snake's bite and keep moving, just as he would almost certainly have to absorb other bites on his way to the door.

He stared into the King's Cobra's black, unblinking eyes. *Okay, motherfucker, get ready to take your best shot, because—*

Something was happening.

Morris thought at first that his vision was going, because the King Cobra in front of him seemed to be... blurring.

Did I pick up a bite from one of these fucking things already and didn't even notice? Am I dying? Is that what this is?

But he realized that his view of the rest of the room remained clear—it was only the snake in front of him that was losing definition and substance. For Morris, it was like watching a Polaroid picture develop, except in reverse. The King Cobra was just fading away.

He risked a glance toward the floor where the other snakes had been slithering around. For an instant his vision seemed to pick up an after-image of their wriggling, hissing forms—and then they were... gone.

Morris looked back toward the King Cobra—but there was nothing to see, except the wrinkled bedspread. The great snake had disappeared.

Remaining where he was, Morris looked carefully around the room, but not a single reptile could be seen. He listened hard, but the only sounds were the hum of the air conditioner and Morris's own labored breathing.

After a few more seconds, Morris felt his knees start to buckle. He let them, and sat down hard on the bed. He started trembling then, all over, like a man pulled from an icy river.

Had that bitch Abernathy been playing with him again? He decided that probably wasn't the case this time. A few more seconds, and Morris would have picked up enough snakebites to put him beyond medical help. No, she hadn't been fooling around—this had been intended as the killing stroke.

What, then?

He realized he still had Libby's mirror in his right hand. In fact, he had grasped it so tightly that he had hair-thin cuts from the mirror's edge across his thumb and palm.

He opened his hand, wincing at the cramps in his fingers, and let the mirror fall on to the mattress. Had Libby's spell on the mirror banished the snakes before they could do their deadly work?

And if the snakes had been dispersed by Libby's magic, *where the hell did they go?*

CHRISTINE ABERNATHY PUT away the last of her magical implements. She thought about doing another scrying to see what Quincey Morris's bloated corpse looked like, but decided it was too much trouble. She'd watch the local news on television later—see what they made of the mysterious death at the Salem Inn. She thought it unlikely that the authorities would consider witchcraft as a *modus operandi,* even though the town was famous for—

She frowned suddenly. What was that noise? It sounded like...

Hissing?

Christine Abernathy spun around to face her work table, just in time to receive a bite from the King Cobra on the side of her neck.

She stumbled backward in surprise, but not before the Black Mamba coiled atop the pentagram delivered two quick strikes to her face.

Another step backward, and suddenly she tripped on a big Bushmaster that was coiling around one of her ankles and then fell heavily among the other snakes which, until very recently, had been slithering around Quincey Morris's hotel room. She received twenty-three more bites in the next few seconds, and even more as she struggled to rise from the floor.

The massive infusion of venom was already starting to work on her, but she still had plenty of time for a long scream full of pain and fear and rage—the kind of sound, so legend has it, that is so often heard just the other side of the gates of Hell.

* * *

MORRIS WAS AWAKE when some conscientious hotel employee slid a complementary copy of the local paper under the door of his room. He had stayed awake all night, Libby Chastain's mirror clasped in his hand like a talisman—which, he knew now, was exactly what it was.

He didn't know if Christine Abernathy would send the snakes again, or perhaps some other form of devilment. Whatever might come, he wanted to be awake to meet it. But the rest of the night had been quiet.

He was glad to be provided with a copy of the newspaper; it would save him the trouble of hunting one up somewhere. Over the course of the long night, Morris had formulated a plan for dealing with Christine Abernathy. He did not know if it was the best plan possible—only that it was the best he was able to come up with.

The main thing he needed was a gun, and getting your hands on one these days usually poses problems. He had a couple of pistols at home, but bringing one on a plane from Texas, even in checked luggage, would have required either a badge or the equivalent of an Act of Congress. Despite the stereotypes about his native state, Morris generally approved of the laws that made it difficult for someone to buy a gun on impulse. But at the moment he regarded them as a damn nuisance.

There are, of course, people who will sell you a gun illegally, but Morris figured there weren't many such folks hanging around Salem, Massachusetts. Boston, maybe—hell, almost certainly. But even there, you'd have to know where to go and who to talk to. Gunrunners don't advertise in the Yellow Pages, and Morris had no contacts in the Boston underworld.

He figured his best bet was to check the classified ads, look under "Sporting Goods," and find someone looking to sell an individual gun for ready cash. In a pinch, a shotgun or rifle would do, but Morris was hoping to get his hands on a pistol—a .38 or .357 revolver, or, better yet, a .45 automatic.

Then, once he was armed, he was going back to Christine Abernathy's house. With Libby's mirror to protect him against Abernathy's magic—at least, Morris hoped it would still be good for that purpose—he was going to do his best to blow Christine Abernathy's pretty little head off.

Even if he succeeded, there was a good chance he would be arrested for murder, but Morris was past the point of caring about that. After the last twenty-four hours or so, he knew how the LaRues must have felt for all those weeks, under the threat of a supernatural force they could neither escape nor fight, and he was well and truly sick of it. Christine Abernathy had to be stopped, and for good.

Morris fetched the paper from the floor and brought it over to the bed. He unfolded it and was about to turn to the classifieds when something on the front page below the fold caught his eye.

LOCAL GIRL DEAD.
FOUL PLAY SUSPECTED.

Morris blinked a couple of times, then read on.

> A teenage girl was found dead in her Salem home last night, and police have not ruled out murder as the cause of her death.
>
> The body of Christine Abernathy, 18, was discovered by police in the basement of the house, located at 328 Chestnut Avenue. Officers were responding to calls from neighbors who said they heard screams coming from the residence around 10:30pm.
>
> A police spokesperson said that the girl's death was considered "suspicious," but would give no further details. An official ruling on cause of death will have to wait for the results of an autopsy, which has been scheduled for later today, sources said.
>
> Ms. Abernathy had been living alone at the Chestnut Avenue address since the death of her mother last year, according to neighbors. They said the young woman usually kept to herself and had little contact with...

A bright, savage smile had formed on Morris's face as he read the article, but as he put the paper down it faded into a thoughtful frown.

He had already seen the magic that Christine Abernathy could work with a newspaper. Could this be a trick to lull him into doing something careless?

After a moment he picked up the telephone, tapped in a single number, then waited.

"Could you connect me with the hotel gift shop please? Thanks."

He waited some more, then:

"Good morning. Listen, you carry *The Salem News* there, don't you? Do you have any of today's left? All right, I have kind of a strange request to make. I haven't seen the paper, but somebody told me that there's a story on the front page this morning about some woman who was found dead here in town overnight. Yes, that sounds like the story. My friend said he thought he remembered the victim's name, and it sounded like a niece of mine, and before I let myself get all upset, I wonder if you could... sure, thanks. Abernathy? That was her name? Chestnut Street? No, that's not my niece, thanks be to God. I appreciate you humoring me, ma'am, that was mighty kind of you..."

Quincey Morris hung up the telephone, then let out his breath in a long sigh.

Three minutes later, he was asleep.

CHAPTER 34

IT WAS JUST past four in the afternoon when Quincey Morris stepped out of the hospital elevator and turned toward the Intensive Care Unit. He carried with him a bouquet of roses, gardenias, and lilies that had set him back forty-five bucks at the florist shop on the ground floor.

Nobody who isn't a doctor or nurse gets to just walk into a hospital ICU, so Morris stepped up to the glass that enclosed the area and peered inside. If Libby was awake and not in the middle of some medical procedure, maybe he could talk his way in to see her for a couple of minutes. He doubted that they would let him leave the flowers in there, but he hoped she could at least see them before he was kicked out again.

It took him only a moment to locate the bed where he had last seen the unconscious form of Libby Chastain.

The bed was empty.

Have they got her back in the operating room?

The bed was made up with what looked like fresh linens. The monitors, which had been registering Libby's vital signs, were disconnected and turned off. The IV drips, on their tall stainless steel poles, were gone.

Okay, they've just moved her to a regular room. That's a good sign, it means she's doing better. That's good news. Nothing to worry about.

Still, he wasted no time walking back to the ICU nurses' station, where a young woman in starched whites was typing at a computer keyboard.

"Excuse me," he said. "A friend of mine was in Intensive Care yesterday, but now it looks like she's been moved. I'm wondering if you can tell me her new room number."

"Certainly, sir. What is the patient's name?"

"Elizabeth Chastain."

The nurse's face froze for just a second, but that was enough to start a glacier forming in Morris's gut.

Without bothering to check her computer, or a list of rooms, or anything else, the nurse looked at Morris and asked, "Are you a family member, sir?"

"No, it's like I said: I'm her friend, I was here yesterday. What's the problem?"

"Well, it's just that... uh, perhaps it would be best if you talked to Doctor Melling. I'll see if he's still in the building." She reached for the telephone.

Morris leaned over the counter. He was about to grab the young nurse's crisp lapels and start shaking information out of her when a familiar female voice said from behind him, "Or perhaps you could just talk to me."

Morris whirled around and found himself looking into the broadly smiling face of a woman who bore no trace of bruises, bandages, or injury of any kind.

It was the face of Libby Chastain.

"Come on," she said, the smile still in place. "Let's go downstairs. I'm just dying... for a cup of coffee."

FENTON HAD INSISTED on driving Van Dreenan to JFK himself.

The two men spoke little in the car, although at one point Van Dreenan said, "You know, I am accustomed to making my own way around. An escort is not necessary."

"Be glad you're not going in fucking cuffs," Fenton snapped. He didn't say anything for the rest of the drive. For that matter, he hadn't said much to Van Dreenan since that night on a lonely stretch of road outside Salem, Massachusetts.

Fenton used his FBI credentials to bypass the long line at the security checkpoint. Once Van Dreenan had picked up a boarding pass and checked his bag, Fenton insisted on walking him to the departure area. The flight for London, with a connection to Johannesburg, would start boarding in forty minutes.

They sat side by side in the half-empty departure lounge for a while, not speaking, until Fenton suddenly said, "I had this speech all prepared about how I don't hold with vigilante shit, about the rights of criminal defendants, and about the need for due process to avoid turning this country into a fucking police state."

"If you feel you must deliver it, I will listen," Van Dreenan said. "I will not even argue with you."

"Like I said, I had this little speech all prepared. But then it occurred to me yesterday to call a couple of guys I know who are pretty high up in the South African Police Forces."

"So, you've arranged to have me fired, instead?" Van Dreenan did not appear particularly dismayed by the prospect.

"No. Like I said, I talked to 'em. About you. One of them knows you personally, and the other one has access to all kinds of official records."

Van Dreenan's face had grown tight. "Yes. And?"

Fenton's voice softened. "And I heard about your daughter. I mean *all* about her."

After a long, aching moment, Van Dreenan sighed deeply. "Yes, well, that was all some time ago."

"Uh-huh. Well, I thought some about what I'd heard. Asked myself what I'd do, if one of my little girls... well, you know."

Van Dreenan just nodded.

"Like I said, I don't hold with vigilante shit. But sometimes... ah, hell, I don't even know what I'm trying to fucking say."

"You don't have to say anything, my friend. It is done now."

"Yeah, well..." Fenton turned to Van Dreenan and stuck out his hand. The South African took it, and squeezed firmly. It was the closest thing to an embrace either of them was capable of having with another man.

The FBI man stood up. "One more thing I wanted to say, Van Dreenan, and this comes from way upstairs at the Bureau: *don't come back.*"

Fenton took a brisk step away, and another, then stopped. He turned back and stood there, hands in his pockets, looking at Van Dreenan impassively before he said, "Unless I call you."

* * *

"THEY WANTED ME to stay around for more tests," Libby said, as she stirred some Sweet'n Low into her cup. "But I've already signed myself out."

"So, why are you still here?" Morris could not stop staring at Libby, comparing her unmarked face with the memory of the battered, bandaged woman he had seen just two days before.

"Waiting for you, naturally. I knew you'd show up here as soon as you could, and I didn't want you to get a fright when you found me gone."

"I appreciate your faith in me. And, yeah, a fright is exactly what I *did* get, once I saw that empty bed in the ICU."

"I know. I'm sorry, Quincey." Libby shook her head ruefully. "It figures. I'd been sitting where I could keep an eye on both the nurse's station and the ICU, then I leave for just five minutes to go to the bathroom, and sure enough..."

"Yeah, your timing always did suck, Libby."

They both laughed, then he went on, "Your magic still works pretty well, though."

"The mirror spell, you mean? Yes, I'm quite pleased with that one. I'd planned to tell you about it on our way to Massachusetts, but... circumstances intervened."

"I thought you said that white magic couldn't be used to hurt someone. Christine Abernathy, wherever she is right about now, would probably take exception to that."

"I told you that white magic could not be used to *initiate* harm," Libby said patiently. "But it does allow you to protect yourself, as you've seen several times already."

Morris nodded. "That's for sure."

"Well, a mirror spell is one form of self-protection. It deflects the evil intent of the black magic and turns it back upon the user. Sort of like judo, where you take the force of your opponent's attack and use it to throw him on his ass."

"So Christine suddenly found herself hosting all those reptiles she had sent to visit me."

"Exactly. She probably could have saved herself if she'd been prepared for the possibility, but she was an arrogant bitch—I could tell that by the kinds of spells she used against us."

"Having met the lady, I think I can confirm your opinion."

"Arrogant, but powerful, no doubt about that. In fact, her magic was so potent, I was able to divert some of the energy as it was transformed by the mirror spell, and use it to heal myself—the results of which you see before you."

"And damn glad to see them, too."

"I was able to manage that little trick because my injuries had been caused by Abernathy's magic in the first place, indirectly. That allowed me to transmute the energy waves along lines of—ah, don't get me started with the mechanics of it. It's boring, to anyone but another adept."

"I bet your doctors aren't bored by it," Morris said.

Libby matched his smile with her own. "Oh my God, you should have seen them! They couldn't decide whether to contact the *Journal of the American Medical Association* or the Vatican. I didn't like causing all that confusion and distress. But if I tried to tell them the truth, I'm pretty sure I'd have found myself transferred posthaste up to the fifth floor."

"Which is—?"

"The psychiatric ward, of course. So, I played dumb. Said I had no idea what had just happened, but since I seemed to be fine now, there was no reason to stick around."

"No wonder they want more tests. You would have made one hell of a journal article, Libby. Or a whole series of them."

"I know. It's very perplexing for the staff, and I feel kind of bad about that. But on the plus side, I think I may have been responsible for at least three religious conversions."

"Well, before they start canonization proceedings, what do you say we get out of here? We'll get your luggage and stuff back to your place, then how about you let me buy you dinner at the best restaurant in town—whatever it is this week."

"You've got yourself a deal, cowboy." She stood up and stretched. "It'll be good to sleep in my own bed again."

Morris nodded. "At least for tonight."

She looked at him quizzically.

"Did you forget?" Morris asked. "We have one more stop to make before this is done."

It took Libby only a second to grasp his meaning. "That's right," she said. "So we do."

* * *

IN A MANSION that was slightly smaller than Alabama, Walter Grobius sat in his favorite armchair, clutching printed copies of two e-mails that had arrived three hours apart. One provided the sad details about the passing from this life of one Christine Abernathy; the other gave the names of two recently deceased individuals whose remains had been pulled from a burned-out car in Massachusetts and recently been identified from DNA analysis.

Walter Grobius was not given to extreme displays of emotion. He had built his immense fortune on cold calculation and iron nerve, and did not waste his time expressing disappointment through vulgar physical displays.

He had, it was true, briefly considered sending one of the servants to buy a dog, so that Grobius could kick it to death. But he had abandoned the idea as unseemly and undignified. *That* was what counted.

He had always responded to setbacks with greater determination to succeed, and this time would be no exception. He viewed the end of the world as he would any other business project; the scale was simply bigger, that was all.

He picked up the telephone next to his chair. As soon as the voice in his ear said "Sir?" Grobius said, "Tell Pardee I want him."

He hung up without waiting for the "Yes, sir" that would be immediately forthcoming.

Adjustments needed to be made, that was all. The project would succeed. The Great Cleansing would take place.

A few moments later, Walter Grobius picked up the telephone again.

He had changed his mind about the dog.

EPILOGUE

Madison, Wisconsin
The Present Day

As Morris pulled up in front of the house, Libby Chastain looked at her watch. "After nine," she said. "I hope the LaRues don't mind us coming over so late."

"Walter said on the phone that they'd prefer it this way. The kids will be in bed, so they won't eavesdrop on our conversation. No point in getting them frightened again, now that they're starting to get back to something like a normal life."

Marcia LaRue answered the door, looking about ten years younger than she had the last time Morris had seen her.

In the living room, Walter LaRue was already standing to greet them, his wide smile a duplicate of his wife's.

"Good to see you again, both of you," he said, shaking hands.

"Yes it is," Marcia said, coming over to stand beside him. After a long moment, she asked, "Is it really over?"

"Yes it is," Libby told her. "Once and for all."

After they were all seated, Morris said, "After all you've been through, Libby and I thought we owed you a full report of what we've been doing since we saw you last."

"More than anything else," Libby said, "we wanted you to understand that this ordeal you've been through really *is* finished. We thought you should know exactly what that means."

"Well, we're eager to hear about it, that's for sure," Walter LaRue said, and his wife nodded.

"Well, here's the way it went," Morris said. "After we left you last time, Libby and I headed off to Boston..."

Twenty-three minutes later, Libby Chastain concluded with, "And I was able to use some of the residual energy from her spell to heal my injuries from the car crash. And so, here we are."

The LaRues sat silently for several moments. Finally, Walter LaRue said, "You've been through quite a lot, on our behalf."

"All part of the service," Morris said, with a smile.

"No, I think I'd call it above and beyond the call of duty," LaRue replied. He reached into his shirt pocket for a piece of paper, unfolded it, and placed it on the coffee table in front of Morris and Chastain. It was a check for twenty thousand dollars.

Morris looked at it, then raised his head, frowning. "That's not why Libby and I came here. I told you before that we had been paid in full."

"I know," LaRue said. "And I accept that. But, from what you've described to us, you two have racked up incredible expenses. Your plane fare alone must have amounted to at least a third of this."

"This really isn't—" Libby began.

"We both agree that we want you to take this," Marcia LaRue said. "There's no amount of money that can pay for what you've done for us, and for the kids, but it's a gesture of appreciation. Let us make it—please."

Morris and Libby looked at each other for a long moment. Then Morris picked up the check and stuffed it in his jacket pocket. "Well... for expenses, then. And thank you."

Marcia LaRue said she had brewed a pot of decaf coffee, and asked if anybody wanted some. She also mentioned a cheesecake that was sitting in her refrigerator. Morris and Libby agreed to some of each.

"Libby, can you give me a hand with the coffee cups and plates, please?" Marcia LaRue asked.

"Sure." Libby rose and followed her into the kitchen.

A couple of minutes later, Libby was slicing wedges of cheesecake when Marcia said to her, "I'm really glad you and Quincey agreed to take the money."

Libby shrugged amicably. "It was kind of you and Walter to offer. I'm sure we'll find a use for it."

"Thing is, there was kind of an ulterior motive involved. On my part, anyway."

Libby looked up, eyebrows raised. "Oh?"

Marcia nodded. "You're accepting the money makes it a little easier for me—emotionally, I mean—to ask you for kind of a special favor."

Libby put the knife down carefully. "What did you have in mind, exactly?"

"Well, do you think sometime, when you're not too busy chasing after demons and zombies with Quincey and all, maybe..."

"What, Marcia?" Libby's voice was gentle.

"Maybe you could, you know, teach me the basics of how to do white magic?"

Libby picked up the knife again and returned to slicing the cheesecake. "Sister mine," she said, "it would be my pleasure."

ABOUT THE AUTHOR

Justin Gustainis is a college professor living in upstate New York. He is the author of the novel *The Hades Project* (2003), as well as a number of short stories. In his misspent youth, Mr. Gustainis was, at various times, a busboy, soldier, speechwriter and professional bodyguard. To balance his karma, he and his wife collect teddy bears.

ACKNOWLEDGEMENTS

MANY PEOPLE HELPED me take this novel on its long journey from my study to your hands.

John Carroll, my oldest friend in the world, gave me the idea for Walter Grobius — about whom more will be said presently. Sorry about that time in First Grade, man.

Jim Butcher was kind enough to take time from getting Harry Dresden in trouble and read an early draft of the book. His encouragement and support kept me trying to find a publisher when I wanted to just give up. Jim's talent as a writer is matched only by his generosity of spirit. I want to be just like him when I grow up.

Christian Dunn at Solaris bought the manuscript of *Black Magic Woman* and then worked with me, very patiently, to make it better. He is a prince among men. At least in my house.

Lawrence Osborn, copy editor without peer, amazed me with both the breadth and depth of his knowledge. Anybody who can find and correct my mistakes in history *and* Latin *and* computer technology is a polymath of the first order.

An unknown judge at the Colorado Gold Writers Contest several years ago gave me some excellent advice on rewriting the Prologue, and a great deal of encouragement, as well.

Michael Kanaly and C.J. Henderson deserve thanks for many favors granted and kindnesses bestowed.

Terry Bear offered nutritional advice and did copious menu planning, most of which was ignored. Pizza delivery drivers fear him.

My wife, Patricia Grogan, is the best thing that ever happened to me. Without her to do the "happy dance" with, none of this would be worth doing. I love you forever, bear.

EVIL WAYS

Read on for an excerpt from Evil Ways, *the next Quincey Morris Supernatural Investigation by Justin Gustainis, coming soon from Solaris.*

CHAPTER 1

QUINCEY MORRIS STOOD alone in the shadow of a decaying eucalyptus tree and wondered if this was the night he was going to die.

Morris was not by nature a pessimist. As an occult investigator, he had an innate faith in the ultimate power of good over evil. But thinking morbid thoughts before beginning a difficult job was his way of guarding against complacency, which was as dangerous to someone in Morris's line of work as it would be to a lion tamer or trapeze artist—with the same fatal results likely to follow.

Except in Morris's case, death might not be the end of it.

The house he was watching from two hundred feet away was built in the Spanish Mission style that Morris always thought of as Southern California Tacky. The property was surrounded by a high concrete wall that would have done any movie star's home proud. But the man who lived there now was no movie star.

Bet he could be if he wanted to, Morris thought. *Horror movies, maybe. Jason and Freddie, watch out, 'cause the real thing's in town, now, y'all.*

Morris had researched the subject, as he always did before carrying out one of these specialized home invasions. He knew that Lucas Fortner was an occultist of mid-level skill and above-average malevolence. He was said to have spent a year in Budapest, studying black magic under the infamous Janos Skorzeny. A year with

Skorzeny made Fortner dangerous. Five years would have made him too deadly to mess around with.

In the moonlight, Morris could just make out the jagged bits of glass that had been set into the top of the stone wall. He knew that the glass was coated with viper venom (Black Mamba, supposedly) that was reapplied weekly—more often, during the rainy season—to keep its potency up.

Morris checked his watch and saw that it was just after 4:00am. Time to go. There were still two hours of darkness left to skulk in, but midnight was long enough past so that some of the Powers guarding Fortner's place would be at less than their full strength.

Morris would not have approached that house at midnight for all the gold in a rapper's teeth.

He patted his pockets to assure himself that all his gear was where it should be, then started across the street. He did not cross in a straight line, but angled to the left—a path that would take him to the property of Fortner's neighbor, a producer at DreamWorks Studios with absolutely no connection to the occult. Morris had checked. He always checked. He was a professional.

The producer's grounds were of interest to Morris for a couple of reasons. One was that the exterior wall was considerably shorter than Fortner's, and free of broken glass, venom-coated or otherwise. The other reason involved an ancient oak tree on the property—the one that rose up tall and stately a mere ten feet from the wall separating the producer's grounds from Fortner's, with several of its branches overhanging Fortner's property.

Morris scaled the producer's wall with little difficulty, swung his legs over the top, and dropped lightly to the ground on the other side. He stood crouched among the plantings and flowers, all his senses alert. There were supposed to be no guard dogs on the property, and no human security either, but you never know these things for sure until you're on the scene. Morris spent the next two minutes absolutely still. He saw no movement except the flowers and shrubbery swaying in the gentle breeze, heard only the drone of crickets and cicadas, smelled nothing except for mimosa and sweet jasmine. Then he straightened slowly and began to make his careful way across the grounds.

As he approached the oak tree, Morris took from his pocket a gemstone, about the size and shape of an almond, that his witch friend Libby Chastain had given him. He stopped, held the stone in his open palm, and waited.

If Fortner had decided to hedge his bets by placing some kind of protective spell on his neighbor's trees, that gemstone would glow bright red.

The stone retained its pale blue color. The tree had not been ensorcelled.

Morris slipped on a pair of thin leather gloves to protect his hands, then began to shimmy up the trunk of the great oak. After ten feet or so, he was able to reach the lowest branches, which made his ascent easier. He continued climbing until he reached a branch that seemed thick enough to bear his weight. He crawled out about half its length, then hung from it with both hands, listening hard for the telltale "crack" that would betray weakness in the limb. But it held him without complaint.

This was important. The second worst thing that could happen tonight was for the branch to give way while Morris was on his way onto Fortner's property.

The worst thing would be for that branch to break while Morris was trying to get *out*.

Sitting on the branch now, with his back carefully braced against the trunk, Morris uncoiled from around his waist a twenty-foot length of rope. It was the kind of line that mountain climbers use, except that Morris's had been dyed jet black.

He crawled slowly along the branch, pausing every few seconds to listen for any sign that the thing was going to give under his weight.

Now he was just over the wall that stood between the producer's grounds and Fortner's. The deadly shards of broken glass grinned at him in the moonlight.

Three feet further, and Morris carefully tied one end of his rope around the branch, using the knots that he had practiced a hundred times while blindfolded.

From between the leaves, Morris could see Fortner's house, a sprawling, two-story structure. No lights burned in the windows, which was unsurprising. Fortner was away in San Francisco for three days, had left that very afternoon. Morris had watched him board the plane, and waited for it to take off, just in case. The man lived alone, which meant that there should be no human presence in that house tonight.

Which did not mean, of course, that the place was unguarded.

Morris stayed on that branch for the next ten minutes, watching Fortner's house and grounds. Finally he decided that whatever might be protecting the property, he wasn't going to learn about it from the safety of the producer's tree.

Morris lowered the rope to the ground inside Fortner's wall. He twitched it a few times, to see if anything below would react to the movement. Nothing.

Wrapping his legs around the rope, Morris used his gloved hands to control the speed of his descent. A few seconds later, he was on the ground, watching and listening before moving on.

Morris was halfway to the house when he picked up movement out of the corner of his eye.

He froze, then slowly turned his head to get a better look. Whatever was out there, it was keeping to the shadows. And it was *big.*

Morris thought about some pictures he had seen in *People* or someplace about movie stars and their exotic taste in pets. One well-known actor had a leopard, shipped all the way from Africa. Another, who had played Tarzan in some movie, was photographed next to the cage containing his pride and joy—a Bengal tiger. Some states had laws forbidding that sort of thing—but not, apparently, California.

If members of the Hollywood crowd could get any of the great predator cats, then presumably Fortner could, too.

The creature moved again, revealing a hint of black fur in the moonlight. A black panther? Fortner would probably enjoy the symbolism of such a sentry. And the damn thing would be dangerous, too. All leopards were formidable, whatever their color. And once they had tasted human flesh...

No, not a panther. It was closer now, and Morris could see that this thing had a short tail, its fur long and shaggy-looking. And it didn't move with a cat's fluid grace. Instead, it had the bouncing muscularity of a—dog?

That was all right. Morris could deal with dogs.

Hell of a big pooch, though, if that's what it was. It looked to be the size of a bull calf.

Then he saw the eyes. They were looking right at him, and they were glowing like hellfire.

Morris looked away instantly. Now he knew what he was dealing with.

Fortner had his grounds guarded by a Black Dog.

Those eyes were the creature's principal weapons. Some of the legends Morris had read claimed that locking eyes with a Black Dog would freeze you in place instantly, a helpless, living statue until dawn. Other accounts said that its gaze could strike a man blind, or speechless, or drive him instantly insane.

But you have to stare into its eyes for any of those things to happen. All the stories were in agreement on that. And after all, who wouldn't gape at such a horrific apparition?

Morris wouldn't, for one.

He closed his eyes tightly, then reached into the side pocket of his jacket, moving as if he were under water. Black Dogs usually relied on their basilisk gaze for both attack and defense, but Morris didn't want any sudden action of his to give this one an excuse to start acting like a real canine and tear his throat out.

He finally found what he wanted in his pocket. Morris removed the object carefully, then slowly went down on one knee. To make this work, he would need to be on the same level as the dog.

Morris could hear it now, drawing closer. He made himself wait, eyes still shut. He was only going to get one chance to make this work.

Now the thing was growling at him, softly, from a few yards away. It was preparing to attack.

In one smooth motion, Morris brought the small hand mirror up in front of his face, the reflective surface facing toward the Black Dog.

The creature's attention would be drawn by the movement, and it was probably looking at Morris's face now anyway, trying to work its mojo on him and wondering why he wasn't screaming, or running away, or doing whatever its victims usually did.

But now the dog's magical gaze was being turned back on itself by the mirror.

The growling stopped suddenly, as if cut off by a switch. There was a brief whimper, then—nothing.

Morris made himself wait for the length of ten breaths, then risked a look.

The dog was frozen in a crouch, as if it had been preparing to spring. The red and yellow light was gone from its eyes, and it made no sound as Morris stood and put the mirror away.

The Black Dog was now no more dangerous than any other lawn statue—at least until dawn.

He could have destroyed the thing, now that it was helpless, but that would have been gratuitous. He was a professional, not some teenage vandal.

And anyway, if Morris were not out of there by sunrise, he would have bigger problems than Poochie to worry about

A minute later, he was searching the house's exterior for the best way in. He had studied the original architect's plans, as well as photos taken from a distance with a telephoto lens. But Morris had a finely developed sense for these things that no image on paper could ever replace.

After a quick but cautious circuit of the place, he decided on the front door. Fortner might well expect any intruder to use a window or one of the auxiliary doors, and would thus concentrate more of his protective energies toward those access points.

Unless, of course, that's what Fortner figured I'd think, in which case the front door is going to have all the heavy artillery trained on it. Which means I'll be blued, screwed, and tattooed.

Morris shook his head impatiently at his own dithering. You could make yourself crazy trying to second-guess someone like Fortner. Sometimes you had to go with your instincts, and Morris's were telling him that the front door was the best bet.

He checked the front steps for traps or tricks, and found none. Then he spent the better part of a minute regarding that door with affection and good will. It might not matter, but he wanted there to be a good karmic relationship between himself and the door before he touched it. It pays never to take inanimate objects for granted.

As doors go, it was nothing special, considering the ostentatious grandeur of the house. No glass in it, of course. Morris was never that lucky. Solid wood, walnut maybe, carved into a series of panels. The knob was plain brass, and the lock was complicated-looking and intimidating—or it would be, to anyone with less experience than Quincey Morris.

He produced the almond-shaped gem again, and passed it slowly over the doorframe, the door itself, and the lock. The stone did not glow red, which meant no magic was being used to protect the door.

Morris scratched his chin reflectively.

Did Fortner leave the door deliberately unguarded, so as to lull the unsuspecting intruder?

He just might, the bastard. You get through the door without breaking a sweat, then stroll inside humming to yourself, only to have an anvil dropped on your stupid head.

Or maybe...

Morris brought out a pencil flashlight and moved its narrow beam around the doorframe, very slowly.

And there it was—the faint bulge under the paint.

Just because Fortner had sorcery at his disposal didn't mean he had to forgo more mundane protections. And now Morris had spotted the wire for the alarm system.

You open the door, you interrupt the circuit, and all hell breaks loose. Morris didn't know whether the alarm would set off a klaxon horn, ring up the nearest police station, or trigger one of Fortner's nastier occult surprises. And he wasn't interested in finding out.

With a sharp knife Morris gouged into the doorframe about a foot above the knob, exposing the blue wire that he knew he would find there. Then, with a pair of insulated pliers, he clipped the wire, disabling the alarm.

The lock itself was relatively easy. Morris didn't even need the magically charged lock picks that Libby had made for him.

He turned the knob and, standing well off to one side of the entranceway, gently pushed the door open.

The darkness and silence within seemed to mock him.

He shined his light inside, revealing the long hallway that the blueprints said would be there. Several pieces of furniture were visible along the walls on either side—brittle-looking antiques in what appeared to be French Provincial. Fortner was said to be a connoisseur.

Spanish Mission architecture with French Provincial furniture. Some connoisseur.

Morris was three-quarters along the hallway when he felt a floorboard give imperceptibly under his foot. This was followed an instant later by the sound of wood moving against wood overhead.

Morris dropped at once to one knee, a posture that would allow him to run, dodge, or roll as needed. Then something flashed above his head from left to right, something long and black and sinuous that appeared to be suspended somehow from the ceiling. It struck the wall with a soft thud and rebounded, swinging back to the left.

When the dangling, wriggling shape bounced off the opposite wall, Morris was ready. He shot out a gloved hand, trying to grasp it a few inches from the end, just behind where the head would be, if his guess was right. Quincey Morris hated snakes.

Black Mamba venom on the glass shards outside. Bastard Fortner has to get it from somewhere. The Black Mamba, deadliest snake in Africa, maybe in the whole world. Jesus Christ, better not miss—

It was made of rubber.

Morris had held on to a few real snakes in his time, very reluctantly. The feel of a live reptile struggling against your grip, fighting to get free so that it can kill you, is something you don't forget. This thing he was holding now was utterly inert. It was not alive, nor had it ever been.

He stood, and examined his prize in the flashlight's narrow beam.

The black rubber snake, about three feet long, was suspended by a cord from a square hole that had opened in the ceiling. The floorboard must have been the trigger for the mechanism that would drop the toy reptile. Gravity and the length of the cord would send it swinging at eye level for a standing man of average height. The thing would be practically right in your face.

And what the hell was the point of that?

The rubber snake would certainly startle an intruder—God knows it had startled the shit out of Morris—but it wouldn't stop one. Nobody who had gotten this far would be likely to run away screaming just because of a toy on a string.

There had to be something more.

All right, you're creeping down this hallway like a good little burglar, you trip the mechanism, the rubber snake drops down and damn near scares you to death—then what do you do?

Your anger and residual adrenaline might cause you to yank the cord in frustration, intending to tear it loose and toss the snake as far as you can throw it.

Morris sent his flashlight beam up toward the opening in the ceiling where the cord was attached. He couldn't see what the cord was tied to up there, but he thought there was a good chance that pulling hard on that length of twine might have very unpleasant consequences.

Note to self: leave the damn cord alone.

But what if you weren't the kind of person to let your temper get the better of you? What would Fortner have in store for you then?

If you didn't have Morris's presence of mind to drop down at the sound of the ceiling trap opening... then the next thing you'd know would be that there was a damn snake right in front of your face. Instinct would be to do—what?

Dodge aside, either left or right.

There was furniture here, on both sides of the narrow hall—an antique writing desk on the left, and opposite, some kind of occasional table.

So you dodge aside, right into the furniture. And then what happens?

Morris took from a pocket a thin metal tube about six inches long. Then he grasped one end and pulled, and the tube stretched to a length of four feet, which is what car radio antennas are supposed to do. Morris wasn't interested in receiving any radio signals, but he'd thought the device might have other uses.

Standing as far away as the extended aerial would allow him, Morris held one end and used the other to gently tap the side of the writing desk.

Nothing.

Morris frowned in the semi-darkness, then drew the aerial back and tapped a little harder.

Still *nada*.

He was probably just being paranoid. But he needed to know for sure, in case he had to come back this way in a hurry. It probably wouldn't hurt to give the writing desk another, slightly more forceful *tap*—and ten razor-sharp blades slid out of hidden recesses in the desk, glinting in the thin beam of Morris's pencil flash.

Morris went over for a closer look. The blades were only four inches long, but they gleamed wetly in the light, each one having been coated with some viscous liquid.

Trying to avoid the fake snake, you blunder into the furniture and get a shot of real snake venom for your trouble. Well, they said Fortner had a complicated mind.

Of course, there was no way to predict whether the unsuspecting intruder would dodge to the left or right. Which meant...

Morris gave the occasional table on the opposite wall a medium-hard rap with his aerial, and was utterly unamazed to see a similar set of blades spring out from their hiding places in the innocent-looking antique.

Note to self: don't bump into the furniture, podner. It just ain't healthy.

He continued down the hallway slowly, carefully, ready to react if another floorboard should move under his weight. But none did.

The hall formed a junction with a perpendicular corridor, and Morris knew enough to turn right, just as he knew the second room on the left was the one he wanted.

Fortner's workroom, where all the fun took place.

The door to the chamber where Fortner performed his black magic rituals was open, and for about three-tenths of a second Morris was relieved about having one less lock to deal with. Then common sense reasserted itself.

This was the most important room in the house. It didn't matter if Fortner had a million bucks in cash and the Kohinoor diamond stashed in his bedroom—this was the place that really mattered to him.

Why wasn't this room locked up tighter than Donald Trump's piggy bank?

Fortner may have been running late when he left. After all, he'd had a plane to catch. Maybe the man just forgot.

He puts snake venom on his walls, conjures up a Black Dog to guard the grounds, booby traps the hallway, then goes off and forgets to lock up the room that's the main reason for it all?

A small smile appeared on Morris's thin face. *Not too likely, I reckon.*

Morris produced the almond-shaped gem yet a third time. As soon as he held it within a foot of the doorway, the stone began to glow red as a stoplight—and for Morris, the message was the same: *stop right there, if you know what's good for you.* The doorway had a spell on it.

Morris used his aerial to probe the floorboards in front of Fortner's workroom. They were all completely solid. He carefully checked both the floor and the ceiling for the telltale edges of a trap door or deadfall. Nothing.

Standing off to one side, he gingerly broke the plane of the doorway with the aerial's tip. No reaction. He waved the aerial around the doorway—slowly at first, then faster.

Zippo.

Could be the stone was responding to the general aura of black magic attached to the room, rather than to the entrance itself. Sure, that's probably it.

Morris was about to walk through the doorway when a thought occurred to him.

He took a step back and brought out a small pocketknife. Pushing one sleeve back, he jabbed his forearm with the tip of the blade—just enough to produce a few drops of blood.

He smeared the blood over the rounded tip of the aerial, then slowly extended it toward the doorway again.

The instant the bloody tip crossed the threshold, there was a blur of movement in the doorway, a sharp *crack*, and the aerial was almost torn from Morris's grip by the force of a blow that left his fingers tingling.

He withdrew the aerial and examined it in the beam of his flashlight. The metal tip had been sheared completely off, as cleanly as if cut by pliers.

Morris looked at the doorframe. A steel blade, about three inches wide and running the entire height of the doorway, was now imbedded in the right side of the frame.

He wondered if Fortner was thorough enough to cover his bets both ways. Morris drew a few more drops of blood from his arm and repeated the intrusion.

This time, a blade concealed in the bottom of the doorframe flashed upward, too fast for the eye to see, and buried itself in the top of the structure. Another two inches was gone from the end of the aerial.

Morris felt his testicles retract involuntarily. If he had been stepping over the threshold at the moment that thing was set off...

Morris tried a third time. No reaction. He brought out the almond-shaped stone. No color change now.

He walked carefully into Fortner's workroom, alert for any other protections the man might have installed, whether occult or mundane. His flashlight revealed the large pentagram drawn on the floor with squat unlit candles at each of the five points, the magical swords and rods in a rack on the wall, the tapestries covered with occult symbols. No surprises there.

The large sink against one wall was a bit unusual, in Morris's experience. He shined his light in there, saw nothing except a lot of brown stains coating the porcelain. *Fortner should get himself some scouring powder, or something.*

There was a large worktable set against the wall opposite from the sink, covered with books and papers. Several tiers of shelves, bearing an assortment of jars, bottles, and vials, occupied the wall above it. Morris decided to start his search with the table.

Luck was with him. It only took a few minutes to find the large envelope with "Willette" scrawled on the front. Inside were several smaller envelopes. One was labeled "hair," another "fingernail clippings," another "handwriting," and still another read "photos"—everything you'd need to cast a devastating black spell on somebody. Somebody like Morris's client. Well, Roy Willette need have no more worries. Fortner would not be using these ingredients to work any hocus-pocus on him.

Morris had been holding the pencil flashlight between his teeth so as to leave both hands free as he riffled through the items on the table. But now he straightened up, which meant the flashlight clenched in his jaws was pointing straight ahead, at the lowest row of shelves.

Morris was busy thinking about his way out, and wasn't interested in whatever else Fortner might keep in his little sanctum, since he wasn't being paid to mess with it. He turned away and was taking his first step toward the door when what he had just seen finally registered on his conscious mind.

He turned back slowly, hoping that he had been mistaken. He directed the flashlight beam once again toward the lowest shelf, and the row of jars that rested on it.

He had not been mistaken.

Each jar contained a heart, floating in some kind of clear liquid.

Morris knew enough anatomy to realize that he was not looking at the hearts of pigs, or calves, or some other animal.

They were human hearts.

And they were small, each of them. Far too small to have come from adults.

They were the hearts of children.

Morris had been in Los Angeles for just over a week, casing the house and grounds and keeping an eye on Fortner's movements. Local TV news, as well as the *L.A. Times,* had featured several stories about the children who had gone missing over the last few months, with no clues to suggest what might have become of them. The police were said to be "following several promising leads," which Morris had recognized for the bullshit that it was.

The most recent disappearance had been reported a week ago, shortly after Morris had arrived in town. The *Times* said that this was the eighth case in the last five months.

There were eight identical jars on Fortner's shelf.

Morris knew that the practice of black magic sometimes involved the use of human body parts, and that some of the more arcane rituals specifically called for the organs of children. He had recently met a South African cop who'd been on the trail of a black magician who was murdering kids for their organs.

Morris didn't know what Fortner had in mind, but it must be something really nasty to require this kind of raw material, and in such a quantity.

Not my business, no sir. I've got what I came for. All I need to worry about is getting out of here in one piece, giving this stuff to Willette, and collecting my money.

He directed the flashlight beam slowly around the room, taking in the tools of the black magician's trade—the grimoires, scrolls, pacts, magical ingredients, and various arcane devices.

It must have taken Fortner years to get all this stuff together. Decades, more likely.

The tools, Morris knew, had been made by Fortner himself. A magician's equipment must be attuned to him, and to him alone. It was a long, laborious process.

The flashlight revealed more mundane materials, too. Some of the shelves contained jars of ordinary chemicals, like magnesium, phosphorus, and sulfuric acid. There were large bottles of alcohol, used in some purification rituals. Morris even spied a box of Blue Angel wooden matches, presumably for lighting the candles, alcohol lamps, and incense burners.

I'm wasting time. Whatever Fortner is up to, it's no business of mine. I'm a professional. Get in, get the goods, and get out again. That's what I'm damn well paid for.

Morris supposed he could inform the police about Fortner. After all, they were eager for information about the child abductions.

Oh, sure. Absolutely. *"Excuse me, officer, but I was burglarizin' this fella's house the other night, and I came upon something you might be interested in. Oh, and did I mention that he's a practitioner of black magic, who's been stealing the kids to use their hearts in his wicked rituals?"*

He'd be lucky if they only laughed at him. A spell in jail or in the local loony bin would be more likely. And an anonymous call would most likely just be filed in the "nut" drawer.

No, there was nothing he could do about Fortner or his little projects. "Let sleeping dogs lie" was good advice, especially when the dog in question was a black magician who did not stint at murder.

It was a professional's attitude, and Morris was, above all else, a professional.

He sent the flashlight beam around the room one last time. *Ain't none of my damn business, anyway.*

Ten minutes later, Morris was shimmying up the rope that he had tied to the producer's tree. He had encountered no further interference on his way out of Fortner's house, or across the grounds.

He reached the branch to which he had secured the rope, grasped it, and quickly hoisted himself up into the tree. Then he unknotted the rope, drew it up, and wound it back around his waist.

Before starting his descent into the producer's property, Morris spared a final glance toward Fortner's house, where the flames were just now becoming visible in the windows, flickering like the eyes of a madman.

Morris nodded to himself. Then he turned away and began his careful climb down the tree. He wanted to be well away before any fire trucks showed up.

Morris was a professional. But that's not all he was.